"Very hot romance. Readers who enjoy an excellent, sizzling Victorian story are going to thoroughly enjoy this one." —*Romance Reviews Today*

"Scorcher! Bernard debuts with an erotic romance that delivers not only a high degree of sensuality, but a strong plotline and a cast of memorable characters. She's sure to find a place alongside Robin Schone, Pam Rosenthal, and Thea Devine." —**Romantic Times*

"*Madame's Deception* is shiverlicious! A captivating plot, charismatic characters, and sexy, tingle-worthy romance . . . Fantastic!" —*Joyfully Reviewed*

"Steamy historical romance is a great debut for this new author . . . Filled with steamy and erotic scenes . . . The plot is solid and the ending holds many surprises . . . Tantalizing." —*Fresh Fiction*

"Sinfully sexy . . . Wickedly witty, sublimely sensual . . . Renee Bernard dazzles readers . . . Clever, sensual, and superb." —*Booklist*

Revenge
Wears Rubies

RENEE BERNARD

BERKLEY SENSATION, NEW YORK

THE BERKLEY PUBLISHING GROUP
Published by the Penguin Group
Penguin Group (USA) Inc.
375 Hudson Street, New York, New York 10014, USA
Penguin Group (Canada), 90 Eglinton Avenue East, Suite 700, Toronto, Ontario M4P 2Y3, Canada
(a division of Pearson Penguin Canada Inc.)
Penguin Books Ltd., 80 Strand, London WC2R 0RL, England
Penguin Group Ireland, 25 St. Stephen's Green, Dublin 2, Ireland (a division of Penguin Books Ltd.)
Penguin Group (Australia), 250 Camberwell Road, Camberwell, Victoria 3124, Australia
(a division of Pearson Australia Group Pty. Ltd.)
Penguin Books India Pvt. Ltd., 11 Community Centre, Panchsheel Park, New Delhi—110 017, India
Penguin Group (NZ), 67 Apollo Drive, Rosedale, North Shore 0632, New Zealand
(a division of Pearson New Zealand Ltd.)
Penguin Books (South Africa) (Pty.) Ltd., 24 Sturdee Avenue, Rosebank, Johannesburg 2196,
South Africa

Penguin Books Ltd., Registered Offices: 80 Strand, London WC2R 0RL, England

This is a work of fiction. Names, characters, places, and incidents either are the product of the author's imagination or are used fictitiously, and any resemblance to actual persons, living or dead, business establishments, events, or locales is entirely coincidental. The publisher does not have any control over and does not assume any responsibility for author or third-party websites or their content.

REVENGE WEARS RUBIES

A Berkley Sensation Book / published by arrangement with the author

PRINTING HISTORY
Berkley Sensation mass-market edition / March 2010

Copyright © 2010 by Renee Bernard.
Excerpt from *Seduction Wears Sapphires* by Renee Bernard copyright © by Renee Bernard.
Cover art by Alan Ayers.
Cover hand lettering by Ron Zinn.
Interior text design by Laura K. Corless.

ISBN: 978-0-425-23337-5

BERKLEY® SENSATION
Berkley Sensation Books are published by The Berkley Publishing Group,
a division of Penguin Group (USA) Inc.,
375 Hudson Street, New York, New York 10014.
BERKLEY® SENSATION and the "B" design are trademarks of Penguin Group (USA) Inc.

PRINTED IN THE UNITED STATES OF AMERICA

10   9   8   7   6   5   4   3   2   1

To my grandmother, who has inspired me in so many ways and demonstrated what true grace and beauty can be. I cannot imagine this world without you, and I've decided I simply won't try. I'll just celebrate you and love you for the rest of my days.

And to Geoffrey, there are no words, my love. Every time you take my favor into battle, I marvel at the luck of finding a Renaissance man of my very own.

Acknowledgments

I often wonder who reads the acknowledgments and imagine it can be like one of those acceptance speeches where an actor is thanking his first grade teacher and every other human being he ever knew . . . and most people aren't listening. But it is a rare chance to truly acknowledge the people that have made a difference and contributed to the strange life of this writer, helping me to achieve my goals and maintain some semblance of sanity. So, here goes!

Kate Duffy once told me that the mark of a great editor is one who quietly but confidently assists you in becoming the writer you were meant to be. (You'll be missed, m'lady.) Kate Seaver, my dear editor, has proven that she is, in every sense, a truly great editor, and I love working with her, as she makes this process so painless.

I want to thank Robin Schone for once again standing by me as a phenomenal mentor and friend. To all my writer friends in the odd world of romance, thank you for making me feel less isolated in the quest and for inexplicably putting up with my quirky sense of humor. To Amanda McIntyre, "thank you" doesn't cover it, so I'll just have to come up with something else.

My thanks go to Sean and Toni, Sierra and Stephen for attempting to occupy the Elf while I'm juggling things on the home front. When they say it takes a village, they aren't kidding! My heartfelt thanks to the entire Shire of Mountains Gate for keeping my clan afloat these last few months and for proving that in any realm of the Knowne World, you are the ultimate definition of family and community.

And finally, I have to thank all the wonderful readers who have sent their personal notes of encouragement to me. It's a humbling thing to receive your compliments, and I've treasured every sentiment and vowed to do my best to never let you down. You inspire me, and for that, I'll be eternally grateful. (And continue to wickedly use your names as secondary characters now and then just for fun!)

Whoever finds love beneath hurt and grief
disappears into emptiness
with a thousand new disguises.

—RUMI

Prologue

Bengal, 1857

They'd just been voices in the dark to each other in the first few days. The familiarity of English accents and the simple relief at not being alone were stark comforts none of them had ever experienced. In an ancient pitch-black oubliette, unsure of their ultimate fate, they'd observed the rituals of introduction and exchanged names and shaken hands as if they were in the foyer of a music hall in Brighton and not standing ankle deep in muck in a raja's dungeon in the bowels of his stronghold.

Galen.

Michael.

Josiah.

Ashe.

John.

Darius.

Rowan.

Sterling.

Eight men from various walks of life, but their paths had led them each to India and now to this. . . . And even without knowing the speaker, their personalities had almost immediately declared themselves as a unique alliance was formed.

"No one else in our travel party was taken, I think. But it happened so quickly, I can't be sure."

"How long have you been here?"

"I lost track, but not more than a few days. Four or five?"

"This is ridiculous. We're British citizens! Our kidnapping is not going to go unanswered by the imperial regiments or—"

"The regiments have their hands full of other duties than tracking every British citizen, I suspect." The interruption resonated with calm authority.

"What the hell is this place?"

"An old cistern, I think. The walls feel carved, as if chiseled out of rock and of course . . ." The sound of a boot being pulled from the wet kiss of the mud around it was unmistakable. "There's evidence of water."

"We'll not last in here."

"That may be the intent, unless you experienced a different welcoming committee than I did."

"Gentlemen," another man spoke, "we're facing two possible outcomes. One, we'll be killed immediately as a show of strength, or to please someone's taste for revenge and rebellion."

"Or?" one of them pressed as if asking about the odds of a game of whist.

"Or we need to figure out how to survive a long stay, considering our host's accommodations and hospitality."

The sound of a rat or some other subterranean inhabitant underlined his words, and the men unconsciously shifted to stand nearer to each other.

"Damn! I hate it when I'm only offered two choices and they're both unacceptable."

"As you wish, a third option. The raja has eight beautiful daughters and each one of us will get to choose an exotic beauty for a wife and live like princes in a penny novel."

"Now that is more like it!"

Soft chuckles broke out and the choking darkness was momentarily forgotten.

"We're going to die."

A long silence answered the words, until one of them summoned a reply. "Undoubtedly, but let's do our best to wait until we're gray old men sitting by a warm fire in England, shall we?"

"To hell with that! I'll have a warm wench astride my lap when I make my farewells! You may keep your dusty hearth to yourself."

"I will. Especially if you're going to pop off and scare the lights out of some poor dolly!"

The men laughed again.

"He's right. You'd better leave a few extra coins in your waistcoat to make it up to the poor creature."

"My God, how many coins cover that sort of thing?"

They'd laughed even harder until the sound of metal on metal had ended their first "party." The door at the head of the steep tunnel entrance had opened, and a single torch had blinded them enough to make it easy for the guards to move in and start to remove them. A few had struggled but were quickly overpowered with punishing blows from short, weighted sticks that the guards carried. They'd been taken out through a labyrinth of dim passageways with stale air and damp walls. Each man's sense of direction was tested as the floors rose and fell, until none of them were sure that they were ten feet or ten thousand feet from the surface.

Finally, they'd been pushed into a four-chambered cell with musty straw on the floor and made to understand that the airless cave with its elaborate iron bars was, for now, home.

Half their number were chained by one wrist to the outer walls, and the others were unshackled. No pallets or provisions were evident, and when the guards closed the heavy door behind them, they took their torches with them and robbed the men once again of light.

Minutes passed in the cloying dark until at last, someone spoke.

"So much for playing cards to pass the time . . ."

And then they'd laughed until they'd cried.

Chapter

1

London, 1859

Galen Hawke's head pounded in a miserably slow fashion that foreshadowed a long afternoon. He eased out of the large bed, stretching his tall, lean frame with caution to allow his muscles to ignore twinges and small aches after a night of little rest. His arrival in London hadn't helped him outrun the restless dreams that still plagued him, and Galen yielded up a long, ragged sigh at the very thought of a lifetime meted out by haunting images of dark holes and suffocating tropical heat.

"You had a nightmare, sir."

Galen winced at the woman's unsympathetic tone and his own lapse in forgetting that he hadn't retired alone. The courtesan stood by the window in a transparent shift, positioned to no doubt let the morning rays highlight the ample curves of her figure and inspire him to lust. Instead, the bright light was making his eyes water, and Galen was in no mood to indulge her. "I never dream. Perhaps it was your snoring that kept me up."

She sniffed in protest, her brass-tinted curls bouncing as

she turned mercifully away from the window to sit down in a graceless move at a side table already laden with a morning repast and the day's paper. One glance at the tray told him that his faithful manservant had come and gone while he'd slept. *Damn. I'll be getting that look from Bradley again. And I'll deserve it since I swear to God, I've forgotten this chit's name . . .*

His guest picked up the paper and fanned herself. "Suit yourself, then. Mind you, from any other man you'd hear otherwise, but since you acquitted yourself so wonderfully last night, I'll let it go."

She'd seemed prettier to him the night before, but Galen wasn't fool enough to express his disappointment openly. "How generous of you." He ran his fingers back through his rebellious black curls before reaching for his robe. "Why don't you have something to eat before you go?"

Galen regretted the words the instant he uttered them. It was a clumsy dismissal, but the need for solitude had temporarily overridden the required pleasantries when trying to get rid of an unwanted breakfast guest. He tried to soften the impact by taking the chair across from her. "Shall I ring for tea?"

She snapped the newspaper open in front of her face, effectively ignoring him. Galen waited for a few moments, oddly grateful for the reprieve from conversation. His headache had just started to ease, so he poured himself a glass of barley water.

It wasn't that he'd had too much to drink the night before. Truthfully, he'd always envied men who could merrily throw caution to the winds when it came to distilled spirits, but his own body had never tolerated more than a sip. Ever since his first taste of liquor at sixteen and the disastrous and nearly fatal illness that had followed, Galen had been forced to accept that drinking was one masculine pursuit he would have to abandon. No, this headache was from hours spent in smoke-filled rooms playing cards and a lack of sleep. Last night, he'd hoped a bit of bed-play would drain him physically enough to allow for the dreamless sleep he craved, but once again, he'd met with failure.

"Aren't you friends with Hastings?" she asked, interrupting his peaceful recovery.

"Why?" Galen set his glass down, instantly wary. *What the hell has Josiah done now?*

"Some little odd reference of him here. See?" She waved the paper toward him. "What's this about a secret club?"

He made no move to take the pages from her. "I'm sure it's nothing."

"Truly?" her smile took on a mischievous flavor. "Talk and rumor of a clandestine gentlemen's club, and it's nothing? Lady Barrow is said to defend 'the Jaded' here, and she is not a woman to be amused by phantoms."

"I do not know the lady well enough to contradict you, but I pay no attention to rumor. And if there is talk, then it's hardly clandestine." Galen shifted back in his seat, confident that the matter was closed.

Her pout was practiced, but not without appeal. "Come, Mr. Hawke. Why not give me a tip? It sounds wicked, this club. Do they exist or is it something your friend made up to keep some blue-nosed beak out of his social calendar?"

I'm going to wring Josiah's neck the next time I see him.

"What makes you think I could answer that question?" he asked, looking across the table with icy regard.

"Because," she answered, squaring her shoulders, "I've heard the Jaded described as a sullen group of impossible men too handsome for their own good, and you—while you are a delectable specimen, you are the dreariest man I've ever met." With another shake of her head, she stood, tossing the paper on top of the tray. "If you aren't one of them, Mr. Hawke, you should be!"

He watched her hastily gather up her clothes and pull them on with unladylike grunts and snarls, amazed at the speed with which she managed the feat on her own. It occurred to him that he might have offered to help or rung for a maid, but Galen was sure that this time a safe distance was the better part of valor.

She snatched up her shoes with one last angry sniff, and carrying them in her hand, she sailed toward the door. Galen kept a subtle eye on her as she did, just in case her temper got the better of her and she realized what lovely weapons those heels could be and decided to launch one at his head.

She threw the door open and disappeared from view, and he closed his eyes in relief. *Well, there's my day off to a lovely start . . .*

He idly picked up the paper, scanning for the article she'd mentioned. "I'm not that damn dreary."

"Of course you are!" Josiah Hastings replied from the still open doorway, leaning against the ornate wood with his arms crossed. "Bradley let me in and said you wouldn't mind the company." He glanced over his shoulder as if to appreciate the retreating figure of Galen's guest, and then looked back at his friend. "Ever since we made it back to England, you've spent months hiding in that dreary country retreat of yours."

"I was ill." A partial truth, though he couldn't really describe the dark depression that had seized him after their return. Instead of the euphoric homecoming he'd anticipated, nothing had felt substantial to him. The memories were like demons holding him captive, and Galen had lost himself for a while.

"Now, I talk you back into Town, thinking it will cheer you, and yet here you are . . . driving away a perfectly luscious guest!"

"I wasn't going to invite her to take up residence," Galen said dryly. "But I'm sure you can still catch the dove if you think she's to your taste."

Josiah straightened from the doorframe and came into the room. "Another time," he said without enthusiasm.

Galen held up the paper. "The Jaded?"

His friend shrugged and moved to occupy the newly vacated seat across from Galen with an eye on the breakfast tray.

"I like the name. It suits us. Not that I'm going to emboss it on my calling cards, mind."

"Talking to the press are we?" Galen wasn't willing to drop the subject too lightly.

"No, we are not," Josiah answered firmly, beginning to set into the plate of pastries and eggs. "And don't start squealing and moaning to me about the impropriety of rumors, Galen. I've had enough lectures from Michael to satisfy a lifetime."

"How did it happen?" Galen asked, his tone more level, as a natural sympathy arose for any man who had survived one of Michael Rutherford's well-aimed speeches. Rutherford was another of the newly dubbed "Jaded" and largely responsible for their survival and escape from India. A fierce friend, Michael hadn't yet entirely relinquished his role of protector of the remaining five men who had shared imprisonment with him.

"Hell, I think I was ambushed! Some informant must have overheard the conversation at Clives, and I can assure you, I said nothing of note. But"—he sighed—"perhaps it was a sin of omission. He who is silent is said to consent, Galen."

Galen smiled. "You are a wiser man, today."

Josiah shrugged. "It may not be such a terrible thing. One small mention, sixteen words, and I'll bet ten sterling we'll have young bucks applying for membership before the week is out."

Galen's smile drained away. "Not if they knew what the entry fee had been for its founders."

"You underestimate the appeal of a good mystery, my friend."

"Are we seeking to appeal?"

Josiah's expression sobered, a dark storm in his eyes mirroring Galen's. "We are seeking to get on with our lives—whatever it takes." He made a dramatic cut of one of the pastries and took a hearty bite. "I don't give a fig what anyone calls us. A rose by any other name smells as sweet, wasn't that what dear William had to say?"

"I don't think Shakespeare had us in mind, but perhaps

you're right. Still, we have good reason to keep as far down-wind of attention as we can manage." Galen's gaze shifted down to the paper, wondering at the subtle turn of a dinner conversation and its power to nudge at the illusion that they were somehow separate from the world around them. But it underlined the unique position they were all in—souls marked and scarred from their hellish experiences in India, each man fragile in his own way but also inexplicably stronger. And none of them had returned to the society that they had remembered and longed for. It seemed that no matter how much the Jaded had changed, the world had temporarily out-paced them.

Or we've outgrown tea parties and insipid exchanges over cocktails about foreign policies and the price of cotton for— Galen's breath caught in his throat and all thought halted as if he'd been struck by lightning.

A name leapt off the page in his hands, innocuous text suddenly yielding a pattern that made his surroundings shrink and then fall away from notice.

Miss Haley Moreland.

A hundred memories, none of them welcome, flooded through him, and it was as if he could hear John Everly at his elbow—his voice low so the guards wouldn't hear, his stories of home hypnotic for all of them, but for Galen, he had al-ways saved the sweetest bits, about the woman John had loved all his life, about the woman who was a shy angel, about the woman John was going to marry as soon as they escaped . . . about Miss Haley Moreland.

Miss Haley Moreland, newly engaged to . . .

Galen struggled to focus, disbelief and fury warring be-hind his eyes. It couldn't be the same woman that John had spoken of! She would be in mourning! She would be some distraught, pale version of a girl bemoaning a life without her one true love, not—

Miss Haley Moreland, newly engaged to the Honorable Mr. Herbert Trumble, is enjoying her first Season and has already caught the eye of many notables for her surprising

*promise and potential as a leading beauty amidst London's
social circles. Mrs. Trumble-to-be is destined to make a respectable mark despite . . .*

"—right, Hawke? Are you unwell?" Josiah's firm hand on
his shoulder finally registered.

"Forgive me." Galen stood abruptly, stepping away from
his friend's reach. "I am . . ." He gripped the paper, as if he
could squeeze away the revelations that hammered inside his
chest.

"Galen?" Josiah's voice was tight with concern.

"I'm fine." He tightened the sash at his waist and turned
back to face Hastings. "I recalled an appointment. I'm loath to
be rude, but I need to dress and tend to some business. If you
can show yourself back out, I would be grateful."

The words sounded stilted and false in his ears, but he knew
that Josiah, of all people, would respond to the urgency and
not to the obviously fabricated details. They'd been through
too much together to nitpick at the little lies a man needed to
tell sometimes—and above all, he knew that they'd long ago
sworn to support each other without question, no matter what
the future might bring.

Josiah bowed in a gallant theatrical gesture, bending his
tall frame but keeping his eyes on Galen. "I shouldn't have
interrupted your morning without notice, friend. I'll take my
leave and await word if you . . . need anything."

The unspoken understanding held, and Galen nodded his
head, dismissing his friend. At last, he was alone.

Miss Haley Moreland.

John's angel had apparently fallen. They'd been back with
the news of John's fate for less than eight months. He'd made
inquiries and located her family to send word of John's loss,
but hadn't worked up the courage to face her in person—his
own grief too raw. The agent he'd sent had confirmed from
some of the locals that John and Haley had been sweethearts
since childhood, but now it appeared that Miss Moreland was
already reengaged and merrily celebrating her upcoming nuptials with a glorious social season in Town. Galen grimaced

as he imagined this heartless creature laughing, carefree at parties, balls, and soirees.

Faithless witch! Galen began to dress himself, his hands shaking with quiet fury. He couldn't recall ever experiencing a rage so white-hot and blinding. John Everly had been a friend unlike any other. He'd been the wit that had made them smile in the worst hours during their imprisonment. John's stories had kept them all going, and the loss of his blithe humor had almost undone them.

Because they'd been so close to freedom when he'd died. Three more days of running, and they'd reached an outpost. *Damn it, I'd have carried him all the way to Bombay if I could. . . .*

And the memory overtook him again, like a fitful dream he couldn't elude.

It was raining, so hard and cold that it was like nettles against his skin. They'd been trying to keep moving, but John couldn't keep up. Carrying him was difficult, they were each so weak—but Galen had refused to give up.

Finally they'd stopped to catch their breath, hiding in the reeds along some filthy ditch. And when he'd looked into John's eyes, he'd known John was dying. Dying, right there, in muck and mud and icy rain, and there was nothing to be done, except crouch over him to try to keep the rain out of his face—and pretend it wasn't happening.

And John smiled up at him. That wry, devil-may-care grin that defied even a monsoon. "Promise me, Galen."

"We're not doing this, John. You're going to outrun all of us when you get a whiff of some mutton pasties and catch a glimpse of the Union Jack."

But the heat in John's eyes began to retreat, and he'd reached up to grip the rags at Galen's throat to pull him closer. "Swear to me, you'll see to her. You'll tell Haley . . . how much I . . . wished for her happiness. That I love her. Swear it, Hawke."

None of the others could hear the exchange. And Galen didn't want them to. It was too intimate and heartbreaking.

*And the vow, so easy to make. "I'll see to her, John. I swear
it to my last . . ."*

*He was going to say "breath." But John's ragged exhale
had silenced Galen, as he'd demonstrated just what a last
breath meant and Galen was left staring down into an empty
shell. And he'd stood up, numb and clumsy in the mud, and
Rowan had steadied him as he was forced to step over the
body. Not one of the six of them had dared a word of memo-
rial or farewell.*

Galen pulled on his morning jacket, marveling that he recognized his own reflection in the gilt mirror in the corner of
the bedroom. Three years in India had altered his appearance,
but not enough, he thought. A man should be more changed
after . . . everything that had happened.

Miss Haley Moreland.

He hadn't forgotten the promise. He'd meant to seek her
out personally and ensure that she knew of John's last words,
knew that his last thoughts had been of her. But he'd put it off
for too long, guilt and shame holding him prisoner.

I'll see to her, John.

Oh, he would "see to her." The words took on an ominous
note that foretold of a world of pain for a certain English miss.
Months of lethargy vanished, and Galen felt a new power and
force of will take shape inside of him. All his instincts to be
cautious vanished in the space of a single breath.

*Oh, Miss Moreland. I believe you are going to get exactly
the Season you deserve. I'll see to you. I'll see that you learn
the cost of cruelty, firsthand. You think to trade one fiancé
for another without regard? I'll see that you end up without
one. You think to play with a man's affections and cast him
off without a care? I'll have your heart and return it to you in
a thousand pieces. I'm going to laugh, Miss Haley Moreland,
when you cry at my feet, for you owe John Everly a river of
tears, and this is a debt I'm going to collect for him.*

I'll have you and then I'll have you.

* * *

"You can at least let the man buy you a hat!" Aunt Alice protested, holding up the lovely bonnet again as if to show off its ribbons and win her arguments.

"I cannot!" Haley's frustration gave way to her lively humor as she stepped forward to pat her aunt's arm consolingly. "It's not as if I need a new bonnet, and even if I did, it's hardly proper to ask Mr. Trumble to pay for such a trifle. But if you'd like, I can ask him to buy *you* one."

"Pish!" Aunt Alice pouted and set the beribboned creation back on the counter, before her own good nature asserted itself again. "I'd look like a gray carriage horse in that thing! And it's my job to fuss about what propriety dictates, Haley. See that you leave your elderly relatives a few things to do, won't you?"

Haley nodded obediently, making no effort to hide her smile. "I will endeavor to be as much trouble as I can."

"Ah! Just what a chaperone longs to hear!" She took Haley's arm as they left the milliner's and made their way down the busy and fashionable shopping street back toward their hired carriage. "Truly, dearest, it's nothing to see a man provide for his future wife's trousseau—not that you aren't lovely in the gowns you already have, mind! But if you play the frugal woman now, he may think to keep his wife with very little expenditure, and when you want to indulge yourself later, he'll remind himself how well you did with nothing."

"It's not . . ." Haley let the argument fall away, unwilling to reveal just how unhappy she felt at the moment. "I'm sure you're right."

Aunt Alice had used the excuse of needing a new set of buttons for her favorite coat to lure Haley into something resembling a shopping trip. But her aunt knew far too well that Haley had spent too many years economizing and stretching any farthing she could harbor to open up her purse strings without good cause.

And Aunt Alice was right in that Mr. Trumble had continuously urged her to use his good credit to buy her heart's desires.

But her heart desired nothing in London's best stores and, secretly, nothing that Herbert possessed. And while she was in no position to ultimately refuse him, it gave her a small amount of comfort to retain the last illusions of independence she could. In a few months, she would be his to dress and dictate to, in all things. As Mrs. Herbert Trumble, the wife of a successful industrialist, she would be his property to manage and care for. And while the thought chilled her to the bone, her aunt had repeatedly assured her that true affection would follow as a natural result of this masculine care.

"You should enjoy this more, Haley. You're young, and a London Season . . . it's what I always wanted for you. And if only my brother, Alfred, had—"

Haley looked away, gently but effectively cutting off her aunt's speech. Haley didn't want to hear another round of wishful thinking or a hurtful and useless condemnation of her beloved father's character flaws.

We are just as we are, and wishing for the moon doesn't bring it any closer.

Her father, Lord Moreland, would have disagreed and then given her a dozen examples of how often he'd once had the world in his pockets (ignoring their current state of emptiness). She'd abandoned the painful pretense of daydreams, and where her father seemed to do little else, Haley had deliberately grounded herself in the practicalities of life.

Nothing about Lord Moreland spoke of restraint. He'd loved Haley's mother beyond measure and wasted his fortune on frippery and foolishness to please her. From all accounts, her mother hadn't had the heart to refuse any gift or extravagance since it gave her husband so much joy to buy her things—and they'd neither one of them seen beyond the moment to the possibility of a grim future when the money ran out.

So when Lady Moreland had died of a sudden illness, her father had plunged into mourning with a tenacity that made most of their country friends shake their heads in wonder. He didn't wish to see a world without her, and so he'd drowned his sorrows with distilled spirits and escaped drab reality whenever possible.

As a child, she'd always known her father had been generous with her mother, but it was only after the funeral on Haley's fifteenth birthday that the full impact of it had struck home. She'd sorted through a mountain of trunks full of dresses she'd never seen her mother wear, laces and notions, ribbons and buttons, bolts of sumptuous fabric all reverently set aside. There'd been countless boxes of stockings and gloves in every hue, enough to outfit an army of ladies. She'd found duplicate gowns in four different shades of red, as if her father had been unable to decide which one best suited his beloved Margaret and so he'd ordered them all.

The sheer audacious waste of it! She'd adored her mother, but once she was gone, Haley had discovered how precarious their existence had become, and the blind, selfish indulgences of her parents had staggered her. Where Lady Moreland had been unwilling or unable to take charge, it was Haley who was ultimately forced behind the scenes to maintain some semblance of sanity. Responsibilities beyond her years had crushed any remnants of her childhood, but Haley had squared her shoulders and taken charge.

She'd sold the carriages and cleared the stables first, learning quickly when her father was deep enough into his cups to cooperate but not so far gone that he couldn't provide a signature on a bill of sale to keep them fed. With the housekeeper, Mrs. Copley, as her ally, she'd cut back on the household staff and released anyone not critical to their upkeep. She'd even gained their land manager's blessings and ridden out to the tenants and the village regularly enough that their people had begun to call her the "Little Mistress" out of affection and loyalty.

But affection and loyalty weren't currency to keep the larders full and the servants paid.

There'd been no money for a debut and little hope for a rescue—at least until Mr. Trumble had rented nearby Frostbrook Manor for the hunting season. Haley hadn't needed anyone to remind her of the practical miracle of a wealthy man in need of a wife who didn't seem to mind a lack of dowry. When he'd asked her to marry him, it had felt like the worst kind of dream because of the suffocating weight of the inevitability of it all. She remembered trying to smile and then crying, and Mr. Trumble had assumed she'd been overcome with joy and he'd run to tell her father the happy news.

What other answer could she have given him? Was it conceivable to refuse him and see her father ousted from his ancestral home and end up begging for shelter and support from her mother's indifferent and disapproving relatives? No daughter who cared a fraction less for her father would have done differently than accept the man even if he'd had three heads. Not that Mr. Trumble had more than the requisite number of limbs and appendages! He was ultimately the most ordinary of men, regular in all his habits and very courteous.

All she could do was pray that her Aunt Alice was right to believe that her heart would inevitably come around to agree with her desperate decision to marry a man prone to drifting off the instant the conversation abandoned breeding dogs and gun collections.

"There are worse fates than a courteous husband," she intoned softly.

"What was that, dearest?"

"Nothing. A stray thought about how fortunate I am, indeed. And Mr. Trumble has been very generous. Surely you can understand my desire to respect that generosity and not overtax him? He has paid for our accommodations and provided carriages and servants for our stay. It seems petty to bother him for trifles when he's already done so much for us."

They'd reached the carriage and the footman moved forward quickly to assist them inside its interior. Aunt Alice sighed as she settled onto the cushioned seat. "I understand more than you think, my dearest."

Haley took the seat across from her, pushing the window open wider to lessen the sense of being confined. She hated small spaces and avoided them whenever she could. It was an irrational fear she'd never overcome, and one she'd never told another soul about, since it was hard for her to admit that her imagination could overpower her intellect so easily. If a lady's character was measured by her amount of self-control and discipline, it was a crippling flaw to lose both in any circumstance—especially in public.

Aunt Alice went on with another theatrical sigh. "Still, fortunate or not, I'd say a bonnet or two wouldn't tip the scales, Haley! You must learn to spoil yourself."

"Are you sure this is what chaperones often dictate? Cause more trouble and spoil yourself?" she teased gently.

"Absolutely! Chaperones with *you* for a charge, undoubtedly!" Aunt Alice laughed. "I can consult a few reference books, but I don't think there's a wise grand dame within thirty miles that would disagree with me."

"Ah! There's a conference I'd love to see!"

"Pish! We'd put ourselves to sleep now that I think on it, and what a mess of tea trolleys and cucumber sandwiches!" Aunt Alice made a playful gesture of dismissal. "You'll just have to rely on my judgment and there's an end to it."

The lively exchange continued and made the ride seem to go very quickly despite the afternoon traffic. Arriving at the brownstone, Aunt Alice excused herself to rest before their evening outing, and Haley took a few moments to enjoy the quiet. She headed up to the first floor sitting room, eager to get back to the novel she'd left on the window cushions that morning.

Her steps slowed at the doorway when she realized her father was already occupying the window seat in question.

"Your mother used to read a great deal." He held up the leather-bound novel she'd been seeking, his eyes watery despite his smile. "I was so jealous of those hours with her pretty nose pressed against those pages."

Haley shook her head and walked forward to gently retrieve her book. "She pressed her pretty nose against your cheek often enough, if I remember rightly, Father."

"She did, didn't she?" He leaned back and Haley noted that his waistcoat buttons were mismatched, a clear sign that he had already had a bit too much to drink before lunch.

"Papa, let's see to this." Haley sat next to him and began to refasten the ivory buttons, patiently setting him to rights. "Martin would be horrified to think you'd left your rooms with your clothes askew."

"Best valet in the known world, my dear."

"Yes, and you should tell Martin so more often. Poor man!" She smiled, too charmed by her father to really fuss at him. "We'll have you looking the dandy in no time."

"Where are all your boxes, Haley? Didn't you go out shopping this morning?" His focus on the present suddenly fell back into place, and Haley was grateful for the distraction of the buttons. She missed these fleeting moments when he truly looked at her and was once again the father she'd long adored.

"I did. And nothing suited." She finished her task and shifted back onto the cushions, doing her best to look him directly in the eye. "Aunt Alice was more disappointed than I was, I think."

"Alice wouldn't hide it, if that is true. Which makes the lack of boxes even more remarkable, I'd say." He put his hands over hers. "Empty the stores, dearest. Our troubles are behind us."

She pulled her hands away and stood. "Almost behind us, Papa."

"You're too practical!" He pouted, standing unsteadily.

"If I were a son, you'd not say so." She reached out to touch his arm to help him gain his balance. "Now, why don't we ring for something to eat to fortify ourselves before tonight's party?"

His gaze drifted past hers to the side table and the decanted wine in a cut crystal pitcher. "I'm not hungry. Go rest and change, Haley, and I'll . . . see you off with Alice later."

"Father, please come with us. Don't you wish to—"

"I wish to be obeyed and left alone!" He retreated past her

to the tray and poured himself a glass of the deep ruby, ending any debate.

Haley collected her novel and began to leave without another word. But her father spoke again and delayed her escape, his tone far more contrite and gentle. "I'm . . . feeling a bit under the weather. You'll make my apologies, won't you, then?"

She forced herself to smile. "Of course."

"Wear the red, Haley. You look like your mother when you wear that dress." His eyes became glasslike with unshed tears, and Haley averted her gaze.

"Yes, Father." She hurried from the room without slowing her steps or looking back. *There are worse fates than a courteous husband. Would I be my mother and love so blindly that I leave devastation in my wake?* She shook her head as she climbed the stairs to the second floor. *Wishing for the moon doesn't bring it any closer, but God help me, why do I keep looking at it?*

Chapter
2

The overcrowded salon was exactly the setting Haley most dreaded, but she kept a light gloved hand on Mr. Trumble's arm so that her nerves wouldn't betray her. At their first party weeks ago, she'd forgotten herself and Herbert had complained that she'd pinched the blood from his fingers because she'd held on to his elbow so tightly. She'd hoped her social skills were improving, but each party felt like the worst sort of gauntlet where one was likely to be undone by mischance or the poor mood of some matron looking for the tiniest fault to criticize her "country manners."

The long, narrow room was filled with guests, forming clusters of lively conversation that echoed off the painted vaulted ceilings. An old-fashioned musicians' gallery ran high along one side of the room betraying the room's original purpose for elegant dances. The balcony's gilt arches pointed toward the lively but indifferent mythological figures cavorting above, and Haley wondered if these demigods trapped in time missed seeing a good quadrille. The house's current owner, Mr. Bascombe, disliked dancing and made no secret of his preference for cards and conversation. Even so, Mr. Bascombe had apparently relented to add to his party's atmosphere and a lone violinist could be heard from his exile on the verandah.

"I cannot stand it, Miss Moreland!" The shrill voice immediately achieved Haley's attention along with that of several other guests, before Lady Pringley's faint smile softened her complaint. "You must reveal your couturier, or I'll be forced to admit to everyone how cruel and selfish you are to keep such secrets!"

Haley's cheeks flooded with heat. The compliment to her gown was so barbed, she wasn't sure how to reply and deflect the woman's interest. "Your ladyship . . . is too kind. I was just envying *your* beautiful gown."

"Indeed!" Lady Pringley shook her head. "*I* am no fashion plate."

"I confess, you all look well enough to me," Mr. Trumble said. "I can't see any difference in one dress or another, but what a lot of fuss and bother my three younger sisters can make over a ribbon! A female mystery, eh?"

Lady Pringley's look of astonishment at the unwelcome opinion of a man she hadn't yet addressed directly was almost comical. Haley did her best to intervene before any more damage was done. "Lady Pringley, you remember my fiancé, Mr. Herbert Trumble? My father had the pleasure of making the introduction at your garden party and—"

"Yes, of course!" Lady Pringley recovered her composure only to pick an even harder topic for Haley. "Is your father here then?"

"No, your ladyship." Haley took a small pause, trying to decide what excuse would end an inquiry, but Lady Pringley was too quick for her.

"Miss Moreland, is your father not feeling well that he would miss a lovely party such as this?" Lady Pringley asked, her expression mock disbelief. "Again unwell?"

"He was very displeased to stay behind, but the London air just doesn't agree with him, I'm afraid." Haley smiled as if she felt nothing but supreme gratitude for Lady Pringley's concern, and not a twinge of icy fury at the old bat trying to pry out a bit of gossip about her father's frequent absences. It was no small thing to keep her father's drinking from his peers' attentions.

"The man is going to miss seeing you grace my ball later in the Season at this pace. You must let me send my physician to attend him! Dr. Rowan West is so gifted, he can put him to rights in a single sitting." Lady Pringley held up a hand as if to wave away any protests. "I'll see to everything!"

"You're too kind, your ladyship," Mr. Trumble bleated, unaware of the intrusion. "Isn't she kind, Miss Moreland?"

"Far too kind." Haley squared her shoulders. "My father has a physician already, Lady Pringley. A day or two of rest, and I'll be sure to let him know that you made such a special point to inquire and remind him about your lovely party. It will be the height of the social season, and we wouldn't miss it for the world."

Lady Pringley's eyes narrowed, but the compliments did their work and her face settled back into a satisfied smile. "Everyone will be there. Well, everyone who is anyone of consequence . . ." She gave Mr. Trumble a patronizing look as if to underscore his amazing good fortune as a man of trade at achieving an invitation. "Or who wishes to improve their circumstances."

Mr. Trumble beamed. "A man can always improve himself!"

"Indeed." Lady Pringley retreated with a prim nod, dismissing the conversation before moving toward another hapless group of guests.

"Did you see that, Miss Moreland?" Herbert asked. "Lady Pringley has taken a special interest. And my father once said that a man born a step below could never do more than strain his neck looking up. But here I am! Not a door closed to me, and—oh, is that our host, Mr. Bascombe?"

Haley followed his gaze and tried to spot the gentleman in question. "I'm not sure I see—"

"Yes! He's there with that Mr. Melrose. I'm going to reintroduce myself. If he's to be in the House of Commons, then

I want to give him my compliments. Besides, I heard he has a Pekinese!" He left her to seize his chance to corner Mr. Melrose about the proper Pekinese, and Haley did her best not to bite her lip in disappointment. She had asked him in the carriage not to leave her unattended, but once again, he'd demonstrated that he had difficulty keeping his promises in his head when it came to the faintest mention of either one of his burning interests.

Toy dogs and antique gun collections! How I'm to compete with such as these apparently remains to be seen . . .

It was awkward to step back without bumping into anyone, and a familiar anxiety began to pour through her as the closeness of the room set in, the noise of conversation swelling with her fears. Nonsensical thoughts about the amount of air left and how tight her corset was fluttered through her in a panicked chase. She looked for the telltale yellow feathers in Aunt Alice's hairpiece, but gave up when the view of a sea of feathered hairpieces only fueled her discomfort.

She tried to maintain an expression of serene detachment, as her gaze swept over the room plotting potential escape routes or seeking a friendly familiar face. Aunt Alice was nowhere to be seen, and had probably assumed that she was in Mr. Trumble's good company.

The rise and fall of feminine chatter and male laughter did nothing to soothe her nerves but began to sound unnaturally jarring and strange, and Haley's grip on her folded fan increased until her fingers were numb.

The sight of Lady Pringley and her companions glancing over at her with smug assessment catapulted her into action. Haley was in no mood to stand still for Lady Pringley's mental catalogue and critique of every stitch and strand of her person. One subtle look at the balconies above cemented her strategy. She shifted without looking back in the direction of Pringley and her cronies and made her way as calmly and carefully as she could from the salon back into the hall until she found the servant's door to the small staircase that led to the deserted gallery above.

She knew her privacy was assured, and the lure of the simple luxury of elbow room was too much to resist. It was an unconventional thing to hide at a party, but Haley was sure that if she kept her eye on the gathering below, she could rejoin Mr. Trumble or Aunt Alice before she was missed and avoid any raised eyebrows.

The narrow gallery was unlit, except for the reflection from the room below, and Haley smiled at the simple elegance of becoming invisible in plain sight. *Well, perhaps not plain sight, for if anyone cared to crane their necks, I'm sure they could spot me easily enough.*

She moved with the unconscious ease of a person completely relieved at her solitude and free of the burden of watchful eyes. Nothing about London's society bid her to risk lowering her guard or allowed the luxury of an impulsive word or action, and Haley was beginning to count the days until it was all over. She'd never thought that the confines of her impending marriage would begin to seem like a slice of freedom compared to this taste of "Town." She shook her head at the absurd idea and headed for one of the deserted chairs along the wall to catch her breath. *Perhaps it's all for the best, accepting Herbert's invitation and suffering a Season, if only so I can look forward to disappearing into obscurity and—*

Haley froze as she realized that she was not entirely alone. At the far end of the gallery, what she'd mistaken for a shadow against the wall was in fact a man. He had his back to her and was apparently enjoying a view of the party below.

Exactly as I'd been planning on doing! An irrational flash of temper at having her scheme preemptively copied almost made her sigh, but then her humor quickly reasserted itself. *I can hardly take offense. After all, it's his privacy and I, it seems, am the hapless intruder.*

She considered a quiet retreat, but the thought of an unsuccessful outcome if he should turn and see her sneaking off like a cowardly dolt decided the matter. Haley was sure that the best course of action would be a quick confession and apology before leaving the man to his watch. She took a few steps closer to avoid raising her voice and alerting the entire party of their awkward location, since the acoustics of the gallery would amplify every word.

"Pardon my intrusion," she said.

He turned swiftly, his hands raised to strike, and she instinctively took a quick step backward. Like a startled predator, he looked like a man about to spring on her in deadly defense. Haley's breath caught in her throat at the fleeting sensation of danger. But he relaxed just as suddenly, no doubt accepting that in an evening gown and impractical slippers, she presented no real threat. She blinked, aware that she was staring at the most impossibly handsome man she'd ever seen. Coal black curls framed a face of aristocratic perfection, with chiseled cheekbones and strong features. She couldn't discern the color of his eyes, but it was a detail that didn't seem to matter at the moment. The light cast his features in a bewitching relief of glow and shadow, exaggerating the masculine lines and shapes of his face and form. Tall and stern, he emanated a latent power that she couldn't fathom, but one that affected her heart rate all the same. Even as he opened his hands as if to prove he was unarmed, Haley surmised that this man was never without a means of defense. "If you're trying to hide, sir, I—"

"I wasn't hiding."

"No, of course not." Haley shook her head, unable to stop a smile from erupting at the tension from such a strange standoff. The sounds of the partygoers below, so near at hand, gave her a false sense of courage. "My mistaken impression at discovering you against the wall in a darkened musicians' gallery. If you'd been lurking behind the drapes, then I might be better justified in the guess."

"I *wasn't* hiding." He crossed his arms defensively, a ghost of a smile tugging at one side of his mouth, and Haley felt a flood of relief at uncovering his good humor.

"*If* one were to hide, I would recommend trying the small library on the second floor."

"And how would you know of this sanctuary?"

Haley shrugged at the reasonable question in the midst of such a unique encounter. "I was a guest here when we first came to London, while we were searching for a suitable house to let. I have it on good authority that Mr. Bascombe may have forgotten he even has a library."

"Not a reader then?"

"Books make him sneeze. Something to do with the dust, if I remember it correctly." She pursed her lips at her own cheekiness, wishing she'd considered the possibility that the stranger and Mr. Bascombe were best friends before she'd spoken. "I'm . . . sure he's a man of good information, all the same."

"Naturally." He stepped forward. "Any man so quick to express his opinions must be well-informed, yes?"

"Absolutely," she replied. He rewarded her with a wicked grin that spawned a hundred molten butterflies inside her chest and made her wish that she could read the forbidden spin of his thoughts. "*Get away, you fool! You're in a private conversation with a complete stranger and losing every rational thought in your head like some brainless flirt every time he smiles!*" an inner voice warned her in panic. She straightened her shoulders and stiffened her spine before taking a symbolic step back. "I meant to merely apologize for . . . intruding." She bent her knees to offer a somewhat shaky, if shallow, curtsy before straightening again. "I'll just go back to the party and leave you to your . . . observations."

"And had you been planning on hiding up here?"

"No. I was—catching my breath." The lie was ridiculous. No one climbed a flight of back stairs to creep about a dusty gallery to "catch their breath." "Well, good night."

She turned and began her retreat, but a feminine curiosity too strong to ignore made her turn and look back. He hadn't moved, and he made no effort to disguise the fact that he was watching her as she withdrew. She lifted her chin defiantly and asked her question. "You never did say what *you* were doing up here, did you?"

"No, I didn't."

The pause lengthened as she waited for him to offer an excuse, and it was clear by his stance and expression that she wasn't going to get one so easily. A small twinge of her first impression of him, as a deadly predator not to be trifled with, returned. "And if I asked you directly?"

"I would probably say I was catching my breath." He smiled again, and this time the heat that bloomed inside of her betrayed itself on her cheeks. Haley put up a gloved hand to suppress the blush and then turned and fled.

There'd been no introductions. It was unthinkable to even consider asking his name or offering hers at such an unorthodox encounter. But what kind of gentleman stood in unlit galleries and made no effort to defend himself? He'd been dressed in evening clothes as any respectable guest would have been, but now she felt a measure of genuine alarm at the idea that he may have been some sort of burglar or criminal lurking in the shadows above them all. *And I directed him to Mr. Bascombe's private library!*

She pushed away the ridiculous notion of courteous burglars in evening coats with a stern internal lecture on the rules of small talk. *The temperature and number of guests—why can I never remember to just mumble something innocuous about how warm the room is or to compliment the party for its popularity?*

At the door at the bottom of the staircase, she hesitated. The crush of the guests awaited her, and Haley took a long, slow deep breath to try to recapture an illusion of calm. If the stairwell had been wider, and there wasn't the imminent threat of that stranger following at any moment, she'd have indulged in lingering there a while longer. But she wasn't foolish enough to risk one more misstep.

Horrifying enough if anyone notes me coming back through this door and then sees him coming after! They'll think it was some preplanned tryst! It was a new thought and one that propelled her quickly through the door.

Luckily, the few guests in the hallway didn't appear to make any special note of her unorthodox reentry, and Haley made an effort to move without any guilty haste to draw their eyes. To avoid Lady Pringley, she deliberately chose another doorway at the far end of the salon nearer the card tables and demurely began a quiet search for Aunt Alice.

After a few minutes the bobbing yellow feathers at last betrayed Aunt Alice's whereabouts, and Haley felt a small measure of her anxiety dissipate at the sound of the woman's familiar chatter. "I don't think they've decided where to settle, Mrs. Bianca. Though my hope is—"

"You cannot let them go north! I know this Mr. Trumble is some sort of industrialist, but what a fate for your dear niece!" Mrs. Bianca's arch tone was softened by an emotional tremble in her voice. "My young cousin abandoned Town for some factory-filled village in the north and her health was destroyed before she'd seen a single spring in that unfeeling burg."

Aunt Alice caught her eye as Haley approached and with a subtle gesture, assisted Mrs. Bianca in realizing that the subject of their speculation was now close at hand. "Have you met my niece, Miss Moreland?"

To the lady's credit, when Mrs. Bianca turned, there was almost no trace of her distress. "I had not the pleasure, till now. How do you do?"

"I am well, thank you, and the pleasure is mine." Haley extended her hand, liking Mrs. Bianca's soft features and warm brown eyes. She was only a little younger than Alice and had certainly meant no harm with her dire warnings. Mrs. Bianca wasn't alone in her disregard for anyone involved with trade. High society reveled in denigrating anyone touched by the industrious northern provinces and the "new" money it generated. Her father's title and family connections had kept certain doors open to them, but she had no doubt that once she was truly Mrs. Herbert Trumble her social environment would change—no matter where they chose to settle. "It is such a lovely party."

"Mr. Bascombe has a talent for drawing together the most interesting guests!" Mrs. Bianca flourished her fan with an experienced hand. "One of which, I shall confess, made a particular point in begging me for an introduction to you once I'd achieved your acquaintance. Your aunt was most intrigued to hear of a Mr. Galen Hawke!"

Aunt Alice readily agreed with a merry nod that sent her yellow feathers dancing. "I'd say so! After all, most men seek an introduction after seeing a young lady, don't they? But this gentleman has determined to meet you without any idea of you at all!" She sighed enviously, a twinkle in her eye giving away her humor. "If only the men of my generation were so forward-thinking!"

Haley shook her head and smiled. "Why not make Mrs. Bianca your conspirator and take the introduction for yourself, Aunt Alice? Since he knows nothing of me, I think you'll make a very fine Miss Moreland to make his acquaintance. Then you can judge for yourself about Mr. Hawke."

Both women openly laughed at the notion, but Mrs. Bianca recovered to reply, "I don't think he'd appreciate the game." Glancing over their heads, she raised one of her hands as if to signal a servant for another glass of champagne. "And I won't be the one to deny him the chance to meet such a charming young woman."

"Do you know him well?" Aunt Alice asked.

"Not well, I'm afraid." Mrs. Bianca seemed to consider her response before continuing, "But his father, the Earl of Stamford, is on good terms with my family, and my cousin's brother by marriage is their vicar. And although Mr. Hawke is the second eldest son, the family is very respected in loftier circles than these, so it's not an inquiry to make light of."

Haley wasn't sure Mrs. Bianca's description of his pedigree had the desired effect the speaker had intended. He sounded like a pompous thing to insist on introductions and cow poor women with distant connections to him into making his wishes manifest. She couldn't remember any circumstantial ties to an Earl of Stamford that would make his son think to "beg" for an introduction—and frankly, after an already eventful evening in an overcrowded room and above it, Haley didn't think she wanted to rectify the situation. "Well, if you

see him, please convey my regret that you weren't able to ful-
fill his request. But I really should find my fiancé and—"

"Leaving so soon?" The deep male voice directly behind
her almost made her yelp in surprise, but Haley's astonishment had more to do with how familiar its timbre was than its
location. *He couldn't be!*

"I was . . ." The words seemed to dry and catch in her
throat as she turned to face her handsome friend from the gallery. *Green. His eyes are impossibly green. Oh, dear!*

"Ah, Mr. Hawke!" Mrs. Bianca stepped in eagerly. "Mrs.
Shaw, Miss Moreland, may I introduce Mr. Galen Hawke?"

Aunt Alice managed to pink up like a girl at her first outing as she extended a gloved hand, openly smitten with the
handsome Hawke. "You may! What a delight to meet you!"

Haley bit the inside of her cheek to ensure she didn't follow suit, or give in to the nervous bubble of laughter at being
so squarely cornered. *If he mentions the gallery, I'm not sure
what I can say to explain myself.*

As he gallantly bowed over her aunt's fingers, his gaze
lifted to meet Haley's, and Haley almost jumped at the sensation of fire and ice down her spine.

He spoke as he straightened to face her. "You'll forgive my
impatience to meet you, Miss Moreland, but I had no faith that
you would simply find me."

Haley gasped, but the reaction was lost on the other women
as they laughed and fawned on the striking younger man in
their midst.

"What is to forgive? Miss Moreland is highly regarded and
it speaks well that you wished to meet her and make her acquaintance, don't you agree, Mrs. Shaw?" Mrs. Bianca spoke
in a breathless rush.

"I shall have to," Aunt Alice said. "We have so few acquaintances in London."

Haley's eyes widened at the mortifying confession, but she
knew there was nothing for it now. Instead, she did her best
to recover what small remnants of calm she could and disregard how much more potent Mr. Galen Hawke was in full

candlelight. "There, you see? An easy introduction, after all, and you've apparently been forgiven, so what more could we say?"

"Tell me how you find London, Miss Moreland."

He spoke as if it were still just the two of them alone in the shadows. He looked only at her as if nothing else mattered— not the setting, nor the dozen people within earshot, or even the two rapt elderly ladies fanning themselves at his elbows.

And without realizing it, Haley felt herself doing the same. "I would rather be home, I think. But you mustn't tell anyone, Mr. Hawke."

"Your secret is safe with me."

"What secrets are we keeping?" Herbert came up to the quartet, his brow a bit moist after enjoying a rousing debate on dog breeding techniques with Mr. Melrose. He held out a hand to Mr. Hawke. "Not that I am one for them, sir! I admit, whatever bits of news I manage to remember, I cannot then also remember whom I should tell and whom I shouldn't. It's quite a quandary, so I warn everyone to keep me out of the game!" He laughed, and then went on cheerfully. "I am Herbert Trumble. And you are?"

Mrs. Bianca interjected herself with a nervous flutter. "This is Mr. Galen Hawke. I was just introducing him to Mrs. Shaw and Miss Moreland."

"At your service, Mr. Trumble." Galen nodded his head, his expression politely neutral as Herbert continued to pump his arm up and down with distracted enthusiasm. "Miss Moreland was telling me how she was finding her time in London."

Herbert grinned. "She loves it! But then what woman doesn't wish for all the social niceties?"

Haley reached out to gently restrain Herbert by the arm. "Perhaps you should . . . let go of Mr. Hawke."

"Ah!" Herbert released Galen, his look apologetic. "I forgot I had ahold of you, sir! My goodness, I hope I haven't just done the same thing to Mr. Melrose! In this press of people, I suppose it's instinct to want to grab onto something and hope you get pulled out of the crush eventually, eh?"

Galen nodded. "A good instinct if you're drowning."

Haley held her breath at the quiet barb but wasn't sure what to do. Mr. Hawke was looking at her again, with an intensity that made her feel vulnerable and conversely powerful at the same time.

Thankfully, Herbert was blissfully unaware of the cross-currents in the conversation. "Just so! Lucky for me I know how to swim!"

"Mrs. Shaw was saying that you wished to widen your circles while in Town," Galen said.

"Indeed, yes! Mr. Bascombe has been very accommodating, but a man can never have too many friends in London," Herbert agreed, and Haley marveled that she alone seemed to feel a growing sense of alarm at how easily Mr. Hawke maneuvered everything. She'd been about to retreat and congratulate herself on escaping relatively unscathed. She'd been about to laud her own good moral character for not making any direct comparisons between the broad-shouldered handsome Hawke and her diminutive and somewhat doughy fiancé. She'd been about to vow never to see the mysterious and dangerous Mr. Hawke ever again and—

"I'll make some arrangements and ensure that you have social calls and invitations enough to make this Season . . . extremely memorable." Galen's smile was diabolical as he bowed to signal his intention to withdraw.

"How generous! Yes, thank you, Mr. Hawke! That would be lovely for Miss Moreland, and much appreciated." Herbert beamed.

"Too generous!" Haley finally found her voice. "I wouldn't want to impose . . . and you hardly know us to—"

"Haley!" Aunt Alice's shocked whisper ended the argument. She turned to Mr. Hawke. "Introductions in country society are harder to come by, you can imagine, and my niece is not yet used to the faster pace of London. But we are overjoyed to discover such an easy welcome in Town and such a kind mentor."

Haley did her best to recover what dignity she could after

her aunt's hinting that she was some country bumpkin overwhelmed by town courtesies. She attempted a smile. "Yes,
overjoyed, Mr. Hawke. And since it is, as you say, no imposi-
tion, then please . . ."

"I'm flattered. And I hope to see you again soon, Miss
Moreland." He inclined his head in a polite nod before turning away and disappearing into the crush.

Mrs. Bianca sighed. "With his family connections, you
could be dining with duchesses before the month is out, my
dears! What a perfect gentleman he is!"

Haley's instinct was to argue the point of Mr. Hawke's gentlemanly perfection, but she knew better. Herbert was beside
himself at the "happy turns" the party had taken, and Haley
wasn't about to spoil his evening with hysterical suspicions
about a stranger's generosity. *I'm being too sensitive, perhaps.
It could all be innocent, the coincidence of running into him
hiding in the shadows and then learning that he'd been seeking an introduction. He couldn't possibly have known that I
would try to get away from the party up there! And there's
nothing sinister in offering to make a few social connections
on our behalf. . . .*

Except there'd been nothing innocent in his looks, or the
wicked smile that had lit up his eyes when he'd made his offer.
He'd ignored everyone else and spoken as if they were alone,
even with Herbert at her side. Haley instinctively knew that
if Mr. Galen Hawke had anything to do with it, she would be
seeing a great deal more of him in the next few weeks.

And it would happen with Mr. Herbert Trumble's happiest
permission.

Chapter
3

Galen avoided his host on the way out, artfully sidestepping the polite bids from others for his attention or for conversation. Instead, he went directly to the main foyer and summoned a servant for his coat and hat and was gone before Bascombe or his political cronies could delay him.

His mind was reeling from the unexpected twists and turns in his first attempt to meet the object of his vengeful plan.

Miss Haley Moreland was quite different from the woman he'd anticipated.

In fact, he'd been so sure of his premonitions that he'd withdrawn from the party confident that he'd be able to recognize her the instant he spotted her below. John had described her in vague poetic terms, but Galen imagined that she would be passably pretty, in a cunning and calculated way. He'd guessed that she would be quite the social butterfly, seeking out the loftier or livelier elements in the room to further her ambitions. He'd pictured a dozen different variations of Miss Moreland, the heartless siren, and then just when he'd decided on the most likely candidate, wearing yellow organza below in the salon, she'd startled him into nearly breaking her neck.

Not that he'd known it was her. Not at that moment.

It seemed that John's fair love possessed a wicked wit and was more prone to hiding in the ferns than elbowing her way to center stage. Even so . . . Mr. Herbert Trumble's amusing lack of social graces spoke volumes to Galen about Miss Moreland's character and apparent willingness to cheerfully marry a mud troll for his money.

Hell, it would serve the girl a delightful measure of justice to be married off to that colorless pigeon! The thought warmed him for a fleeting moment, but then the dull chill of his strategy returned in full force. Leaving her to the long, dusty grind of a loveless marriage didn't suit Galen's plans.

And now that he'd seen the lovely Miss Haley Moreland, he was truly looking forward to the game. Not that his own pleasure was a consideration, but as he'd stood before her in the salon and observed the delicious change in her coloring at every compliment, Galen wasn't oblivious to the curl of anticipation that had unfurled inside of him. Granted, she was a tall beauty with a sleek, ripe figure that defied a man to keep his sinful thoughts to himself despite an army of chaperones (much less one elderly aunt's watchful eyes). And Miss Moreland did possess the requisite porcelain skin and classic patrician features that seemed all the fashion these days. But unlike the golden curls that so many women sought to copy, her hair was a defiantly stunning mahogany brown. Heavy silk curls hung down between her shoulder blades and back from her face to frame eyes the color of the sea, and Galen guessed that few men could withstand their storms. And there again she strayed from the fashion plates—no sleepy-lidded doe eyes staring out with innocent indifference. Wide eyes with a beguiling spark of wit met the world, and Galen wondered how a soul could be so malicious and still look out at the world with such a clear appeal.

But what truly warmed his blood were the signs that Miss Moreland might be, in fact, a unique creature in their midst.

She hadn't fluttered or fawned, and unlike any woman he had known, she had spoken the truth before censoring herself or considering her audience. She'd been so refreshingly direct that he couldn't help but wonder how far the trait might extend. Would she be as direct in her desires? Would she be so natural when faced with raw passion? This seduction would be sweet and slow, by his choice, not by necessity.

She'd been like two different women, in the gallery and then in the crowd below. At first, a mischievous sprite far out of bounds but apparently unafraid of the dark—or him. And then on the main floor of the salon, she'd been all polite graces, a regal beauty determined to keep her calm despite all his attempts to unsettle her. But it was the sprite he suspected John had loved, and it was that fearless side of her he needed to draw out if he was going to win her over and achieve his aim.

For if there had been a small tendril of mercy, a faint hint of regret inside of him, he'd let it die at the sight of her in that glorious red dress. She was a bloodred ruby brought to life with an allure and a power all her own. She was a vision of fire and beauty, but like a gem, cold to the touch and heartless. She was a siren with dark secrets of her own, and Galen's soul felt scorched by the desire she inspired in him.

Perhaps if he had seen even a faint nod to the state of mourning she had abandoned—a simple black ribbon trim or a plainer gown in a muted color. But instead she'd adorned herself in a fiery silk that defied every weeping widow and mocked true sentiment. Every flounce and fold of expensive ruby material sang of her indifference, and Galen's fingers had itched to tear her out of the offensive thing.

You'll be out of your clothes at my command, soon enough, Miss Moreland.

The carriage rolled to a stop, and Galen alighted without waiting for the footmen to bother with the door. They moved aside without question, long used to the unconventional habits of their employer's friends.

He headed directly upstairs, briskly taking two risers at

a time. Muted voices from a room above assured him that at least a few of the others had also sought out the oasis of West's library. Reaching the ornate doors, Galen felt a familiar wash of comfort at the sight of his friends.

"Hastings said you weren't coming this evening," Rowan said from his seat by the fireplace. "Some nonsense about attending a party at Bascombe's," he added with a wry grin.

"At which point, I believe, the good Dr. West was kind enough to suggest that Josiah had lost his sanity." Ashe straightened from his chair to extend a welcoming hand. "Come take my seat and help me win my wager."

Galen shook his head. "I'll stand for a bit." He crossed over to the long side table where a few refreshments were laid out. He reached for a decanter of lemon water, ritually ignoring the slight tremor of his hands. The hour was late and fatigue fueled the weakness in his extremities. "So what is this wager, Mr. Blackwell?"

"That despite Rowan's firm belief that you would rather be flayed alive than cross a gilt room in evening clothes with that social set, I had a strange feeling that it was just unexpected enough to be true." Ashe resettled with an easy grace, stretching out his long legs in front of him. "You never do what's expected, Galen."

"Then I'm a predictable bore!" Galen put the glass down before turning, unwilling to risk dropping it in front of the others. "But in this instance, it's Josiah's honor and apparently, his sanity I have to defend. I did attend Bascombe's."

"Whatever for?" Ashe asked. "And don't tell me for stimulating conversation! I've met Rand Bascombe."

"I had my reasons." Galen was in no mood to share.

"Careful, then," Rowan said, his tone diplomatic and calm. "Bascombe and his cronies have strong ties to the East India Company. It may not be wise to draw too much attention just now."

"It's too late for that." Ashe broke off the lecture with a wave of his hand. "Come, let's ask him how the mothers of the Ton reacted to his social debut."

"Oh, please!" Galen cracked a smile at last. "As usual, they have a tendency to pull their girls out of my path as quickly as they can, thank God!"

"Poor Galen, the curse of a handsome second son!" Ashe sighed theatrically, one hand over his heart. "No fresh flowers falling at your feet, but if your peers knew how plump your accounts have grown, I don't think you could take ten steps without some desperate mother shoving her daughter into your arms."

"They don't know anything of me, Blackwell, that I don't wish them to." Galen's irritation was compounded by the memory of Josiah's cavalier enjoyment of their group's notoriety. "And I couldn't care less about some simpering debutantes wrangling for their next victim."

"Leave him be, Ashe. Hawke is right." Rowan leaned forward, the amber in his eyes warming with the sincerity of his tone. "You can certainly attend any party you wish, old friend, without explaining yourself to the likes of us!"

Ashe shrugged. "I'm just cross because I suspect I've lost my favorite chaperone."

Rowan laughed. "Oh, yes! There's a position to aspire to! Chasing your worrisome carcass all over London and yanking you out of harm's way!"

"Hastings might volunteer for it," Galen said, instantly aware of the disastrous mischief the two wildest men in their company might achieve if left to their own devices. "Josiah might enjoy playing the overseer, for once."

Ashe shook his head quickly and downed the whiskey he was holding. "Lucifer would make a better guardian."

"I think the devil already has his hands full," Rowan countered, still laughing. "What about Darius, then? If you can pry him from his books, he could offer you a bit of scholarly balance, I'd guess."

"Thorne's out of town, again! Some nonsense about tracking down some rare first edition volumes. . . . How much can a man's head hold of all those dry philosophies and dreary bits of science before suffering an apoplectic fit?"

Galen gave Rowan a sympathetic look, since he and Darius had a shared love of knowledge and books. "Is that the cause of fits, Doctor West?"

"Hardly." Rowan shook his head then named the final candidate for Ashe's dilemma. "Should we ask Michael?"

"No!" Ashe held up his hand to stop the game, standing to cross over to the side table to pour himself another drink. "Hell, the reason I preferred Galen is that he hardly ever pays attention to the land of the living to tell a man 'nay'! Michael never misses a thing, and how the blazes is that supposed to add to the fun?"

"I'd say you're out of short pants, then." Galen clapped him on the back.

"Well, I shall just look out for myself—and the rest of you when I can." Ashe raised his glass in a mock toast. "Not that I expect to have the time when all the delicious ladies of London demand my personal attention."

The men settled into their chairs, their camaraderie fortified by the light banter and easy conversation of the evening. Galen absorbed it, grateful for the haven of Rowan's small library—the usual setting for the impromptu gatherings of the Jaded. He'd often marveled at their ability to arrive without prior notice and almost always find another member or two here. Rowan's wasn't the finest residence among them, but it seemed to cheerfully ward off the worst of the world outside, and the doctor's study was a unique haven filled with eclectic touches and distracting comforts that they all had come to cherish. Culled from generations of intrepid adventurers in the West family, the small library's treasures had more to do with Rowan's ancestors' desire for knowledge than any quest for wealth. (A sad clue, Rowan had once confessed, to the reason for the West family never quite achieving more than a footnote here and there in dusty texts. Not that Rowan dismissed intellectual achievement, but poverty could drain scholarly joy from any man and force him into a trade as it had Rowan.) No doubt, it was a nightmare for the maid to dust all the trinkets and sculpted bookends, but every object held a magical story that the men had come to value.

But even here, Galen was distracted by thoughts of red silk and an elusive idea that perhaps the elderly canary Mrs. Shaw could be useful in gaining Miss Moreland's trust. If Miss Moreland had been unengaged, the older women would have zealously guarded the young woman from his attention. As a rule, any second son without a specified income was too much of a risk for a woman seeking to marry well. But with Miss Moreland's altered status as a "woman claimed," the rules were relaxed somewhat, though not entirely forgotten. Hints from Mrs. Bianca that Trumble was eager to rise had proven helpful, and he'd felt no guilt at mentioning his family's connections to further his cause. Trumble wouldn't complain if he stayed close, and he would need the man's ignorant cooperation if he was going to make any headway.

Though it wouldn't do to get caught too soon, now would it?

"—for a lark, Galen."

Galen shifted in his chair, embarrassed at his lapse in attention. "I'm sorry. What were you saying?"

Ashe sighed. "I was attempting to lure you out since there is still time tonight for an amusement or two, but I'd say you were a thousand miles from London, Hawke."

Galen shook his head, despising the instinct to lie and keep his thoughts to himself. *Hell! I don't need the blessings of the Jaded to see to my own damn business!* "A lack of sleep, Ashe, has made me poor company."

"We are all of us entitled to be poor company now and again." Rowan's look was one of calm understanding. The cause of their sleepless nights and restless moods was well known in the group. It was one of the reasons they continued to find themselves in the library. There was never any need to explain themselves—one of the unbelievable benefits of sharing the same past. They could offer sympathy, but not tainted by pity and sideways looks as there would be from any other audience.

Ashe set his drink aside and stood. "Well, if you're not going to sleep, you may as well enjoy yourself. A visit to the ladies of—"

"No, thank you." Galen held up a hand to ward off any more invitations. "It's getting late, and that last foray with you proved I'm not made for your brand of entertainment."

"I shall do my best to make up for your absence!" He made a gallant bow, sparing a wicked wink before heading out the door. "Perhaps the twins are available this evening!"

Rowan and Galen both shook their heads as the door closed behind him. "No one makes an exit like Ashe," said Rowan.

"Oh, I don't know. I think Josiah's entrances would hold their own in comparison." Galen stood to make his own departure, suddenly anxious to be alone with his thoughts.

Rowan walked with him as a courtesy and for one more exchange, this one a quiet inquiry. "Not to push, but may I take this foray of yours back into society as a good sign?"

"I couldn't say." Galen did his best to speak as honestly as he could. "But I'm certainly not going to abandon my new social calendar just to keep you from losing any more bets."

Rowan laughed. "Point well taken!" But the merriment dimmed in his eyes as they reached the main foyer and Galen pulled on his coat. Rowan cleared his throat. "The warning about the East India agents wasn't an idle one. They are always hungry for treasure, and if they've caught sign or scent that we can lead them to more . . ."

It was the Jaded's ultimate secret that made the East India Company their nemesis. The raja who had gone mad and collected them like chess pieces in his dungeon for a game the Englishmen never understood had also stored a vast treasure in his labyrinth. All hell had broken loose when the raja's own men had rebelled, and the Englishmen had seized the opportunity to escape, struggling to find their way out of the dark. It was then that they'd accidentally stumbled onto a treasure room. Even in the dim light, they'd seen enough golden ornate boxes of gems and precious metals to give them pause. In the shadowed room, the moral debate had been brief, and they'd filled their ragged pockets and used a coat for a larger bundle to carry what they could—only to secure a passage home or to use for bribes.

When they were safely aboard a ship sailing for home, they'd met in Michael's cramped stateroom and first realized that they'd managed to crawl out of the jungles of Bengal with far more than they'd thought. It was a startling sight lying out on the wool blanket on the bunk—diamonds, emeralds, sapphires, rubies, and pearls of a size and quality that none of them could deny. It was a breathtaking and unbelievable fortune that they solemnly divided equally amidst their number. But there was almost no celebration. There would be no sympathy or sanctuary offered from either side of the question. Because the raja, if he'd survived the coup, was sure to notice he'd been robbed, and if he didn't, others might. The natives of India were tired of the greed of England stealing away the riches of their country, and the East India Company was the ruthless engineer of too many crimes to count. Their interest in finding new caches of wealth went beyond benign curiosity, and there wasn't a man among them who wanted to be drawn back into a dangerous and bloody quest into Bengal. They wanted no part of any further pillaging of their host, no matter what transgressions had transpired. So they'd vowed to keep their silence and the bulk of their newfound wealth as far from the prying eyes and ears of the Company as possible. They trusted each other to spend their shares wisely and protect the secret of their fortune's origin.

Rowan continued, "Michael hasn't said much, but he made a point of saying that something was stirring and we should all be on our guard."

"Then I'll be on my guard. But let's see if the safest place to be isn't in a crowd, shall we?"

"Are you sleeping?"

Galen stiffened defensively. "Are you?"

Rowan crossed his arms and said nothing.

Galen yielded the point and answered the doctor's question. "Not yet, but I may have found the solution I need to finding some elusive peace."

"I'm glad. So long as the remedy doesn't come in a small green bottle, I won't nag you any further."

"You're a good friend, Dr. West." Galen headed out the door. "And I don't believe for a moment that anything I say will prevent you from worrying about us to your last breath."

Rowan waved as his friend climbed back into his carriage and replied almost to himself, "On that you can wager your life, friend."

Chapter
4

🌷

Haley's long fingers smoothed out the emerald silk she'd cut, and with an eye on the picture she'd propped up on the bureau, she began to pin antique lace to the corsage, moving it from one position to another while her imagination kept pace with her design as it emerged. It was a complex puzzle spread about the floor, but Haley knew where each seam would come together. She welcomed the pleasant calm that came over her whenever she worked on her dresses.

She used what fashion plates she could, or pictures from various fashion journals, as a vague guide, trusting her intuition more than the often imperious opinions of their French sources. Drawing inspiration from her mother's legacy of dresses, fabrics, and notions, Haley only hoped that Lady Pringley never learned that she was her own couturier.

She had always made her own clothes at home, out of sheer necessity for economy. But it had become a great solace and something she truly enjoyed. It was as if the fabrics her father had so lovingly bought for her mother brought her spirit closer as Haley reworked them into the dresses of her dreams.

And so, even in London, she had decided to keep her own wardrobe and face the Lions of Fashion in her own humble creations.

She leaned back to sit on her heels and eyed the green silk spread around her. Haley had envisioned it as the perfect evening dress for an upcoming concert that Mr. Trumble had invited her to attend. But now, all she could see was that the green was the same distracting shade as a certain gentleman's eyes.

Did my heart skip a beat because he was so dashing, or because he seemed so dangerous up there in the dark?

Haley gave her shoulders a little shake, trying to push aside thoughts of a man who was most certainly out of bounds. Instead, she began to wonder if there might still be time to make another outfit. *Perhaps something in brown that won't remind me of anything at all!*

"You'll be a vision in that color, dearest." Aunt Alice came into the room, gingerly taking a seat on a nearby chair. "Something for a ball?"

"For the concert next week. I modified the redingote pattern to make it more of an evening style, and I think the lace will soften the line of the corsage." She held up the lace for her aunt to see.

"Soften it and draw the eye, I'd say. A lovely choice."

Haley blushed. "I'm not trying to draw anyone's eyes."

"Naturally not." Alice shook her head, still smiling as if she were in on some secret jest. "I knew a woman who used to sew tiny bells along her décolletage to ensure that not a man within earshot would miss the chance to take a peek."

"You cannot be serious!" Haley returned to her dress, pinning the lace to the fabric. "I swear you say these things to shock me."

"Me? I was merely conveying a provocative tale from my youth, and perhaps inspiring you to risk a bell or two of your own." Alice regally leaned back as if she had announced the need for tea. "They were etched silver and very pretty. I think I still have them in a trinket box in my bureau drawer if you'd like to use them."

"Aunt Alice!"

"Oh, very well! Another day," she said in mock disappointment before giving way to a smile. "I think Mr. Hawke may have kept his word. So many calling cards and invitations today! He is so very kind, don't you think?"

Haley shook her head. "I don't see what he stands to gain from all this generosity. Perhaps he desires an investment opportunity in Mr. Trumble's factories or—"

"Or," Aunt Alice cut her off, "he is simply being a true gentleman and making good on his promises."

"An unlikely possibility." Haley stood to set the emerald pieces aside. "People are rarely kind without cause."

"Oh, dear! I'm afraid you've taken too many of your father's hardships to heart. Be careful, dearest. Cynicism is unbecoming in a woman."

"I'm not cynical. I'm just . . . cautious." At the comical look of disbelief on her aunt's face, Haley gave in to a smile and decided against further argument. "Very well, then! Mr. Hawke is a veritable saint and I will lay flowers at his feet at our very next meeting. Satisfied?"

"Completely."

One of the maids knocked discreetly at the open doorway. "Mr. Trumble is downstairs to collect you for the exhibition, Miss Moreland."

"Thank you, Agnes. I'll be down directly." She smoothed out her skirts and reached up to make sure her hair wasn't awry. "Weren't you coming, my dear chaperone?"

"For a man who needs bells to find your bosom? I should think not!"

"You are deliberately trying to get me flustered." Haley crossed to sit next to her aunt, aware of just how stubborn Alice could be. "Please come. It's supposed to be a lovely outing, something to do with the botanicals of the South American jungles, I believe."

"My head is pounding already, just thinking about it." Aunt Alice took Haley's hand to pat it apologetically. "I'm sure that Mr. Trumble won't take advantage of my absence, and even if he did, would that not be an improvement? A small hint of relief that his feelings toward you may include a touch of passion after all?"

Haley pulled her hand away, a guilty flush creeping into her cheeks. She didn't see how Herbert making advances was any form of improvement, but admitting such a thing meant facing that it was her own passions that were untouched and cold when it came to her current engagement. "He is demonstrating gentlemanly restraint and I happen to admire him for it!"

Aunt Alice continued, "Forgive me, dearest. I didn't mean to embarrass you! But I'm afraid I would age ten years staring at jungle ferns and listening to some professor-type wax poetic about river algae."

"You're a terrible chaperone, Aunt Alice, but I don't think I have the strength to argue the point this afternoon." She stood to go, retrieving her bonnet from a table by the door. "Please let Father know I will be home before dinner."

"I'll make sure he knows not to worry. Do have fun, Haley, or at least try! You're far too young for all this remarkable discipline and practical nonsense!"

Haley shook her head but smiled. "I will make every effort to look for mischief to get into."

Aunt Alice beamed and waved her out the door. "That's my girl!"

Haley deliberately kept her chin up as she headed for the stairs. If her aunt and others perceived her as a practical person, then it was all for the best. She certainly was striving to keep a level head and not let sentimentality disrupt her plans, but it was getting harder and harder to ignore her misgivings. *Perhaps I am my mother's daughter more than I would wish to be—all this longing for things I cannot have, and odd thoughts about men who have no business in balconies.*

Herbert crossed the open hall downstairs, looking up eagerly for her. "There you are! I was just boasting to Mr. Bascombe at the coffeehouse that you were always prompt. A fine quality in a wife, I told him."

"I'm sure punctuality is a fine quality for anyone to strive for, but thank you, Mr. Trumble." Haley reached the bottom of the stairs to take her wrap from one of the servants. She was used to his odd compliments. Mr. Trumble never spoke of her appearance, perhaps because he thought it might be too direct. If Mr. Trumble was anything, Haley knew he was reserved in his courtship—if not in his social conduct otherwise.

"Where is your aunt?" He looked nervously behind her. "Fashionably late again?"

"I'm afraid she won't be joining us this afternoon. A slight headache has detained her abovestairs."

"Oh, well . . . that is . . . regrettable." He tugged on the lapels of his coat, as if bracing himself for the trials ahead. "We'll just have to do our best to enjoy the fruits of Mr. Millstein and Mr. Brown's expedition to the Amazon on our own. Shall we go then?" He held out his arm to stiffly escort her down to the carriage, and the pair was finally off.

Haley was relieved to see it was the open chaise and suddenly felt a small hint of excitement to be out of the house and away. *Perhaps Aunt Alice was right, if not in her specifics, then in the direction of her advice. I need to try to be happier.* "What a lovely day, Mr. Trumble!" she said as she took her seat and arranged her skirts.

"The wind is blowing in the proper direction, for once," he returned with a jolly certainty. "London air is not the sweetest, but who would complain? And with such company? Although . . ." He hesitated to situate himself as conscientiously as he could on the seat next to her. "I do hope no one thinks I've spirited you away from your keepers."

He was openly uncomfortable without Aunt Alice along—and a sheen of nervous perspiration across his upper lip only compounded the trouble, forcing him to anxiously dab at his face at odd moments with a linen handkerchief. "Not that this is not reasonably proper since we are formally engaged, but . . . these Londoners do have their own ideas about what is proper and what isn't. We'll be sure to meet friends as soon as we're there, and then no one will be able to say that we were genuinely alone." He shifted another inch or two away from her on the carriage seat, as if even the touch of her skirts against his breeches might cause offense. "I'm thinking only of you, naturally."

Haley had to bite the inside of her lip to keep from laughing. With his handkerchief sporadically popping up and down, he looked like an old bishop waving to the populace as they drove by. "You're too thoughtful, Mr. Trumble."

"Manners make the man, my father always said." He wiped off his lips again but clearly began to warm to the conversation. "I imagine it's manners that make the cut anywhere, but I'm thrilled to discover such a welcome in high society."

Haley nodded, unsure of what to say. Mr. Trumble, for all his courtesies, was hardly a paragon of etiquette, and she knew that their welcome had more to do with his fortune and her father's title than anything else.

"Even Mr. Bascombe remarked on our good fortune!" Herbert continued cheerfully.

"Did he?" she asked.

"He said he was extremely impressed that we'd garnered Mr. Hawke's attention. 'A rare blessing to gain three words in conversation as of late,' he said. Never a prayer he'll be seen making social calls, and all that, but now—Mr. Bascombe was asking me how I'd managed it! I told him it was the pair of you exchanging secrets that must have done it."

"We were hardly exchanging—"

"Ah, here we are!"

He held out a gloved hand to help her alight from the carriage. "Melrose's sister is a judge, so we must be sure to inquire after her. She was the one who mentioned that this was the perfect genteel outing for a bride-to-be."

"How so?" Haley deliberately pressed, her curiosity getting the better of her as she was unsure of how Miss Melrose made the link between tropical botany and English brides.

"Oh, well . . ." Herbert's brow furrowed as he considered the puzzle briefly before his expression cleared and returned to its usual jolly state. "All ladies love flowers."

Haley wouldn't have corrected him for the world but took the gloved hand he offered to help her down from the carriage. Together they headed up the shallow steps to the exhibition hall, and Haley did her best to take in the grand setting. The explorers seemed to have collected an entire jungle to display for the curious of London, and it was difficult not to wonder if they had left anything behind in the Amazon to shade the native inhabitants there. Behind orderly ropes and descriptive signs, floras of every size and shape were doing their best to evoke an exotic aura and make onlookers forget that they were steps away from Regent's Park.

But as Herbert nervously escorted her through the gathering, it was clear he was far more interested in finding his friends than stopping to take in the sights. She did her best to stay serenely at his side, but his sudden bursts of speed when he thought he'd spotted this or that acquaintance made it challenging—not to mention his sudden stops when he realized that he was virtually running up to greet complete strangers.

"Ouch!" Her toes took a direct blow as Mr. Trumble changed directions without warning.

"Pardon me, Miss Moreland!" He took out his handkerchief to wipe at his sweat-soaked brow. "I had no idea that the exhibit would be so popular with the general public."

"I imagine it's their only chance to experience the Amazon, Mr. Trumble." Haley forced a smile and ignored the throbbing pinch of her toes and the quizzical looks of a few bystanders. "Shall we just stroll and see if friends will simply find us?"

His brow furrowed at the proposal. "I don't see that they would stand a chance with all these vines blocking a man's view of the horizon." His expression cleared as he came up with his own brilliant plan. "Let's reserve your strength, my dear, and spare your poor feet! There are benches in these smaller rooms. Why don't you stay here, where it is quiet, and I will make the effort to locate suitable company? Then we can review the exhibits without anxiety!"

"As you say," she said, swallowing a sigh of disappointment. *So much for my afternoon outing! I could have sat at home and in better quiet, but I suppose one has to make the best of it.* "It's very considerate of you, Mr. Trumble."

"There you are! No one will bother you here, and I shall be back within moments! I'll ask for Miss Melrose!" He made a little bow and gave an odd wave of his handkerchief before heading out on his quest. Haley watched him go with a wistful smile.

She was abandoned, yet again. The minutes stretched out into a dull and tedious chain, and Haley's thoughts wandered to the more interesting study of the attendees than the botanical wonders in the hall. It was a true slice of London society, and she did her best to memorize the lively flow so that she could relate it again when Aunt Alice asked.

The hoi polloi made a fascinating show, but one well-to-do couple in particular caught her eye as they sauntered nearby. Haley's hands unconsciously clenched in her lap as she watched the pair of lovers, clearly enamored, with their eyes locked on each other. They paid no attention to their surroundings, but instead made it seem as if the world around them no longer existed. In a subtle dance of polite gestures and movements of their bodies and hands, they strolled past her at a dreamlike pace. It was all somehow genteel and civilized, but it was as if they were yet connected to each other, beyond conventional rules.

Haley would have looked away when the gentleman reached out to trace his lady's cheek and brush back a curl from her face, but then he leaned in to run his tongue along the outside shell of the woman's ear—and Haley was sure the world had stopped to hold its breath. She gasped at the intimate act, breathless at their boldness and shocked at her own envy. *What would it be like to be touched like that? To want to touch someone so badly that it wouldn't matter where you were or who was watching?*

"Are you a voyeur, Miss Moreland?"

She jumped from the bench, startled beyond words to have

been caught staring—and by Mr. Hawke! "N-not at all! I was just . . . admiring the . . ." She could feel the heat of her blood in her cheeks as she realized that she couldn't name a single plant in the vicinity to make her lie plausible. "Greenery," she finished lamely.

"Were you?"

His tone had a friendly teasing edge to it, and Haley couldn't help but smile at it. "I am a great fan of greenery," she finally managed. It was mortifying to be caught gawking at strangers, and her guilt heightened every sensation and made her feel breathless and awkward. "And you?"

He took a small step closer, effectively cutting off her view of almost everything and everyone in the hall. "I think Mr. Millstein and Mr. Brown are apparently obsessed with ferns, and that a man can waste a great deal of time looking for beauty on far-off continents only to realize that it was within his reach right here at home."

Haley almost hiccupped at his provocative words, and even more at the strange heat in his eyes as he looked at her so directly. "I'm not sure they have the same ferns in Hampshire."

Galen glanced back over his shoulder at the pair she'd been studying, watching them move away toward the main hall, before he looked back at her to ask, "Have you ever been in love like that, Miss Moreland?"

"What a—that's an inappropriate question, Mr. Hawke!"

"Is it?" He shrugged, taking a step back to innocently gesture for her to return to her place on the bench, so that he could sit next to her. "I didn't mean to pry."

Haley took the seat tentatively, reminding herself that they were in a public hall and it was probably her own nerves making her feel so strangely charged and defensive. "It is a personal and private subject, sir."

His gaze fixed on her with an intensity that made the world fade away. Once again, she could feel her practical nature just slipping away in his presence. There was a touch of something savage in his emerald eyes, something wicked and unfettered that belied the word *gentleman*. His appearance was flaw-lessly civilized, but the glimmer in his eyes mocked the very idea. His elegant façade did nothing to mute the effect but only managed to highlight it. And instead of being frightened, Haley felt a surge of desire at the sight of it.

For one fleeting second, she thought she saw a hint of . . . dislike? But it was gone before she could name it, and he shifted closer and there was nothing to note but the raw masculine presence mere inches from her.

"What are you doing, Mr. Hawke?"

"I'm trying to understand you better. You are not an easy woman to make out, Miss Moreland." He tilted his head to one side, as if contemplating a great mystery. "Is love such a forbidden thing to ever mention?"

"Not forbidden, just . . ." Haley wasn't even sure what to say. "It's a topic that could be misinterpreted."

"Perhaps I do venture too far to ask these things." He straightened, his manner once again casual. "Your face when you were watching those lovers, Miss Moreland, made me wonder whether you were thinking of a love you'd lost, or wishing for another. You looked like a beggar at a bakery window."

"I did not!" She narrowly reined in the urge to strike him in the arm. "I am not—starving for affection!"

He laughed and held up one hand defensively as if aware of how close he'd come to a well-earned bruise. "I apologize! My mistake, Miss Moreland. But who wouldn't envy them, even secretly?"

She took a deep breath, ignoring the cascade of butterflies in her stomach. "There is nothing to envy. Love is . . . foolish. A woman has to keep her wits about her, if she wishes to avoid . . ." Haley bit her lip before her mind could summon the right word. "If she wishes to avoid catastrophe."

"Ah, yes! Catastrophe." He leaned forward, his voice dropping to an intimate growl. "I think a man in love with you would sacrifice anything to keep you from, as you so eloquently described it, catastrophe."

Haley nearly jumped from her place as his hand casually

moved into the voluminous folds of her skirt so that just the tips of his fingers grazed the outside curve of her hip. Layers of cloth did little to lessen the imprint of the heat of his fingers at her thigh, and worst of all, she couldn't seem to bring herself to move away.

"I wouldn't—"

He withdrew his hand to shift on the bench, making the touch seem entirely accidental, and Haley lost her train of thought.

"Yes?" he prompted gently.

"I wouldn't want someone to sacrifice anything on my behalf. I don't need—" She couldn't make herself say "love," and then she wasn't sure what to say at all. She was drowning in needs and fighting every instinct to seize onto Galen and beg him to never stop looking at her this way, to put his hand back and to do more—to do all the things that the beautiful caged creature behind his eyes would do if there were no consequences. "Not everyone is interested in such things, Mr. Hawke."

He shook his head, lessening the spell but not breaking it. "You hide more than any woman I have ever met."

"I'm hardly hiding, Mr. Hawke."

"No?"

"No." Haley did her best to look cavalier and close the subject. "I am entitled to seek a few moments of quiet, if I wish to."

"To catch your breath," he amended playfully. "I can see how one might mistake the practice for something else."

"You are an expert on the matter, Mr. Hawke." Haley smiled, enjoying the banter in spite of herself.

"May I see your hand?"

"Whatever for?" Her smile vanished at the unexpected request.

"For science, Miss Moreland."

"Science," she echoed, completely caught off guard. "I'm sure I shouldn't allow a stranger to hold my hand in public."

"I'm hardly a stranger, Miss Moreland. We've been formally introduced, and I'm not trying to make love to you in front of a display of philodendrons. I'm just trying to satisfy a small and innocent curiosity."

Nothing about you is innocent, Mr. Hawke. She repressed the quick rejoinder by a narrow margin. "A curiosity about what, exactly?"

"Your hand, please."

Haley held out her gloved hand, unsure of exactly what the man intended.

He shook his head. "I'll need to see your bare palm for this to work, Miss Moreland."

Well, this certainly qualifies as mischief. . . . Haley tugged at the tip of each finger to pull off the glove on her right hand and then deliberately held it up, palm outward, fingers splayed to show him her hand. She silently congratulated herself on complying with his outlandish request without any risk of an onlooker mistaking it for anything inappropriate. *Odd, perhaps, but not scandalous!*

His gaze shifted to her palm, and he looked at it as if she were holding up a pamphlet for him to peruse. Haley felt a stab of uncertainty. "Mr. Hawke?"

"In the east, I met a man who claimed that each experience leaves a mark on the hand, and that there was wisdom in each line if a man knew how to read it." Galen reached up to extend his own index finger to trace an almost invisible groove along the fleshy and sensitive topography of her palm. The touch was electric and so light, evoking pleasure that she hadn't expected. "If you were ever in love, Miss Moreland, it would be here."

"Would it?" she whispered.

"Love should leave a mark, don't you think?" His finger continued its journey, a magic that kept her spellbound. "Something that powerful, with that kind of passion. There should be a sign of some kind, some indelible scar that is unmistakable—or it wasn't love. But then, a scar likens it to something that you would avoid. A catastrophe to be warded off, instead of a quest for completion."

"You're a romantic, Mr. Hawke."

"Not at all." He withdrew his fingertip, leaving only the echo of sensation on her skin. "And we've proved our eastern friend wrong."

"Oh?" She lowered her hand slowly, surprised at the taste of disappointment.

"Not a trace to be seen, but you undoubtedly know what it is to love."

"I do?" Haley gasped at her own mistake. "I do! Yes, undoubtedly!"

A look of pure sin rewarded her confession as he leaned forward as if to make a confession of his own. Haley's heart pounded at the prospect of it, and she began to incline her own face to better hear him when—

Herbert's hail boomed along the corridor. "Just where I left you! But look, you found a friend without my aid. What a relief!" Mr. Trumble approached with every sign of pleasure at finding Mr. Hawke at her side. They stood to greet him, and Haley had to swallow a miserable lump of guilt at being caught in so foolish a position. She did her best to smoothly replace her glove, praying that Herbert wouldn't ask about its removal.

"I've been striding about looking for a familiar face and now learn that I had only to leave it to the Fates! How are you, Mr. Hawke?" Herbert said, extending his hand.

Galen offered his hand with a friendly grace to counter Herbert's eager grip. "I am well."

"Have you seen the exhibits, sir? I'm sure we'd be glad of the company if you care to take the part of chaperone. Miss Moreland's aunt has left us unaccompanied and we couldn't—"

"I'm afraid I've already seen what I desired most to see, and I have another appointment, or I would gladly do my best to keep you at arm's length from your lovely fiancée." Galen's smile was the essence of charm, but Haley had to bite her tongue at the soft undercut in his words.

Naturally, Mr. Trumble was less astute. "A shame! Next time, eh?"

"Yes." Galen bowed gallantly, deliberately not looking at her. "There will most definitely be a next time."

With another nod, he left, and Haley let out the breath she'd been holding as Herbert unwittingly invited the fox to watch the henhouse.

"Well! There's a gentleman, I warrant!" Herbert's exuberance shone on his face. "It would be rude to inquire about his clubs, but I'd say he wouldn't mind it if I mentioned him as an acquaintance when I make my own foray at the coffeehouses."

She wasn't sure if she could answer. What kind of gentleman was so forward and stirred a woman's blood until she was an inner storm of fire and muddled emotions? What kind of gentleman looked at a woman with raw desire when he knew she was spoken for? What kind of gentleman ignored the rules of civility but made her feel as if the rules needn't apply? *I don't want rules when he looks at me like that.*

"Don't you agree, Miss Moreland?" Herbert prompted when she failed to respond.

"Yes, of course." Haley did her best to reoccupy the present moment and ignore thoughts of Mr. Hawke. "But you have acquaintances that know you far better and would offer a word on your behalf if you wished it. I'm sure you have no need to mention Mr. Hawke to gain entrance to any gentleman's club that interests you, Mr. Trumble."

He shook his head and smiled, patting her hand as if she were a child to be indulged. "You are a dear thing and have been sheltered in the country, quite rightly, from all this nonsense. Men have a better head for these matters, business and introductions and such. A friendship with the son of an earl is no small thing, and I won't be the man to miss the opportunity."

"Mr. Trumble, I don't think it—"

He cut her off, his smile still friendly, but his voice firm. "I won't have anyone saying I can't hold my own with those born a notch or two above. I'm not oblivious to the advantages of a blue-blooded wife, but I won't have anyone doubting that

I can't make ties and connections of my own—and on my own merit!"

The last lingering pleasure she had in the outing dissipated. He'd never spoken so frankly about his ambitions, or her role as a well-bred pawn, but if any part of her had hoped that affection might also play a part in their relationship, he'd just rough-handedly destroyed it. *Destroyed it with a smile on his face and a simpering look afterward to make sure I'm not distraught at his tone. Oh, God.* "No one will ever say such things, Mr. Trumble."

"Let's make an early afternoon of it. I don't think your aunt would approve of you being out in this crush, and of course, better to make it a brief outing since we are unfortunately on our own, don't you think?"

"Yes, I think that's best." Haley took his arm and allowed him to lead her out of the hall.

I'm not trying to make love to you, Galen had said. Haley wasn't sure what to think. She'd been off balance through every turn of the conversation, and at each instant where she was sure he'd trespassed, she'd never mustered the momentum to stop him. Instead, she felt more like a restless child trying to play a game without knowing the rules. And now, there was only one thing she knew of Mr. Galen Hawke for certain. *I don't think he's the kind of man who needs bells.*

Chapter
5

❦

Sleep was like an elusive dragon he could just catch sight of but never quite capture. Galen wrestled with the wisps of tantalizing rest that promised restoration only to fall into a maze of images that wounded and bruised his spirit and provided no peace.

"More tea, Galen?"

In the pouring rain, she sat wearing a white linen frock soaked to the point of lust-inspiring translucence. A calm English goddess in the storm . . .

Haley was offering him tea, sitting on a wool blanket with a picnic basket next to her and china plates and silver spread out between them . . . but he couldn't take the cup because he was holding on to John. And John was dying in his arms.

"No, thank you." He heard himself answer as if there was nothing out of place. As if cucumber sandwiches and monsoons, blood and embroidered napkins made for the perfect outing.

And then she wasn't wearing white linen anymore. It was the red gown she'd been wearing the first night they'd met, and she was even more beautiful. "You should eat something sweet, Galen."

John was moaning, writhing in pain, and Galen had to struggle to hold him still—and then her dress began to change into a river of blood and it filled every plate and cup and soaked everything in sight. And the worst of it was that he couldn't take his eyes off of her. That he wanted her more than anything else. And John was getting too heavy to hold. John was slipping from his fingers. "I can't."

And she was smiling, sitting primly and looking at him, with blood in her hair, and the rain stung his skin and she began to laugh.

He was awakened by his own strangled cry of distress, a rush of shame nearly choking him. He hated this weakness that made him cry out like a child in the dark. It had been a senseless dream, and he was nauseated by the lingering heat of his still stiff cock from the macabre and erotic images of Miss Haley Moreland.

He kicked against the twist of sweat-tangled sheets that trapped his legs and took long, shaky breaths to try to regain his senses. He stood from the bed to distance himself from the visions that haunted him and began to pace, naked as the day he was born, about his bedroom.

Exhaustion gave an edge to his thoughts, but Galen wasn't sure how a man remedied such things when he dreaded his dreams more than he craved sleep. A glance at the clock on the fireplace's mantel told him that it wasn't even midnight. He raked his hand through his hair, marveling at how a woman could present such a puzzle.

He'd studied her that afternoon at the exhibition hall, searching for any flicker of guilt or remorse at the choices she'd made. Instead, she'd dismissed love as a foolish business with a naïve mercenary streak that took a man's breath away. And when he'd made his advances, she'd been all innocent blushes and clear, sweet looks of curiosity and awakening interest in his presence. He'd flirted outrageously and risked frightening her away, but the reward of experiencing her sub-

tly leaning into his touch had been worth it. And when dear
Mr. Trumble had stumbled over to interrupt their tryst, Galen
had indulged in a moment of triumph at the flash of pure disappointment in her eyes.

Galen pulled on his robe and made his way over to a small
writing desk near the windows. "Time to step out of the
shadows, Haley." He spoke his thoughts aloud as he lit the
lamps. "Let's see if we can't let your aunt think she's in on
the game."

He pulled out a piece of personalized stationery and began
his composition. After only a few moments he was calmed by
the mental exercise. The sound of the pen against the paper
seemed like a quiet anchor, tying him again to the waking
world and dismissing the last echoes of his nightmares.

Dear Mrs. Shaw,

*I hope it does not seem too forward to write this note, as I
have only recently been introduced to you and your niece.
I wished to express my concern at hearing this afternoon
that you were not feeling well enough to attend the exhibition with Mr. Trumble and Miss Moreland.*

*I also wanted to take this opportunity to ensure that
my good word has been upheld and that your social calendar has improved. Please send word if you can which
invitations have arrived so that I can press again for
those that lag behind. You and your beautiful niece are
too delightful to pass a London Season quietly, and I
am humbly pleased to offer what services I can to your
family.*

*But I would not have you think my interest is intended
to forward my own character in a Certain Lady's eyes.
Therefore I must ask that you not mention our correspon-
dence to your niece. I sense that she perceives my help as
unwarranted out of delicate sense of pride, but I do not
criticize. I admire a lady with such personal pride and
would not normally trespass. But as I stated, she seems*

*to be too lovely a girl to miss the best that London has
to offer.*

> *Yours respectfully,*
> *Galen Hawke Esquire.*

Galen read it over again to make sure he'd struck the
right note between discreet politeness and an overt invitation
to conspiracy. It was a deliberately clumsy play for a list of
Haley's social appointments, and Mrs. Shaw was no fool. She
would have to realize that he could have made discreet inquiries and gotten whatever information he wanted without
resorting to writing a letter. But asking for it tipped his hand,
and, he hoped, signaled his desire for an ally in the chase.

"And if I read you correctly, Mrs. Shaw, you're like most
women and are more than eager for a little conspiracy of your
own." Galen folded it carefully, adding his personal seal.

"What's that about conspiracies?"

Galen uncoiled from his chair at the unexpected voice
coming from the corner. Michael Rutherford was an imposing
figure as he stood unmoving just inside the room, his broad
frame unmistakable, even in the shadows.

"Damn it, Michael! You could knock, couldn't you?"

Michael smiled. "And spoil my only pleasure? Besides, I
didn't want to ring the bell and bother your servants. They
deserve a good night's rest, don't they?"

"Late for social calls, isn't it?" Galen tried to disguise his
relief at the intrusion, grateful for the diversion. He knew better than to ask how Rutherford had managed to gain entrance
to his bedroom without alerting a single soul belowstairs.
"Here, take a seat like a civilized caller and stop lurking over
there."

Michael shrugged, then moved farther into the room. "A
bit late, yes. I was driving by and saw your light and knew
you weren't sleeping." He leaned over the unlit fireplace, as
if he could still absorb heat from a phantom fire. "I ran into
Ashe earlier and he said that he was looking for Josiah. He

was apparently confident that Josiah, out of all of us, wouldn't censure his quest for entertainment."

"They could both of them benefit from restraint, but I'll not be the one to criticize. I'm hardly . . . innocent myself."

"No one is," Michael conceded, turning back from the fireplace but waving away the offered seat. "So what is this conspiracy you're planning?"

Galen considered lying for a fleeting moment, but one look in Michael's icy gray eyes and he knew it was pointless. The man had an incredible knack for discerning insincerity, and frankly, Galen valued his friendship too much to risk it. Bad enough that he'd held back with Rowan . . .

"A small bit of revenge, Rutherford. Nothing more."

Michael's look was tinged with skepticism. "Revenge is never a small matter, Hawke."

"Perhaps you're right. But in any case, I'm taking care of this personally and didn't wish to involve the others."

"Have you been wronged then? Personally?" Michael pressed, taking the seat now in one graceful movement to settle across from Galen.

"I made a promise to John. I'm acting on his behalf."

Michael leaned back against the padded carved arch of the chair, his look thoughtful. "Really? In what way?"

Galen took a deep breath before he plunged ahead. "Before he died, he asked me to see after his fiancée when we returned. But before I could even begin to seek her out, I saw a notice of her appearance in Town and of her new engagement."

"I see."

"Do you? Since we returned and word was sent of his death, it's not been a year. Not eight months. And yet his *true* love has decided to kick up her heels and take on another lover without so much as a public sniffle!" Galen felt the anger in him unleashing and gaining momentum. "It's the worst sort of betrayal, and I won't stand idly by and watch Miss Moreland dance on his grave."

"Galen, I'm not sure you—" Michael stopped himself, then went on in a more careful tone. "What could you do?

She's made her choice. Even if you despise that choice, it's hers to make."

"Yes, hers to make. But mine not to play the spectator. Not this time, Michael. If Miss Moreland wishes to ignore decency then I don't see why I can't do the same."

"What do you intend?"

"I'll expose her for the heartless witch she is and let the lady live with her choices."

"Expose her?"

Galen left his chair to cross over to his desk, retrieving a packet of papers from the top drawer. He brought them back and handed them over to Michael. "Drafts, of course. The artist I commissioned this morning to do the caricature promised to refine it later if I wished, but the text for the article alone should do the trick when the time comes."

"My God," Michael exclaimed softly. "You're going to crucify her in the press."

"They adore gossip, and this tidbit will be fact by the time I'm finished." Galen sat back down, the tension in his body unrelenting with his emotions. "She'll get no less than she deserves."

"So you say! I'm not sure you can appoint yourself her judge, jury, and executioner, Galen!"

"I didn't. John did."

Michael handed back the papers as if they scorched his fingers. "You'll go too far, Galen."

"I'll go as far as I need to, Michael, to set this girl on her heels and make it up to John."

"John's dead. I don't think he cares."

Galen's jaw clenched in fury. "I care. I made him a promise to see to her, and by God, I'll see to her as I wish. This is not your concern anymore, Michael. She was the only thing that John cared about, and she repays him by wearing party dresses and cheerfully breezing through the social season as if she hadn't a care in world?"

"Like the Lucknow widows? Weren't there a few tongues wagging at how cheerful they were? Perhaps women react differently sometimes, to death. Perhaps Miss Moreland . . . wants to embrace life instead of dwelling on John's miserable end." Michael leaned forward, desperate to convince his friend to change course.

"She isn't embracing life!" Galen left his seat, unable to sit still any longer. He paced angrily as he spoke. "She's embracing a fat little troll's bank accounts! She throws away the heart of the most decent man I've ever known, and for what? Money? My God, Michael! I know that London is no stranger to the practice, but—I cannot let it stand, not this time."

"You could, Galen."

"I won't!" he roared back, instantly aware of how it all sounded, especially with Michael's calm voice in counter to his. He took a step back and let out a long breath to try to decrease the chokehold of anger that made his hands shake. "I can't, Michael. I know it probably makes me a lesser man, but I think of John and I cannot see any other course open to me."

Michael stood, carefully unfolding as if wary of making any sudden movements. But when their eyes met, there was no trace of uncertainty. "Your cartoon alluded that she was onto would-be husband number three. Are you throwing young bucks in her path then? Or are you taking a more direct hand in it, Galen?"

Galen held his ground, his silence supplying the answer.

Michael sighed. "And what if Miss Moreland doesn't fall for the trap? Will you abandon your quest and accept her choice?"

"She won't fall," Galen said, his eyes glittering like a predator's. "She'll run into my arms. And then we won't hear arguments about her good character and questionable choices, will we?"

Michael shook his head and began to move toward the concealed servant's entrance he'd come through. But Galen called after him, and his steps slowed.

"I'm asking for your silence, Michael. Even if you don't agree with what I'm doing, swear to me that you won't interfere."

Michael turned back, assessing his friend. They'd been

through so much. But Galen had borne the brunt of their captor's attentions more than most. Galen had been John's protector in prison, shielding him whenever he could. Michael suspected it was because John reminded him of the younger brother that Hawke had seen die in their childhood. So after months of torture and starvation, and the strange twists of their escape, John's death had hit Galen particularly hard.

And now he'd seized on the idea that he could set things right by punishing this girl—for not grieving? For not being faithful to John? For not sharing Galen's pain? Michael knew it was an unfathomable blend of all those things and a dozen more that Galen couldn't name.

Easier to hate this woman and distract himself with revenge than accept fate, Michael mused. Every fiber in his being knew that Galen was off in the fog, but fighting him wouldn't help. And Michael had seen too many battles to invoke one now. *I'm just worried you'll go too far, Galen . . . but even if you're heading for Hades, I suppose I wouldn't be much of a friend if I didn't acknowledge that I'll still follow and do my best to keep you safe.* "I swear I'll leave you to your game. And as for the rest of the Jaded . . ."

Galen smiled to hear Michael use the term.

Michael acknowledged the look before completing his vow. "Yes, the Jaded. I'll keep our exchange tonight to myself. But if they ask, I'm not lying. I'll keep your motives out of it, but the rest of it will be public knowledge soon enough, won't it?"

"When I'm ready, yes." Galen folded his arms. "Thank you, Michael."

"Don't thank me, Galen. Just be careful."

He was gone before Galen could respond to try to defuse the tension between them. Even so, Galen wasn't sure what he could have said to have soothed the rift. Michael just didn't understand. It was a grisly business, and nothing he was ready to boast about, but Galen knew that Michael would be true to his word, and for now, he would have the freedom he needed to complete his mission.

There was a firm knock at the door.

"Are you in need of anything, sir?" Bradley's voice was filled with a concern the solid door did nothing to muffle.

"Come in." Galen sighed. "Come in and see for yourself that I am fine and in fact, don't need for a thing."

Bradley came through the door, a heavy brass candlestick holder aloft as if he'd anticipated a good brawl. "I heard shouting and could have sworn you were under attack!"

Galen shook his head. "The danger is passed, good sir. Now put that thing down before you set your nightcap on fire."

"Trouble sleeping, then? Was it a nightmare?" Bradley pressed, lowering his candle. "Shall I send for Dr. West?"

"I don't need a nursemaid, Bradley!"

Bradley was nonplussed. "May I make you some tea? The green tea seemed to suit you last time. Perhaps it will calm your nerves, sir."

Galen felt a twitch of amusement at the man's cheek, but also at the strange notion that a cup of green tea didn't sound unappealing. *Damn it. So much for proclaiming my independence! Bradley's getting too good at this. I'll have to increase his wages at this pace.*

"Tea, then," Galen said. "And a plate of anything handy downstairs. I may as well eat while I'm at it. But don't wake the cook!"

"I'm the soul of stealth, sir." Bradley bowed curtly and retreated to fetch the tray.

"Wonderful," he spoke aloud to the closed door. "Everyone is the soul of stealth and may come and go in this house as they wish."

Everyone, except me.

Chapter
6

The sound of a Mozart concerto filled the elegant ballroom, now appointed as an intimate music hall for the Earl of Marchfield's guests. Aunt Alice had insisted that they were seated at the back of the room to allow them to leave discreetly if her headache should return. Haley was convinced that her dear aunt might be using these headaches more and more frequently to achieve her own aims, but it was hard to confront her chaperone since Haley wasn't clear on Alice's overall scheme.

For the moment, Haley was battling to politely ignore the long, heavy breathing sounds of a very sleepy Mr. Trumble seated next to her. A distracting internal debate as to how one might subtly awake him before the rumbling breaths became out-and-out snores and drew the attention of everyone in the hall was overshadowing any pleasure she may have had in the concert. So far, he'd tipped his head forward onto his chest in what she prayed might be mistaken for a meditative pose.

She leaned forward to try to catch Aunt Alice's eye on the other side of Mr. Trumble for assistance, but her aunt had, in fact, achieved a similar repose, though with a more ladylike smile on her face and less of a tendency to snore and give herself away.

So much for classical music uplifting the soul! Apparently, I'm the only one who's still conscious!

Haley lifted her fan and made a careful study of the guests in front of her and further down the row to make sure that no one else was aware of her dilemma. It wasn't uncommon for a guest to nod off during a lengthy performance, but if the slip in etiquette intruded on someone else's enjoyment of the evening, it was far less forgivable an offense.

She sighed with temporary relief when no one's eyes met hers with disapproval or amusement and leaned back to consider her next strategy. *A pinch on his elbow? But if he's startled and yelps, then I've humiliated him and that's too horrible to—*

A man softly cleared his throat to her left, and Haley froze. When she'd summoned the nerve to look up, there he was. Leaning against the wall was a jaguar with glittering emerald eyes that conveyed pure mischief. *He must have arrived late and just taken his place there by coincidence.*

It was hard to credit the handsome presence of Galen Hawke standing six feet away to mere coincidence, but Haley wasn't sure what to think as she looked away quickly as if riveted by the violinist. Herbert chose that moment to let out a soft snort, and Haley felt a flood of embarrassment stain her cheeks.

After what felt like a small eternity, Haley glanced back again, a small part of her wondering if he'd seen enough of her misery and decided to move on. But he was still there.

And he was looking directly at her.

*   *   *

Galen had waited patiently, watching her struggle for decorum as Mr. Trumble slid further and further into what was guaranteed to be an ill-timed sleep in front of all their newest acquaintances. The humor of it, as her fiancé and aunt both nodded in their chairs, was difficult to ignore. But the sight of her—so beautiful and so proud, a regal thing perched on her seat trying to act as if there was nothing amiss in the world, affected him in a way he'd not expected. She was in a jewel green evening gown, with lace dyed to match along the décolletage that drew his eyes along the creamy slopes of her shoulder blades and neck. A glittering hair comb in the shape of a peacock held her lustrous brown curls aloft, and Galen's fingers itched to pluck it free and watch her hair fall down her back.

And when she glanced back at him the second time, with her cheeks flushed pink, he made no effort to look away. Instead, he held her gaze and let the erotic fantasy in his mind unfold—aware that it must show in his face, that the raw heat of his need would blaze in his eyes, challenging her not to look away.

It's just us in the world, isn't it? And if it were just us . . . in this room . . . it would echo with your sighs, Miss Haley Moreland. I can just see it. Can you? I'm going to take down that hair and fist my hands in that silk and kiss you until you know what it is to be well and truly kissed. You'll have no thoughts of the mud troll, my dear. No thoughts of any other man before me. . . . How long till that reserve is gone, I wonder? I'm going to taste you until I'm satisfied. And only then will I see to those buttons and laces. . . .

I shall strip you bare and lay out that green dress on the floor and push you back against it. I'm going to survey every inch of your body, and then I'm going to taste every inch until I'm satisfied. Galen had to shift his balance slightly, aware of his body's raging reaction to the workings of his mind. His cock was rock hard as he imagined her arching beneath him, pressing those breasts upward like a pagan offering for his worshipping mouth, her thighs parting wide to show him the ripe, glistening pink flesh that would be his to claim. *You'll be wet and wanton and this illusion of prim reserve will shatter forever when you come for me. . . .*

He wanted her in a thousand ways, and the erotic tangle of

it unfolded in a sweet cascade of images that taunted him as he held his place against the wall.

I'm going to have you, Haley Moreland. All of you. Every glorious inch, and then we'll see what the tigress is capable of when she has nowhere to turn. . . .

Her lips parted, as if she'd heard him, but still she didn't look away. He could see her breath coming faster, the crescendo in the music masking her situation from the man at her side. The color of her dress brought out the green in her eyes, and he watched in open fascination at the storm of emotions that lit them from within. One pale hand moved up to cover her heart, as if her trembling fingers could slow its beat and shield it from him; yet still, she didn't look away.

I want you. I want you. I want you. He let the thought echo again and again, in rhythm with the music, deliberately seeking to cast a spell and consign her to her fate.

Haley wasn't sure how long she'd been caught in his gaze. It was so otherworldly and impossible, to find herself staring back at him, basking in the heat of his eyes like a cat basking in the sun. She kept thinking that she should feel some measure of shame or offense, but her outrage never seemed to coalesce in the whirlwind of her emotions. This wasn't the leering or lecherous look of an uncouth ruffian—this was that primitive fire she'd first glimpsed in him at the exhibition hall, unleashed. She felt naked as his eyes raked over her body, as if he were touching her, or even somehow devouring her. For his look was raw hunger, and she knew instinctively that she was the main course. But fear gave way to something else she couldn't name, her body surging with heat and a restless hunger of its own that answered his and begged him to step away from the wall.

It was ridiculous to think such things, to entertain this bizarre exchange in such a public place and without a care to the slumbering man at her side, but once again in his presence, Haley felt the world slide away into an inconsequential background that left only the two of them together.

Wicked thoughts of what it would mean to surrender to impulse, to allow him to do more than look, suffused her cheeks with color and Haley had to put a hand over her heart to prevent it from pounding out of her chest. *A girl could drown in those eyes and never cry for help. It's indecent, the way he's openly staring. It's obscene the way I'm enjoying this—every thrilling, horrifying second of this. . . . I should—*

But the internal momentum of her protest faltered at "should" as an odd spasm of delicious tension made her aware of every taut inch of her body, from the tiny hairs raised on the back of her neck to the molten damp well between her legs. It was too much.

She began to rise from her chair to escape on unsteady legs, determined to end it, once and for all. But just at that instant, the musical piece ended in a flourish and applause broke out. Herbert awoke with a distinct snort, and then immediately joined in to clap his hands with guilty enthusiasm as Aunt Alice calmly opened her eyes as if pleasantly surprised to find her dreams ending in public acclaim.

Haley was forced to keep her seat, fanning herself with her eyes forward. *If I'm lucky, he'll just take this opportunity to slip away before Herbert or anyone else notices him. After all, he cannot be so reckless as to want to draw attention to himself just standing there . . . staring at me, can he?*

"Well, that was most refreshing!" Herbert exclaimed. "Very re—Ah! Mr. Hawke! I didn't see you there, sir!" Herbert stepped in front of Haley to reach out and offer his hand, the clumsy maneuver sacrificing her toes and pushing her closer to Mr. Hawke. "It was a delightful performance, was it not?"

"Delightful," he echoed, his eyes looking sympathetically at Haley's struggles to keep her skirts and extremities out of her fiancé's careless path, before he looked back to Herbert and accepted the handshake. "I cannot imagine a better performance, Mr. Trumble."

"Are you staying for the reception? Won't you join our small party?" Herbert asked. "Lord Moreland leaves us a gentleman short this evening, and so I'm sure Mrs. Shaw would enjoy having an escort on her arm."

Haley was sure her heart was going to simply stop at the strain. Bad enough to have Herbert pawing at the man like an overeager puppy, but she wasn't sure she could risk any more of Galen Hawke's incendiary looks in her direction before someone else took note. "I-I think Aunt Alice might be too tired for—"

"Nonsense! I've had a lovely nap and I'm feeling like a girl of sixteen!" Aunt Alice smiled, the flash of mischief in her eyes impossible to miss.

"And tonight, you look it, Mrs. Shaw," Galen said, giving her a quick but gallant bow and extracting his hand from Herbert's sporadic grip.

Aunt Alice practically giggled. "There's a gentleman who knows how to win a woman's heart!"

"Well, that settles it," Herbert said. "I believe they've set up refreshments in the salon. Shall we?"

When it was clear that Mr. Trumble was going to head toward the salon at Galen's side, it was Galen who subtly held back to offer Aunt Alice his arm, giving Herbert the chance to correct his mistake and retrieve his forgotten ladylove.

"I'm sorry, Miss Moreland," Herbert mumbled. "All this ferrying about is quite something to get used to, isn't it?"

She nodded, not sure how to answer, mortified that Mr. Hawke was witnessing every misstep. The contrasts between the two men were becoming painfully stark and difficult to ignore, and Haley felt a miserable rush of guilt for her own misbehavior. Even so, it was punishment enough to play along and hold her place in the awkward scene that was unfolding around her.

The salon was a broad room adjacent to the ballroom and was intended for just such a party with its various seats and sofas for conversation and games of wit. At the far end, a display of food and delights was set out to impress even the most hedonistic London palate. There was even a display of sparkling champagne at the center of the long sideboard, and servants were circulating with crystal glasses to make sure that no one missed a chance to indulge.

Herbert let go of her arm once they'd reached a few vacant chairs in one corner of the room. "There, isn't this nice? Are you hungry, Mrs. Shaw? Can I fetch you some cake?"

Alice shook her head. "None for me, but perhaps a bite of everything for Haley. She's been peckish for days, and I'd hate to see her faint away and miss the best part of the evening!"

Haley gasped. "I'm not—no one is fainting!" She flipped open her fan with a telling snap, trying desperately to signal her aunt to behave. "I do not faint. Ever."

"When I was young, Mr. Hawke"—Alice turned to her co-conspirator—"I used to swoon with great skill and, I assure you, great charm. It is a lost art."

Galen smiled. "I'd have loved to have seen it."

Aunt Alice rewarded him with a flirtatious blush that would have been a credit to a woman half her age. "You would have been just the kind of man I'd have deliberately overtightened my corset for, Mr. Hawke."

"Aunt Alice!" Haley squeaked. "You mustn't . . . Mr. Hawke may not appreciate your rare sense of humor the way we do, Aunt Alice. Please!"

"On the contrary"—Galen looked directly at Haley, openly enjoying her discomfort—"I find your aunt delightful, although Mr. Trumble may be the one in need of smelling salts."

All the talk of swooning had indeed brought out a nervous sheen of sweat on Mr. Trumble's brow, and he looked for all the world like a man who would rather be on an inquisitor's rack than in a discussion that mentioned ladies' undergarments. His color had gone a little gray, but he plucked out his white handkerchief and gave his forehead a characteristic pat. "No! No! But I think I'll head off to get a plate, after all. I heard that the earl spent a pretty penny on all of it, and I wouldn't want to see it wasted!"

He turned to carry out his mission and disappeared from view amidst the gathering attendees.

Haley took a deep breath and wondered what conversation was appropriate after what had taken place between them.

Though Alice had no such hesitations. "Doesn't my niece look fetching in her emerald silk?"

"Extremely fetching," he said, a smoldering look at Haley underlining his words. "I would be surprised if she hasn't fetched every heart in London into her hands by now."

"I am not . . . in the habit, of collecting hearts, Mr. Hawke," Haley said.

"I'm glad to hear it." Galen's eyes seem to darken as he looked at her. "So many women seem to think it a game, gathering men's hearts like trinkets."

"Lah! But what a lot of clutter!" Aunt Alice interrupted. "Where in the world would a person put all those trinkets? Although, if I had wisely gotten expensive trinkets instead of hearts, perhaps I'd be a wealthier old woman today."

"Aunt Alice." Haley had to bite the inside of her cheek to hold back a lecture on appropriate moments to reminisce on instances of youthful indiscretion. "Please."

Herbert returned without the promised plate of food, startling a few nearby guests as he hailed them. "Look who I found near the sandwiches! What a jolly surprise to see him here as well!"

Rand Bascombe smiled at his elbow, apparently flattered to be the subject of a remarkable discovery. "Common enough to see me by now, I would think, Mr. Trumble, but thank you. Is it possible that this is the elusive Mr. Hawke?"

"It is!" Herbert beamed. "Mr. Hawke, Mr. Rand Bascombe was your host a few days ago at his home, so I assumed you knew each other well enough. Bascombe was kind enough to harbor my future in-laws and fiancée until I could find suitable lodgings for them when we first arrived in London, and I am forever in his debt."

"Not forever, Mr. Trumble," Bascombe corrected him with lofty charm, "but perhaps for a Season or two until I can think of a favor you can do me in return." He turned to Galen. "It is a pleasure to finally meet you face-to-face, Mr. Hawke."

Galen nodded, his expression more neutral. "Mr. Bascombe."

Mr. Bascombe waved over a servant with a tray full of sparkling crystal flutes of champagne. "Let's toast to your return, Mr. Hawke."

"I wasn't aware the man had been away!" Mrs. Shaw said, only to be roundly ignored by Mr. Bascombe.

"What a lively idea! A toast!" Herbert replied to Rand, as if never in his life had anyone proposed a toast in his presence.

"Yes, back from . . . where in India was it?" Bascombe asked Galen, his gaze intent.

Galen seemed to ignore the question and held up a hand of refusal, even as Herbert eagerly took a glass. "I don't drink, but thank you."

Rand's hand hesitated for a moment, but then he also took a goblet. "Are you a religious man, then, Mr. Hawke?"

Galen shook his head slowly. "Not at all."

"Don't tease him, Mr. Bascombe!" Mrs. Shaw chimed in. "Besides, I never saw why God would object to a good glass of sherry now and again!"

"Mr. Melrose said he never trusts a man who doesn't demonstrate a good command of his faculties after a bottle or two," Herbert added cheerfully. "But he must not trust too many men then, for I swear I don't know any man who demonstrates any good sense after two bottles of distilled spirits! I hardly make sense after two glasses, and where's the reason in that?"

"Reason to try temperance, I'd say," Mrs. Shaw said softly enough that only Haley could hear her.

"You are a music lover, then, sir?" Mr. Bascombe readdressed Galen. "Is that what draws you back out from hiding in your hermit's cave?"

"I wasn't aware I was hiding," he said. A small twitch of a smile tugged at the corner of his mouth, and Haley knew he was thinking of their first encounter on that dark balcony.

"You were a fixture in Town before you went to India, and no one has seen a breath of you since your return—until these last two weeks, that is! I cannot help but wonder what brings you out so late in the Season," Bascombe said, openly speculating. "Dispelling rumors, Mr. Hawke? Or are you trying to create new ones?"

Haley's shock at this rude line of questioning ended her silence. "Mr. Hawke is too gentlemanly to pay any heed to wagging tongues, I'm sure, Mr. Bascombe."

"Is he?" Rand looked at her as if he'd just noticed her standing in their midst. "Yes. Yes, of course he is, Miss Moreland. I meant to jest."

"A pitfall of befriending all those politicians," Aunt Alice said with an innocent smile. "No one can ever tell when you're jesting, or what you mean when you do."

Herbert laughed. "Then almost everyone I meet in London is a politician, for I swear I can't make out what anyone means by anything in this town."

"You should hire a translator, Trumble," Rand said, his warm smile not touching the ice in his eyes. "Though you may be better off in ignorant bliss."

Galen stiffened, neutrality fading from his expression. But Herbert spoke before Galen could give his displeasure a voice. "You jest, again! But we mustn't give the ladies the impression that we aren't the best of friends, eh?"

Bascombe nodded and snatched another glass of champagne from a passing servant's tray. He held it out to Galen. "Yes. Come, Hawke. Drink to friendship."

Galen didn't move. "As I said, I don't drink."

"Make an exception! How can you not for such lively company and on such a night?" Herbert said merrily, unaware of the disastrous tension in the air.

"Good evening." He somberly turned to Mrs. Shaw and Haley, dismissing the men outright. "I look forward to seeing you again." He took Haley's hand and bowed over it, his eyes rising to meet hers one last time. "Soon, I hope."

He released her fingers and turned away without another word.

A long, awkward pause was ended with Aunt Alice's sigh.

"How gallant he is!" She fanned herself, ignoring Rand's disgruntled look of disappointment. "He reminds me of my husband, God rest his soul."

"Why? Was your husband a dreary teetotaler?" Mr. Bascombe jibed, but then seemed to remember his audience. "Forgive me. It's just that I am most curious about Mr. Hawke's experiences in India during the Troubles, and he is extremely uncooperative and reticent about the affair . . . to everyone apparently."

"He is quite happy to talk to Miss Moreland," Herbert volunteered. "They share secrets as readily as children share mud cakes."

"Oh, really? And what secrets are those?" Bascombe asked, holding out the unclaimed goblet of sparkling champagne to Haley. "Do tell, Miss Moreland."

Haley had had enough. With a look to her aunt, she knew she had an ally for whatever rebellion she wished to attempt. She snapped her fan closed. "*If* I had Mr. Hawke's confidence, I hope you would think better of me than to expect me to simply betray him at your command, Mr. Bascombe." She stepped away from Herbert, frustrated and furious at the confusion on his face. "I'm feeling a little fatigued and I wish to retire."

"S-so early?" Herbert asked. "But you haven't even tasted the salmon!"

"By all means, stay, Mr. Trumble, and enjoy Marchfield's hospitality," Aunt Alice offered, taking Haley by the arm. "I can take her home in the carriage and you can find your own way later. Besides, it's sweet of her to offer me an excuse to get these aching bones home before midnight, wouldn't you agree?"

"Yes, of course!" Herbert said with relief. "I shall stay then, if you don't mind, Miss Moreland, and you can rest as you wish. You are looking a little drawn and pained."

Haley winced, unwilling to admit that her "pain" might be the dawning realization that when Mr. Hawke had walked away, she'd struggled not to simply follow him. "Yes, I don't mind. Enjoy yourself, Mr. Trumble. Good evening, Mr. Bascombe."

She managed an unsteady curtsy and then made as graceful a retreat as she could with her Aunt Alice in tow.

* * *

Aunt Alice was remarkably silent until they were well away from Marchfield's manor home. But Haley knew better than to expect it to last.

"Well, *that* was an interesting evening," Aunt Alice finally said inside the dark confines of the carriage.

Haley just nodded, unsure how to voice her agreement without giving too much away.

"I like Mr. Hawke," Aunt Alice continued, undeterred by Haley's lack of response. "Not just for those striking eyes, mind you! But I swear, there was a fleeting moment when I thought he was going to punch Mr. Bascombe; and that must count in the boy's favor!"

Haley's mouth fell open for a moment. "Aunt Alice!"

"Oh, come now! You saw it, too, and must have felt a small shiver of hope that that pompous fop was going to have his due."

"You do this on purpose." Haley couldn't stop the smile that interrupted her well-worn speech. *What a sight that would have been! Bascombe landing on his oversized bottom with all the world watching!* "I don't want to talk about Mr. Hawke."

"I understand," Aunt Alice said, readjusting her wrap with a sigh. "A young woman has every right to keep her thoughts to herself."

Haley almost pointed out that she wasn't going to think about the man either, but she caught herself. "Thank you."

The silent respite was fleeting. "I think Mr. Hawke is the most handsome man I've ever seen. And mind you, I wasn't without a good eye in my youth!"

"Didn't we just agree not to talk about him?"

"No, we agreed *you* wouldn't talk about him. I made no

such promises." Aunt Alice reached up to touch her curls and adjust her feathers. "I am a woman of a certain age, and I have the privilege of talking about whatever I wish."

Haley crossed her arms and pushed back into the cushions, refusing to argue and encourage her any further.

Aunt Alice smiled in the darkness. "Oh, come now! Admit that you like him."

"I'll admit no such thing! I'm engaged to be married! Or had you forgotten that minor detail?"

"I've forgotten nothing, dearest," Aunt Alice said quietly, her tone changing softly and losing its reckless cheer. "I've not forgotten what a joyous sprite you used to be, and I still long to see a glimpse of that girl who used to tie up her skirts and run about the countryside with such happy abandon. What a mischief maker you were!"

"If this is another request for mischief, I—"

"But my brother robbed you and made more mischief than any man has a right to, Haley." Aunt Alice refused to relent. "And you've been paying for it ever since by being so responsible and practical that I swear it makes my bones ache just to look at you."

"Oh." The sound came on a single exhale.

"And so you're engaged. And I'll carry banners and stand on my head if you ask me to on your wedding day, my love. But"—she shifted over in her seat and drew Haley over to nestle next to her—"what if on your wedding day, you could be as happy as that barefoot girl without a regret in your head?"

Haley put her cheek on her aunt's shoulder. "You're like Father, Aunt Alice. You're a dreamer."

"I'm a chaperone, and I've made a few inquiries as any proper companion would. So dreamer or no, I'm old enough to give a little guidance when it's needed."

Haley lifted her head, instantly wary. "What kind of inquiries?"

"Mr. Galen Hawke is the second son, as you know, of an earl. And I discovered that he has a fair little income from his generous older brother, a Lord Winters, who has probably en-

joyed living vicariously through Galen's London adventures."
Alice beamed. "But even better, it seems the family's investments in India must have done well, because there is suddenly
talk of repairs and improvements at their estate, new horses in
the stables, and increases all around."

"Oh, dear." Haley straightened her back. "Mr. Hawke's financial status is nothing to me, Aunt Alice. It doesn't matter
if he's as rich as Croesus or—"

"It does matter! Because no one would fault you, Haley,
if he's sincere. If he's sincere in his interest, then a match to
a family of noble blood and strong financial accounts could
also be the remedy your family desperately needs." Aunt
Alice caught Haley's hands in hers. "The advantages are as
plain as the handsome nose on his face."

"You're urging me to do the unthinkable, to betray Mr.
Trumble and cast aside—"

"Unthinkable? If you haven't thought of it by now, I'm ter-
rified for the state of your heart! I know you have your honor
to consider, but changing your mind is not a capital offense
and these things happen every day, Haley."

Speech deserted her. It was an outrageous conversation,
but it was impossible to ignore. *Is he sincere? Is it really possible that there could be a happier solution to all our worries? Wait—how can I even think of it after everything that
Herbert has done for my father?*

"Life is risk, my dearest, even for the most practical creatures in our midst. But if you have a chance for true passion
and happiness in this brief lifetime, then you must be coura-
geous and seek it with both hands!" Alice gave her fingers a
warm squeeze and then let them go. "Or you can spend a lifetime with your hands in your pockets. I shall leave the choice
to you."

Haley moved back to the seat across from her aunt, withdrawing with her thoughts. The memory of the look in Galen's
eyes haunted her, and she wasn't sure if contemplating their
dangerous depths made her feel any better about what her aunt
had said. She allowed herself to imagine what it might be like

to be publicly on Hawke's arm, or in his arms privately . . . and a rush of longing brought tears to her eyes. *So much for the practical Miss Moreland. But I don't think I can follow in my mother's footsteps, not knowing the tragedy and suffering that can come of it all. Aunt Alice speaks of passion as if it's a happy achievement and not an unstoppable force that turned my father into a stranger and ended up destroying the life I'd known. Yet here I am, wishing for the moon. . . .*

Of one thing she was entirely certain: Mr. Trumble wouldn't see it the same way her aunt did; and he wasn't going to appreciate an impractical bride. *It's too easy to feel the lure of Alice's fantasies and the heat in Mr. Hawke's eyes. . . . It's time to make my choice.*

Chapter

7

The next morning, the weather was too fine not to draw out London's elite to Hyde Park to show off their latest fashions and see what other acquisitions and acquaintances could excite interest. As usual during the social season, invitations would be made, alliances created, and a few relationships severed.

Haley adjusted the sheer veil across her face as she rode along the path, wishing that Mr. Hawke had selected a more private place for conversation. But his note had requested a meeting here, and after their encounter last night and the sleepless hours that had followed, she'd decided that it was better to meet him quickly and be done with it while her courage lasted.

"Most people come here to be seen, Miss Moreland. But I think I would know you anywhere, even if you were swathed from head to toe."

She barely managed to swallow a squeak of surprise as he seemed to appear out of thin air on a stallion at her side. "Mr. Hawke, I . . . I would prefer not to be seen."

"Then you should have foregone the veil. It's easier to hide in plain sight if you look as if you have nothing to hide at all," he said, his wry humor ringing softly in his tone.

She smiled. "Once again, you seem to be an expert on the topic."

"I seem to get more practice since meeting you, Miss Moreland," he countered.

She tried not to laugh. "Why am I having trouble believing that?"

"I can't imagine."

Haley shook her head and looked away from him. It was harder to recall her purpose if she looked at him, so dashing in the tailored cut of his riding clothes. The dark coat over his white shirt accented his broad shoulders and narrow waist, and the flex of his thighs was all too visible beneath his doeskin pants as he controlled his mount. *Can a man be that good-looking and not be vain?* Haley seized on the thought, as if hoping to find fault in a flawless picture. But when she glanced over to scrutinize him, the hope died as she took in his crooked cravat and the obvious lack of time he'd taken with those black curls.

He guided his horse off the path and then reined in to make sure she was following. "Come, Miss Moreland. We'll escape public eyes and ears and see if we can't have a private conversation."

Haley hesitated. An audience of curious peers represented great risk if they were overheard, but they also meant security if she stayed within earshot of them. If he intended to take advantage . . .

Mr. Hawke gave her a knowing look full of challenge. "We can always talk on the main circle and then you'd have a hundred chaperones, or a hundred witnesses, depending on your point of view."

She pulled on the reins and urged her horse to follow him. "I'm not afraid of you, Mr. Hawke."

"I am glad to hear it." He spurred his horse into a gentle canter, and for a few minutes, the pair simply rode through the trees until they found a private copse where the ground dipped lower, making it a completely secluded location.

"There, you see?" he commented as he dismounted and secured his horse's reins to a branch. "We're in a public park and yet entirely alone."

She dismounted as well, determined not to let him see how nervous she'd become, and lifted her veil to push it back onto the brim of her riding hat. "Your note was . . ." Haley squared her shoulders and began again. "I agreed to meet you only because I need to entreat you privately, and in earnest, to cease and desist!"

"Cease and desist what, exactly?"

The lecture she had rehearsed in her head all night long faltered in one unsteady breath. "Y-you know perfectly well!"

He shook his head, his look a mockery of innocence. "I'm afraid I can't cease doing something if I don't know what it is, Miss Moreland." He raised an eyebrow, the very image of a challenge. "Can you not be more specific?"

"You . . ." She stamped her foot in frustration. "Your outrageous flirting and attention! If people haven't noticed, they soon will, and I don't want—"

"Flirting?" he asked nonchalantly. "I can't remember ever being accused of outrageous flirting before. Is there a circumspect level of flirtation that I wasn't aware of? Should I ask Mr. Trumble? I don't think I've even seen the man attempt to kiss your hand, so perhaps he would know."

"You'll ask him nothing of the kind!"

"I'll ask him whatever I wish, unless you agree to answer one question honestly." He stepped away from his horse, closing the distance between them. "Not that I often practice blackmail, but you, Miss Moreland, force a man to think creatively."

"One truthful answer? I suppose it's a small price to pay, but if you were a true gentleman you would agree to be discreet without demanding anything in trade." Haley crossed her arms. "What question then?"

"Why Herbert?"

Haley's cheeks burned with humiliation, but she finally

answered him as honestly as she dared. "I will never lose my head with Mr. Trumble. I will never . . . be swept off my feet. And for all the endless verses of the poets, I am fairly sure that a practical life without blinding passion is not the tragedy they would have you believe. It is dangerous to want more than the world is capable of giving, Mr. Hawke."

"You need to be swept off your feet. You of all the women I have ever met, Miss Moreland, need to be thoroughly and dangerously blinded by passion. And I think you want to be, more than anything else."

"You don't know me at all."

He drew even closer, standing within arm's reach, but made no move to touch her. And she realized that she was all too aware of him, of every physical detail, every button on his coat, every glorious angle of his face and the emerald fire in his eyes. She was close enough to smell the soap on his skin and suddenly her knees were numb and unresponsive. *Too close. Oh, God, not close enough!*

"Call me a liar, Miss Moreland."

"You are . . ." Whatever accusation she'd intended faded at the maelstrom of her thoughts. *Who is he? This impossible man . . . making my insides spin fire and ice . . .*

"I am . . . ?"

"You're a sinful, depraved man and I want nothing to do with you."

His response was a single look of wicked regard. "Really? Are you so sure?" He shifted forward, in one graceful movement asserting his dominance, her view filled only with the wall of his chest as he was mere inches from her nose, the heady male scent filling her nostrils. "And what about you, Miss Moreland?"

"What do you mean?"

"If I am depraved, as you say, then what are you?"

"You go too far."

"What should I think of a woman whose eyes met mine last night at Marchfield's? You never moved to alert anyone else. You didn't look away from me, my dear."

"I was . . . too shocked." The words sounded feeble, even to her, and Haley knew that the lie wouldn't hold. Even now the memory of it—reinforced by the way he was looking at her now with raw, potent, shameless desire—made something inside of her begin to tighten and ache with a hunger equal to his.

"And now? I'm close enough to have earned a slap by now, Miss Moreland. But you aren't running away." He leaned down, his breath sweeping across the bare skin of her throat. "We are the same, you and I. And I suspect you realize that you have met your match."

She gasped, struggling to recover her composure. "You presume too much! I am engaged to be married, Mr. Hawke. I am—"

"You are here, with me, and we can argue presumptions another time." His hands reached out to pull her close against him, the gentle heat of his hands on her arms enough to tip her easily into his embrace, effectively punctuating his argument about her willingness. "Kiss me, Haley, and then should you command me to, I'll obediently retreat forever."

"What makes you think that I would . . . do such a thing and not insist that you retreat now?"

"Because obedience comes at a price, and because my insolence gives you the perfect excuse to prove that you are immune to my charms—with a single kiss."

Galen watched the storm in her eyes crescendo and subside, and he knew she'd given up on the inevitable feminine debate of yes or no. *Yes! Miss Moreland, to me, you will always say "yes."* He lowered his head slowly, savoring this moment of fleeting victory, and kissed her for the first time.

For a first kiss, it was remarkably indolent. He let her dictate the pace, and discovered immediately how potent Miss Haley Moreland could be. Unlike so many women, she made no rushed, nervous grab at his arms for balance, nor pressed into him to "accidentally" ensure he was aware of all of her charms. This was not the practiced kiss of a woman playing the maiden; this was a maiden practicing her arts on a man for the first time, and Galen was completely at her mercy.

Never before had he allowed a woman to take charge, but with Haley, every instinct insisted that he give her this chance. Even so, his body began to fight against the logic of self-control as the fire she evoked started to rage through his veins.

This kiss held no trace of a tremble of haste or a push for a quick end. Not *this* kiss. This kiss was the slow and leisurely exploration of every soft corner of his mouth, of every variation of his touch and taste until he'd thought he'd die from the pleasure of it.

Her tongue was velvet, and he mirrored each movement, suckling and guiding her, tasting her as she had him, but with a gentle force to try to draw out her trust and build her virginal confidence in the power of her actions.

One kiss became a dozen, and one of Galen's hands slid up her back to cradle her against him, the other tracing the sweet lines of her face and throat, sampling the silk of her skin and the intoxicating tangle of her soft hair in his fingers. She yielded to let him take control with a sigh, and Galen's palms itched to explore more of her, to remove the layers of impractical feminine clothing that kept her body from his; but he knew better than to pop a single button. The knoll's isolation wasn't impenetrable by any measurement, and if they were discovered too soon, it would foil his greater plan. As bold as Miss Moreland was, Galen knew that her courage would evaporate the minute he went further than reason allowed.

But reason was abandoning them both.

She moaned softly and he drank it in, marveling at its sweetness, the vibration resonating through his body and tightening the knot of heat between his legs until his cock was stiff and heavy with it.

He guided her backward until they were halted by a giant oak, and Galen tried to ignore the thought that he now had whatever physical leverage he needed to take her if he chose to. An erotic image of the serene Miss Haley Moreland with her legs wrapped around his waist while he rode her into oblivion against a tree was so sharp and sweet he almost spent himself in his pants.

He finally pulled back from the kiss, but only to blaze a trail with his mouth down her chin to the wild pulse at her throat, flickering his tongue along her skin while his hot breath made her writhe against him. She arched her back, her breasts pressed against him, and he held her as close as he could to savor the hot curves of her body against him. His thigh instinctively slid in between the yielding haven of hers, and even with the barrier of her skirts and his riding breeches, he could feel the scorching heat of her most intimate flesh. He shifted his leg up, deliberately adding to the friction and pressure against her clit, and returned to her mouth to deepen his kiss at the same time to drive her further down the sensual path that would give him what he most desired.

And then without warning, she was pushing him away. Every fiber in his body protested, but Galen released her instantly. It wouldn't pay to play the bully now, no matter how much she'd heated his blood.

"I can't! I won't do this, Mr. Hawke!" Her breath was coming quickly, and she staggered away, forcing him to hold out his hand to steady her on her feet.

"You'll forgive me if I point out that your kisses didn't seem so equivocal," he said softly, adjusting his coat to make sure she wouldn't be alarmed at the sight of his swollen cock outlined by his tight breeches.

She looked up at him, her expression full of pain, fresh and raw, and Galen experienced a mixture of concern and vindication. *I've wounded her . . . so quickly . . . and all I can feel is a sense of power and . . . desire.*

"I owe you an apology, Mr. Hawke."

"Do you?" It was the last thing he'd expected her to say.

"I wanted—to know what it was like, to kiss you. To experience what it could be to . . ." She hesitated, her eyes gaining a sheen of unshed tears, but her voice grew stronger and steadier as she spoke. "I apologize if I misled you. It won't

happen again. I have to protect Herbert and my reputation—
no matter how much of a temptation you present. I am not
some stupid ninny to be ruled by passion and risk ruin."

"I see." He struggled to keep his expression neutral, as if
he truly believed a single word of it. Though there was one
truth in all of it—she was most definitely *not* a stupid ninny.
As for the rest, it was too comical to take in, but he did his
best to nod. *What a beautiful liar you are, Miss Moreland.*
"As you wish."

She walked to her horse and then made one or two unsuccessful attempts to remount before Galen crossed behind her.
"Please, Miss Moreland. Allow me to help you."

"Thank you," she said softly, without looking at him.

Galen smiled behind her. *You can't look at me because
you're afraid you'll kiss me again, and then what will have happened to that delightfully prim speech you just managed?*

He knelt to let her use his thigh as a step, but then made
sure he reached his hand up to firmly give her pert little backside an extra boost. She squeaked in surprise, but the maneuver was complete before she could really protest, and Galen
stood to dutifully see to her saddle and make sure her skirts
were clear of the straps.

He enjoyed the role of groomsman, taking a few liberties
as he allowed his hand to slide up her calf while he placed her
foot in the stirrup and along the outside of her thighs to make
sure she was properly seated. He was just careful enough not
to give her the excuse of indignation, but firm enough with his
caresses to keep her off balance.

"Miss Moreland?"

"Yes?"

"Don't you wish an answer to your question?" he asked.

"W-which question was that?" With her lips swollen from
his kisses, he could see her trying to shake off the effects of
passion to recall what question he might be referring to.

"You asked me to cease and desist." He held out the reins
for her to take.

"Oh, yes . . . of course."

He smiled, relishing the wicked thoughts that surged through him and tried to ignore the tight, hot sensation of his cock thrusting up in futility against his breeches. "The answer is no."

He slapped her horse's backside before she could think of a retort and sent the lady on her way, though he could hear her indignant sputtering through the trees.

* * *

"Did you enjoy your ride, dearest?" her father asked, crossing the room to plant a sloppy kiss on her cheek. Haley could smell the brandy on his breath and closed her eyes while he embraced her, praying for patience.

"Father . . . you should get outdoors." She tried to keep her tone light, as he held her at arm's length. "It's too beautiful a day to sit inside by yourself."

"Pish!" His protest came cheerfully, and he let go of her shoulders. "I can see it well enough from here. That's why God invented windows! And I wasn't by myself." The drink slurred his last word, and Haley gently guided him to a nearby chair.

"Did you have a caller?" she asked, hoping that Aunt Alice had had the sense to intervene if he'd been drinking and they'd received any social calls.

"Just Trumble!" He leaned back against the cushions, his eyes losing a little of their focus. "A bit of business between gentlemen, dearest. Nothing to trouble yourself with."

"Business?" She took the seat across from him, a new sense of dread curling in her stomach.

"Now, now . . . you needn't worry about every entry in my ledgers anymore! A man can borrow money as he wishes from his future son-in-law and I don't need your nagging!" He rose, instantly agitated, like a child guiltily trying to deflect her attention from a broken vase.

Words failed her. *Another loan. More debt—it's a nightmare that never seems to end. And I was . . . Oh, God, for a moment, I let myself forget Herbert and the loans and the smell of brandy. I kissed Mr. Hawke and for one glorious moment, I forgot all of it. But never again . . . I can never allow it to happen again.*

"I used to ride with your mother. What a horsewoman she was!" He sighed. "I used to buy horses only if their color would compliment her lovely riding dress. Do you remember?"

"Yes, I remember." She clasped her hands, unsure of what else to say.

"Herbert said he was taking you to the opera tomorrow night. You should wear the red dress. You look like your mother in the red—"

Haley stood abruptly, cutting off the familiar pattern of his melancholy request. "I'll ask the cook to make you something to eat. You need to eat, Father. I'll be in my room if you require anything."

"I wasn't . . ." His look was pure contrition. "Yes, I should eat."

She turned away, unwilling to be drawn into another round of apologies and reassurances, and hurried out of the room and up the broad staircase as quickly as she could. Her emotions were too raw and unsettled after her appointment with Hawke, the taste of him still fresh in her memory. *I am not some stupid ninny to be ruled by passion and risk ruin.*

Or am I?

Chapter
8

The small box at the theatre gave them a wonderful view of the stage, but also of the glittering attendees. Every hue of the rainbow met the eye, and Haley wasn't surprised to see more than one lady in the audience turning her opera glasses to view her rivals in full dress rather than bothering with the performance. It was an acceptable sport for women, this obsession with fashion and jewels, but Haley's eyes were drawn to the drama of the stage.

Her aunt sat next to her near the railing, while Herbert sat behind them, dozing as the opening night's performance unfolded. Haley was lost in the story, swept up in the romance of it, and the ethereal sounds of so many voices intertwined in song—and the costumes were so otherworldly, it was easy to forget her troubles.

The incomparable soprano Miss Beatrice Langston was beginning another aria when Aunt Alice leaned over to whisper, "Isn't Betsy a delight?"

"Such sadness and longing in her voice." Haley nodded.

"Why are operas always so tragic? Can't someone sing

about something other than wretched heartbreak and death?"
Alice fretted behind her fan. "Perhaps a livelier tune would
keep your Mr. Trumble awake."

Haley winced but didn't turn to let her aunt see it. Dutiful
resignation to her fate hadn't fostered any sense of peace, and
no matter how often she told herself that she had rightfully
made the correct and honorable decision to allow Mr. Hawke
no more liberties, her heart just wasn't having it. Mr. Trumble's usual sincere and bumbling habits were wearing against
her nerves a thousandfold, each misstep and clumsy touch
underlining her sense of impending doom. And with every
clammy hand he offered, she'd been haunted by the memory
of that kiss. . . .

Instead of its power fading with each passing hour since
she'd left the glade two days ago, it seemed to grow in her
mind, endlessly replaying each sensation and evocative second
that he'd touched her, that she'd given in to her baser nature
and explored what it would be like to be "*that woman*"—with
secret smiles and no fear.

*This is ridiculous! I'm not the first bride to marry without
passion. And before Aunt Alice became so enamored of Mr.
Hawke, she told me a hundred times that my heart was bound
to follow my head at some point. Of course, now her advice is
all about wearing bells on my breasts and throwing all caution to the winds. . . .*

She nervously scanned the neighboring boxes, wondering
if Mr. Hawke would make good on this threats not to give
up the hunt. He'd appeared so often recently without warning
that Haley began to feel a pang of disappointment that tonight
it looked as if he'd failed to repeat the trick.

*What am I doing? Wishing for the man to appear and lay
waste to the last little shred of peace I have?* She forced herself to look back at the stage, but the blur of sparkling costumes and cavorting players did little to dampen the torrent
of her thoughts.

*I'm sold like a broodmare from my father's stables and
chafing at the bit and bridle. The bargain's made and I gave*

*my word of honor as a gentleman's daughter. And if I ever
see Mr. Hawke again, I shall be sure to remind him of it.*
She sighed, aware that she'd once again let her thoughts circle
back to the forbidden subject of Mr. Galen Hawke.

The performance drew to a finish, and the audience ap-
plauded warmly, awaking Herbert instantly so that he could
clap louder than anyone else. "Bravo!"

Aunt Alice gave him a look of amusement. "Mr. Trumble,
be careful you don't show too much enthusiasm. If Miss Langston asks you anything of the plot, you'll be in a terrible bind!"

He laughed, taking her jibe in the friendly spirit in which it
was intended. "I shall just say that I am speechless as a result
of her talent, and she'll think me very glib!" He stood to hold
out his arm for Haley. "Shall we meet the players, then, and
rub a few elbows?"

Haley gathered her fan and stood to join him. "Not too
many elbows, I hope. Perhaps if it's too crowded we can make
an early departure?"

"Yes, yes, of course!" He led her out of the box, and Aunt
Alice followed as they made their way to the soiree to be
held in a first-floor salon where the attendees could meet and
mingle with the talent of the night's performance. "I have
never met theatre folk before, but I understand they are quite
friendly!" Herbert said in anticipation.

"Oh, yes!" Alice countered knowingly. "I have met several, and they are . . . quite friendly!"

Haley glanced over her shoulder to catch the wicked little
smile that followed her aunt's reminiscence and tried not to
roll her eyes. It was just like Aunt Alice to have a ribald tale
involving some handsome actor she'd encountered in her hey-
day! Like her brother, Mrs. Shaw had also known a great love
in her spouse, but when she'd lost him after only a year of marriage, she'd indulged in her own brand of mourning and lived
the life of a merry widow. But Haley wasn't sure which stories
were true and which were wishful thinking, since they seemed
to grow more and more shocking as the years went on.

They reached the party just as the actors were entering,

many still in their costumes, which seemed to add to the gathering's excitement. It was as if exotic creatures had landed in their midst, and Haley watched several ladies lift their fans to hide their appraisals of the charming male performers. The male guests were far less worried about hiding their appreciation of the actresses, although a few of them seemed to make an effort to stay true to the dictates of good decorum.

Herbert craned his neck, looking about the room. "I don't see Miss Langston!"

"She is the star of the evening, Mr. Trumble. No doubt she wishes to make an entrance of her own," Aunt Alice advised sagely.

"Ah! I see," Herbert said, then clapped his hands in excitement. "And there she is, just as you said! How enchanting!"

"Would you like an introduction, good sir?" a gentleman nearby offered, bowing briefly. He had paste diamonds at the center of each button on his coat, and Haley sensed immediately he had all to do with the theatrical company.

"I would, indeed! I am Herbert Trumble, and this is my fiancée, Miss Moreland, and her aunt, Mrs. Shaw." Herbert seized the man's hand and gave it his customarily thorough shake. "How do you do?"

"I am Edmond Blakely, Miss Langston's manager, and"— his eyes opened in dramatic surprise—"Is that Herbert Trumble of *the* Trumble Textiles and Imports?"

"It is!" Herbert beamed with pride. "I see you have heard of my father's company?"

"Heard of?" He shook his head. "How can anyone not know of your industrial empire, sir?"

Haley bit the inside of her lip to keep her expression neutral as Mr. Trumble puffed up at Mr. Blakely's attentions and instantly seemed to forget everything else around him.

Miss Langston came over at her manager's signal, and Haley was forced to let go of Mr. Trumble's arm as he stepped away from her to meet the lovely singer. "What an honor, Miss Langston!"

"This is Mr. Herbert Trumble and party, Miss Langston,"

Mr. Blakely blithely introduced them, and Aunt Alice chuckled softly behind Haley as Herbert made no sound at correcting the man and providing their names or dutifully indicating that she was, in fact, the future Mrs. Trumble of Trumble Textiles and Imports.

"Did you enjoy our humble efforts, Mr. Trumble?" Miss Langston asked, her voice as smooth as silk.

"You are a siren! And I saw nothing humble in any of it!" Herbert almost gushed with praise.

"Ah! You see? A man who knows fine art when he beholds it!" Blakely pronounced. "Would that other investors shared your distinct passion, Mr. Trumble!"

Alice leaned over and whispered in Haley's ear, "An interesting turn, eh? It's Herbert's turn to feel at home, I'd say, and we're just the tagalongs while they work him over for an investment or two."

"It's . . . refreshing for him to be able to speak informally and not feel judged, I'm sure." Haley tried to come to his defense.

"Well, as refreshing as it is, perhaps you should take heart in it! After all, this may be more of a taste of what's to come for you than the other London parties we've attended. Not that he's ever lacked for cheer!"

Haley whispered back, "Mr. Trumble makes friends wherever he goes, and you shouldn't hold it against him if he doesn't discriminate against—"

"She'd be delighted! Wouldn't you, Miss Moreland?" Herbert's words brought her instantly back to the conversation, but she'd missed the transition.

"I-I'm sorry, what will delight me?" she asked, her cheeks flushing in embarrassment.

"A tour of the very private and exciting spaces behind the stage! Mr. Blakely is offering to lead us into the heart of the magical beast, as he calls it!"

"It is quite a labyrinth, but I vow to return you safely to the world you know," Mr. Blakely added, waving his hand with the flourish of a practiced showman.

Haley had no desire to face the nightmare of a labyrinth of narrow brick passageways and the confines of a theatre's makeshift catacombs, but Aunt Alice perked up before she could respond. "A tour! How fascinating!"

Haley shook her head. "I'll . . . stay here. I'm not sure I'm ready to abandon the world I know."

"Nonsense!" Herbert looked at her as if she'd suddenly grown a third eye. "It would be rude to refuse such a generous offer, and I'm sure you wouldn't want to insult our friends!"

"No." Haley took a deep breath. "Of course not. Just promise you won't leave me."

Herbert smiled, instantly placated. "Never!" He looked merrily at Miss Langston and held out his arm. "May I?"

The actress took his arm, and Haley had to blink twice to maintain her composure as he walked off on her arm without a thought in his head. Mrs. Shaw started to voice her sympathy, but when Mr. Blakely offered his arm in turn, her attention was also diverted from the issue at hand.

Haley had no choice but to follow behind the quartet and leave the party for an impromptu journey into the "heart of the magical beast."

*　*　*

It was worse than she'd imagined. Less than twenty minutes into their tour, she'd been forced to stop to unsnag her petticoats from a nail on a wooden prop box, and by the time she'd looked back up the dim corridor, she was completely alone.

Surely Aunt Alice is going to look back and realize I'm not there! But after a minute or two, doubt smothered hope as she accepted that when it came to a man spouting inane bits of prose about her "flowering beauty," Aunt Alice wouldn't notice a house fire.

Separated from their small party, her worst visions had come true. Old scenery flats leaning against the walls enhanced the optical illusion that the walls were collapsing around her. The narrow halls and manmade labyrinth of spiral staircases, rolls of canvas, and odd little passages were like an alien landscape, and Haley's panic began to grow with each step.

She tried to call out for her aunt, but her throat closed tight. She thought she saw shadowed faces in some of the corners; that they were ogre-like added to her terror. The monsters of childish fairy tales took shape around each corner, and she began to shake at the powerful coil of fear that began to tighten inside of her.

This is ridiculous! I'm a grown woman and I'm scaring myself with goblins! I'll just take a deep breath and go back to the party, and then when the others arrive, I'll make up an excuse and that will be that!

She tried to retrace her steps, but everything began to look alike in the same oppressive, menacing manner of half-constructed ruins and false walls and doors, as if the very building had been designed to keep her trapped and confused.

The idea made it harder for her to breathe, and Haley knew she was getting closer and closer to an outright state of panic. Thinking about a lack of air was as suffocating a thought as any other, and Haley had to put out a hand against a small, disassembled staircase leaning against the wall to try to regain control.

I'm fine. Lots of air. I'm—

She screamed as the skittering kiss of a rat's feet and tail moved across her fingers in the dark, and she fainted dead away.

* * *

Galen watched with relief as her eyelashes fluttered, heralding her recovery. She was in Indian ruby red again, and the impact of it on his senses hadn't lessened. He'd laid her on a narrow velvet couch with gilt griffons at her head, pressed a cool wet cloth at the back of her neck, and decided it was better to wait than gently harass her back to the waking world. When her sea-colored eyes took him in, he watched the flood of color in her face and knew she was suffering from a surge of miserable embarrassment at being seen this way. She closed her eyes again briefly as if to wish him away.

"For a woman who never faints, I would say that was well done."

Her eyes opened with a quick start, her feisty spirit returning. "I'm . . . where is this place?" She sat up, temporarily distracted by the shocking sight of a dressing screen draped with corsets and lacy undergarments, brocade curtains that adorned stone walls instead of windows, and, no doubt, the sinking suspicion that she'd landed in another woman's most intimate closet.

"Miss Langston's dressing room." Galen struggled not to smile. "It was the nearest and best place to lay you down. I thought you'd prefer to recover in some privacy."

"What are you doing here?"

"Besides hiding?" he teased, deliberately holding his position next to the small sofa so that she would keep her seat and have a few more minutes to recover her equilibrium. "I confess I arrived too late for the main performance, but I couldn't stay away when I saw that there might be a chance to see you alone. Though"—he shook his head—"this wasn't exactly what I'd envisioned, Miss Moreland. Are you ill?"

"No." She straightened her skirts nervously then reached up to make sure the ivory combs holding back her curls were still intact. "I don't . . . like tight spaces."

For a moment, the memory of chains and blackness came rushing back, and Galen could only nod in sympathy.

She stood, forcing him to also stand. "I should return to the party and wait for the others there."

"I'll escort you out."

She started to reach out to accept the arm he'd proffered, but then she stopped. "What if someone sees us? How will I explain—this?"

"Mere coincidence should do it. I was also at the theatre, and if you wish to deflect anyone's questions, you could hint that I must have been waiting in Miss Langston's dressing room when I heard you outside." Galen savored the look on her face as she absorbed the implications of his offer.

"But that would mean . . ." Her eyes widened. "Were you waiting for her in here?"

"Are you jealous?"

"No!" But he'd caught her in a lie, and they both knew it. Haley stamped her foot in frustration. "I don't care if you meet every actress from here to the Strand!"

"I shall make a note to that effect." He crossed his arms, deliberately giving her a look that conveyed his disbelief.

"I thought you said you would retreat forever if I kissed you in the park!"

"I said I would if you commanded it after you'd kissed me, but as I remember it . . . you never said anything remotely close afterward."

"Well, I'm saying it now!"

He gave her a look full of regret. "Too late. The offer expired as soon as you rode off."

Her eyes narrowed, and he was sure if she could have spit flames, she'd have set his waistcoat on fire.

It was too tempting. "If you'd care to kiss me again, I could make a similar offer and this time you can send me to the ends of the earth if you remember to."

"I am *never* going to kiss you again, Mr. Hawke. What do you say to that?"

"Galen."

Haley's eyes widened in apparent confusion. "Pardon?"

"My name." Galen shifted the weight of his body to the balls of his feet, subtly ensuring that he could move in any direction and with any speed he needed to reach her when the moment called for it. "Vows involving the subject of kissing should always use a man's Christian name. I'm fairly sure it's English law."

"You're deliberately trying to provoke me." Her voice was low, her eyes darkening, and Galen held perfectly still, a hunter afraid of frightening off his prey.

"Yes."

"Why?" she asked.

"Because I enjoy the way the color in your eyes changes

when you are . . . impassioned." It was the truth, and Galen continued, hoping that just enough of the truth would bind her a little tighter to him. "Because it allows me to catch a glimpse of what you might look like, Miss Moreland, if you ever let yourself go wherever 'provocation' might take you."

"To . . . to what end?" she whispered, then unconsciously moistened her lips with the very tip of her tongue, sending a wrenching arc of need through her opponent to taste her mouth again.

"To allow me to imagine. To allow me to hope," he replied in the same intimate tone, holding his hands at his sides by sheer force of will, "that a lady"—he took a step toward her, the front of his waistcoat less than two inches from the tiny pleated ruffles on her décolletage—"could change her mind."

"I . . ." Her confusion was a beautiful sight to behold, cheeks flushed and eyes shining, her lovely chest heaving with the effort to keep up with her pounding heart, but Galen decided it was enough for now.

"Come, let's get you safely upstairs." He stepped back and held out his arm. "And since the last thing we want is a scandal, I promise I'll leave you before we reach the public party and ensure that no one knows that you didn't make your own way out of these backstage rooms alone."

"Thank you, Mr. Hawke." She took his arm, her fingers wrapping around the crook of his elbow, and Galen smiled.

* * *

"It's confirmed. He seems to be in pursuit of one particular woman, a Miss Haley Moreland, but we're not the only ones who are interested in his movements."

"Naturally."

"Others are trying to track him."

"Let them. They are not our concern."

"They are, if they can engage him and learn what he knows. We have kept the infidels away until now, but if they learn of the treasure's location . . ."

"They won't. We will see to these Jaded before they have

*the chance, and then the thieves can take their knowledge
with them to the grave."*

"Yes."

*"Wait for the right moment, and see to his death
personally."*

"Yes."

Chapter
9

Lord Moreland escorted his daughter proudly down the stairs, almost sober for the occasion as a small peace offering to his child. "Isn't she a vision, Trumble?"

Herbert glanced up to dutifully observe her dress. "Quite right! Which reminds me, Lady Pringley was asking again for your couturier, so be sure to write it down for me so that I can recall it the next time she inquires."

Haley tried to squeeze her father's arm to signal him, but neither man seemed to excel in discretion.

"Why, it is my daughter's own creation! Can you imagine?" He patted her fingers, openly proud of her feminine accomplishments. The ball gown was pale hyacinth purple satin piped with the fewest number of required flounces and pleats, over a silver-threaded ivory organdy underskirt. Each point was adorned with tiny embroidered silver flowers inset with small crystals to give the impression that she was dusted in a magical dew that shimmered with each step. Her shoulders were bared, and Haley had dotted her hair with matching silver flowers.

They reached the foyer and the waiting Mr. Trumble, who now seemed less cheerful than usual. "Oh, dear! Well, that is all well and good, but . . ."

"But what?" her father asked. "She looks like a queen!"

"A queen does not make her own dresses, Lord Moreland." Mr. Trumble's forehead furrowed as if he were contemplating an impossible problem. "What in the world will I tell Lady Pringley?"

"You could tell her that you didn't know the name of my couturier, Mr. Trumble," Haley offered as diplomatically as she could. "And since I have none, it would be the truth."

"Yes, that may do it, but"—he took a deep breath, then smiled as the solution presented itself—"in the future, you will make use of London's finest and then we'll have no need of little white lies. No offense, dearest, but no wife of mine will stoop to such labor if she doesn't have to. I'm not marrying one of my mill girls, after all!"

"I . . . I enjoy my creations, Mr. Trumble. It calms me to construct my dresses and—"

"I'm sure your father will agree that it is far more calming to have someone else see to it. I think you'll discover that shopping is much more enjoyable! I had set up credit for you and expected that you would have already made this discovery, Miss Moreland."

Haley looked at her father but realized that he'd conceded the battle.

"Many women make their own clothes!" she said, hating the note of desperation in her voice.

"Not ladies of good breeding, surely! You'll not have the time after the wedding, in any case, and"—he straightened his shoulders and she recognized that he was finished with the debate—"it pleases me as your future husband to spoil you in this regard."

"You deserve to be spoiled, darling." Her father smiled sadly. "So much like your mother."

Haley hid her misery with long years of practice, as Aunt Alice finally joined them to allow for their departure. She serenely glided past Mr. Trumble on her father's arm toward the door and the waiting carriage, and did her best to keep her eyes forward.

* * *

"I cannot believe I'm here." Michael Rutherford growled beneath his breath, for Galen's hearing alone. He tugged at the lapels of his evening coat, clearly uncomfortable in such formal garb. "You should have asked Josiah to come with you to this damn thing!"

"I haven't seen him for several days, and frankly, I'm starting to worry." Galen looked away from his friend, scanning the room for any sign of his quarry. They'd arrived unfashionably early to the ball to make sure of Miss Moreland's attendance. "Feel free to go and look for him, Michael. Since honestly, I don't think I'm the one who insisted that you come with me."

"Like hell, you didn't! But if you're giving me a choice now, I'd prefer feeling useful and making sure that Josiah is safe to standing around amidst . . . *this*!"

"*This*" was the Duke of Bellham's grand ball, and one of the most elite and lively gatherings of the year. The duke's young wife had made sure that her older husband's deep pockets were exercised to the breaking point to achieve her desire to host the most extravagant party of the Season.

The duchess had outdone herself this year, and there were rumors that the crown princess herself would be in attendance. The entire house was bathed in gaslight and every surface in gold brocade, a glittering backdrop outshone by its bejeweled inhabitants as they cavorted and paraded in their finest clothes.

It wasn't difficult to see it from Michael's perspective, since he shared the cynical view of a world that paid more attention to appearance than character—but vengeance crowded his thoughts and he desired nothing more than Miss Moreland.

"Do what you wish," Galen said, his breath caught in his throat as he spied her for the first time. "I will meet up with you later."

He moved away from Rutherford, his senses coming alive with the awareness that she was once again nearby. She was on the arm of an older gentleman, and Galen didn't see Trumble, which suited him even better. It was tedious to remain polite while the man bandied about him with the grace of a three-legged Pomeranian, yipping away nonsensically.

As he drew closer, he began to see a vague resemblance between the pair that supplied Lord Moreland's identity without the ritual of an introduction. Galen noted the subtle signs of a man prematurely aged by poor habits but made no judgment. It was too common among the peerage, and in many ways, a sign of their status that they could cavort themselves into an early grave, or at the very least, enjoy a good case of the gout.

But before he could cross the room, Trumble appeared to lead Miss Moreland off to the dance floor. Galen slowed only for a moment, then decided to take advantage of a different kind of opportunity.

No better way to know the woman than to know a little more about her father. What's the old argument? If Henry VIII had bothered to sit down with Thomas Boleyn for a good chat, we'd have a different story to tell.

"Good evening, your lordship. If I may, I have had the pleasure of meeting your daughter and Mr. Trumble, and thought I would introduce myself." Galen kept his approach even-keeled, assessing the man as he went. "I'm Galen Hawke."

"Ah! Mr. Hawke! Alice sings your praises so much I almost thought you'd be quite a bit older." Lord Moreland held out his hand cordially. "Not that your youth will protect you! My sister is a notorious flirt."

"Mrs. Shaw has been very kind, and a man of any age would be flattered."

Lord Moreland's eyes rose appreciatively. "You *are* good!"

Galen did his best to humbly defer the compliment. "She is your sister, Lord Moreland. If I said any less, wouldn't you be worried?"

"True! I suppose you're cornered into making the smoothest speeches you can manage, or I'll be forced to stamp on your toes in defense of my sister's honor."

"Just so." Galen put his hands behind his back, glancing at the dancers. "Does Miss Moreland dance presently?"

"Yes, with her fiancé," Lord Moreland said, pointing out the pair. "She is there in that pale purple–colored dress. The spitting image of her dear, dear mother," he sighed. "Mr. Trumble, as you know, has a vast fortune from his father's factories, and so I am very pleased with Haley's choice."

"Did they court long?" Galen asked.

"Not too long," Lord Moreland noted, a wistful note coming into his voice. "He lighted on her quickly after his arrival in the country, and it was a matter of weeks before we were making plans to come to London. Love has its own timetables, Mr. Hawke."

"I suppose it does." Galen watched her, absorbing this new tidbit of information as she moved about the floor in a graceful quadrille. *Weeks. Why is there a part of me that was hoping for something . . . else? What would make it better? That she'd known the mud troll for a long time and simply turned to him in despair after learning of John's death? Probably not much to mute the blow, but still—Trumble is hardly a candidate for a credible whirlwind romance. Which brings it all back to money again. . . .*

Unaware of the turn of Galen's thoughts, Lord Moreland went on, "My girl deserves the very best, and Trumble will spoil her as she should be spoiled. Nothing else matters, does it?"

"Well . . ."

"When you're a father, you'll see it differently. You'll want only the best for your child." Lord Moreland kept his eyes on his daughter. "Though I'm not sure what I'll do without her."

"Time enough before the wedding to enjoy her company!" Galen tried to turn him away from the melancholy direction of his words. "Shall we head to the salon upstairs for refreshments and leave the young lovers to their dance?"

Lord Moreland's eyes took on a feral edge, and Galen's earlier suspicions were confirmed when he replied, "Well, I'd promised Haley I wouldn't overdo it, but . . . it seems a bit too rude to snub the duke's attempts at hospitality, does it not?"

"A man should keep his promises. If you've given your daughter your word, I'm sure—"

"Just one drink won't breach my vows! I told her I wouldn't overindulge, but I'm sure I didn't swear to sip tea all night." Lord Moreland turned to leave the ballroom with Galen, his expression that of a child aware that he was heading out of bounds, but simply delighted at the prospect.

Galen felt a small stab of concern that he'd inadvertently set the man in the one direction he probably shouldn't go, but there was no way to diplomatically argue against it now. Instead, he would just have to see what else he could learn and perhaps do what he could to rein him in before he was too deep into his cups.

Unfortunately, since Galen couldn't drink, Lord Moreland seemed only too happy to take on his new friend's unclaimed ration of spirits as well, and before long, Galen was wishing he'd kept Michael closer at hand.

* * *

Haley limped as subtly as she could away from Herbert and the male circle of conversation he'd insisted on joining. Endless minutes of a discussion on the developments in textile production and the advantages of automation versus the ending of genteel civilization and all she could think of was the throbbing agony of her feet after enduring three dances in a row with Mr. Trumble.

The Duke of Bellham's house was extravagantly decorated in gold until it was easy to imagine that one had stumbled into Midas's great hall. Haley shook her head in amazement at the vast expense and waste of it all. *I'd have been able to redo the roof on the house and keep up the property for several years on what the duchess must have spent on this single night's entertainments. Why, the cost of the orchestra alone would have redone the gardens!*

She wandered for a few minutes, trying to take in the sights of the ball but also trying to avoid any invitations into the crush of conversation. By staying on the periphery of the crowd, she began to feel a little better, but her aching feet complained until she accepted that she would need to find a quiet place to sit down and recover. She was confident that Herbert wouldn't stray far from the conversation he'd found, so he would be easy enough to locate later.

Her father was another matter, but Haley saw no sign of him and could only pray he hadn't gotten into any mischief. Her chaperone had also wandered off, no doubt in a merry search for mischief of her own, but she was sure Aunt Alice could manage to enjoy herself without causing too much damage.

Haley didn't feel comfortable exploring the house for a suitable hiding place and risking looking either like a nosy guest or a would-be thief, so she eyed the glass-paned French doors that led out to a stone verandah overlooking the gardens. She escaped into the cool night air with a huge sense of relief.

Fortunately, it was a moonless night and the weather had threatened rain earlier, so there wasn't a single soul to intrude on her precious solitude. There was just enough light from the windows of the house for her to make out the lush layout of the garden below, and she spied a rustic gazebo styled to look like a miniature Grecian temple against a far wall that looked promising. She was sure that she'd be able to sit there undisturbed and still be able to enjoy a good view of the house to make sure she wasn't caught unaware if Herbert sent a search party.

This is better than the musicians' gallery, and this time, I have ensured that I won't run into a certain gentleman with emerald eyes! Not that she'd seen him in the ballroom, but the man did have a way of turning up when she least expected him.

With one last look back through the glass doors to ensure no one was watching, Haley made her way as quickly and quietly as she could down the dark steps leading into the garden. It was slower going on the gravel paths, as her eyes adjusted and she had to force herself not to look back at the bright windows since it made the garden seem almost pitch-black for seconds afterward. But at last, she'd reached her little haven, and just as she'd hoped it housed a convenient teak bench with cushions, though probably intended for an afternoon's reading rather than an errant guest trying to escape conversations on blights of cotton weevils.

She sat down carefully and drank in the fairylike atmosphere. The garden was covered in a light mist suspended in the night air, and the music from the ballroom drifted out to echo across the hedges. Haley sighed at the beauty of it.

Her eyes dropped to the folds of her overskirt, and her throat tightened as she remembered Herbert's proclamations about what he deemed improper work for his future wife. She'd always secretly taken pride in her designs, gaining a sense of pleasure and accomplishment at turning closets of raw materials into things of beauty—sure that her mother would have approved of her industry and thrift. It was a talent that turned her father's previous impulsive purchases into a better legacy, redeeming some of the past with the pull of each thread and creation of each lovely piece.

But Herbert had apparently made up his mind and insisted that he knew better regarding the things she should enjoy. Just as her father always insisted that he knew best how his daughter should be spoiled . . .

Everyone, even her Aunt Alice, seemed to have an idea of what would be best for her, or how she should be. Everyone except . . . Galen Hawke.

She felt warmer at the very thought of him and smiled down at her idle hands. Whenever he looked at her, she forgot all the things that she was supposed to be. Exposed to the heat in his eyes, every practical restriction melted away. It was as if whatever hidden siren lurked inside of her, longing for all the impossible and wicked things in this world, came to life when Galen was near. And none of her internal warnings about the inevitable disaster of yielding held any sway.

A part of her seemed to not only know he was dangerous, but to revel in it, to be drawn to that fire and hunger for it, even if it meant the end of her.

She'd met him in the park to end their friendship and instead had ignited a longing for so much more. Haley sighed. A part of her wanted to become that practical woman who could truly dismiss such men from her mind and take the correct and proper course without looking back and wishing for everything she couldn't have. But more and more, as the Season began to wane and her marriage with Herbert loomed, she was thrilled to think that Galen might have meant what he said—that he might not give up his pursuit.

She looked up and indulged in a childish game of summons, wishing for Mr. Hawke to come. It was a trick one of her early governesses had taught her, to think of someone and try to bring the person to you without uttering a word. It was only later she'd realized that it was probably just a way to make a boisterous pupil sit still for several minutes and afford her poor teacher some quiet—but even so, she remembered thinking it was a secret talent she possessed to draw her father to her side or explain an unexpected visit from a friend.

So where are you, Galen Hawke? Here I am . . . alone in the dark . . . and is this not the perfect place for you to make one of your unexpected appearances? I wish you would. I know I shouldn't, but I do. Because I wore the hyacinth, and as I was dressing, I wondered what you would think of it. Because I put my hair up and thought of you. Because there seems to be nothing that I do, no ordinary act, that doesn't summon you to mind since that kiss.

Her heartbeat careened out of control as she recognized his silhouette, the width of his shoulders and the pantherlike steps that carried him out onto the verandah. The silly game took an exciting and terrifying turn as he appeared to scan the garden as if looking for something . . . or someone.

This is ridiculous! I can't wish for a man and make him appear! It's a coincidence, and in just a moment, he'll turn back around and head inside for—

He started down the steps, and Haley stood, fighting an impulse to run. She'd wished for him with all her heart, but seeing the reality of the man coming toward her in the dark now made her feel an odd mixture of excitement and pure panic.

I should run.

But it was too late, and she wasn't sure how it would look, to flee from him like a coward. Would it give too much away to let him realize how much he unsettled her? Would it not be better to hold her ground and demonstrate that his arrival didn't affect her in the slightest? It was a paper-thin lie, but by the time she decided that her first impulse to run may have been wiser, it was too late.

He was walking directly toward her, and Haley held onto one of the columns praying that the dark would hide her expression—since she could feel the heat in her cheeks and the flush across her skin.

"Miss Moreland?" He was a dark shadow in the frame of the gazebo steps, drawn against the light of the house behind him. She couldn't read his expression at all. "Are you hiding again?"

"I was . . . admiring the garden." The instant the words left her lips, she smiled at the audacity of the lie. "And you? Did you come out here to admire the roses?"

"I came out here to see you."

Haley's breath caught in her throat at his raw honesty, his voice low and level. "There must be . . . I must be blatantly flawed in my character, Mr. Hawke, that you think me so . . . I thought I told you that I wasn't going to see you again, Mr. Hawke."

"It's dark enough out here, you could hardly say you'd seen me even if you wanted to."

"Don't be glib! You know what I meant."

"Yes, I know. But you never said any such thing," he said calmly.

"Didn't I?" His outrageous claim completely distracted her.

"No. However, you did promise not to mislead me ever again, and I thought that very charming. And then there was something about requesting me not to flirt, which once I really thought about it, I decided you may have been right to require such a thing."

"You . . . decided I was right?"

"Yes." He took a step closer, and the scent of him once again encroached on her awareness—the sweet, smoky scent of sandalwood making her toes curl with pleasure. "Flirtation implies a frivolous attention that never truly leads anywhere, and I can assure you, Miss Moreland, that I have every serious intention of taking action where you are concerned."

"Mr. Hawke"—Haley slowly let go of the column, determined to stand on her own—"as much as I would love to . . . discuss the implications of your decision, I'm afraid I have to rejoin the ball before anyone misunderstands the nature of our private conversation and . . ." Her words trailed off as she realized that it had begun to rain, effectively sealing them off from the party and complicating her return.

There would be no mistaking it if they were the only two rain-soaked attendees at the ball, and the speculation that followed could destroy her reputation in a single evening.

"Oh," he went on, the humor in his voice impossible to miss, "I almost forgot. I also came to see you to tell you that I thought it might rain."

"How unfortunate that it slipped your mind until this moment!" She did her best not to smile.

"It's your fault."

"Mine?"

"You distracted me. It's too potent talking to you in the dark, Miss Moreland—especially when you whisper hints that only a woman with a flawed character would feel desire or draw my attention." He shifted over to the bench and took a seat. "So, I'm afraid it falls to you to come up with distracting small talk until the rain lets up."

She almost argued, but his point was too well made. She'd intimated just that—that it was a flaw of hers to draw him to her side, to wish for him or to want him. And he'd just matter-of-factly stripped her of the notion and then offered to let her steer the conversation in any direction she liked. *Impossible man to be so reasonable and unreasonable at the same time!*

"Very well." She took a seat on the bench at its opposite end. "Are you a recluse, Mr. Hawke?"

"No."

"Yet so many people seem to be under that impression," she informed him, relaxing as this odd game of small talk took shape in the darkness. She felt freer to ask whatever she wished, the rain closing them off from the rest of the world. "How is that possible?"

"I wasn't in the mood for society for a few months, and I think it gave people something to talk about," he speculated. "Perhaps I should feel flattered that anyone missed me at all to even notice."

"Well, you're a terrible hermit from what I can see, since I seem to run into you everywhere I go."

He laughed softly. "There! It's all perception, and my career as a recluse is at an end!"

"What altered your mood, Mr. Hawke?" she asked.

It took him a little longer to answer, the light wit in his manner bleeding away. "A friend died."

"I'm so sorry!" She instinctively reached out to touch his hand, the need to offer him comfort overriding everything else. "How could anyone question your need for solitude? It's terrible!"

"Let us speak of something else, Miss Moreland. The night is gloomy enough without inviting a ghost to our small party." His own hand briefly covered hers, tracing the fingers she'd placed on his wrist, and a tendril of electricity moved up her arm and across her breasts, her heart racing to outrun it before he withdrew his touch.

"Yes, very well." She did her best to think of a more cheerful topic, marveling at the power his lightest caress wielded. "How did you know I would be out here?"

"It suited your pattern."

"I beg your pardon?"

"I've never seen a woman avoid crowds so actively as you do, Miss Moreland. From hiding in musicians' galleries to clutching at walls whenever the room is full of a crush of partygoers, I don't think I've ever seen you in the center of a room." He began to take off his evening coat as he went on, "And then at the theatre, you explained everything."

"Did I?"

"You confessed you didn't like tight places." He moved to gently place the coat around her shoulders, and Haley was grateful for the warmth, the heat of his body still imprinted on the cloth that now enveloped her. "So when I saw how crowded it was this evening, I kept an eye on the verandah since it was the most likely and least populated place I could think of, and just happened to see you slip out."

"Do you remember *everything* I say, Mr. Hawke?"

He nodded solemnly, sitting closer to her, shielding her body from a breeze that had come up with the rain. "Every single word, Miss Moreland."

"Then I should attempt to pay greater attention to what I say."

"Not at all." The bass of his voice resonated through her. "I like you better when you simply speak your mind without censure, even if it's to order me into the rain."

Haley reached up to draw his coat closer, savoring the comfort as the revelation of his words struck her. *It never even occurred to me to banish him! How is it that it's the devil himself who is pointing out what a more prudent woman would have done?* "I would hate to see you catch your death, Mr. Hawke."

"Ah! I knew you liked me."

She opened her mouth to protest but decided against it. It was getting harder and harder to lie—and the world that held debts and obligations seemed further and further away.

"I would be a terrible person if I wished anyone pneumonia, but I suppose it's safe to say, you are a difficult man to dislike, Mr. Hawke."

"Careful, Miss Moreland." He lowered his voice and Haley drew closer almost without realizing it so that she could catch his words over the patter of the rain on the roof overhead. "You'll profess your adoration, and then there will be nothing to stop you."

"To stop me from what?" She pulled back, attempting a prim retreat more out of habit than desire.

"From dancing with me."

Haley's mouth fell open for a moment, unsure that she had heard him correctly. She'd expected another audacious proposition or some sly invitation to repeat the kiss they'd shared in Hyde Park. Before she could think of a witty response, he stood, and even in the semidarkness, she could see the hand he outstretched toward her.

"Dance with me, Miss Moreland."

As if the orchestra inside the grand house was in league with him, it struck up a new tune, and Haley began to suspect that the man had a touch of the magician in him. She reached out and took his hand, and the last tenuous thread that held her to the world outside their small haven disintegrated in a small sigh.

Galen gently guided her into his arms, amazed anew at how naturally she moved against him, gracefully matching his steps as they began to dance slowly in the confines of the gazebo. He couldn't remember the last time he'd asked a woman to dance, but certainly never before in such a manner and without a soul to keep a watchful eye.

The simple act of leading her in the steps of a waltz took on a primal and powerful new meaning, as she yielded to him at the slightest pressure of his fingertips on her back, following him and turning at his unspoken command. At first, it was innocent enough, but with each sweeping circle around the confines of the miniature temple, Galen drew her closer and closer until there was no space at all between them. Within seconds, it was if they were entirely attuned to each other, and he marveled at the pleasure of it, even as the erotic consequences began to ignite his every nerve ending.

He'd anticipated kissing her again, and now he deliberately toyed with the gentle torture of prolonging this embrace—unwilling to hurry a single step of the seduction now that he held the reins.

"I want to kiss you, Miss Moreland."

"I can't—Galen, I shouldn't."

His lips moved against her temple, the lightest caress over the tiny pulse there that betrayed her sweet response, and he whispered against her skin. "Then don't. Don't kiss me, but if you let me kiss you . . . then you'll keep your vow not to misbehave."

It was wanton logic at its finest.

"Let me kiss you, as I wish, and you . . . need do nothing."

It was reckless, wicked logic that would never have held sway under the bright lights of a ballroom, but alone in the dark, Galen relied on the heat between them and the magic of the shadows to lure her into allowing him to take what he wanted.

When she sighed, it was the softest sound of acquiescence, setting off a cascade through his body with the roar of an avalanche that demanded he seize this chance as if no other would ever present itself.

Even so, he began with the most innocent kiss on the satiny heat of her forehead, before trailing a soft string of kisses across her face, deliberately lighting on the tip of her nose before skimming across her cheek and seeking out the sensitive shell of her ear to nibble and tease her until her breath quickened. He caught the fleshy curve of her earlobe between his teeth, only to suckle her briefly, making her writhe against him at the unexpected sensation. Galen dropped his mouth down to her bare shoulder, moving to the sensitive juncture at her neck, and Haley began to push against him as he found the magical intersection that sent a chill across her skin and undoubtedly sent a new tendril of fire through her frame.

"What are you doing?"

"I'm kissing you, Miss Moreland."

"I'm sure I thought you meant . . . a proper kiss . . ." She was obviously having trouble collecting her thoughts, and Galen wasted no time in pressing the advantage by complying with her request for a "proper kiss." He caught her mouth with his, forgetting about the game, losing himself in the fiery sweet taste of her lips and tongue, drawing her closer until she was melded against his body. Each movement, she matched, innocently fueling his desire until he was sure there was nothing else in existence but the siren in his arms and his need to possess her.

His right hand dropped to find the curve of her bottom, lifting her slightly, pressing her against his arousal, instinctively seeking the warm core between her thighs, feeling the heat of her even through layers of clothing. She made no protest, her thighs parting for his, riding against him and reacting to the friction against her sensitive folds. He deepened the kiss and strode forward, easily pushing her back onto the cushions of the long bench with his evening coat beneath her, as his explorations left any guise of gentlemanly restraint behind.

The stiff structure of her bodice thwarted any thought he might have of exploring the delectable mounds of her breasts or tasting them as he would have wanted—at least, not without risking damage to her dress that couldn't be undone or explained away later. Instead, his hands started to caress the sweet curve of her thighs, lifting her skirts to reach under the endless layers of silk and taffeta to find the bare flesh inside the opening of her underclothes, and her hidden soft slit, already ripe and wet and eager for his touch.

She stiffened, shock and pleasure warring to make her moan, off balance by the maelstrom of sensations roaring through her. She wasn't sure how to protest as his mouth sought and found every sensitive corner of her mouth until she only knew that she never wanted it to end—and when his hand slid up her thigh, slipping easily past the top of her stockings and finding the wet, silky skin between her legs, Haley waited for some sensible part of her to cry for a halt, but it never really happened.

Instead, every inch of her passionate nature unfurled like a flower in the sun, and she surrendered to each impulse that brought her closer to the heat and fire she craved. She clung to him, instinctively seeking to touch him, her hands sliding around his waist and up the warm planes and curves of his back, circling the strong muscles underneath her fingers and savoring his warmth even through the silk of his shirt and waistcoat.

She was trapped between two impossible pleasures, each feeding into the other, his hot mouth and the movement of his tongue echoing playfully off the rhythm of his fingers on the tight bud of her clit, sliding back and forth over the bundle of nerves just beneath her skin, teasing it with each pass. It was like a dance, a keening melody of desire going faster and faster with each wicked touch until she was writhing, moaning, arching against him, transformed into someone else.

A coil of need twisted and tightened inside of her, a searing spiral that suddenly seemed to connect every part of her at once until she was afraid she would shatter, and then she didn't care if she did, aware only that some unknown bliss was just barely out of reach—that if she only knew what it was, then paradise would be hers for the taking.

But Galen seemed to know, his fingers increasing their speed and goading her on, as his lips left hers to tease the outer shell of her ear, his teeth grazing the plump flesh of her earlobe to suckle her, and Haley cried out as the white-hot coil inside her unraveled in an ecstatic explosion that careened past her control, tearing away the illusion, once and for all, that there was a boundary between desire and discipline.

She wasn't sure what to say. "You . . ."

His breath was coming as quickly as hers, the ragged sound of it making her wonder how much further he could have gone—and the toll it took on a man to provide for her pleasure but not necessarily for his own. "Mr. Hawke, I—"

He put his fingers over her lips, surprising her as he quickly shifted away without warning, a rush of cold air against her skin accenting the sudden distance between them. But before she could even raise herself from the cushions to protest his rude dismissal, the cause became clear.

"Mr. Hawke? Is that you?" Aunt Alice queried from the verandah, her voice carrying in the night air.

Haley closed her eyes in instant mortification, a horrifying shame she had never experienced almost making her cry out. But Galen stood, shielding her more effectively from view, as he stepped into the temple's narrow doorway.

"Yes, Mrs. Shaw. I was just enjoying a smoke away from the party."

"Have you seen my niece?"

"No, I can honestly say I have not."

Haley nearly squeaked at the lie, but then remembered his jest about it being too dark to have truly "seen" each other, and put her fingers over her mouth to stifle a groan. *Ruined— or nearly ruined! And I'm only regretting that he stopped . . . what kind of woman have I become?*

"Well, if you see her, do let her know that her father is . . . under the weather and ready to leave."

"I will. Thank you, Mrs. Shaw." He held his place for a few moments, then turned to help Haley to her feet. "That was harrowing."

Haley stood, struggling to regain her composure. To be almost discovered with her skirts around her waist, and even now, to feel the residual echoes of each passionate tremor and the cool night air whispering across her still damp thighs— it was like a feverish dream. Haley looked back toward the house and realized that the rain had stopped. *When? When did it stop? How long when I could have escaped before . . .*

"Miss Moreland?" he asked, stepping behind her, his warm breath caressing her bare shoulder. "Are you all right?"

It was too much. Haley fled the temple without looking

back and ran through the garden toward the verandah and the house. She ran as if speed and distance alone could resolve the tangle of her emotions and free her from the spell of his touch—and banish him from her heart.

* * *

Leaving the garden, Galen rebuttoned his coat and moved back toward the glow of the party and reentered as carefully and quietly as he could. He turned the handle slowly and held his breath as the wood creaked. He looked up to see if any of the servants had noticed and then nearly yelled out when he realized that Michael Rutherford was standing just inside the door.

"Damn it, Michael! How does a man the size of a mountain do that?"

"Do what?" Michael asked, his mood unimproved after a night in such "good company."

"I thought you'd left!"

"I said I wanted to, but frankly, it's not Josiah who has me concerned."

"I'm in no danger, Michael."

"And there's the problem." Rutherford crossed his arms. "You are, and you're not paying any attention."

"I don't think Miss Moreland is—"

"Not the girl!" Michael let out a sigh, then fixed an icy cold gaze the color of steel on his friend to ensure that he had his complete attention. "You're so focused on the girl, I think I could have paraded a regiment in full colors through this party and you'd have missed it. Trumble's friend, Bascombe, is a known associate of agents with the East India Company and if I guess right, then he's taken you on as a special favor to them, or for someone in the government. He's asking too many questions, Galen, and he's too heavy-handed for you to ignore."

"He's an ass, but he's too clumsy to pose much of a threat to me."

"Normally, I would agree with you, but since you seem to

be blinded to all else in the world but Miss Moreland, I'm not so sure."

"He wasn't even in attendance tonight, Rutherford. Why are we talking about Rand Bascombe of all people?"

"He was in attendance, and I'm fairly certain he saw your ladylove coming back from the garden."

Galen's breath hissed through his teeth, but he wasn't going to admit defeat. "But not me?"

Michael shook his head. "But you may want to put off your plans and—"

"No."

Michael shook his head and sighed in resignation. "Then on that particular topic, allow me to make one final observation."

"Do as you wish."

"Your attentions to the girl have been obvious enough already to give your campaign credibility. In other words, if you still insist on it, then you can ruin her with a word. But you don't have to ruin her in truth, Galen. A fine line, I know, but one that your conscience may later appreciate."

"My conscience . . ." Galen repeated the word, unsure of anything except that Haley fogged his every thought and was beginning to make him doubt his motives and his sanity. He could still smell her and taste her from their encounter in the garden, and it had been too easy to forget why he'd meant to achieve her ruin. Her father's drunken speeches about marble fireplaces and how vast his stables would be had only muddied matters. Lord Moreland's maudlin proclamations about his dead wife had been endlessly intermixed with strange mercenary hints that he appreciated every penny weighting his future son-in-law's pockets and was looking forward to spending them.

But more damning had been the moment when Galen had asked of John Everly. Lord Moreland had nostalgically described his daughter's first fiancé and mumbled something about the loss of a good man, but nothing of regret that she'd forgotten to mourn in order to enjoy her good fortune. It was as if Lord Moreland shared the same propensity to amnesia so long as the financial benefits were within his reach. And even when he'd mentioned the loss of his friend to Haley, she'd said nothing to indicate that she, too, had experienced a recent loss.

She should explain it, be forced to face her cold and callous decision to dismiss John's memory so handily. But perhaps Michael is right. Another overt public flirtation or two, and I can say whatever I want. No one wants to believe the best in anyone, and the public is always hungry for a delicious scandal. I could serve her up to them without laying another finger on her person. . . .

And tonight, when he could have easily allowed them to be discovered and ended it all, he'd instead instinctively protected her—and for that, he had no explanation at all.

Michael interrupted his internal debate. "Whatever you intend, Hawke, do it quickly. I'm not sure I can stand back endlessly while this tragedy unfolds."

"Are you threatening to intervene, Rutherford?"

Michael's look would have made any other man shake in his boots, but Galen had seen too much to fear his friend.

"No, Galen. But my conscience is starting to rob me of my rest, and I'm not going to promise that I'll allow *that* to continue for very long. Pull the trigger or let her go."

Michael turned and stalked off without another word, leaving Galen to the tangle of his thoughts and the dawning realization that he was starting to dislike either choice.

Chapter
10

Haley's maid stood patiently waiting for her mistress to signal that she was ready to undress, but Haley finally waved her away. "I'll manage, Emily. Go on to bed, and by all means, linger in the morning if you wish. You've been kept up late enough to earn a morning of leisure."

"Thank you, Miss Moreland!" Emily curtsied with a cheerful grin. "It's kind of you!"

Emily left and closed the door softly behind her, and Haley was alone at last. She stood, unmoving in the center of the room, a woman in the eye of an emotional storm. Long, silent seconds unfurled until everything inside of her finally calmed and a single quotation from a poem by Keats she'd once read repeated in her mind. *Was it a vision, or a waking dream? Fled is that music—do I wake or sleep?*

In dreams, she knew, there could be a boldness that would never withstand the harsh light of day, and so a part of her longed to claim that it had all been an illusion, that she'd fallen asleep in that temple on those cushions and had every excuse for all that had taken place. But if it was a dream, then another, newly awakened part of her protested, because it robbed her of her courage and denied her new, fragile hope that Aunt Alice had been right in encouraging her to risk more for a chance at a greater happiness.

Advance or retreat.

Either path seemed fraught with danger. But then a new idea struck her.

Herbert would expect to touch her as Galen had. He would be her husband. He would go as far and further.

Haley closed her eyes, repulsed and sickened by her impending nuptials in a way she had never been before. Because there was nothing of the electricity and fire between them . . . and now that she'd tasted true passion with Galen Hawke . . .

Every look Galen gave her, his every touch was not about polite courtship or cautious civility. If she gave into her growing need for him, he would consume her body and soul and there would be no turning back.

Life is risk. I've followed my head for all these years and now I am come to this moment. The bargain I've struck with Herbert sours with each passing day, and I don't think I can face it. But if I'm mistaken in Galen, then I risk more than my own disgrace.

But to not take the risk suddenly seemed an impossible course.

This is no dream. No one has forced me into this predicament. Aunt Alice said, who would blame a girl for falling in love with such a man?

But I already know the answer. I'll have none to blame but my own heart.

*   *   *

Alone in his library, Galen sipped a cup of green tea and watched the fire in the fireplace begin to die. Bradley had insisted on starting one to add a little more warmth and cheer to the room, and then given him that look that said he had a firm opinion on a certain lack of cheer from his employer.

Galen sipped the hot tea and considered why Bradley put

up with him for all his wretched qualities. *He's a mother hen trying to coddle a tiger! If the man didn't move so fast, he'd risk—*

"Mr. Hawke, beg your pardon." Bradley appeared in the doorway, his posture absolutely perfect, but his shirt wasn't quite tucked in, revealing his rush and unreadiness to make announcements at one o'clock in the morning.

"I thought you went to bed, Bradley! For God's sake, man! You don't have to hover and offer me cakes at this hour!" Galen snapped, feeling more than a little surly after the events at Bellham's. He put his teacup on the mantel and then waited to hear what in the world would have stirred Bradley to disturb him.

"There is a young lady who has come to call," Bradley replied. "I'd have insisted on turning her round, but she . . . She was quite polite." It was a lame explanation, but Galen suddenly had an inkling of an idea of exactly who could put Bradley into such a flushed state of imbalance.

Polite? She's charmed his befuddled stockings off and Bradley of all people is about to melt into a puddle! If it were one of Ashe's women, my first word of it would be the screeching noise outside when Bradley shoved her into the refuse piles on the street. . . .

But what the hell is Haley Moreland doing here at this time of night?

"Show her up, Bradley. And then by all means, go to bed."

Bradley radiated disapproval but hurried to fetch the "polite young lady" from the foyer where he'd asked her to wait. One did not leave a lady of genteel breeding to stand on a darkened stoop at such an unheard of hour, and Galen could hear him muttering as he went to carry out his duties.

He'll put arsenic in my tea in her defense, I think. Incredible! Well, no worries, Bradley, I've already resolved to let the lamb go untouched. Michael is right, and it's not as if—

His resolution not to take things any further was instantly forgotten. Haley appeared in the doorway, still wearing her ball gown, and he almost swore under his breath at how stunningly beautiful she was, so calm with those remarkable eyes reflecting back the glow of the fire.

"It is . . . late for a social call, Miss Moreland."

She nodded and reached up to slowly remove a single gilt hairpin. "Is it?" She dropped the ornament to the carpeted floor and took a step toward him.

"Won't your family be looking for you?"

She shook her head, and then another silver flower followed to tumble at her feet. "My father would sleep through a round of cannonade this evening, and I have the feeling that Aunt Alice wouldn't alert anyone, even if she did bother to check my room."

"What a forward-thinking woman, your aunt." He exhaled, mesmerized as yet another glittering tiny pin fell and her mahogany hair began to cascade slowly over her shoulder. "And your servants? Won't they talk?"

As she reached up again, she innocently arched her back and he was treated to the remarkable silhouette of her breasts lifted up, accenting the lines of her figure. Two more flowers fell, and the rest of her curls fell in a silky curtain down her back, to her waist. "Our roles are reversed, Mr. Hawke. I thought it was usually the woman who presented obstacles and objections?"

After all his scheming, Galen knew he was conquered.

"Miss Moreland? If you came to command me to exile to the ends of the earth, you—"

"I came to . . . finish what we started."

He froze, wanting to absolutely ensure that he hadn't somehow misunderstood. "Don't—torment me. This isn't a simple game, Miss Moreland. What happened in that garden . . . you've already risked your reputation and your engagement. Coming here, alone, at this hour, I don't think you realize what you're doing. And I'm not—I'm not going to make a single promise of restraint if you so much as take one more step."

"Mr. Hawke—"

"Be sure."

"You are an unconventional person, Mr. Hawke. And I . . ." She pulled out the last of the silver flowers from behind one of her ears, dropping it slowly on the carpet at his feet. "I cannot seem to remember convention when you are near."

He stared at the shiny little ornament for a moment, his heart racing at the prospect of her actions. "A mutual problem we share, Miss Moreland."

She reached up again, with unsteady fingers, to push her hair back from her face. "I have spent too many years being practical, Mr. Hawke. Too many years trying to be something I suspect I never was. So I hope you'll forgive me if I am . . . clumsy at this."

She took a single step forward.

His eyes locked onto her face, amazed at the serene calm on her delicate features despite the shy trembling of her hands. She was the embodiment of grace, and he felt like a pagan about to kneel and beg her for every sensual favor that a goddess could grant. "Consider yourself forgiven."

He lifted her into his arms in one swift movement that elicited a small squeak of surprise from her as she lost her satin shoes in the process, and he carried her against his chest directly out of the library and out into the hall toward the stairs.

"I . . . I could walk," she offered shyly, her arms gripping his neck and shoulders for balance.

He ignored her, unwilling to admit that he didn't trust himself to release her—that he didn't trust himself to do anything beyond carting her delectable person into his bedroom and burying himself inside of her until he couldn't think anymore.

He practically kicked open the door to his bedroom, and had a small measure of satisfaction when it slammed shut behind him by way of sheer momentum. Her eyes had grown a little wary from his brooding silence and the speed of her arrival in this inner sanctum of his life, and Galen reminded himself that there was nothing to be gained in a hurry that couldn't be enjoyed even more at a slower pace.

He kissed her, a thorough, tender exploration that lay claim even as he carried her toward the giant four-poster bed that dominated one end of the chamber. As her posterior settled against the pillows, he lifted his head to allow her to realize exactly where she'd landed.

Her eyelashes fluttered open and she bit her lower lip. "I'm . . ."

"Second thoughts?" he asked, praying she didn't realize that he was probably not capable at this point of letting her go.

She smiled, a vision looking up at him with the most inno-cent and potent invitation in her eyes. "You have never kissed me indoors before, Mr. Hawke."

He smiled as well, a flood of relief robbing him of some of his tension. "And was there a remarkable difference?"

She shook her head. "Only a lack of a breeze, or inclement weather . . ."

"I'm hurt you would have noticed such a thing, Miss More-land," he teased, lowering his lips back toward hers. "I shall have to try a little harder to distract you."

He kissed her again, this time lingering over the silky con-fines of her mouth, while his fingers began to trail down over her body, assessing the layers of feminine clothing and seek-ing to find ways to reach the sweet flesh underneath. Unlike in the garden, he had no desire to work around women's fashion but burned to see her without a single stitch on her body and to feel every inch of her against him.

He found the tie of her laced bodice beneath her hair and pulled the curls back to kiss the base of her neck there, be-tween her shoulder blades, wetting her skin with his tongue and then deliberately blowing against it to send a shiver down her spine. Galen loosened the bow, and then in a trick as old as London itself, he simply ran his fingers across and under the laces to free their hold just enough to let him slide out the cording as he pleased.

At last, he pulled back to bring her forward onto her knees, allowing him to gently tug the bodice off her shoulders and remove her arms so that he could lift the gown up over her head in an easy sweeping maneuver so that it lightly landed at the foot of the bed.

The undergown followed suit, and he surveyed the delightful puzzle of stays and petticoats, crinoline and underpinnings that now faced him. Haley was clearly trying not to laugh but openly enjoying his efforts since they were highlighted by shocking caresses and fiery kisses. "I could . . . do this myself."

He grunted, playfully sliding a hand up her outer thigh to follow the firm curve of her bottom. "Such independence, Miss Moreland! You're spoiling my concentration."

She laughed, but the soft peals ended quickly when he pushed her down against the bed and made quick and efficient work of her undergarments until she was breathlessly left with nothing but her semitransparent cotton chemise and her stockings.

Galen surveyed her for a moment, a wicked gleam in his eyes, as the last layer teased him, opaquely draping across the curves of her body, hinting at the triangular shadow of curls between her legs and the darker tips of her nipples. He caught the first hint of the scent of her arousal, and his cock tightened almost to the point of pain. Galen started to unbutton his shirt and then his fingers slowed as he realized that her courage had faltered slightly and her eyes were tightly closed.

"Do you intend to keep your eyes closed the entire time, Miss Moreland?"

"Haley."

"Pardon me?" he asked softly, smiling at the quick, witty workings of her mind, even under such circumstances.

"It's English law. If we're discussing whether it's proper to look or not . . . you have to use my Christian name." She spoke with her eyes still shut tight, until Galen laughed and the sound of it made them flutter open in curiosity. "Are you laughing at me, Mr. Hawke?"

"No, Haley."

"Oh," she sighed. "That sounded so much better than I'd expected."

"Pardon?"

"My name. I like the sound of my name when you say it."

The heat in his eyes surged, and he knelt on the bed next to her. "Is it so easy to please you? Is that possible, Haley?"

"I'm afraid so. Were you . . . hoping for more demands?"

He shook his head. "I was about to stop hoping at all. But let's readdress this business about closing your eyes. I have an idea."

"And what would that be?"

"Why don't you undress me yourself? Then you can open or close them as you wish and control the pace. But you will have your hands to help you make the decision . . . whether or not to peek."

"That seems like a—wicked suggestion."

But he could see the light of excitement in her gaze, the appeal of the proposition impossible for her to ignore. He slid off of the bed to make it easier, making a quick and subtle business of removing his shoes and stockings first, refusing to allow her first intimate impression of him as being stark naked with a rampant erection wearing his white stockings.

"Come to me, Haley."

She moved closer to the edge of the bed, kneeling to face him as an equal, and he waited until she reached out to splay the long, soft blades of her hand against his heartbeat. For long seconds, they remained there and he allowed her to drink in the desire of his eyes until she was finally emboldened to slide a hand up to remove his cravat and slide her hand inside his collar, just below his throat.

"Your skin is hot." She spoke softly, her eyes falling to the small well at his throat to watch the pulse there as it jumped at her words while her fingers skimmed the small triangle of smooth flesh she'd discovered.

"Buttons, Haley, I beg you," he whispered back. "I'm not sure my wicked suggestion will hold if you don't move a little faster."

Despite a flash of mischief in her eyes, she obeyed him and her fingers began the powerful ritual that released each button in turn. She lingered in the small thatch of thick, soft hair on his chest, absorbing the texture with a smile, then tracing its path downward with each fastening she released. But he noticed that the grace of her fingers deteriorated as she approached his stomach, no doubt her nerves getting the better of her. Galen took mercy and guided her hands and pulled his shirt out of his pants to try to ease her past her hesitations.

She reveled in an exploration of his chest, delicately trailing her fingers over each indentation and rise as if memorizing his body before she pushed the shirt back off of his shoulders and slid it effortlessly from his arms. Her cheeks colored, but she relentlessly began to trail her fingernails lightly across the muscles of his shoulders and his stomach, rocketing pleasure through him. When her palms grazed the sensitive crests of his nipples, his entire body stiffened in reaction.

"Did I hurt you?"

"Not even close." He kissed her, drawing out her tongue to tease and taste her, inciting her to move faster. "Your touch gives me great pleasure."

Her hands had come to rest on the rippled plane of his stomach, and Galen watched her consider her virginal strategy at how best to proceed. In the meantime, his own hands began to mirror the movements she'd made, and Galen decided that while he'd allowed for a game so that she could undress him at her leisure, he'd never said one word about keeping his hands at his sides.

He pressed his palms over the hardened peaks that beckoned him to touch, and he was rewarded by a sweet gasp and an involuntary shudder that pushed the round orbs against him harder, as if they, too, wished to protest the indolent speed of the proceedings.

"Y-you're distracting me, Galen!"

"I'm sure that was my intent."

She tried to ignore his words and the electrical arc between his touch and her body's core, sure her wits were already scrambling to take in this new world of sensual delights. She could feel his every twitch and reaction as she continued her venture of learning his body. The slow movement of her fingers transmitted the heat of his flesh to hers, and when she added the lightest drag of her fingernails to the game, it set off a catch in his breathing and made his heartbeat increase. Haley marveled at her new power to affect him with the softest pressure of her hands. Like their first kiss, she didn't want to rush, wanting nothing more than a languid foray into this new world—for even more than a simple kiss, this exchange held far more meaning.

But her own body was fighting her, fueled by the taste of bliss he'd given her in Bellham's garden, and she could feel her thighs getting slick in anticipation. Haley trembled, but not with fear. She felt like a horse straining at the slips, eager to be off and finally know true freedom—to give herself up to this delicious and dangerous path, into his hands, yielding her innocence and entering into an intimacy that should have, by rights, been only her husband's privilege. But she wanted Galen, and no other—and there was no turning back.

Her fingers dipped below the line of his waist, and at the realization of the size of his anatomy, outlined by the cloth and pressed against the buttons, she bit her lower lip and hesitated.

"Haley, a man can die from this kind of torment," he noted in a sage growl that made her smile.

"Then let's see if we can save your life," she whispered back, and he gasped in ragged shock at her words. But her eyes were on the buttons as she gently tugged to unfasten his breeches and began to free him at last. His sex was so large, the head of him was pushing up at the very waist of his pants, and Haley marveled at her first glimpse of the dark purple head of it, like a plum. When the buttons gave way, his cock sprang forward, heavy and hot into her hands, jutting proudly, so taut and rampant from a nest of black curls that she forgot her intentions to close her eyes at this critical moment.

Haley had seen male statues, Greek ideals of male beauty, and not always with the modest fig leaf placed "just so"—but nothing of cold white marble had prepared her for the sight of Galen's male prowess. Rigid and virile, with every breath his cock bobbed and pulsed, a living part of him in a colorful display that demanded admiration. Velvet soft skin in a darker hue was stretched over a thick molten steel core, and Haley knew its purpose. She forgot her maidenly shyness and openly stared, her own inner muscles clenching in desire, hungry to consume and hold this part of him inside of her. . . . Her hand reached up to trail from the outside of his thigh, working up the courage to touch what her eyes were devouring. Curiosity was making her more and more eager for experience—but the sheer size of him made her wonder at the practical logistics.

Perhaps it doesn't actually go all the way inside . . . or . . .

Haley looked up at him shyly, instantly aware that he was reading her thoughts.

He slid his trousers the rest of the way down, kicking them off with a practiced grace, and Haley held still and took in the view of her own Adonis, naked and unashamed. His untamed curls were pushed back from his face as he returned to the bed, and his emerald green eyes glittered in the lamplight. Long muscular lines and smooth skin were highlighted only by a black swirl of hair on his chest and the thatch around his sex, and Haley admired the lean shape of his thighs and calves and even the tight swell of his bottom. There wasn't an ounce of softness on his body, and she marveled at how different he seemed, and yet, how some part of her recognized and joyfully welcomed every difference.

Galen's desire insisted that the time for maidenly hesitation and leisurely study had drawn to an end. He returned to the bed, a panther on a merciless prowl, eager to feast on his delectable prey. Haley sighed at his first touch, and he lifted her up by her arms to kiss her in an assault that indicated the last of the civilized world melting away from his reach. He lifted her into his arms to taste her mouth, pressing her body against his, and pushed her back onto the bed.

The barrier of her chemise added to the sweet friction but also tantalized him as his cock sought the molten notch between her thighs and her hard little nipples pushed against his chest in searing points that begged him to take all he wanted.

And God help him, he wanted all of her.

He lifted off of her with a groan, hating to end the kiss and lose the heat of her body against his, but his impatience with the chemise brooked no more delays. He pulled it up over her head and flung it off the bed onto the floor. Galen leaned back, kneeling above her, and was sure that no man had ever been faced with such a vision.

Her hair was fanned out beneath her head, trailing off the edge of the bed in mahogany soft curls, and she was looking up at him with such innocent lust, such unpracticed wanton that he almost spent himself. She was completely bared for him and put up no resistance as he untied the ribbons of her garter and peeled off her stockings to press open her thighs and allow him to survey the spoils of his conquest.

He drank it all in, surveying the bounty of Miss Haley Moreland sprawled across his bed. Her narrow ankles and curved calves, dimpled knees and pillow-soft thighs, willowy figure with its pert apple-sized breasts and tight little coral nipples thickened and hard from arousal just beckoning a man to taste and suckle pure ecstasy. But he stared for an extra moment at the sweet sight of her sex; ripe pink flushing to red, her thick soft lips were already slick, and he watched as a trail of clear honey dripped from her, coating the glistening flesh underneath her dark brown curls.

Nothing was hidden from him, and Galen reached out to run his fingers up into the sensitive flesh, instantly eliciting a moan from her as he dipped his finger into the hot well of her core to spread the viscous soft evidence of her arousal up over the tiny jutting button of her clit.

"Galen, please!" She reached for him, eager for the comfort of his arms, and no doubt remembering the particulars of their embrace earlier at Bellham's.

"What do you want?" he whispered, wickedly hoping for a certain answer.

"Kiss me, Galen," she begged innocently, her hands trying to pull him up to guide him toward her pouting lips.

Ah, just what a man wants to hear!

"Your wish is my command." He let his breath fan over her damp flesh, giving her the first hint of exactly where this "proper kiss" was going to land. As exotic as an orchid, but far more beautiful in Galen's eyes, her skin tightened at the hot sweep of his exhale, and he watched the colors deepen as her body anticipated what her mind had yet to grasp. He spread one of his hands over the soft swell of her belly to hold her in place and kept the other free to augment his "kiss" when the time came. Galen gently pulled his mouth up her slit, tracing the folds with his tongue before settling his mouth against her bud to use the pressure of his tongue against her clit, darting up and down the miniature bundle of nerves beneath her skin and circling, faster and faster, until he was lost in the dance of it. The sweet, musky taste of her arousal was as intoxicating as any wine for him, and Galen savored the scent and flavor of her sex as she began to sigh and moan in mindless pleasure.

Her hips bucked beneath him, but his hands held her in place while his mouth ensured her willing captivity. Galen increased the speed of his tongue but softened the pressure to draw out her journey to the culmination of this act.

She sighed again, writhing to increase the contact of his mouth, wordlessly begging for him to give her more of what her body was screaming for. Galen drew his fingers up to circle the tight pucker of her nethers before sliding a single finger upward into the welcoming wet of her channel. The tight grip of her muscles encircling the slight thickness of his finger made his cock surge with new heat, at this foreshadowing of how incredibly tight and sweet her body would be for him.

He moved his finger, withdrawing it and then driving it forward to press against her, again and again caressing her with each stroke, deeper and deeper. He curled his finger against the textured walls until the pad of his index finger found the juncture inside of her he sought. He changed the pressure of his hands, and his mouth, using them together in concert to elicit the first hint of a tremor through her body.

Galen lifted his head to catch his breath and appreciated the view he was afforded from his vantage point between her thighs. She was a goddess spread out before him, and her scent was in his nostrils and in his mouth, and she was about to spend at his command and it was a power he'd never known. In the past, he'd seen almost obliquely to his partner's enjoyment, but never had he unraveled a woman's desire and focused on her climax alone with such intensity.

You're mine!

He lowered his mouth with renewed vigor, enjoying his delicate feast and the lush bounty of her body. He wanted to drive her past reason and control, past words and logic, and bring forth the passionate temptress he'd recognized from the very first time he'd seen her. He mastered himself, and sought to master her with his tongue, his lips, his fingers pressing up into her saturated inner muscles, all working together in a rhythmic dance as old as time, and she was helpless against it. She cried out, a long, sweet cry that echoed through him in triumph as she bucked and trembled, flooding his mouth with the salty-sweet rush of her orgasm.

"Galen . . ." She spoke his name, breathless and unsure. "That . . . wasn't . . . a kiss. . . ."

"Wasn't it?" He lifted himself up on his elbows and crawled up to cover her body with his, his throbbing erection jutting against her soft belly. "Are you sure?"

She blushed furiously, but her gaze never dropped from his, and Galen admired her anew for that forthright fire in her sea-colored eyes. Ever so slowly, he lowered his lips to hers, willing her to open to him and taste herself on his lips.

Haley met his kiss, her mouth already parted, and when he hovered for a moment, drawing the satin of his lips across hers, her tongue darted out to shyly sample all that he offered.

The gesture ignited him as no other had.

Suddenly, the kiss was a bruising connection and he moaned at the sweet hunger of her lips against his as she matched his need, clinging to him with an unbridled lust that affected him to his very core.

Her thighs parted instinctively to accommodate him, but Galen knew what she did not—that her virgin passage was so small that he wasn't going to risk hurting her unnecessarily. Better to work her back to another peak before breaching her maidenhead, although she was wet enough that he considered it briefly, especially when the little minx innocently began to trail hot kisses down his throat and then back up to nip at his ear.

Even so, he reached down and began to tease her with the tip of his cock, reveling in the sensation of his swollen head working against the velvet soft folds, coating himself in her honey and deliberately pressing up against the tight bud of her clit. He experimented with the sweet friction until he found the melody again, and this time she was already close to the edge, her body still primed and eager to climax again.

She clutched at his shoulders, her cries more urgent as the tremor worked through her frame, and Galen could feel another rush of honeyed wetness against his cock—and he knew that he was the one in danger of being lost.

Chapter
11

He shuddered in pleasure, struggling for control as her juice coated the sensitive skin of his sheath, coating him and begging him for more. But his control was tenuous at the first press of his ripe head inside of her, and Galen held his breath at the overwhelming sensation—even after coming, she was so much tighter than he'd anticipated, but it was a carnal bliss that began to outweigh chivalric considerations.

Damn it! I don't think a saint would leave this bed without laying this woman within an inch of her life.

He was trapped by the unforgiving hold of her channel, but it was so tantalizing as her climax continued, and Galen simply used it to his advantage, pressing in with each spasm, using the grip of her body to hold him and draw him in even farther.

Inch by inch, he gained entry, aware of everything at once and awed at the intensity of the experience. He could still taste her on his tongue, could feel her every movement against him, could feel the swollen head of his cock stretching her, making his way deeper inside her to claim every untouched inch of her body. He moved ever so slowly, kissing her constantly wher-ever he could reach, trying to rebuild the fires within her, and ensuring that each pulsing grip and pull of her channel against him from the echoes of her fading climax wasn't wasted.

But then he felt the unmistakable barrier of her maidenhead—and Galen held himself in place as she regis-tered the first touch of pain, stiffening beneath him, and he watched the tiny bit of wariness enter her eyes.

He'd known she was a virgin, or rather he'd assumed it. For John had made no hint that he'd yet trespassed with his angel, and Galen couldn't imagine Trumble being so bold—beyond that, she'd given him a hundred subtle signs that she was un-schooled when it came to the acts of love. Still, reaching her maidenhead, it gave him pause. It was hard to think, and then the world entirely fell away as her legs wrapped around his waist and she lifted her hips in supplication.

"Galen, please . . ."

He eased back, for just a few seconds, teasing her as he pressed in just an inch or two against the sensitive opening, feeling the tight grip of her hungry channel and ensuring her readiness. "You never keep your word, Miss Moreland."

"How c-can you say that?"

"You said you'd never kiss me again."

"Oh!"

He kissed her, a bruising, branding claim meant to push every thought from her head and ratcheting up her desire, sucking her tongue and tasting her until she was breath-less and moaning, and he instinctively drove forward in one smooth maneuver that rendered her maidenhead before she could remember her fear. Galen slowly waited for the space of a breath or two for her body to realize the pleasure yet to come, and he softened his kisses before moving against the exquisite confines of her body around his.

Slow, deep strokes meted out their rapture, and Galen quietly worked to help her find the way of it, countering his thrusts and discovering her own capacity for raw surrender and sensual delights. Long, hard, relentless strokes shadowed the beating of his heart until at last he was buried to the hilt. Galen withdrew almost completely, only to drive forward to knock on the very door of her womb, his possession of her complete and potent, freeing him with each movement to take all that he could of this fleeting ecstasy.

Rocking into her, holding her hips, he drove himself harder and harder, and then he forgot himself—forgot about conquest and vengeance, about anything that might have defined him or anchored him to his civil self. He slipped into a primal world that held only this need, this fire, this hard cock, this wet slit, these eager hands, this woman's cries as she spent again and again and he could feel himself drowning in the seraphic hold of her body and his. Galen groaned as the crescendo hit him at last, a wall of bliss that tore the crème from his body, and he could feel it jetting in white-hot streams inside of her, the pleasure of it so sharp it brought tears to his eyes.

Finally, he could only rest his weight on his elbows, sagging against her to catch his breath in great ragged gulps, while he waited for his heart to return to him.

Oh my God . . . Well, I'd say I just officially ruined this girl, in more ways than one . . . Hell, I feel a little ruined myself, if that will make Bradley feel better.

He gingerly pulled away, tenderly trying not to cause her any more discomfort. He pushed her hair back from her damp brow, warily studying her for any early signs of hysterics or regret. He offered her a smile. "How was that for a distraction?"

She laughed softly and shook her head, pulling the sheet over herself in a show of modesty. "I can't see how anyone ever . . . leaves their bed." She blushed at the admission, and Galen relaxed at this strong indication that she wasn't going to bolt for the door.

"How do you feel?"

She squirmed at the intimate inquiry, even knowing that there was now nothing of her body that he hadn't seen. She took a moment to assess, surprised at how little there was to report in all honesty. "I feel . . . a little stretched and perhaps bruised, but then, I cannot say it is an uncomfortable sensation. Instead I feel . . ." She blushed at the confession she'd been about to make, that she was wishing she could do it all over again and at this very moment.

"Yes?"

A clock on the mantel of the fireplace across the room began to chime three times, and Haley realized that the realities of time weren't going to allow for any more distractions. "I feel as if I should get dressed before you tempt me again," she said evasively, sitting up and taking one of the sheets with her. She slid from the bed and began a quick search for her chemise. "I don't want anyone at the house to realize I've . . . been away."

He brought her a small pitcher of water and a soft cloth, and showed her to the dressing room and bath, pointing out the water closet and then leaving her briefly to her private ministrations to clean and restore herself before dressing. He pulled on his own trousers and his shirt, leaving it open, and then began to gather up the various layers of her dress that he'd so carelessly discarded, brushing them off with quick efficiency before he returned to her side.

"May I assist you, my lady?"

"I . . ." She hesitated, weighing out the practicalities and risks of having such a handsome ladies' maid. "If you would, Galen, thank you."

"How is it these things are easier to remove?" he mumbled as he reattached the tabs on her crinoline.

"I have never considered it." She smiled, enjoying the process while he surreptitiously slid his hands over her skin, grumbling softly over each tie and lace as they made a game of setting her to rights.

"I cannot seem to find your shoes," he confessed, then kissed the top of her shoulder left bare by the evening gown's corsage.

"They are downstairs, in the library." She felt her face grow hotter remembering that he had literally swept her off her feet and out of her satin slippers. "Where we . . . began our conversation."

His emerald eyes lit with mischief. "Ah! Yes, our conversation! I do love conversing with you, Miss Moreland." He shifted easily to pick her up, again holding her against his chest as if she weighed nothing at all. "I'll just have to return you as I found you, then."

"I am capable of managing the stairs!" she laughed.

"Nonsense." He nuzzled her neck and headed out of the bedroom, retracing the path they'd taken earlier. "Hush and don't spoil a man's pleasures, Miss Moreland."

"I would hardly think it's pleasurable to haul me around like a great lump."

"You are not a great lump, and considering your delectable derriere is resting in my arms and I have a considerable view of your breasts from this angle . . . I'd say there are pleasures enough to compensate me for my efforts."

"Galen!" She wriggled in protest, but not too vigorously, far too aware of her own bliss at being carried in his strong arms against the firm wall of his warm chest, her fingers sliding over his skin and threatening to reignite her own desires.

He carried her back into the library and set her down in almost exactly the same spot that she'd originally occupied. He knelt to retrieve her shoes as she began to gather up the jeweled pins from her hair that were strewn about the carpet.

She laughed as she gathered the ornaments from the floor. "I once told Aunt Alice I would throw flowers at your feet, but I confess, this wasn't what I had in mind."

"No?" He lifted her up, his hands at her elbows to steady her as he guided her back into his arms. "I rather liked it."

"Did you?" she teased, daring a small kiss on his cheek, and feeling oddly awkward with him. They'd crossed every line of decent behavior and she'd held nothing back from him, but suddenly she was dressed and retrieving hairpins and starting to worry that she might not be ready to face what she'd done.

"Like Julius Caesar entering Rome. Didn't they throw flowers?"

She nodded, unable to resist teasing him. "Yes. Just before they stabbed him to death."

"Ah! A good lesson, that!" He leaned over, then gently cupped her chin with his hand, forcing her eyes to meet his. "Promise me that you'll let me see you again."

"I . . . of course! I thought we—I mean, I assumed that you—" Panic coursed through her at the awkward admission. *Is he asking because he hadn't thought to see me again until this moment? Did I misunderstand all his pursuit and attention for more than it was?*

He quickly reached up to smooth her cheeks. "I want far more than one night, Miss Moreland. You were not mistaken. I should have spoken more graciously just now, but you have me bemused. So, you must swear to be kind and not overthink every phrase."

She sighed with contentment. "I am new to . . . *this*."

"Good." The sound of a passing carriage on the street below broke the spell, and Galen glanced up at the clock on the mantel. "I would keep you here, if I could, Haley, but . . . it will be dawn soon."

"Don't worry. I made sure that I could slip back into the house without anyone noticing." She retrieved her shoes, suddenly shy when he knelt before her to place them on her feet. "You don't have to—"

"I want to. It's an excuse to touch you."

She smiled, then sat up in the chair, her back stiffening as a new thought occurred to her. "Herbert—I'll have to tell him this afternoon when he calls!"

"You can't," he said, leaning back slowly to sit on his heels before her.

"It's the honorable thing to do."

"No, wait, Haley." He kissed her fingertips. "I don't think the man has any idea—about much of anything—but certainly about us. It may cause a scandal if it's known that we . . . that I was the reason you ended the engagement."

"I don't think I can lie. I'm a terrible liar, Galen."

"Hear me out. Trumble may not take an abrupt drop as well as you think. If he acts aggressively against you or your father—"

"I don't think he's a violent man."

"Not violent, but he may be more petty minded than you realize. If he's paid for your Season . . ."

"Oh." She felt her color change, the calculation of debt making her stomach hurt. *If he called in his debts and demanded payment, we'd be ruined!* "I hadn't thought of that."

"Don't worry. If we let him down gently, I'm sure he'll negotiate or even forgive it all as a gesture of goodwill."

"Do you think so?"

"I do." He began to gently massage the back of her calves, taking advantage of his position to caress and calm her. "I have spent too much time in London not to know the ways of the world. Trust me, Haley. If you suddenly broke with Trumble and then appeared on my arm the next day, it would be a smear we might never recover from."

"What do you think we should do?"

"Let's be patient." He leaned forward and kissed her lightly, a whisper-soft caress of his lips against hers. "There is nothing to keep us from seeing each other, and when the time is right, you can tell Herbert your decision—but not that you've found another lover. If he cares for you, he won't want to hurt you or your father, but if you tell him the whole truth . . ."

"And after I break it off with him, what then?"

"We wait until the dust settles and I will set things right and publicly see to your honor."

She looked at him with tender relief. "I'm looking forward to that, Galen."

"As am I," he said solemnly, his expression serious. Galen stood up. "But if we rush, then the sharp eyes of society may still put the puzzle pieces together, and we'll be right back where we started." He smoothed out her hair, moving the curls back from her forehead. "I won't have you suffer a single harsh look, my dear—not on my behalf."

On John Everly's behalf is another matter, Miss Moreland, but we'll leave that for now.

He could guess her thoughts. She'd given herself to him, and gone too far to turn back now. . . . Her situation was precarious, at best, but Galen was doing his best to give her the assurances she needed. He held out his hand to her.

At last, the storm in her eyes subsided, and she looked back at him, calm and serene, and reached for his hand so that he could pull her up from the chair. "It's not forever, this arrangement."

"No, not forever." He kissed her again, tasting her more deeply and sealing their bargain. "And perhaps you'll find something to enjoy, something to please you about our secret. What do you think?"

She melted into him, "I think I may already have an inkling of an advantage, or two."

"For now, just trust me."

"Yes, Galen. I trust you completely."

And I have you, Miss Moreland. I have you.

* * *

The carriage ride home through the dark and deserted streets of London was like a dream. She kept wondering when she would feel shame or terror at her actions, but instead she felt only a wild kind of liberation and happiness. She had seized her chance for joy with both hands and thrown caution to the winds. And she just knew it would all work out as it should.

He'd all but proposed to her that very night, but for his sensitivity and thoughtfulness when it came to her current predicament. He'd proven his affections beyond anything she'd ever imagined possible, and—they would meet again soon!

It was illicit and forbidden, and so intoxicatingly romantic, this taboo passion! Aunt Alice would be strangely proud, if she knew what Haley had done, but Haley hoped to keep it from her as long as possible. Dear Aunt Alice wasn't known for her discretion.

And now I have a naughty tale of my very own to shock a grandchild with one day. Haley leaned back against the cushions and almost cried with happiness.

* * *

The man dropped his cheroot and extinguished it at his feet, then watched the woman's carriage pull out of sight. If Galen Hawke was truly one of the members of this secret circle called the Jaded, as Bascombe seemed to think, then there were many possibilities. But the Jaded were strong, looking out for one another and trusting no outsider with their secrets—so far the Company hadn't even been able to ascertain their membership roster. But a woman could change everything—and she already had. She'd brought Galen into the public eye, and now he wouldn't be as careful.

For now, they would just wait and see if Galen would lead them to the others before some sahib's assassins could spoil everything.

And Bascombe had promised he'd be able to use the girl to their advantage.

But if not . . . they had their own ideas about how Galen Hawke could be brought to heel.

Chapter
12

"There's a note for you, Miss." Emily brought it in on the little silver tray. Usually it was the butler, Mr. Weathers, who brought the cards and notes in, but the housekeeper had already informed her that the poor man was terribly ill this morning.

"Emily, will you ask Mrs. Biron to send for a doctor for Mr. Weathers, please?"

"Yes, Miss." Emily grinned as she curtsied, and then left to carry out her mistress's bidding.

Haley studied the sealed note for a moment, admiring the strong, graceful handwriting—unfamiliar to her, but undoubtedly Mr. Hawke's. Then she turned it over to lift the seal and unfold the paper.

It has been hours since we parted and I have decided that I am impatient to be in your company again. Come out to Bell Street to the market square tomorrow morning at ten under the guise of needing some feminine trifle from the shops and my carriage will be waiting.

Come to me.

G

Relief flooded through her and she pressed the paper to her pounding heart. *It wasn't a dream! I'm to see him again, and he was true to his word!*

"I've been invited by Mr. Melrose's secretary to see to a bit of local color!" Herbert announced, flopping onto the broad padded cushions of the sofa of the downstairs sitting room. He'd entered the room with the informal familiarity of a man so used to calling that he hadn't even bothered to pause in the doorway. "A dog show! I hear they're notoriously dangerous and seedy, but what a chance to gather for myself what the common man thinks he's up to with the most popular breeds!"

Haley tried not to let her anxiety at his sudden appearance show and tucked Galen's note away into a hidden pocket in her skirt. She could still smell Galen on her skin, and since she'd miraculously gotten back into the house undetected for only a few hours of restless sleep, her morning had all but evaporated as the rest of the house demanded her attention. All the promises she'd made to Galen echoed in her head, but the sight of Mr. Trumble's sweat-covered brow and his cheerful belligerence made it hard to hold her place. "Herbert, there's something I wanted to—"

"I heard they have bred dogs so small that they can sit in a man's beer mug! But," he leaned forward earnestly, "I think they're shaving guinea pigs and trying to pass them off to win a few coins from idiots who don't know any better!"

"Herbert," she tried again. "I was hoping to—"

"No women allowed!" Herbert put up both of his hands, nervously waving her off. "I'll be lucky to leave without getting my wallet pinched, much less with my dear life, from what Melrose's man told me! So, there is no possibility of your attendance for—"

"I don't want to go." Haley resorted to his own method of speech and interrupted his tirade. "I need to tell you something, Herbert."

He seemed to realize his mistake, instantly appearing contrite. "Yes, of course."

Haley took a slow, steadying breath to compose her thoughts. No matter what Galen had said, she did trust him and she knew that everything he'd said made perfect sense; but she couldn't keep Herbert in the dark—or misuse his engagement. And she was sure there was a way to break it off with him without throwing her future with Galen away. Hopefully, Galen would understand her decision to give in to her own instincts and be as truthful as she could be.

"I need you to please . . . forgive me, Mr. Trumble. I'm afraid that I can't marry you after all. I'm relying on your good nature and mercy, and hoping that you'll understand."

"What is there to—but I don't understand, Miss Moreland! What could possibly have changed? Unless . . ."

"Unless?" Haley prompted him breathlessly, suddenly afraid that he'd guessed the truth.

"Unless it's that nonsense about my investing in Miss Langston's next production. I was afraid you wouldn't approve, but I can assure you that it's a respectable business arrangement! I even asked a few colleagues and they said that the royals have been known to support the arts!" His face was flushed as he spoke, and Haley held up a hand to stop him from saying any more.

"My mind, Herbert. I changed my mind." She took his hand, trying to reassure him, but speaking as honestly as she could. "The more time we spent together, the more I began to doubt that I could ever make you truly happy. I am . . . not an ideal match for you, Mr. Trumble."

"That's ridiculous!" He shook his head. "You are well-bred and your family is well-respected. You are exactly what I want in a wife and exactly the kind of wife who can help me make my way in the world and improve my station. I know I may not be the most polished bloke in the Empire, but you have quality enough to make up for my shortcomings! We are a perfect match!"

She pulled her hand away, wishing there had been another way to protect her ragged conscience without hurting the poor man. "You don't love me, Herbert."

"That's ridiculous! I've spent hundreds of pounds! I've opened credit lines for—"

"And I don't love you, Mr. Trumble," she whispered, the quiet truth finally reaching him.

He stood, turning his back on her to stare out the window onto the street below. "Affection can grow over time."

"I don't think so. Every instinct tells me . . . no, Herbert."

He turned back, confusion giving way to a strange look of belligerent challenge on his face. "This may be a feminine impulse of the moment, Miss Moreland. My sisters are notorious for changing their minds and then tearfully changing them back as soon as they realize their mistakes." He straightened his coat, pride lifting his chin a small fraction. "I'll await a note from you within the next three days before I say anything to anyone. That should spare you the embarrassment of explanations and hold off any misunderstandings."

"Mr. Trumble, I don't need three—"

"Three days! I do hope you'll reconsider all the advantages I have to offer, Miss Moreland. I am a generous man, and can promise that I'm not going to hold this sudden and uncharacteristic change in temperament against you after we are wed."

He made an awkward bow and turned, leaving without saying another word.

Haley sat for a few minutes, stunned by the strange turn of events. She'd expected him to protest but not to completely deny her breaking off of the engagement.

Still, once his deadline had passed, she was more hopeful that he would, in fact, be kind when it came to voiding their contract.

As for now, he'd given her the gift of three days to catch her breath and not be forced to make any decisions at all. Three days without dreading any more confrontations, three days to brace herself for the inevitable disaster of telling her father that his financial security might have to wait for just a while longer.

"Miss?" One of the maids spoke from the doorway. "Miss,

your father is asking for you. He's . . . feeling a little poorly this morning."

Haley stood up, setting her shoulders for the task ahead. "Feeling poorly" meant his head was still bothering him after drinking far too much at last night's ball, and she would have to put off her own chance to rest for just a while longer to attend him. "I'll be right there, Emily, thank you."

Haley headed up the stairs to the second floor and her father's rooms. It was nearly noon, but the draperies were still drawn, robbing the room of all light. She was familiar enough not to trip over the furniture to reach him, mildly concerned at his soft moans.

"Father? Can I get you anything?" she asked softly.

"A shroud," he mumbled. "A burial shroud."

She smiled, leaning over to light an oil lamp by his bed stand, only to suffer his complaints.

"No lights! My eyes will burn out of my head!"

"Nonsense." Haley retrieved a small pan of water from the table by the door where the maid must have set it before retreating to fetch her, and she returned to see about wetting a small cloth to put over his eyes. "Here, this will soothe."

He took the cloth, sparing her a grateful glance before returning to his laments. "I was a fool to drink with that Mr. Hawke."

"Mr. Hawke doesn't drink." Haley swallowed hard, surprised to hear Galen's name.

"True! Wretched soul!" he moaned, pressing the cloth against his eyes. "What torture for him to walk this miserable earth without allowing himself even the solace of spirits!"

"Father, I hardly think Mr. Hawke's soul is wretched from a lack of drinking. And as for torture, the only soul who looks to be in agony at the moment is you."

"Don't mock me," he whispered dramatically. "This could very well be the end of me."

She sighed. "I've never heard of anyone dying of a hangover, unless, of course, they were smothered by a daughter who was furious at her father for not keeping his word—they may note that differently in the papers!"

His pout was usually endearing, but Haley had seen too many of them to find the childish gesture anything but repugnant under the circumstances.

"You're being cruel." He stuck out his lower lip, lifting the cloth to give her a pitiful look. "I was . . . overwhelmed at the ball. All those couples only reminded me of my solitary state and I . . . couldn't help myself."

She dropped a fresh cloth in the pan of cold water and forced herself to look at him again. This time, to see him as a stranger might see him. Sprawled on his silk sheets, eyes sunken and his face drawn from a night of endless indulgence, his nose almost permanently stained a comical tint of red, the handsome man she'd once adored was like a phantom with his pale skin and shaking hands.

"Father"—she took one of his hands, stilling it and warming it with her own—"what do you think Mother loved about you best?"

He smiled. "She always said she loved my heart best."

"And now?"

His smile faded, the question confusing him. "Now?"

"Now, what would she love about you best? If she were to come into the room, what would she say?" Haley tried to tighten her hold on his hand as he started to pull away, but petulance lent him strength and he churlishly retrieved his fingers from her touch.

"I'll not be lectured by my only child as if I am in short pants!"

Tears filled her eyes. "I love your heart best, too! It's no lecture to tell you that, Father. It's no lecture to beg you, one last time, to stop looking backward and using her as an excuse. If you loved her, I cannot believe that *this* is the way you choose to remember her."

She laid her hand over his briefly and stood to leave the bedside. But she stopped at the door, her back to him. "And you're right. I apologize. You are not in short pants and I am not the parent. In the future, I will do my best to hold to my place and for better or worse, leave you to your own devices." She turned back, letting the tears fall as she looked at him, his jaw dropped open in shock as he sat dumbfounded in the middle of the bed in his nightshirt. "I will never again ask you not to drink."

*　*　*

Haley threw herself onto her bed, exhaustion finally taking its toll. She felt as if she'd been through the strangest storm of her life within a single night and day—with highs and lows she could never have anticipated. She'd lost her heart and taken the ultimate risk with Galen, but knew for the first time what her life could be, what happiness might yet be hers to claim. She'd severed her engagement and now faced an uncertain future. But the relief of knowing that Herbert Trumble wasn't the one holding the reins made it feel like the sweetest liberty.

And she'd finally relinquished control over her father's choices and spoken the words she'd longed to tell him for so many years.

For the first time, she experienced a curl of delightful anticipation for the days ahead and smiled at the memory of her beautiful Hawke sweeping her into her arms as sleep began to claim her.

At last . . . I know what my mother had with my father, and I'm not afraid to seek it with Galen, and risk everything for his love. And if all of it was just a dream, then I don't ever want to wake up.

Chapter
13

Galen tapped his foot and checked his pocket watch for the third time. He'd meant to just send the carriage for her and wait at the house, but at the last minute, an uncontrolled restlessness had suddenly overruled him.

He tried to tell himself that it was out of a natural concern that she would be suffering from regret at giving in to him and yielding her innocence so quickly. He tried to tell himself that it was out of this practical concern that he'd insisted on seeing her again so quickly.

But the logic wasn't holding.

He listened to the traffic and tried to keep a subtle eye on the pedestrians, watching for her. He tried to tell himself that his darkening mood had everything to do with the villainy of his plans and naught to do with an oppressive sense of guilt that had robbed him of any guise of sleep. After all, what guilt should he harbor? Galen reminded himself that no matter how sweetly she played it, she'd heartlessly cast John aside and done nothing to dispute or dissuade him from believing otherwise. She'd fallen into his hands, just as he'd predicted to Michael, and willingly thrown off her engagement at a better prospect—again just as he'd said she would.

His scheme had taken on a life of its own, and he wanted to enjoy the accomplishment, but instead he was simply left with a bone-gnawing lust and the sinking feeling that he cared less and less about the reasons behind his actions—so long as she was once again beneath him and crying out his name.

At last, he felt the footman start to descend from the back of the carriage and realized that she was just outside the door. He waved the man off and opened the door for her, his throat closing at the sight of her in a beautiful day dress of daffodil yellow with a soft green underskirt. Her delight at seeing him lit her eyes, her face framed by the simple straw bonnet she wore, and she smiled as she took his hand and gracefully ascended to sit beside him.

"You're late." He almost winced at his own words as he closed the carriage door and drew the curtains, but he couldn't take them back and he couldn't say why he was suddenly choking on his own desire. It flared through him in an irrational flash, and a small part of him wondered if he weren't about to deliberately scare her away. He knocked on the wall, and the carriage pulled smoothly away down the lane.

"I came as soon as I could," she demurred shyly. "You can't imagine how—"

"Take off your bonnet."

"Galen?"

All he could do was look at her, knowing that the hunger in his face would be impossible for her to mistake. And without another word, she reached up to untie the green silk ribbon of her bonnet, setting it aside on the seat next to her.

Her lips parted and her pink tongue nervously darted out to wet the soft wedge of her lower lip, and Galen's grip on the cushions tightened until his knuckles showed white.

Without another spoken word, she moved toward him, awareness in her blue green eyes, like a doe approaching the hunter, a willing and eager sacrifice. And his body mercilessly responded, every nerve ending insisting that he take all that she offered and more.

"Damn it!" he muttered involuntarily.

Her eyes widened at the quiet curse, but he reached for her, averse to waiting for a protest. For time had lost its meaning since she'd left his bed and Galen was half-convinced she'd bewitched him somehow. He felt compelled to prove that he was still master of his own will and that he truly had the upper hand with her. He grasped her upper arms and pulled her against him, kissing her as if he'd waited a century to taste her again. As if she alone possessed the nectar of life, he drank it from her lips with an insatiable thirst. She responded with an enthusiasm that incinerated the last vestige of his self-control.

He cradled her face in his hands, his fingers sliding into her hair and fisting in her curls as if he could absorb her into himself. This was a kiss meant to conquer, and Haley surrendered to him. He inhaled the scent of her skin and detected a trace of honeysuckle, but beneath the flowers there was something earthier, and he knew instantly it was the scent of her arousal. His hand slid up her skirt, over the alluring curves of her calves and thighs to slip through the open seam in her underclothes. Galen's fingers found her soaking wet and ready for him. He shifted his fingers up to tease her clit before pushing one of his fingers up into the slick of her quim, and Galen was struck again by how tight she was—

He couldn't wait any longer. At the first thought of how close he was to having her again, he was in danger of wasting himself in his clothes. Galen was furious at himself for this new weakness, but helpless to deny it.

He pushed her away, only to instantly turn her around so that her back was to him, awkwardly perched for a moment in between the seats.

"Galen?" she asked breathlessly.

He held her hips to hold her steady with alternating hands as he quickly worked her skirts up over her hips and untied her drawers to bare her tantalizing bottom. She gasped but made no protest, instinctively leaning forward to place her hands on the seat cushions for balance, as he spread her legs apart so that she stood across his lap. Galen's cock jerked against his breech buttons at the sight of her ass, like a ripe peach spread before him, with the wet pink of her sex just waiting for him.

He made quick work of his buttons and freed his cock, holding the head with one hand and reaching up to start to pull her back down onto him. Galen grit his teeth as he guided her hips until their flesh touched in a unique damp kiss. He pushed the swollen tip of his cock into the searing hold of her channel's slick opening and then bucked upward as he gripped her hips to pull her down in a merciless stroke.

She cried out softly, and he could feel the muscles of her body seizing onto him, accommodating him with a hold that made him want to weep at the glorious embrace on his cockstand. Galen held onto her hips and bucked up, again and again, driving up into her as she moved with him to deepen each touch, increasing the friction and length of every pounding caress. Faster and faster, he worked his body into hers, until he knew he couldn't prevent his climax.

He came so hard, he groaned at the force of the cascade of ecstasy that shimmered and exploded out from the base of his spine and throughout his frame. Galen felt each pulse as his crème rushed into her, rocking his hips into each spasm to prolong his pleasure. After a few minutes, he gently kissed the back of her neck while the rest of his sensibilities finally began to function again.

Well, that was the best temper tantrum I've ever thrown. . . . God, I'm an idiot!

If he'd meant to assure himself that his memory had enhanced their first encounter, he'd only succeeded in proving that she was capable of reducing him to a mindless rutting bull after a single glimpse of her tongue. She'd matched him perfectly, yielding to the raw onslaught of a searing, bruising passion, responding to his every move and equaling his desire. But he wasn't sure her reaction excused him, or if any excuse could save a small shred of his pride.

He gingerly disengaged himself from between her thighs, drawing his breath through his teeth at the sensation of cool air against his sensitive wet cock. As quickly as he could he refastened his pants, then assisted her in pulling her skirts and petticoats back down, attempting to restore some order to her appearance. She began to blush as he reached to turn down the hem of her underskirt.

"Galen?"

He pulled her back into his arms, this time to gently tip her back to cradle her against his chest. He dipped his tongue into the sensitive corner of her lips, making her gasp before he gave her what he knew she deemed "a proper kiss." He did everything he could to soothe where before his kisses may have bruised, until she sighed her pleasure and sagged against him. He lifted his head, unsure of what a man could possibly say after losing control as he had.

"I'm so sorry . . . I'm sure I had some bit of conversation prepared . . . or the diversion of a witty story of poor Bradley's efforts to fuss about the house without speaking to me. But, Haley, I meant to be—more tender this time." He ran his fingers through his hair in a frustrated gesture. "I had every intention of making love to you very slowly *after* we'd gotten back to the house. . . ."

"You've changed your plans then?"

His cock became hard again at the shy gleam in her eyes, and for several seconds, there was no sound inside the carriage but their ragged breathing. "No, I don't think I have."

* * *

Haley stretched slowly out on his bed, lying on her stomach, even wiggling her toes in innocent pleasure at how delightful Galen's attentions were—at any speed. She turned her face into the pillow to breathe in the sandalwood scent. His rush in the carriage had caught her by surprise, but no less than her own rush to have him inside of her again. She was sure it wasn't the behavior of a lady to melt at the very idea of being rogered soundly with the London public on the other side of a thin carriage wall and curtains—but she'd melted nonetheless.

She'd even forgotten her discomfort with small spaces, as she'd clutched at the seat and walls for balance while he pressed into her so deeply she'd almost cried at the myriad of sensations.

He'd looked at her exactly as he had when he'd watched her during the music concert, and Haley had fearlessly given herself into his hands, reveling in his raw lust for her body—and accepted that Galen had been right when he'd spoken in Hyde Park. *I needed to be swept off my feet, and if this afternoon's romp doesn't qualify, then I'm sure Galen will demonstrate it soon enough.*

"What are you thinking over there, Miss Moreland?"

"I'm wondering how it's possible that I can . . . be so wicked. . . ." She blushed. "This all seems so . . . unlike me. But when you look at me like that . . . I can't remember being any different." She covered her eyes. "I'm not making sense. And it's foolish to think I've come this far and can still feel so . . . conflicted."

"It's only natural. A lifetime of civilized habits can't be dropped without a few echoes of hesitation and doubt, can they?"

"You don't seem to hesitate, Galen."

"I know what I want." He came back to the bed, stretching himself out alongside her body, and began lazily trailing his fingers down the bare skin of her back and making her shudder in delight. He circled back upward over her shoulder blades before following the line of her spine and teasing the soft rise of her bottom with his whisper-light strokes.

"What do you want?" Haley glanced at him flirtatiously over her shoulder. "And be as specific as you can, sir."

His emerald eyes seemed to darken for a moment, and it was as if they were back on that darkened balcony. He looked dangerous, and at the same time so alluring, her breath caught in her throat.

"At the end of the day, I want all the scales to finally balance so that I can sleep," he said, and then planted a lingering kiss on her shoulder. "No less than any man, Haley."

"I'm having trouble picturing you just as 'any man,' Galen. For I cannot think of anyone I've met who . . . looks at me as you do."

"And how do I look at you?" he asked, gently pushing her onto her back so that he could continue the light sweep of his fingers across her skin. He slowly circled her breast, spiraling in on each coral-tipped point until they were stiff and sensitive under his hands.

Haley arched her back, instantly feeling a connection between the hardened tips of her breasts and the pooling warmth between her legs. She reached for him, using his own trick on him as she mirrored his touch through the soft black swirls of hair on his chest to tease his flesh and was rewarded as he pulled her into his arms.

"Ever since I first met you on that balcony, I should have known you were going to be like Greek fire—impossible to put out the flames once ignited."

She smiled. "Am I so insatiable?"

"In the best and most challenging ways, Miss Moreland."

Her brow furrowed briefly. "May I ask . . . why were you seeking me that night? You didn't know who I was on the balcony, but Mrs. Bianca said you'd asked for me, for an introduction at the start of the evening. Why?"

The question caught him off guard. "I'd already heard another man commenting on your beauty in the foyer when I arrived, and I admit I was curious."

She smiled but sat up in the bed, lifting the sheets to wrap around her breasts. "But what brought you out to Bascombe's that night? You clearly despise the man, and if what he said was true about your reluctance to attend public events . . ."

"I'd heard an old friend might also be there that night, and I thought it was time to show my face again." Galen seized her hips and lifted her back onto him, distracting her with the move that pulled the sheet from her hands and nestled the wet silk of her slit back up against his reawakening cock.

"All these questions, Madame Inquisitor? I can think of better ways to torture information out of me."

"Yes, but . . ." She caught her breath as he slid her forward so that the molten tip of his swollen head was pressing against her clit. "I'm . . . forgetting my . . . questions. . . ."

"Ah! Then it's working . . ." He laughed and positioned her above his erection, notching himself just inside of her body while he held her hips to suspend her in place. "Let the torture begin, my lady."

He pulled her down, impaling her in one stroke, and Haley groaned as the last of her questions was forgotten entirely.

* * *

Haley set her bonnet aside, her fingers trailing over the soft ribbons, and she caught a glimpse of herself in the mirror, smiling. It was the secretive and supremely happy look of a woman in love, and Haley almost didn't recognize her reflection. For one fleeting second, she could have sworn she saw her mother there.

"Would you need anything, Miss?" Emily asked quietly from the doorway. "I finished basting the new morning gown, if you'd care to see it."

"Already finished?" Haley shook her head in disbelief. "I'd love to see it."

Emily brought it out from behind her back, shyly holding it up for inspection.

Haley turned the seams and admired the handiwork. "You've quite a talent, Emily, and such speed! Although"— she looked at Emily, suddenly concerned—"you didn't lose precious sleep over this dress, did you?"

"I may have lost track of the hours, but . . . it were a pleasure, Miss. And I wasn't sure if you'd need it sooner," Emily explained as if to apologize for the dark circles under her eyes.

Haley held up the simple morning dress, seeing each turned flounce and feathered pleat with new eyes. *Lost track of the hours because I was too distracted to tell her that there was no hurry at all—and now she has a full day ahead of her, poor thing!*

She looked back at Emily, seeing her anew. "There is nothing I need that is important enough to rob you of your sleep. But it's truly beautiful work, Emily." She handed it back to the maid. "Please finish it *at your leisure* and then we'll make a day dress, for your days off."

"F-for me?" Emily's eyes widened. "A *new* dress?"

It was customary to give one's ladies' maid castoffs or off-season outfits that a lady no longer desired, but Haley's wardrobe was so new, she could hardly see what difference it made. Emily had been taking the part of ladies' maid since her arrival in London, and Haley didn't want to seem ungenerous. But Emily being so petite and round, making a dress to fit her seemed a far kinder gift. Still, her father was constantly fussing that she was too soft-hearted a mistress and she didn't want to lose Emily's respect. "Yes, as part of your lessons, of course. Then when someone wishes a hem or an adjustment, why you'll know so many tricks from having built your own creation that they will want to keep you forever as a treasure. Won't that be lovely?"

Emily nodded, her eyes watering with joyful tears. "Yes, Miss Moreland."

Aunt Alice appeared behind the girl, and watched in bemusement as Emily hurried off clutching the morning dress as if it were the Holy Grail itself. "Did you just make that creature cry?"

"You know I didn't!" Haley moved to her vanity table, hoping Alice wouldn't notice anything different about her, and began to rearrange her hair to comb it out. "Not in the way you're suggesting!"

"No, I suppose not." Alice smiled. "You're spoiling the servants, Haley."

"I am not!" Haley turned on her chair. "Has . . . there been some complaint or lapse that I'm not aware of?"

"None!" Alice ran a finger over the top of a shelf and held up her clean finger as if to underline her point. "Indeed, Mr.

Weathers is recovered, and while I'm not sure the man is capable of smiling, he actually looked as if he might when I saw him last. Mrs. Biron is singing your praises and made inquiries to see if you will be taking any staff with you to your new home."

"My new home?"

Alice's eyes narrowed with suspicion. "Yes, when you marry . . ."

"Oh, yes! My new home!" Haley was astonished at how far her mind had wandered, her face heated with embarrassment. She hated lying to her dear aunt, but she wasn't sure how much more she should say until Mr. Trumble made an announcement of his own. "Honestly, I hadn't thought of that."

"Well." Alice stepped closer. "I'm afraid that's what's worrying me. You've got to take a hand in these things! Surely you're not going to let Herbert determine every household decision? Granted, men are masters of the universe and all that rot, but no niece of mine is going to blithely forget to insist on hiring her own cook!"

Haley tried to maintain a serious and interested expression. "I'm sure I won't."

Aunt Alice didn't appear convinced. "I know you think I'm a tyrant to go on about starting out the way you mean to finish, but it's true, dearest. You've been as meek as a lamb lately, and despite all these afternoons of shopping, you've not mended your ways! I don't see a single package, and there have certainly been no deliveries, Haley!" Her aunt sat down with a heartfelt sigh. "Frugality can be extremely unattractive, dearest. Please, appease a treacherous and greedy old woman and spend the man's money! I'm beginning to worry that this self-denial is becoming a terrible habit."

Haley had to bite the inside of her cheek to keep from laughing. She had just spent an afternoon in the most indulgent and decadent manner, but she could hardly point out that she had recently abandoned self-denial in its most basic form. "There's no need to worry on that account."

"What in the world is keeping you from loading up your

carriage with all the latest London fashions?" Alice pressed, her brow furrowing.

"If you must know, I just like to look. I can study what I wish, and then when I want, I'll make my own creations—and be happier for the effort."

Alice's expression changed to genuine concern. "Herbert made his position clear on that matter, Haley. Unless you've had another conversation on the subject, I'm not sure this is—"

"I'm not married yet, and until I am, I will do as I please and please myself while I can, Aunt Alice." She held her breath for an instant, a little surprised at her own cheek. "How's that for mischief?"

Alice nodded, a smile lighting up her face and making her look young again. "If I'd known you were up to no good, I'd have banished you out of the house and sent you window-shopping on your own from our first day in Town!"

Haley blushed and turned back to her dressing table to comb out her long hair. "I'm blessed to have you for a chaperone, Aunt Alice."

"From now on, I shall fuss if you are *not* out pleasing yourself!" Aunt Alice went on, oblivious to the impact her encouragement was having on poor Haley's efforts to look calm.

"Yes, Aunt Alice."

Chapter
14

The next afternoon, they were stealing a few more hours, lolling about in Galen's four-poster bed. He was fingering one long curl of her hair, wrapping and unwrapping it around his wrist and hands, enjoying the silky sensation of it.

Once more, in the wake of having her, instead of simply feeling satiated, Galen wrestled with an increasing attachment to her, a desire to keep her close and linger in her presence. The more he experienced her, the more beautiful and enticing she was growing, and the puzzle of it was as intoxicating as the woman.

Her leg was hooked over him, and when she drew her calf across his hips and grazed the base of his shaft, his body instantly hardened. It was easy to slowly reposition himself so that his cock was nudging her thighs apart, and he shifted Haley over so that her back was on the bed, but her bottom was nestled up against his arousal. He imagined they made an odd pinwheel, but he loved the view of her sprawling away from him, with her sex up against his.

It was a lazy game that suddenly became increasingly sensual as Galen noticed that his hands were still free to do as he wished. Spreading her thighs further apart, he touched her, exploring her at his leisure and admiring how amazingly soft her skin was, warming to his attention and pinking up as he watched. She was the most exotic of flowers, and the honey she exuded was an opiate that made him forget everything but the celestial transport her body offered him.

Haley wriggled against him, closing her eyes at the sudden renewal of her own need for him. It was ridiculous—this inexorable pull to join her body to his. It was as if her practical self was connected to the world around her by the smallest threads, and every time he touched her or even looked at her a certain way, she was cut adrift.

He dipped his fingers into his mouth, and then the soft workings of his fingertips around and over her clit felt mysteriously like a tongue. It was the most wicked illusion she'd ever experienced, for his warm, hard cock was buried inside of her, gently rocking into her and stroking up against the side of her wall, finding a sensitive place that sent her reeling, the tense little coil of pleasure inside of her instantly tightening.

She felt like the most licentious sultana to lie back and allow herself to be stroked and pressed, his shaft so delightfully thick and his fingers so skilled, her eyes filled with tears. Just when she thought she might find her release, he teased her and changed the rhythm or lightened the friction of his fingers over her engorged clit, and Haley gave herself over to the dance, following his lead and enjoying this decadent waltz.

It felt a little strange to be angled away from him: she could reach his chest and press her splayed fingers against his heartbeat, but her touch was limited. "Galen, I . . . I seem to be . . . receiving far more benefit . . . than you. . . ."

"Nonsense," he said softly, but moved his hips to remind her that he was very much enjoying the connection between them, and she gasped as his shaft seemed to thicken inside her as he increased the speed of his fingers. "But if the lady is keeping a tally . . ."

Something inside of her began an inevitable cascade,

tumbling and gaining momentum with each fluttering pass of his hand over her clit, until there was no part of her body that wasn't directly linked to that tiny bud, until she was sure that finding and mounting that invisible peak would shatter her completely—and she didn't care. There was only the promise of release, and Haley arched her back as the first white-hot jolt of her orgasm unleashed itself and radiated up her spine. The intensity made her cry out, but it was as if another woman were moaning somewhere, and Haley could only ride wave after wave and pray that she would recover herself when it was all over.

And then even gravity's hold betrayed her, and Haley had the dizzying experience of being lifted and turned until she was on her knees, and Galen had repositioned himself behind her, quickly refilling the void inside her with his hungry cock. She cried out again, this time in a trembling sigh as the waves began to subside.

But Galen caught her, leaning over her as he buried himself to the hilt, and one of his hands recaptured her sensitive clit and immediately reignited the fire there. She bucked against him, biting her lip to keep from begging him to stop because already she knew she didn't want him to cease a single movement. The cascade swept away her thoughts and she pulled her knees together to tighten her hold on him, to increase the strength of her spasms, and it was all she could do to cling to the bedding and breathe through unthinkable pleasure.

Galen began to move back and forth, gritting his teeth against the force of her orgasms, taking her in strokes that were so slow and so deep, he could feel her channel's every twitch and release. He drew out until only the tip of his cock was inside of her, ringed by the tight pink of her opening, and then he deliberately pushed forward in a relentlessly slow invasion of her body until she finally moaned.

"Galen, please . . . faster . . . faster . . ."

He obliged her with the merciless skill of a man who wished to draw out her own pleasure, and his own. He increased his momentum, driving into her, faster and harder by degrees, until at last there was no sound in the room but the slap of flesh as their bodies came together in a crescendo of carnal lust.

Galen tipped his head back, his orgasm ripping through him and robbing him of the last vestiges of his control. He spent himself in a hot rush of crème that never seemed to end. He squeezed his eyes closed tightly and marveled that he could feel his own heartbeat in every inch and extremity of his body—his fingertips and toes, his eyelids and . . . *Hell, I think I can feel my hair. . . .*

It was such a ridiculous thought, he laughed at the sheer joy of being so completely undone, and discovered that even that small spasm of laughter added to the power of his orgasm and stopped his breath in his throat.

"Oh, my!" He gripped her hips to prevent her from shifting as he waited for the last rivulet of his spendings to leave his body—and for his heartbeat to slow. "Don't move."

"I . . . I shall have to move at some point, Mr. Hawke," she teased, then laughed softly and undid all his efforts. They both gasped at the movement and fell apart in peals of laughter to fall into each other's arms on the bed.

"I cannot help but think that this is a most unconventional affair, Galen." She pushed her hair back from her forehead. "We talk so little—"

"Conversation would seem a waste of these minutes we steal, don't you think?"

"Not a waste." She bit her lower lip, then smiled up at him. "I suppose there will be time enough for talk later, and if you aren't forthcoming, I shall have to get better at torturing things out of you."

"Ah, torture!" He smiled, too, then felt his humor bleed away. "What use are stories of the past? They either say too much about a person or too little to matter. Although I do often wonder what you were like when you were younger . . ."

"We are none of us recognizable from our past, I think," she sighed. "People are like chameleons, changing over time. . . ."

"Because they're faithless and disloyal?" He couldn't help himself.

"No!" She laughed, playfully punching him in the arm. "Because when you're eight and you swear you wish to grow up to be a fairy king, I don't think you should be condemned as an adult to living in a house made out of mushrooms."

"Some promises are meant to be kept."

"Do *you* always keep your promises, Galen?" she asked him, drawing up to perch on his chest, her nose level with his and her expression suddenly more serious.

He could feel her heart pounding against his, the firm press of her ripe breasts against his chest and the sweet naked length of her body lodged on top of his as if she'd been molded for him. *Do you always keep your promises, Galen? Dear God, which ones—the ones to dead brothers and friends; or the ones to you, Haley?* "I keep as many as I can."

"You never speak of yourself."

"It is an uninteresting topic."

She laughed again, and he was smiling before he realized it. "It is not uninteresting to me, Galen."

"We have already established that you are easily pleased, Haley," he teased, bucking her over without warning so that now it was his body that covered hers. "But you'll have to trust me that I never aspired to be a mushroom king."

"And what do you aspire to?"

He kissed her to distract her from the question and ended up rewarding himself with another rampant erection. "Come to the house tomorrow."

She shook her head. "Aren't you worried my father is going to start asking about my sudden penchant for window-shopping?"

"Come to me tomorrow, Haley."

"I wish I could, Galen, but Aunt Alice has committed us to viewing the Diorama in Regent's Park and then we're attending a party afterward. I don't think I can excuse myself without creating suspicion." She disengaged from his embrace, shyly beginning to retrieve her clothes. "Indeed, I should go home now before the afternoon is gone completely."

One glance at the clock confirmed that she was right, but Galen didn't feel any more ready to let her go. "Tomorrow."

She shook her head and held her clothes in front of her. "Not unless you have an invitation to Lady MacLean's dinner party, and frankly, I'm not sure I can maintain my composure after . . . It's not like before, Galen."

"Isn't it?"

"I think you are dangerous enough behind closed doors, Mr. Hawke." She turned to head toward the dressing room. "But lucky for me, it's too small a dinner party for you to work your dark magic and make an appearance."

Galen smiled, the wicked smile of a man who liked nothing better than a challenge.

* * *

Late that same night, he was alone and distracted in the dark of his room. He'd expected to be sleeping like the dead. But instead he was wrapped in sheets that held the faint scent of their lovemaking, and struggling to find peace.

I should be basking in triumph. I should feel better. I'm supposed to be dreaming about innocuous green fields and fluffy clouds, damn it!

Not that he'd expected John's ghost to mystically appear with a blessing once he had the girl in hand, but . . . a sense of fulfillment? Of relief? Of accomplishment? Anything but this melancholy state of alertness defined by the dragging sound of the clock ticking on the mantel and the burning memories of her beautiful presence in his arms.

A part of him acknowledged that he was the worst kind of villain, even foregoing using French letters to prevent a possible pregnancy—as if leaving her with a bastard child would be the coup de grace. Michael's warnings about sparing his conscience later haunted him now.

But Haley Moreland was nothing he'd anticipated, and

not even the scream of his conscience would make him stop now.

She'd surpassed his expectations. She'd eclipsed the fleeting fantasies of his imagination and surprised him at almost every turn with the candor and playful spirit of her lovemaking. She'd expressed her every delight, innocently hiding nothing from him, and naïvely spurred him on to please her even more, to find new ways to make her moan and sigh.

Just thinking about her, his body reacted, a soft weight like hot sand in his belly slowly hardening his cock. Galen reached down, closing his eyes as his hand circled the thickening shaft, marveling that he could burn for her again so quickly.

He inhaled her lingering scent, the orchid sweet musk enveloped him, and it was all too easy to conjure the memory of her, complete and compelling enough to make him groan. He closed his eyes, sliding his hand down to the base of his shaft, tightening on the sensitive base where his flesh contracted across his balls, and then began moving in a languid motion to draw out the pleasure.

He imagined her in the red dress, the one she'd worn the first night he'd seen her, but this time, in his fantasies he adorned her in a ruby necklace dripping with diamonds and envisioned a very different encounter in that balcony.

In his mind's eye, he watched her draw closer and closer. This time there was no element of surprise. He was waiting for her in the dark. She was seeking him there. And the anticipation of her, the sight of her moving toward him in that red silk dress, so demure and impossibly sexy at the same time, heated his blood and made his cock start to turn rock hard.

She knelt in front of him, her dress fanning out in a lush backdrop that mirrored her pouting red mouth. She reached up to feel him through the cloth of his pants and then brazenly opened his buttons to admire his cock.

"It's beautiful, Galen." He could feel the heat from her breath as she whispered, each exhale caressing his skin and teasing him with phantom light kisses. And she held perfectly

still, just there, her breath tantalizing and tormenting his ripe head, before she looked up at him through her long sable brown lashes. "May I?"

He'd only had to nod and her mouth began to move closer and closer. His swollen head was already weeping and she licked off the first drop, then looked up at him again, her lips glossed by his desire. She smiled, wanton and treacherous, innocent and heartless—everything in the world he loved and hated in one glorious figure.

She took him further into the soft cavern of her mouth, pulling, drawing, sucking in long, slow strokes that made his knees want to buckle. Her long, tapered fingers reached up to cup his testicles, and then she drew her fingernails lightly around them until they seized against her palms and she found the most sensitive point at the base of his shaft, pressing against it just as her tongue changed rhythm and began to lave him along the ridge underneath his cock.

She grazed him with her teeth, just enough to send a shiver up his spine and confirm her control of him. She latched onto the base of him and began to suck until it became a pinpoint of such intense sensations that it bordered on pain. But she soothed him instantly, releasing him only to slide the hot, wet fires of her mouth back up to gently devour him once again.

Her grip on his balls tightened and then softened, in a strange echo of every flicker of her tongue against him. And he groaned, as he could feel the telltale fisting of pleasure in the pit of his stomach and knew he was about to spend himself. He could feel the core of his cock changing into something molten, and then it was heaven, and she had all of him at once—she was commanding him to spend, supplicating him with every touch, every pull of her mouth and the sight of her skirts spread out around her, his queen kneeling at his feet in surrender—and yet she was in complete control, and he yielded to it . . . until she met his eyes again, and he knew what he wanted.

He reached down to undo the pins of her hair, fisting his hands into the heavy brown silk to guide her mouth up and down his shaft. And she relinquished her newly won power and the very thought of it pushed him over the edge. He came in uneven surges, and she drank every last swallow from him, clinging to his thighs and squeezing his balls as if to rend the last drop from his body.

Galen came in a glorious spasm, the crème jetting from his body in an ecstasy that bordered on pain, and he covered himself quickly with the sheet, dismayed at the sense of shame that shuddered through him on the heels of his release.

He'd never been so consumed by a woman, and he worried that he hadn't even begun to slake his lust where Haley Moreland was concerned.

I should set her aside now, before this becomes some kind of obsession.

Yes. Just set her aside.

But not yet.

Not just yet.

*   *   *

The carriage let her off at the head of a street of fashionable shops to allow her to walk a short distance and then safely hire her own hansom cab to get home. Haley smiled at the scheme to protect her reputation, warmed by Galen's care and attention to detail.

Her steps took her past the colorful wares in the many-paned windows, but Haley kept her eye on her steps to avoid the mud and puddles on the thoroughfare, and her thoughts were still with her lover.

"Miss Moreland!"

Haley looked up in surprise at the unexpected greeting.

"Out for a bit of shopping?" Rand Bascombe asked cheerfully. "But where is your maid or even your dear Mrs. Shaw? May I escort you to your carriage?"

"My aunt . . ." Haley took a deep breath, wishing once again that she'd mastered the art of deception that others seemed to take for granted. "My aunt thought she might need it for errands, so I was going to use a hackney carriage."

"Allow me to assist you, then, for it can be a bit harrowing for a lady to hire one alone." He held out his arm. "That is, if you've finished your shopping?"

Haley nodded and put her hand lightly on his arm, unwilling to carry the charade too far and risk saying something that would betray herself. "Yes, thank you."

"London is not a town I would recommend a lady going about on her own, Miss Moreland. But then you strike me as a resourceful creature, and very astute for a girl so remarkably fresh from the countryside."

Haley wasn't sure how to accept a compliment that came so close to an insult by implying that any other girl from the country would have suffered a lack of acuity. "I'm sure common sense is a portable enough quality, Mr. Bascombe, to serve a woman anywhere she might find herself."

"Quite right!" He began to guide her through the passersby as he continued. "And it's that candor and intelligence that I'm sure won Mr. Trumble's heart. Naturally, you realize, I admire your fiancé's ambitions and his knack for making friends."

Their broken engagement was not yet public knowledge, and Haley had no intention of correcting the man. Even so, she felt uncomfortable in a lie and tried to skirt the topic. "He's a good man."

"And your knack for making new friends is no less admirable, Miss Moreland."

"I . . . would guess a person's social circle can always be widened and improved." Haley suddenly felt unsure of where Mr. Bascombe was driving the conversation.

"Oh, yes! But please tell me, what is *your* impression of Mr. Galen Hawke?"

Haley could only pray her expression didn't reflect the extent of her shock and panic at his casual inquiry. *He doesn't know anything! And if I start sputtering like a schoolgirl, it will be exactly the disaster that Galen cautioned me to avoid!* "He seems very . . . interesting. But, then we've made so many new and interesting acquaintances since coming to London."

"He is more than interesting!" Rand slowed his steps as

they reached the corner. "He is an absolute mystery, my dear. I suspect he was a hero of some kind, during the Troubles in India, for there have been whispers of a most unique nature about him."

"A hero?" she asked, captivated by the idea despite herself.

"It's humility, to be certain, that keeps him from speaking of it, or of the fortune he seems to have made there. Or is there something else more sinister?"

"How can you even suggest such a thing?" Her alarm at the conversation escalated in a single heartbeat.

He stopped and gave her a knowing look that did nothing to dampen her discomfort. "It's difficult to know what to suggest when a man refuses to share even the smallest detail about his adventures and continues to rebuff almost every invitation that's issued—unless, of course, *your* name is on the guest list."

She said nothing, frozen in place by her fear of what he would say next.

Rand Bascombe smiled. "It's a happy coincidence, and I was a fool the other evening to press you to betray whatever confidences he's shared with you. Have you forgiven me, Miss Moreland?"

She nodded, not trusting her voice to speak.

"Ah, here is a carriage for you!" He raised his hand to hail the driver to stop directly in front of them, handing the man up a coin with instructions to take her to the rented brownstone address. Then he turned back to her, as if all were right in the world. "We are friends again, and I am glad for it, Miss Moreland. I shall continue to look for you and your dear family when I am out, and I hope"—he bowed slightly and touched the rim of his hat—"that you will continue to enjoy your time in Town, and make the very most of it."

"Thank you, Mr. Bascombe." She was numb as she climbed into the carriage, shaken but unsure. It was possible that she was simply filtering an innocent exchange through her own guilty conscience and reacting to insinuations that Mr. Bascombe hadn't intended.

She was at a loss. If he knew of her affair with Hawke, she could hardly say anything without confirming his suspicions, or worse; if he knew nothing, and she overreacted, then she would create the rumor herself.

She let out a long, slow, shaky breath and regained her composure. If anything, the strange incident with Bascombe strengthened Galen's case for continuing in secret for the time being. And as the carriage pulled away from the street, Haley began to feel better, and even reminded herself that bumping into an acquaintance while shopping only provided more of an alibi should anyone ever ask where she was spending her afternoons.

Oh, dear, I'm growing craftier by the hour. Is that a change for the better? She sighed, unsure of anything but her feelings when it came to Galen. She leaned back against the cushions and indulged in the newest memories of his body to hers. Every touch made her feel safe and desired, and she clung to that sensation as she returned alone to her precarious life. *I have to weather the storm when Father learns I've broken my engagement . . . if only to make Galen proud of me later when he learns of what I've done. Then I'll be able to tell Galen that I kept both our secret and my own honor by not deceiving Herbert.*

As for Bascombe, *whatever his interest in Galen, it has naught to do with me.*

Chapter
15

❦

"What a delight to add you to our intimate dinner, Mr. Hawke!" Lady MacLean marveled aloud yet again, and Galen watched out of the corner of his eye as Haley's blush renewed its bloom.

It hadn't been entirely easy, but it was worth it to see Haley's reaction to his presence. And Galen was also enjoying the unexpected bonus of seeing Miss Haley Moreland once again in the exact same red dress he'd imagined her wearing in such erotic detail. He'd meant to just be present, and tease her if he could manage it without alerting the hostess too much, but the sight of her, so beautiful and so familiar—and within reach—was proving to be quite the temptation.

Aunt Alice had eagerly welcomed his presence and, as usual, was doing her best to assist him in any way she could. "So lucky that you could join us, especially as Mr. Trumble was unable to make it and poor Haley has no dinner partner!"

"Yes, extremely lucky—for me." He bowed over his hostess's hand, and was rewarded with Trumble's vacant chair. Throughout the meal, that put him less than four place settings away from the delectable Miss Moreland, and Galen did his best to just savor it.

She was a skilled wit, and he watched her charm an older colonel into sharing some of his adventures in the Congo, and then just as sweetly keep the widower to her left amused and included in the exchange, until Galen was sure that both older men were besotted enough to envy the absent Mr. Trumble's good fortune.

Almost as entertaining was watching that same man try to steer clear of Mrs. Shaw's flirtatious hints and shocking pronouncements that for any widower looking to marry for a third time, he should consider a wife with a little snow on the roof as she had already demonstrated an ability to survive. Even the colonel and Lord MacLean kept their heads down rather than enter into the fray.

As for his conversation partners, Lady MacLean was very gracious and all too happy to share with him the details on their current renovations of their property in the country. Galen did his best to nod and make the appropriate comments when it came to landscaping and the dire consequences of a lack of irrigation, all the while keeping his eyes on the siren in red across the table.

"Why are you looking so smug over there, Miss Moreland?" he asked softly, observing the catlike look of satisfaction on her face as they took their places in the drawing room after dinner. He carefully joined her in a window seat away from the others, but they were still well within sight of the party and were forced to keep their voices down.

"Because I think you've accidentally delivered yourself into my hands."

Galen held very still, suddenly wary. "In what way?"

"Because now we are in public and you will be forced to make small talk and answer questions and . . . your methods of distraction are powerless here, Mr. Hawke."

"Not powerless," he threatened softly, looking at her as if he had every intention of sweeping her up to strip her naked and take her in front of a drawing room of guests.

Haley's eyes widened, and her cheeks reddened, but she bravely held her place next to him. "You're bluffing, Mr. Hawke. Now, behave!"

He shrugged and smiled. "It was worth a try. I suspect you wouldn't respect me if I didn't even attempt to ward you off with a reference to how delicious I find your juices."

"Galen!" She gasped in shock, then realized the game and composed herself quickly. "Enough of that, Mr. Hawke." She tilted her head as if assessing him anew. "All this evasiveness might give a woman pause to wonder what you're hiding."

"I'm not hiding."

She smiled. "You always say that, and I always have the feeling that it isn't true."

"Very well, you have me at your mercy, Miss Moreland. Ask what you will. But I warn you, I think Lady MacLean is starting to eye me so that she can come over and show us sketches of her proposed herb garden." He crossed his arms and gave her a look of pure challenge. "Unless you've lost your nerve?"

She hesitated and fingered the silk of her skirt for a moment. "I don't know where to begin." She looked back up at him, and he caught himself on the verge of sighing at the stunning color of her blue green eyes. Galen straightened in his seat, attempting to regain his own composure as she bit the plump flesh of her lower lip.

Damn it! You're not some love-starved pup, Hawke! It's after-dinner conversation, not pillow talk!

"Something easy then," she said. "A favorite poem? Or some anecdote from your youth? Or even better, a sweet story about your first kiss . . ."

Galen's brow furrowed as he tried to decide if anything was easy when it came to conversing with Haley. There was so much he'd kept to himself and now, as he looked at her, it was harder to remember why. "Lately, Shakespeare's twenty-seventh sonnet comes more often to mind, as it's about insomnia and I . . . have trouble sleeping more often than not."

"Do you?" She looked at him with an honest sympathy. "Does the sonnet help?"

He shook his head. "No, but it lets me consider my plight in lofty pentameter, and that can make me feel more noble about suffering at three in the morning."

"I'll have to look it up!" She laughed softly, and Galen's shoulder relaxed at the melodious sound of it.

"If you wish, for I'm not going to recite it here!" He leaned forward conspiratorially. "Don't they warn young women about the dangers of poetry?"

She nodded. "They do. But I still don't see the harm. For you are . . ." She hesitated and then lowered her voice even more. "As impossible to resist as you are, I don't see how you reading poetry to me could be any more potent!"

The urge to kiss her was almost too strong to set aside, but Galen forced himself to just smile. "An experiment for another day, Miss Moreland."

Mrs. Shaw came up quickly enough to catch them both off guard, and Galen straightened the instant Haley's gasp alerted him to the intrusion. "Did you not wish a glass of port, Mr. Hawke? Some of the other gentlemen are yet enjoying a taste or two in the library."

"I never drink, Mrs. Shaw."

"Oh, yes! You said something like that before, and I've naturally credited your reluctance to the company at hand," she said as she cheerfully took a seat across from the couple. "I don't think a bar mouse would have taken a glass of champagne with Rand Bascombe after he was so odd."

"Aunt Alice!" Haley rolled her eyes. "Must you?"

"What?" Aunt Alice ignored her niece and turned her full attention back to Galen. "I wasn't misbehaving, was I, Mr. Hawke?"

"Not in the slightest, Mrs. Shaw." Galen settled into the cushions as if he had nowhere else in the world he'd rather be, deliberately hoping that the tables would turn to show Haley that he might not be the only one cornered into conversation. *I'll ask Mrs. Shaw about Haley and see if—*

"What was India like? Were you there during the Troubles?"

"I don't want to speak of it. India is . . . India." He shook his head, grimly accepting that. "Others seem to bask in the exotic and flourish, but I was never one of them. I always felt like I was trespassing. So"—he took a deep breath—"I shall leave it at that, and adventure no further than Bristol or Bath, if pressed."

"Why do you think everyone is so curious about your time there?" Alice asked.

"Are they?"

Haley looked away, an awkward pause telling him that she'd heard more than she was saying.

"Mr. Rand Bascombe was extremely persistent, and I can't help but wonder why he would bother—why concern himself so much?"

"Perhaps the answer is a simple one, more befitting the nature of the man who's asking," he offered as directly as he could. "I think Bascombe has no adventures of his own to bandy about and seeks to live vicariously through the mishaps of others and fortify his dinner conversations."

She laughed. "He could certainly benefit from a new anecdote or two!"

"And there you have it!" Galen leaned forward, rewarding Haley's aunt with a wicked grin that was sure to give her a thrill. "But you strike me as the kind of woman who has no need to live vicariously at all! I suspect you have a tale or two of your own that could top any fiction, Mrs. Shaw."

"One or two! Of course, there is one in particular that . . ." Her aunt went on, but Haley's thoughts drifted. She could feel her levity bleeding away almost instantly, despite the skilled turn of the conversation and Aunt Alice's lively stories. She wondered why she instinctively knew that there was so much more to him—so much he wasn't saying. He was like a wounded animal, protecting his weak side in case she should suddenly strike out against him. And the idea brought tears to her eyes.

Haley had to clench her fingers together in her lap to keep from reaching out to gently pull her fingers across his forehead and down to caress the handsome lines of his face, wishing that by a tender touch or word alone she could reach him, even heal him.

He touches me or instantly diverts me every time I ask a question, or get too close, I suspect. He distracts me with the undeniable attraction between us—this powerful desire that makes me forget everything else. At least, for a while . . .

Haley sighed, leaning back against the cool stone of the alcove, letting the ancient masonry draw some of the fever from her blood—and studied the profile of the man she knew almost nothing of but who now held her entire future in his hands.

Chapter
16

Alice pressed her ear against the smooth, thick wood of the library door, determined to discover what Mr. Trumble and her brother were discussing in such uneven tones. She could pick out her brother's voice more easily, as he practically shouted on the other side of the door.

"Like hell, she has! I've not heard a word of it!"

And then there was something sternly mumbled by Trumble, and Alice winced as she heard the reply, "Oh, my God, no!"

The rest was all spoken too softly for her to make out, but the intensity of the exchange never wavered. She could hear her brother moaning at one point, and then it was as if Mr. Trumble was doing his best to comfort him.

I'd bet my last farthing that the engagement's off! The question is, who broke it off and where is Mr. Hawke?

Alice was straining to try to catch the gist of their words when Trumble opened the door without warning. Alice gave out a startled yelp and nearly fell into the threshold before catching herself to stand aside to allow Herbert to make a hurried and unhappy exit from the house.

"Oh, my! I was just . . . in the hallway when I thought I heard you in pain, Alfred. Are you all right?" Alice came in, approaching her brother, who was still seated in a chair by the window. "Did you . . . have a lovely visit with Mr. Trumble?"

Alfred glared at her, clearly in no mood for her attempt at innocence. "You were listening at the door!"

"Unsuccessfully!" Alice sat down across from him, abandoning theatrics in an eager attempt to get at the truth. "I could tell you were yelling, but then you were both very inconsiderate to speak so softly, and I thought I'd have the vapors before he finally opened the door!"

"You are an impossible woman," he noted, distracted for just a moment from the matter at hand. "How is it that no one has strangled you before now?"

"I can be very charming, Alfred. Now, as for Trumble?" she prompted.

"He said that Haley broke the engagement! She told him three days ago, and he waited to give her time to reconsider, but—"

"She said nothing!" Alice said in astonishment.

"He said he was waiting for a note from her, but he's heard not a word and so wanted to tell me that the engagement is, in fact, off!" His voice echoed with disbelief. "How could she? All my hopes and plans, dashed in a single act! Is it vengeance? Because I've been such a terrible father? Because I—"

"Oh, pish!" Alice's optimistic nature wasn't going to allow him his speech. "You've lost your senses if you think that dear child has a single malicious bone in her body!"

"I'd have said not a deceptive bone, either, but Trumble said it was days ago!" He put his face in his hands. "Where are the tears? Don't women cry when they lose a chance at a good marriage?" He dropped his hands, lifting eyes narrowed with suspicion as a new possibility struck him. "Alice? Is there something you'd like to tell me?"

Alice took a deep breath. "Perhaps."

"Alice, as your brother and sole support in this wicked

world, I'm going to tell you that I'm in no mood to have to pull this out of you piece by piece, so let's have it."

"I can assure you that I believe there may be a better man waiting in the wings," Alice said, doing her best to match his serious tone despite the tickle of happy mischief inside her. "A man you're sure to approve of, and who has money enough to at least stem the tides of disaster and keep us all afloat."

"Really?"

"I'm more certain of it with each passing moment. After all, this is Haley we're discussing! Not some crazed loon prone to chasing after ghosts."

Alfred managed a weak smile. "You're deliberately trying to make light of this!"

"Not at all! I am the soul of discretion, and I am looking forward to seeing this new suitor make his calls."

"Well, I hope he emerges soon! Trumble has generously agreed not to evict us from the house or dismiss the servants since he'd paid for all in advance. But the man expects to be repaid! Oh"—he closed his eyes at a new thought—"and all those loans! Oh, I think I'm going to be ill!"

"There, now. Would you like a brandy?"

"No." He shook his head adamantly. "None for me."

"Oh!" Alice exclaimed in quiet surprise. "All the better, Alfred. Now, no worries! Haley is too levelheaded a girl not to have good instincts, and I want you to trust her."

"Trust? In what? Is there any chance you know the name of this better prospect that would lead her to make such an insane gamble?" he asked.

"I might, but I'm not about to blurt out a wrong guess and send you off on a wild-goose chase. Let's just wait and see how things unfold, and when she is ready to tell us, why then, you just do your best to look entirely surprised!"

"I will be surprised!"

"All the better!" Alice clapped her hands, as if the matter were now completely settled. "Now see that you don't go marching into her rooms to start bellowing! It's hardly conducive to the first tender stages of romance to have the father throwing tantrums."

He sighed. "I'm going to just accept it as a bad sign that everyone continues to speak to me as if I were five years old."

"You're young at heart, dear Alfred." Alice leaned over to pat his hand and then stood to go. "It's one of your best qualities. Now, I'm going to see to my niece and make sure she's dressed for the evening!"

* * *

"Is it true? You broke your engagement to Mr. Trumble?" Alice asked without any preamble, sweeping into Haley's room.

Haley jumped at the sudden question but kept her place and tried to hold onto her needle while draping a side panel onto her dress form. "Yes, I did. It seemed like the right thing to do."

"Why didn't you say anything? To me! Of all the women in the world, wouldn't I be the one to understand?" Alice asked.

"I wasn't . . . ready to tell anyone. And I'm not necessarily ready to discuss it now!" Haley blushed, doing her best to keep her eyes on the cloth she was stitching on her dress.

"But you must tell me why! Was it Hawke? Is it possible you've—"

Haley dropped the cloth and turned quickly to face her aunt. "I'm not sure I should tell you anything! I love you, but nothing is settled! And if Father were to find out too soon, it could all go horribly wrong!"

"Of course! Of course! My goodness, it's this sudden burst of shopping you've been about, isn't it? And I've been glumly sending you out without a whiff of the truth!" She pouted for a moment. "I don't think I've seen a single new ribbon, but I was too distracted to notice till now!"

"Aunt Alice, please!"

"Well, you can tell me everything now and then I won't feel so left out. And as for Alfred, I've already assured my brother that whoever presents himself will be a man of your choosing, and he's agreed to wait as patiently as he can—so now what do you think of your doddering old aunt?"

"He's not angry?"

"Ah! Let's give him the rest of the evening to fret and mull it all over, but I would say he's taken it remarkably well for a man in his position." A slow, wicked smile crept over her features. "So, it is Hawke, then?"

"Yes."

"Aha! I knew it! I saw the two of you sitting together at MacLean's and I swear my heart was just pounding at the prospect!" She clapped her hands like a child at a puppet show. "It's too romantic! A secret affair and now the way is clear for you to accept and marry the man you desire!"

"It must remain a secret for a while longer! Promise me you'll say nothing to anyone!" Haley captured her aunt's hands in hers, desperate to have her attention. "Swear it!"

"I swear, I vow, I promise! I would offer my firstborn on the bargain if I had one!" she replied gleefully. "How much longer do you think, though?"

"Long enough for any ruffled feathers over my broken engagement to be soothed, and so that Galen's courtship won't appear to be linked to the matter. He doesn't want anyone to judge me harshly for . . ."

"For falling in love with someone else while you were still betrothed?"

Haley's heart skipped a beat. "When you say it like that, it sounds perfectly awful!"

"Which is just why your young man is being so clear-headed! La!" She fanned herself with a bare hand. "And in the meantime, you'll have the distinct pleasure of enjoying your first torrid affair!"

"My first and *last*!" Haley playfully fanned her own face with her fingertips, mirroring her aunt. "Although, I will have to be clever to escape the watchful eyes of my chaperone."

Aunt Alice giggled. "Too bad you don't have a wicked old

woman for a chaperone who would turn a blind eye to your comings and goings!"

Haley tried to keep a straight face, but within the space of a single breath, they fell into peals of laughter until they were both speechless from their merriment.

*   *   *

Bradley came into the library with a formal bow. "Mr. Blackwell has come to call, sir. Shall I tell him you're not in?"

Galen stifled the urge to throw his pen at the man. Bradley didn't approve of Ashe, and his less than subtle ways of demonstrating his feelings were almost comical. "No, Bradley. I'm always in for Mr. Blackwell."

"Always? I shall make a note of that." He turned and left to retrieve the guest, and Galen set aside the letter he was working on. Truthfully, he was grateful for the interruption since his mind kept wandering from the confines of his desk and back to the irresistible curves of Haley's inner thighs.

He strode over to meet his friend in the doorway. "Ashe, did you come to tell me that you've found a chaperone after all? It occurred to me that you should simply hire one."

"Now, there's a novel idea! I'll hire myself the fiercest dragon I can find to keep me in line and wouldn't that give the Ton something to talk about!" Ashe laughed. "But no, for tonight, I've come with news of Josiah."

"Is he all right?"

"He's fine. If you consider it fine that he's holed up with his paintbrushes and paints staring at a blank canvas in a loft in the worst part of town. I've already told Michael, so he's called off the search."

"Thank God."

"Speaking of which, you look like hell."

"All this flattery makes me wonder what a man would say if he weren't such a good friend," Galen said.

"Darius once said if you cannot rely on your nearest friends to tell you the unvarnished truth, then the world makes a terrible mirror."

"That sounds like something Thorne would say," Galen conceded. "And if you must know, I'm having a little difficulty sleeping."

"Still?"

"Still." Galen didn't offer to elaborate. "Drink, Ashe?"

He nodded. "You're a good man to have it around even if you don't partake."

"I try to be as hospitable as I can. Besides, one man's poison . . ." He held out the glass of scotch he'd just poured.

"Is another man's pleasure!" Ashe took the glass with a grateful smile. "So"—he sat down—"tell me about this woman. Word has it you're up to no good."

"Who said that?" Galen nearly spilled the barley water he'd been pouring himself.

"Michael." Ashe shrugged. "But he wouldn't elaborate, so I assumed he merely meant that she was completely unsuitable—which consequently means, of course, I'm thrilled for you."

"It's not a question of suitability."

"Ah, but there *is* a question?"

"No," Galen said firmly. "No questions."

"But there *is* a woman?"

Galen sighed, sensing his defeat was inevitable. "Yes. There is a woman."

"Well, unless you're pursuing Lord Russell's daughter, I'm having trouble understanding why Michael was so grim and secretive about it. Hell! He never sighs like that when I tell him I'm flipping up the skirts of half the chorus at the Royal Theatre!"

"Sadly, I think we're coming to just expect it of you, Ashe," Galen teased.

"Ah! The predictability of always getting cast in the role of the rake and ne'er-do-well—it's a curse, I tell you."

"If it were such a curse, you'd alter course."

"True, but we each have our tonics, don't we?" Ashe tossed back his drink, demonstrating his capacity for all manners of indulgences. "And I sleep like a baby, my friend."

Galen didn't believe him, but he wasn't going to dispute the claim. "Yes, I suppose we each have our own method of . . . adjusting back into the world."

"Naturally! Darius has his books, Rowan his profession, Josiah his art, I have my pleasures, and Michael has the Jaded to watch over, and you. . . I'm still not sure what you have, Galen."

Revenge. Galen took a sip of his barley water, wishing that Ashe were less astute and more of the fool he pretended to be.

Ashe gave him a searching look, as if he could read the answer if he looked hard enough at his friend. "Is it solitude, Galen? Is that what you have? For I swear, you always seem to hold everyone at arm's length. Even amidst the Jaded, I'd say, you're always careful about revealing too much of yourself."

"You're becoming quite the philosopher. Darius must have worn off on you all those weeks in the dark." Ashe and Darius had shared a cell together for a time, and despite their stark differences, Galen knew they were strangely close. But Galen also knew that he'd deliberately tried to draw Ashe off with a painful reference to the past, and consequently, proven the man was right in his guess.

And the look in Ashe's eyes conveyed that he knew it, too. "Hard to keep a woman at arm's length, isn't it? Especially after you've tumbled them once or twice."

"Ashe." Galen gave him a warning look. "I can manage my own affairs."

"Well"—Ashe set down his empty glass—"any man who can truly 'manage' a woman should be sure to share his methods with the rest of us. I've never met anyone who could really make that claim, Galen."

"You manage well enough."

"I do nothing of the kind! I sample, savor, and select from the garden of sensual little flowers within reach, but I'm not sure I've ever claimed to be in control." Ashe's eyes flashed with wicked mischief. "Perhaps it's that humility that keeps all my lovely blossoms so happy."

"Oh, yes! How could I have forgotten about your humility, Lord Gardener?"

Ashe stood, gracefully unfolding from the chair. "Hmmm, Lord Gardener . . . I'll keep the persona in mind for the next masque ball I attend. Thank you for the rousing ideas, Galen. Well, I'm off to Rowan's to make sure he's heard about our poor painter."

"So soon?"

Ashe laughed. "Don't pretend you're not glad to see me go! I've violated your sacred solitude long enough for one afternoon, but . . ." His smile faded, and for one moment, Ashe's look was somber and sincere. "I'm hoping this girl will change all this for you, Galen. And from the way you sputter denials and expend those icy glares when I even come *close* to mentioning Miss Haley Moreland, I have a feeling that she just might—if she survives the attempt."

The small shock of hearing her name on Ashe's lips was enough to stun him into silence as Ashe retreated without another word exchanged. But Ashe's final words were too haunting and far too close to his current dilemma to give any comfort at all.

Galen gave himself a quick shake, as if he could brush off the effects of the conversation. *If she changes me, it will only be as the instrument that settles old scores and allows me to feel human again. I'm going to sleep like a baby, too, Ashe! And as for her survival, I'm sure no matter how temporarily crushing a blow it will be to have her heartless nature exposed for all the world to see, she'll find her feet eventually.*

But nothing about Haley felt heartless, and it was harder and harder to see the path ahead. She'd denied him nothing— except the truth about her past or any admission of guilt about casting John off. The temptation to confront her directly about John was fleeting and he again dismissed it. She would only deny their betrothal or come up with a lie. There was a part of him that didn't wish to bring John's ghost into the room only to see him betrayed. But now only one thing was clear: the longer he held her, the harder it was going to be to let go.

Chapter
17

"Mr. Weathers wished me to thank you, Mistress, for your thoughtfulness the other day. He said he couldn't remember another employer so kind," Mrs. Biron said as she waited for Haley's menu selections for the remainder of the week.

Haley shook her head. "I cannot believe that, but please tell him there's no need for thanks."

"Every maid has made a point to praise you, especially Emily, as you've been showing her tricks with your dressmaking to help her better herself." Mrs. Biron beamed. "Not a cross word in all this time from you!"

"Why would I be cross?" Haley asked with a light touch of confusion. "You've all been so good to us, and I know it must be challenging to take on a household so quickly and to . . ." Haley tried to think of the most diplomatic way to describe her immediate family's odd quirks and tiresome requirements. "Accommodate us as you have."

"You've no worries, there, Miss Moreland!" Mrs. Biron's voice dropped, ensuring that they wouldn't be overheard. "You've the loyalty of the entire staff, and there's no doubt of that." Without another word she placed a small brass key on the table between them on top of the menus. "That's the old laundry service door near the south entrance. Not a soul uses it, really, and so I thought you should have it for safekeeping."

"Oh." She stared down at it, then looked up to make sure she'd understood. "Not a soul, you say?"

"I should get these off to the cook as soon as possible." Mrs. Biron collected the pages, discreetly leaving the key behind. "If there's anything else, be sure to let me know."

She bobbed a quick curtsy and left before Haley could think of a dignified reply.

Oh, dear. I've been less careful than I thought if Mrs. Biron has noticed, but . . . it seems she and the servants have agreed to look the other way. Her fingers closed around the key, and a thrill shivered down her spine.

It would be easier now. Even with Aunt Alice's cooperation, it was harrowing to come up with excuses every afternoon with the worry of what the servants might say when no matter how many times she went out shopping, she came home empty-handed. But if what Mrs. Biron said was true, she could come and go as she pleased with few limitations. She smiled in anticipation, eager to enjoy her new freedom. *I could even be with him at night! Father retires so early, I could slip out and return without anyone seeing me.*

She took up a fresh sheet of paper and began to compose a note to Hawke. *Tonight, my heart, I will be there tonight!*

* * *

He was in the Black again, and the air was so thick with the smell of rotting flesh and excrement that he was sure he would choke to death. He hated the Black. A man could forget who he was, or what he was, if he was trapped there for too long— and Galen had been there too long. He knew it. And there were torches coming.

And he wasn't glad to see them.

It wasn't the bone-gnawing terror of knowing that they were going to torture him again, barking in a language he didn't know and inflicting so much pain that he wouldn't even be able to weep or beg for mercy.

He wasn't glad to see the lights coming closer because he'd been in the Black too long. And he was afraid of what the torches would reveal.

"They're coming again." It was Haley's voice in the Black, soft and sweet and out of place, but in the dream, he didn't question it. Of course, she was here. She'd been in all his dreams since the first time he'd set eyes on her. His beautiful angel. His erotic demon. She was always here.

"Yes." He answered her, even though it meant he had to taste the foul air on his tongue.

"You could close your eyes," she suggested in a whisper, and panic seized him because they were coming closer and closer and the light was starting to hurt his eyes and he was trapped. And even she would see . . .

And he reached for her, and the torches were there— blazing cruel light so that he could see her face and watch the terror that came to life in her eyes when she realized what he'd become. He reached out to touch her cheek, to comfort her or deny it, but then he could see his own hand. Fingers rotting, covered in black beetles and maggots . . . and he was touching her and she was screaming.

"Galen! Wake up! Wake up!"

He almost struck out against her, but her soft, cool fingers on his face finally anchored him back into the waking world. "I'm . . . it was . . . a bad dream."

She knelt next to him, instinctively protecting him by cradling his head against her chest, her fingers stroking his hair and face in gentle soothing circles. "You were screaming. I don't think I've ever been so frightened in my life, my poor Galen! What was it?"

He opened his mouth to reply, but nothing came out as he realized that none of the residual terror he usually felt was there. He'd made love to her and then fallen asleep. Normally, after any of his nightmares, he would have been compelled to leap up and light every lamp in the room to dispel its effects.

But this time it was different. His heart had already slowed, and his attention was absorbed into the scent of her hair and the sweet silk of her warm skin against his. "It was nothing."

"Nothing? How can that be?"

He stared into the dark, not really sure of the answer. *How is it possible that I'm not tearing this bedroom apart and ringing for poor Bradley? The only difference—is Haley.* "Ghosts and nightmares, Haley, apparently don't have the same power as I look at you."

"You can't look at me, Galen. It's too dark, but it's a sweet sentiment." She kissed him on the forehead, in an almost maternal gesture, but his body responded nonetheless and Galen wasn't about to let her think of him as helpless for a single second longer.

He reared up, using his strength and speed to exchange positions with her, tucking her against his side and pinning her to the bedding. "I've memorized you, Miss Moreland. Lights are desirable, but I can navigate without them."

"How . . . resourceful of you!" She sighed, arching into his hands as he began to demonstrate his mastery in the dark. He splayed his hands up over her rib cage and covered her breasts with his palms, relishing the way their pert tips came to life in hot, ripe points against his touch. "Every inch, Miss Moreland, of that voluptuous body of yours is mapped."

"N-not every inch!" her voice was suddenly shy. "A lady likes to think she has a few mysteries left, Galen."

"You have your mysteries, Haley. Never fear," he whispered. Galen lifted himself off the bed and burrowed under the light covers to position himself at her feet.

"G-Galen? What are you doing?" she asked warily.

"Conducting a survey of the landscape," he answered, his voice muffled by the sheets.

He started with her toes, playfully kissing each one before he dragged his nails lightly along the arch of her feet and made her giggle. Galen's campaign was relentless, as he gently bit her instep only to circle her ankle with his tongue, making her yelp with surprise. He gave each foot equal attention, until she no longer seemed startled by any of his maneuvers. He massaged the small muscles in her heels and then easily slid his hands up to her calves to press his hands up over the curves there, contracting his fingers as he drew them back down until he'd reached her heel again—only to leisurely repeat the process.

"Oh, it's heaven!" she sighed, and Galen began to relish the game. He had never considered the potential of a woman's body beyond the obvious, and it was thrilling to know that he could please her in new ways. Even so, he wasn't about to miss the obvious . . .

He gently gripped her knees, careful not to apply any pressure and cause himself a black eye with an unplanned spasm. He crawled forward, his face level with her knees, and risked a hot kiss on the tender crease behind each one, tasting the soft skin there and savoring the tremors he was sending up her body with each flick of his tongue. From there, he kissed a trail up each thigh, intermittently grazing the firm curves with his teeth as the sweet musky smell of her arousal filled his nostrils.

He crawled forward, her thighs parted by his bulk, until his nose was just above the luxurious spread of her sex. With the sheets covering him, Galen felt like an explorer in a humid, lush cave, and the thought made him smile as he lowered his lips to hers. She was already wet and wanting, and he dipped his tongue into the well between her silken folds and tasted the slick ambrosia of her need. He penetrated her lightly with his tongue, then sampled the entire length of her vulva, nibbling and laving every change in texture and sucking on her nether lips to make them even more swollen and sensitive to his touch.

She lifted her hips to try to guide him up to the greedy little button that was demanding his attention, and Galen obliged her, but only in a teasing pass of his mouth, tonguing the jutting tip of her as he moved up to press his nose against the soft curls on her mons. Galen didn't want her to spend too quickly, though he deliberately let his chin push into her clit and then was mindful that at least part of him was "inadvertently" touching her there at all times, as he continued his journey upward.

He spread his fingers over her hip bones and studied the shape of her body there. He loved the way it rose and fell, every curve a delight and every dip guiding his hands to uncover more of her. Galen kissed each hip then used his tongue to trace the soft swell of her belly, to dip his tongue into her belly button. Haley laughed softly, wiggling at the sensation of his mouth against the miniature well, and he abandoned it to hover over her to taste the points where her waist narrowed while his fingers splayed over her ribs, measuring her slight span and absorbing the rise and fall of each breath.

He moved up, carefully keeping his full weight off of her but dragging his body across hers as he settled in over her breasts. He touched them with the reverence of a man admiring the sculptured work of a master. They were ripe and firm, the size of apples, ample enough to make his mouth water. He caressed the underside of each, letting his warm breath touch her skin to echo the path of his fingers. He pushed them upward to expose the soft crease underneath and then kissed her there. His hands roamed around the sides of each mound, lightly touching her until her skin marbled beneath his fingertips. Haley arched her back in a spasm of pleasure, pressing her breasts upward into his hands, eager for more.

Galen squeezed each one, then tweaked the hardened peaks in a pinch that made her buck more wildly. He lowered his mouth to one, sampling the ambrosia of her body, all the while aware that he could feast on this woman all day, but the delicious mounds would never diminish—the enchanted well between her legs would never run dry. She was a living goddess of sensual bounty, and his hunger for her was endless. He bent over and caught the other nipple in his mouth, capturing the taut pebbled circle completely and drawing on it, suckling her and consuming the hardened flesh as if her body alone was sustaining his life.

At last, he forced himself to let go, blowing cool air across her skin, and returned to his quest, kissing the valley between her breasts and up to her throat where he could taste the pulse in her throat and the faint salt of her sweat. At last, he found the firm, eager satin of her lips, and instead of a culmination of his feast, Galen was rewarded with a kiss that set off a ruthless hunger edged in the hypnotic promise of fulfillment yet to come. His cock was so hard and heavy between his legs, the slightest movement made his breath catch in his throat.

"I like the dark," she whispered.

"Do you now?" He tried his best version of a Scottish brogue. "Well, lass, it does a let a man explore the bonnie heights!"

"What's good for the goose . . ." She nipped at his ear and then shifted away, inspired to do a bit of exploration herself—as only seemed fair in light of the delicious torment she'd just endured. The dark emboldened her, and Haley decided to take advantage of the opportunity. Freed from the embarrassment of him seeing what she was sure was an unladylike lust, she pressed him back on the bed and moved down to the warm length of his sex and knelt between his thighs to satisfy her curiosity. By touch alone, she measured out the jutting prowess of his erection, amazed anew that such a marvelously large member fit her channel so perfectly. She could barely get her fingers around him, he was so thick, and his cock jumped in her hand when she squeezed to make the connection of her fingertips around the base of him.

She leaned forward, slowly planting a tentative kiss on his ripened head.

The dark is very liberating—I think I shall insist on it more often. . . .

She could smell the musk of his skin, and as her lips parted, she could taste the salty-sweet silk of his essence as his cock responded to her attentions. Her hair fell forward, and Haley deliberately allowed her long curls to caress his bare thighs and stomach as she deepened the kiss. Her tongue found the sensitive juncture at the underside of his swollen head, and she licked him there, flicking and pressing against him before circling his entire tip. She could feel his hips tensing, and it only added to her desire. She pulled him deeper into her mouth until she held all of his ripe plum-shaped hood in the hot pocket of her mouth, and the world melted away and became only this act of need—for she truly needed to taste him and please him and command the hunger in her to cease.

His hips strained, and she suspected he was trying not to buck against her mouth—and it thrilled her to think that she could be the one to drive him past his self-control. She released him, but only to use her tongue to locate every vein on his shaft and follow it down his engorged length. She mapped every texture with her mouth, kissing and sucking him until she knew exactly where he was most sensitive, and then added her hands to the game. She pulled her hands up and down his shaft, increasing the pressure slowly up and down the sinew that ran down the underside of his cock, massaging the butter-soft skin that encased the hot, unyielding core of his shaft.

She cupped the odd sac underneath, enjoying its soft fur and vaguely realizing that it too moved in her hands, tightening and contracting as her breath fanned its surface. Haley prodded him with careful fingers and uncovered the pressure points to make him writhe and groan. She leaned over to place her mouth against it, and Galen's entire body stiffened.

"Did I wound you?"

"God, no! Don't stop, Haley!"

She smiled and immediately set out to comply with his wishes. She kissed and suckled him till she was almost dizzy with her own brazen actions, reveling in Galen's every sigh. Then suddenly, he'd disengaged himself and tumbled her over and for a second she was disoriented—and distraught to think she'd done something wrong—before realizing the delightfully wicked workings of his mind.

He was astride her face, and her lips could feel his impatient cock pressing against her, requesting her renewed attentions. But even more forbidden, his head was firmly planted between her thighs, and his tongue wasted no time in finding her clit as his hands spread open the petals of her sex so that there was nothing his mouth couldn't reach.

She almost giggled, but the magic of the dark held sway and she drank in the raw power of her hunger for him, and banished her blushes as she took him back into the eager confines of her mouth and parted her thighs to silently bid him to feast as he wished.

Galen lost himself in the decadent dance of giving and receiving pleasure until he wasn't sure how much more he could take. She'd surpassed his fantasies, and the reality of her mouth and hands on his cock was more potent than any opiate—and just as addictive. The fire pooling behind in his balls was a pressure so sweet it was setting his teeth on edge. And while he couldn't keep himself from savoring the promised bliss, he hesitated to allow himself to release—fearful of shocking her with a flood of crème in her mouth.

He pulled out with a groan and repositioned her with a primal growl in his throat so that she was astride his lap, facing him. Kneeling together, he penetrated the tight, wet confines of her body almost instantly and, only then, remembered to breathe again. They were intertwined so tightly, Galen relished the perfection of the fit between them. His hips pressed his cock up into her quivering channel, battering against the opening of her womb, until the rough curls above his shaft were teasing her clit, and he kissed her breasts as they bounced against him—laving and teasing the tips, using his teeth and tongue to pinch and stimulate her, until she cried for more.

Rocking up into her, Galen felt the fire inside of him roar into an inferno of blue white desire that lingered just out of reach, deliberately lashing him forward in a primeval dance of conquest and surrender.

Closer and closer, he pushed and pressed without hammering, for he couldn't withdraw to strike up into her. This was more of an endless caress. They were locked together so perfectly. Like a mortar and pestle, each movement was minimized but the slightest shift touched everything. It was friction everywhere, and Haley began to almost keen as he slowly meted out his thrusts in time with the beat of her heart.

She threw her head back and he could feel her orgasm all around him as her body released a flow of its own, coating his cock in the rich honey of her climax.

His own release came on the heels of hers, and he held onto her as the fire imploded through him and he was robbed of speech and thought for long moments, even after the last spasm had wrenched the crème from his cock.

They were both quiet as they settled back against the pillows, trying to recover themselves as their hearts finally slowed. Not a word was spoken as she tucked back against his side, and Galen waited while her breathing evened out and she dropped off into a deep sleep.

He held her in the dark and stared up into the void. *This is like some twisted version of Psyche and Cupid.* The nightmare's visions unfurled in his head, and Galen pulled her closer against him. *I don't want you to see what I am, Haley.*

* * *

Galen paced around the small room, stopping only to pick up one or two strange objects from Rowan's collection before setting them back down again. "Do you think objects can be cursed?"

"Why? Do you think we lined our pockets with bad luck, my friend?"

"I don't want to believe anything of the kind. Just the opposite, Rowan. I want to believe that something good truly did come out of all of it in the end. That there is some justice in the world."

"You want to believe? My goodness, Galen, how far have we fallen?"

"Far enough that I think I'm trying to make sense of everything on my own. I just don't trust the Fates to balance it all out."

"Are you sleeping at all, these days?"

Galen smiled, unwilling to admit that most of his current

lack of sleep was due to the distracting and beautiful Haley Moreland. "Some."

"I'll send you home with a packet to steep in some hot water. Try a cup before you retire and see if it provides any relief."

"I thought you'd advised against tonics."

"Most of them have an alcohol base, Galen, and will send you to your grave for a little more rest than you're bargaining for. The packet I'll make for you is natural herbs and a bit of tea. You can add a bit of honey if the flavor doesn't suit," Rowan said in his most professional manner.

"No wonder your patients adore you." Galen abandoned his study of the curios to occupy his favorite chair. "You could coddle a man to death, Dr. West."

"Yes, but he'd never complain," Darius said as he knocked at the doorway, nodding a greeting before entering to join them without formality.

"Trust me, they complain," Rowan countered, stretching out his legs as Darius poured himself a drink and sat down.

"Why do I feel as if all of us are dancing on the edge of a cliff? As if whatever tragedy we escaped on the other side of the world is stalking us even now?"

Rowan sighed and took a small sip of his brandy. "Who can say? I think each of us brought a demon or two with us into the dark, Galen. Nothing is banished or resolved through suffering, and then to find ourselves so . . . unexpectedly fortunate when we stumbled onto that treasure. Some have spent a portion of our shares discreetly while others prefer to wait as we agreed. We've all saved the more spectacular gems for the future, but we wouldn't be human if we didn't worry about the consequences of cheating fate so completely."

"A demon or two . . ." Galen considered it, then looked at his friend with new eyes. "Did you bring a demon with you to India?"

"I did."

Galen waited, but Rowan said nothing more. He looked at

Darius, who simply nodded. Finally, Galen spoke aloud the question that haunted him. "Can a man cheat the Fates?"

"The Greeks didn't think so," Darius noted quietly.

"And what do you think, Dr. West?" Galen asked.

"You don't want to know what I think, Galen."

"I asked, didn't I?"

Rowan finished the rest of his drink in one smooth swallow and set the glass down. "I don't believe in fate. I believe that we can, by choice, manifest the best or the worst for ourselves—and those demons, Galen, they feed off of the worst parts of our soul and grow only when we allow them to. If I . . ." His words faltered for a moment, his eyes taking on a faraway look from some unspoken memory. "If I dwell on the mistakes I've made, or the disappointments . . ." Rowan caught himself in the dark reverie and instantly smiled. "Then what a glum friend I would make!"

"And your philosophy, Thorne?" Galen asked.

"I think the Greeks had it right enough, but perhaps not the way you're looking at it." Darius set his drink down. "It was more like destiny. I like to think of it as the path best suited to our purpose—and not some punishment we can't avoid like an errant child. After all, maybe the worst scrapes are when we're not fulfilling our divine potential, and the Fates are there to push us back onto the path."

Galen shook his head. "I like my friends, no matter their moods and philosophies, and I'm grateful they tolerate mine." He pushed up from the smooth soft leather chair, restlessly returning to one of the shelves to look at a small statuette of the Egyptian god Horus. "But I worry now that I've given too much to that worst part of me—that demon in the dark. And if there's a path, I think I'm so far off into the woods that it's becoming more and more difficult to recognize the man I once thought I would become." He turned back, attempting a bit of black humor. "Do villains even have friends?"

"You aren't a villain, Galen," Darius stated immediately.

Rowan was equally quick to protest. "The fact that you would even worry about such a thing disqualifies you."

Rowan also stood to cross to Galen. "Similar I think to men who wonder if they're insane. No one who stands drooling in corners ever seems to question it or worry what their friends will say."

Galen closed his eyes for a moment, then smiled. "You have a talent for imagery that never fails."

"Hawke"—Rowan's tone grew more serious—"you've told us almost nothing of what is troubling you, and out of respect, I've not pressed you for any details. But if it's atonement you're seeking, then I'm afraid it's in your own hands."

"Atonement." Galen tasted the word, savoring the bitter-sweet feel of it on his tongue.

"It's your demon to do with what you will, Galen." Rowan crossed his arms and sat on the edge of his desk. "And I'm sure I'm not the first man to advise a friend to just set the damn thing down and give yourself permission to be happy—and to sleep."

"You make it sound so simple, Dr. West."

"You're not cursed, Hawke. You're just stubborn," Darius added sagely before a smile undermined his serious pronouncement.

"Like hell!" Galen muttered the oath before he thought better of it, and then they all laughed at the inescapable truth of it.

* * *

On the short ride back to his home, Galen leaned his head back against the seat and closed his eyes. *My demon . . . so I need my permission . . . is it that simple, really?*

Galen sat up suddenly, the epiphany happening in a quick rush that almost made him cough. *Why can't it be that simple? I want her, I need her . . . I love her. Oh, God, I'm in love with Haley Moreland.*

And there's . . . nothing standing in my way.

Galen's brow furrowed as he measured out the truth of that last thought. From Haley's perspective, the matter was entirely settled in his favor. As lecherous and impossible as he'd been, she'd given herself into his hands and . . . she was quietly and rightfully expecting his proposal any day now.

There's nothing standing in my way!

Except, a part of him chimed in darkly, for the lies, deception, and the matter of a certain vow he'd made. But Galen shook his head and ignored the voice. *It won't matter if I make her happy.*

And by God, I'm going to spend the rest of my life making Haley Moreland very, very happy.

Chapter
18

On impulse, Galen ordered the carriage to let them out at the corner near his home. She'd been so tender with him the previous night when he'd battled his demons, he couldn't wait to throw off the restrictions of a clandestine affair—and all the lies he'd told. He'd been feeling more and more like a thief, and it wasn't a sensation he'd enjoyed. But now he'd accepted that every minute with Haley had an appeal he didn't have to relinquish.

Haley gave him a questioning look. "Has there been a change in plans?"

"I suddenly thought that I would like to walk in the moonlight for a few minutes before going inside." He traced the outline of her thighs and knees through the layers of her skirts. "There's hardly anyone about at this hour, but we can pretend it's a noontime stroll and that we've nothing to hide."

"I'm looking forward to walking out with you, Galen."

He smiled, enjoying the lighthearted impulse and glad he hadn't worried too much about how foolish it might make him look to request so simple a thing. "Then let's walk for practice and see how it will feel."

He climbed out first and then held her hand as she descended to the ground beside him. The moon was full, and the normal haze of the city had lifted to give the air a pleasant aspect. Shadows through the treelined lane added to the atmosphere, and Haley played along with his proposed fantasy, taking his arm as if they were indeed just out for a turn.

"Why, thank you, Mr. Hawke! What a gentleman you are!"

"Ah! Wouldn't my father be pleased to hear you say such a thing!" Galen spoke easily, then realized he'd volunteered a topic that would generally have been forbidden. He had an apprehensive truce with his father, ever since the Earl of Stamford had learned that the youngest son he'd accused of being a wastrel had quietly been assisting his older brother, Trevor, with his businesses and investments. It had been Trevor's idea to send him to India—and Galen had gone knowing that he was, in the grander scheme of things, the more expendable of the two. In his extended absence, his father had learned the truth of Trevor's dependence on his brother and the reason behind Trevor's "generosity" to his younger sibling; and so it had been his father who had met him on the dock when Galen made it back to England.

"Does your father not realize what a man of quality you are?" she asked, innocently mystified.

"Mine seems to have set his opinion on quite a few things several years ago, and he hasn't considered the passage of time," Galen said. "A common occurrence, I think. Some parents may see you when you're at some awkward stage and then they never look again—most likely out of a fear of being further disappointed."

"And your mother?"

"Long gone." Galen squeezed her hand. "She died at the same time my younger brother caught ill and—"

"Hawke!"

Galen wheeled around instinctively, drawing Haley behind him to protect her, and in a single instant, recognized the very real threat of the man lunging at them from behind one of the elms, the dim gleam off of the wicked curve of a wide blade held in his fist.

The man hissed through his teeth, muttering something in Hindi as he closed the gap between them, and Galen recognized the word for *thief* and *bastard* before his world narrowed to the man's eyes glittering with loathing in the pale light and the movement of his shoulders and hands. He didn't focus on the knife, knowing full well that by the time he registered its movement, it would be too late to step out of its path. So instead, he absorbed the full figure's intentions, and each telling shift of his weight, praying his instincts were right.

This was a punching blade, but Galen didn't have time to be grateful that it hadn't been designed for throwing. It would be almost impossible to escape injury, as the blade could catch him on a strike or a withdrawal, and deflecting it without a shield or weapon of his own . . .

His internal debate was on how to draw the assassin in close enough to disarm him without finding that razor-sharp edge buried in his rib cage. He was going to need a miracle.

Haley screamed for Bradley behind them, as she ran toward the house, and his assailant's eyes darted away for a single second at the unexpected noise and movement. It wasn't much, but Galen decided it was the only miracle he was going to get. He darted forward, at the same time pulling his evening coat over his left forearm to try to pad it for defense and using his right elbow to the man's jaw to stun him. The blow managed to graze the man's jaw, and Galen tried to grab his wrist.

The attacker was wiry and strong, so instead of attempting to stop the knife, Galen stepped sideways, like a matador, and redirected the blade past his vulnerable midsection, then twisted around to drive them both to the ground.

It was a brief wrestling match, as Galen felt the knife drive home off bone and into flesh. For a moment, there was no sound but the wind through the elms, and Galen stared into his would-be assassin's face and watched him slowly register pain.

"Welcome to London," Galen muttered in disgust, loosening his grip to climb off the man—only to watch in shock as the injured assassin scrambled away to his feet like a crab and ran off down the darkened street. The urge to chase him never fully materialized, and Galen stood slowly, brushing off his pants and coat, before remembering Haley.

Galen looked back to find her on his doorstep, her hand upraised as if to pound on the door, but she was frozen, her eyes wide looking back at him—no doubt having watched the exciting conclusion to Galen's close encounter with death. "Well, that wasn't the romantic moonlight stroll I had in mind!"

"G-Galen!" She came back down the steps and rushed into his arms. He could feel her damp, hot tears through his waistcoat as she laid her head on his shoulder.

"Muggers . . ." He sighed, deliberately keeping his tone light. "Though it wouldn't be London without them."

"H-he could have killed you!"

"No," he lied easily. "Did you see how clumsy and fat he was? Why, I don't think he could have scratched a tree trunk without injuring himself! No doubt he's in a bar right now, deciding it would be safer to pick the pockets of a juniper bush next time."

"Th-that makes no sense, Galen." She hiccupped, her eyes losing a little of their shocked, disconnected look.

"Really?" he asked, in a pretense of astonishment. "I thought I was being perfectly reasonable."

"What was that language he spoke?"

Galen shrugged, unready to tell her too much. "Welsh, I think."

She started to smile, but then the light from a streetlight shone onto him as they turned back toward the steps and her eyes widened in panic. "Galen, there's blood! You're injured!"

Galen glanced down and realized his shirtfront had taken the worst of it. "No! I'm fine!" He deliberately closed his coat and then kept his tone calm and level, pulling her closer. "It's not my blood, Haley. I think he must have cut his hand in the struggle and was rude enough to ruin my favorite shirt."

"You're sure? You're not injured?"

"Let me see," he said, then leaned over to kiss her, a distracting maneuver for them both. By instinct, he glided his lips over hers, the softest caress he could manage, evoking every tender thread in his psyche, wanting nothing more than to reassure her and reaffirm that he was truly alive. This was a gentle dance, and he kissed her slowly and patiently until at last, she sighed and melded against him. He lifted his head, wishing all his problems could be so delightfully resolved. "No, not a single scratch."

"He knew your name, Galen. This was no random act! We should contact the authorities!"

"He could have overheard it from the coachman when he let us out at the corner, or even from you when we spoke. Not one of my best ideas, but somehow a short walk in the trees in the moonlight didn't seem like a death-defying proposition earlier. And as for what we should do now, let's get into the house and see if we can't get cleaned up before getting you home safely."

He guided her inside, but as they crossed the threshold, she seemed to weaken, tearful hiccups overcoming her, and Galen scooped her up and cradled her against his chest. "There, there now . . . you're safe, and all is well, for I have you now."

Bradley stepped forward, openly concerned. "Sir! Is everything all right? I thought I heard—"

"Yes. Just see to it there's hot water in the pipes upstairs. Miss Moreland will be taking a bath, and we're not to be disturbed." Galen began to carry her upstairs, instantly more focused on Haley than Bradley's mad scramble to race on the ground floor to relight the water furnace. She was so astute, but he wasn't going to share his fears that she was right about the attack being planned.

Hell, the knife he was using gave the game away long before that little burst of Hindi!

He knew he would have to let Michael know, but there

would be time to send word later. For now, he was far more interested in Haley's well-being.

He reached his master bath and closed the door firmly behind them with the back of his heel, determined to shut out the jarring chaos a would-be assassin had introduced into his life. Kneeling, he lowered her onto a soft chair in the corner, reassessing her condition.

Galen was relieved to see that she looked more embarrassed than anything else, the spark of wit in her eyes returning in force. "I'm . . . fine! It's not as if I . . . was going to faint."

"Of course! You never faint, remember?"

"The theatre doesn't count." A last trailing hiccup undermined her show of strength. "There was a rat!"

"Oh!" He tried to keep a straight face, looking at her as if this new information about a rodent changed his entire perception of his place in the universe.

She hit him playfully on the arm before her eyes unexpectedly filled with tears. "I don't know what I would have done . . . if anything had happened to you . . ."

"But nothing has!" He took out his handkerchief and wiped away her tears as best he could, staggered by his own reaction to her genuine fear for him. He reached up to hold her face in his hands, cradling her as tenderly as he could to reassure her, looking into her eyes still shining with unshed tears. "Nor will it so long as I have you."

Galen knew that he would rather have taken a bullet than have seen her harmed in any way. Michael had been warning them about nebulous threats for so long that Galen hadn't really paid attention recently. Instead, he'd been caught in the web of his own making—unable to confess to Miss Moreland, unable to retreat and leave her exposed, and most of all, wondering whether even if he'd decided to let the ghosts of the past go, they were willing to leave.

He left her in the chair for just a moment and went over to turn on the hot water and see about filling up the tub. He knew Bradley hadn't had time to make too much progress, but at this point, anything above freezing would do. He just wanted to go through the ritual, and in his experience, nothing soothed like a simple bath.

His fingertips confirmed that it was warm, but only a few degrees above tepid, so he wasn't complaining. He poured in a little oil, then set the bottle aside along with towels and his bathing tray so that everything would be within reach.

"There! We're almost ready for you," he said, kneeling at her feet to begin untying her shoes.

"Are you playing valet now?"

He smiled, gently taking off her slippers. "I suppose I have to. You weren't impressed with my skills as a ladies' maid."

"You kept trying to take my clothes off when I needed them back on, Galen." Haley's voice sounded stronger and more like her usual self, and Galen silently offered up a grateful prayer.

His hands slid up to untie her stockings, pulling the ribbons. "And here I am again . . ."

"I don't wish to bathe alone."

He relaxed his shoulders and pulled off his evening coat, dropping it casually over another chair in the corner. "I don't wish you to, either."

He helped her to her feet and began unbuttoning the jet buttons of her mantle. "Ah, the mysteries of women's fashion . . ." He pulled it from her shoulders, treating it more carefully than he had his jacket, aware that even passion might not forgive a ruined ladies' ensemble. He gently turned her around to address the lacings down the back of her green evening dress. "You wore this dress to that music concert, and I remember thinking that you looked like a jewel in it."

"Is that what you were thinking?" she teased, and he knew she was remembering how he'd deliberately made love to her with his gaze that night.

He smiled, caught in the lie. "Well, that's not *entirely* the bulk of my thoughts that evening, but I'm sure at some point I likened you to a jewel." He finished loosening the dress and pushed it forward off of her shoulders. "Why do women wear so many layers?"

"Men wear almost as many, although you have the advantage of foregoing petticoats," she noted dryly.

"Thank God." He lowered his lips to her bare shoulder as he pulled her arms from the half sleeves of her gown. "Besides, it all looks far better on you."

His tongue darted out to make a light trail of moisture, deliberately letting his breath set off a shiver down her spine as her skin pebbled. She turned to face him and smiled up at him as her fingers loosened his cravat and began to tug at the buttons of his shirt until his chest was bared for her.

She kissed his chest, lingering over his heartbeat, and then dropped down to lightly suck the brown points of his chest, nipping at the hard, warm planes and making him gasp at the innocent audacity of her explorations.

He wanted to touch all of her, smoothing and soothing the outlines of her frame, slowly trailing his fingertips down her arms and then back up to tease her through the barrier of her underclothes.

She caught one of his hands in hers and turned his palm upward to trace the lines in his hands. "Teach me."

"Teach you what?"

"To read your hands, as you read mine. I want to see if *you* have known a great love."

"But the trick doesn't work. Remember? It failed to show your great love, didn't it?"

She turned to him. "Have you known love before me, Galen?"

"I don't want to talk about the past anymore, Haley. Not tonight."

He turned his attention to the silk and lace confections of her underclothes, biting the inside of his cheek in concentration as he carefully untied her stays. Her figure certainly didn't require a corset, but he was wiser than to voice his opinion. No lady of quality would ever abandon the contraption, and he was just grateful that Haley's practical nature had kept her from contorting her natural beauty. Without rushing, Galen removed each layer in turn, enjoying the process that would bare her for him and setting aside her camisole, petticoats, silk chemise, and finally, her stockings.

Galen stepped back to admire the results of his efforts. She was as naked as a nymph, and as beautifully shameless. Her mahogany hair cascaded down her back, and her skin pinked under his study, but she made no move to cover herself.

"You're wearing too many clothes for a bath, Galen."

She stepped closer, and their roles reversed as she slowly and gently finished undressing him. Neither one of them hurried, but it was only moments before they were stripped of every ornament of civilization and facing each other as they'd been born.

Galen bent over to kiss the curves of her breasts, lingering and enjoying the weight of them in his hands, sucking the sensitive sides and the crease underneath, tweaking those pert little nipples. He began to kiss each bared inch, and knelt before her to place her right foot on his shoulder, opening her sex to his full view. The pink lips glistened in the lamplight, and he could already see the jutting pink pearl of her clit above its small cap of red flesh. With every breath he inhaled her musk, and with every exhale he watched her swell and ripen in anticipation of his touch.

He leaned forward to taste her, his hands holding her hips to help her keep her balance. And Galen quickly lost track of time as he made a languid journey to sample her sex, tormenting her silk pearl with his tongue until she was struggling to stay upright.

Her thighs were shaking, and her hands fisted into the curls of his head. "Galen, please . . . I don't want to rush . . ."

"No, dearest." He kissed the inside of her thigh, nipping at the quivering tendon that betrayed the tension there. He stood slowly, sharing her need to take their time and make the night's pleasure last for as long as it could. He stepped over the side of the tub, and then held onto her to help her safely into the water, so that they were facing each other with the water reaching their knees. "One day you must teach me a better trick, Haley. You must teach me how to put the past out of my mind, as you do. You must teach me to forget. . . ."

"I forget nothing."

Galen surrendered to the lie, because it was too sweet, and he needed to believe her.

Chapter
19

"I want to see you this time. I want to taste you again, Galen."

She loved his body, so vastly different from her own, yet the same. His cock was a thing of beauty, and just looking at it increased the tension in the heated coil between her hip bones. As she reached for him, it pulsed and jumped against her palm, and she marveled at its power, watching its color deepen with his arousal. It was a part of his body, but it seemed to have a life of its own as it flexed and stiffened at her touch.

I don't need the darkness to hide from him. I want to see him, and I want him to see how much I adore him.

Fingers traced its lines, following the map of veins and sinew, then gripping him intermittently, enjoying his sighs and grunts, aware of the effects of her hands, but newly discovering how far she might take this game.

She kissed the swollen tip, rewarded with the salty-sweet taste of him on her lips, licking it off of him and then pulling him into the warm harbor of her mouth, tasting, savoring, while her fingers began to stroke his shaft. Her other hand slid up his bare thigh and then reached up to cup his sac, working the flesh there and the weight of his testicles until she could feel them drawing up and tightening in ecstasy.

She tried to use the same tricks he'd used on her, his mouth to her most sensitive flesh, finding the junctures of his anatomy that yielded the best responses, his hips moving involuntarily, his hands gently reaching down to hold her hair, and Haley knew he was deliberately not pressing her—allowing her to find her own way and add to his own enjoyment.

"Haley, hold . . . I'm going to—"

But this time, she wasn't going to let him stop her. This time, Haley wanted to experience all of him. She wanted to drink his very essence and savor her lover's crème. Like a starving child, she wasn't going to be denied this sweetest of sweets, and Haley simply clung to him, moving ever faster, until she knew he couldn't deny her what she desired.

He came in luxurious hot jets, and she drank from him, relishing the delightful heat of his body, draining him completely until she was sure she could taste his rapture.

He knelt in the bathtub, pulling her down with him into the water, so that she was lying atop him, his breathing heavy and hard.

"That was wonderful," she sighed.

"I'm sure I was about to say the same thing," he noted with a wicked smile of satisfaction. He kissed her, lightly at first, but then it was a soft whirlwind as new tendrils of hunger spawned and strengthened inside them both. Her hand slid down under the surface of the cool water and encircled his cock, and Galen was amazed at how quickly his body responded, the familiar heat invoked without effort, as his already sensitive penis began to stiffen and swell once again.

The water gave him an advantage, allowing him to shift her underneath him with her head on a cloth on the edge, buoyantly floating her hips up to meet his. Her legs parted, and Galen lifted her calves up onto the sides of the tub for leverage and positioned himself until he could reach down and tease her with the head of his cock. The bath augmented every moment but also slowed them down with gentle resistance, and Galen watched her face as her sex grew slicker and slicker at his ministrations. She tried to buck her hips upward to catch him, but he wouldn't allow it.

He pressed forward only as far as her entrance, watching her taut lips grip him, each small thrust making her shudder with need, and she arched her back and Galen buried himself inside of her, ramming his cock home only to grip her hips and hold her there while he allowed his mind to catch up to his body. The coolness of the water made her core seem molten, and Galen closed his eyes at the magic of it.

"God, you're so hot inside . . . a man wants to die in this kind of fire, woman."

Her muscles clenched him, and he felt her excitement recoat his cock in a silent invitation to take all that she offered—and more.

"Haley, I must have all of you."

"Yes."

She was on the brink of release but felt no frenzied race to finish what he'd started. Every nerve ending was singing, and Haley felt a languid bliss like no other. He stood in the water, carefully bracing his feet against the sides of the tub, and held out his hand to help her to hers. Like a mermaid rising from the seas, she moved proudly out of the water, relishing the way his eyes roamed over her skin and lingered on her breasts and mons. His open appreciation of her charms sent a new wave of shimmering heat down across her skin to pool between her hips.

She anticipated his desires, and when he turned her and placed her hands on the smooth lip of the tub, she sighed in anticipation as she bent over and spread her legs for balance. *It will be like the carriage—only better . . .*

At the unexpected sensation of warm oil pouring into the crease of her bottom, Haley gasped. But when his fingers slid across her bottom, circling each ripe curve and then sliding against the folds, she gave into the hypnotic feel of his large hands working her flesh and finding every responsive part of her.

Haley closed her eyes as more oil followed, and his thumb circled the tiny pucker there, pressing it and allowing her to adjust to his touch on this most intimate of portals. His touch was relentless but gentle, and she groaned at the surprising thrill it was giving her.

His right hand slipped around her hip and then down over her velvet soft curls to reach her clit, and Haley opened her legs even wider to seek more of his touch. The oil had coated her, but he dipped his fingers inside of her core to ensure that she was fully aroused. Then his fingers gently squeezed the skin over her clit, sending an electrical arc of fire and desire across her skin, and Haley tilted her hips to try to give him the access he needed.

Galen's fingertips began to flicker against the tight bud of her clit, the friction made delicious by the slippery oil and her own juices—all the while, he'd never neglected her bottom, and Haley began to want more of him there, too. She groaned as the coil inside of her began to slowly tighten, and Haley marveled at his powers to command her body to respond to his.

Then the pressure changed, and Haley realized that the swollen head of his cock had taken his thumb's place, and she started to stiffen in surprise. "Galen, I—"

"Haley," he whispered, his voice low and soothing, "I . . . must have all of you."

"Yes." She dropped her head in a sigh, giving in to all of it, aware only that she trusted him completely.

His fingers moved faster over her clit, each time barely brushing over the tip only to jostle the nerves beneath until she was sure she would climax. And when the large ripe head of his cock breached her, the cascade began. But this time, it was a tangled spiral of pain and pleasure blending until she thought she'd faint as she climaxed against his fingers as his cock pressed deeper and deeper inside of her.

It was like the first time, as her body adjusted to the invasion, accepting the heat of him and slowly stretching to accommodate him. The oil made him slick and he began to ease forward and backward, demonstrating once again how this simple movement could provide her endless fulfillment.

Her climax echoed on as he drove into her with languid, careful strokes timed with the spasms of pleasure that edged into pain. He teased her clit and then penetrated her with two fingers, matching the rhythm of his cock, and Haley cried out as her release suddenly increased its speed, racing past her control, growing stronger and stronger instead of ebbing as she'd expected.

At her cry, he held onto her hips with both hands, as his cock seemed to demand that he work the tighter passage in earnest. Galen groaned behind her, and Haley could only clutch the porcelain surface of the bath as the sweet wash of his crème splashed up inside of her, adding another dimension of fire to the moment. She was so tight and full of him in such an impossible way that she wondered who could ever have imagined such bliss in the first place. She knew the taboos, but he'd shattered her reserve and she felt like a woman adrift. *How can something so odd be such a slice of paradise?*

"Did I hurt you?" he asked quietly, withdrawing very slowly but with more ease as his cock's girth had naturally lessened.

"Yes—No!" she answered quickly, hearing the surprise in her own voice. "I mean . . . I . . . liked it."

He bent over her and placed a kiss reverently on each cheek before helping her to straighten. He used a bathing pitcher to pour water over both of them, and Haley laughed as the cool water sluiced across her skin. Within seconds, the evidence of their lovemaking was washed away, and Galen poured an extra pitcher over his own head. "You make a man dizzy, just looking at you, Haley." He pressed the excess water from his curls. "Especially like that."

"Like this?" Haley glanced down, unsure if disheveled and wet could garner any man's truthful praise or if he was teasing.

"Wet and wanton, shameless and beautiful"—he stepped closer to her—"I could look at you forever."

He pulled her against his chest and held her in a simple embrace, so caring and complete. She closed her eyes at the thrill of his body to hers in quiet communion. But at last, he released her to begin their exodus from the bathtub.

He climbed out first, wrapping a towel around his waist, then helped her out to sit on the edge of the tub. Without preamble, Galen gently began to dry her with the towels he'd set aside, and she started to blush at the domestic act—so tender and unexpected.

He lightly pulled the dry cloth around her back and down her arms and legs, across her breasts, lingering wherever his touch elicited a quickened breath or a sigh, and Haley closed her eyes as he parted her thighs and the warm cloth dipped even there, and she shuddered as his hand lingered long enough to reawaken the tension between her hips. Haley reached down to still his wrist, her eyelashes fluttering open as she realized what was happening. "Galen . . . you should stop . . . I'm . . . I don't think I can . . . again . . ."

He shook his head. "Come again for me, Haley."

He knelt before her, then put her hands over his to ensure that she was indeed still in command. "Let me give you pleasure."

Galen used a damp cloth and continued to follow the shape of her open sex in the lightest stroke, while his index finger offered a teasing whisper of pleasure alongside the hidden core of her, never pressing her directly, but tormenting her with a phantom hand across her clit.

It was a long, slow release, almost elegant in its structure, so fragile and perfect she wept. Galen pulled her down into his arms and kissed her, as gently as if she were made of glass, a fragile, fey creature he'd somehow captured and now hoped to keep.

It was a sweet kiss, and her lips parted under his at the first touch of his satin soft skin to hers. His tongue barely touched hers, and even this careful contact heightened her craving to submit to him again and again. But this time the yearning was familiar and comforting, and Haley clung to him and the knowledge that she alone possessed his heart.

He wrapped her up in long Turkish towels and carried her back to the bedroom where his large bed awaited them.

"Galen?"

"Yes," he said, kissing her forehead as they settled against the pillows.

"Before . . . when you spoke of the trick with the lines on my hand . . . you said it hadn't worked." She propped herself up on one elbow to look into his smoldering emerald eyes. "But it did. I had never known what it was to love before I met you."

His expression was unreadable. "How is that possible? That I am the first . . . There must have been—there *was* someone else. You're too beautiful not to have known love before now, Haley."

"I know my own heart, Galen." She laughed, playfully kissing the stubborn line of his jaw. Haley wondered briefly if it were possible for him to harbor any jealousy at all toward poor Mr. Trumble, but dismissed the idea as quickly as it came. "Why is this so difficult to believe?"

"I think you're telling me that I'm the first to win your heart, because you suspect it will mean more . . . but you needn't. If you admitted that you had loved someone else—"

"I haven't!" She kissed his cheek again, then gently nipped his ear with her teeth. "My poor Galen. I can only guess that someone has hurt you to make you so wary even now. . . ."

He didn't answer, instead reaching up his hand to gently draw his fingers over her cheek and down her throat, as if studying her features to memorize her in this moment. Haley took courage in the tender caress, amazed at his solemn approach to the topic, and spoke before her practical mind could rein in her tongue. "I love you, Galen."

He kissed her, so tenderly and so thoroughly that she could feel her eyes overflowing with tears of joy, her emotions too close to the surface to hide from him. He drew her close, into the crook of his arm, to nest alongside him again, and Haley knew that all the happiness she had once disavowed had come to her a thousandfold with Galen's love.

His breath evened out, and she sensed him sleeping soundly at last. She lingered in the warm pocket their bodies had created in the large, soft feather mattress, marveling that such simple comfort existed. To lie in his arms and know such peace, it had been beyond her imagination only weeks earlier.

He'd saved her life. Only hours ago, he'd stepped in front of a knife-wielding monster, as calmly as a man stepping forward to claim a carriage. It didn't seem possible. More frightening than the strange-looking knife was Galen's cavalier attitude toward his own safety—as if he valued himself as nothing.

I love you, Galen. You are everything to me.

A large clock somewhere in the house softly chimed the hour, and Haley realized with a start that it was three o'clock in the morning. She'd never intended to stay so late. Newly aware that the cook often arose around four, Haley knew that even with her key, she didn't want to press her luck.

Still, it was hard to go. She carefully eased away from him, determined not to disturb his slumber. The moon was bright enough through the open curtains to illuminate the room in a cool wash of magical gray and ivory shadows. She slid her feet over the side of the bed and began to retrace her steps to the dressing room and adjoining bath to retrieve her clothes.

Behind the door, it was easy enough to reconstruct her clothes and put back on all the layers that Galen had so skillfully removed. Haley congratulated herself on wisely beginning to choose dresses that she could manage on her own without the aid of a second pair of hands. She stepped into her shoes and then rolled her still damp hair up into a simple chignon.

Walking back into the bedroom, she watched him sleep for a few moments, admiring his masculine beauty as he lay across the bed with the moonlight touching his back and showing off his physique.

She glanced at a small writing desk against the windows and decided to pen a small love note to excuse her lack of a farewell and reassure him that she would seek him again as soon as she could manage it.

She slid open the wide drawer underneath the leather pressed table and pulled out a sheath of paper, but as she lifted it to look for a blank sheet she could use, her heart began to pound out of control.

It was a caricature, like one saw in the *Times*, well drawn but deliberately crude and bawdy to catch the eye—and its subject was unmistakable. Like a nightmare, her initials appeared underneath the rendering of a dark-haired woman tossing up her skirts as she was climbing from one sorrel pony's saddle to another sturdier-looking mount, even as another stallion pawed the ground in the background. The captions were horrifying—identifying each horse as another man she'd chosen "to ride to the bank," and a man on the ground looking up the woman's skirts no doubt in the guise of helping her to keep her balance proclaimed she was the "finest rider in all of England—or I've never seen a fortune-hunting gel!"

Fortune-hunting whore.

It was graphic and base, and—Haley stopped breathing for an instant as she saw that a note of submission to the *Times* was attached to it with Galen's signature.

She dropped the papers to the floor, stunned by a pain so intense her knees buckled. Haley gripped the desk to maintain her balance and closed her eyes to try to shut out the image of the bright-cheeked whore laughing up at her from the floor.

A wave of nausea nearly overtook her, but it held no power against the icy wall of agony that had moved into her chest.

I told him I loved him. I . . . oh, God . . . what have I not willingly and blindly done for this man? And he . . .

Her mind couldn't fathom it. It was a betrayal so hateful and shocking that she wasn't sure what to think or do. The ice began to numb her and Haley was grateful for it. She looked back where he was lying, still so breathtakingly handsome, and wondered why she wasn't weeping.

Later. I'll have all the time I need to cry, won't I?

Haley moved toward the bed, almost touching his hand, but she pulled her fingers back at the last instant. She stood absolutely still and waited for the strength she needed to leave him—and then she turned and walked out.

* * *

Galen sighed as the last blissful layer of sleep began to drift away, and he stretched out against the pillows trying to will himself back into the glorious dreamless rest he'd been having. But even that brought him closer to a state of consciousness as the realization of what had just happened slowly sank in.

I slept. Merciful gods, I slept! And not that restless soul-wearying, nightmare-filled semblance of sleep! His eyes flew open. *This was real! No dark dreams! No green tea with Bradley at four o'clock in the morning!*

He sat up quickly, multiple questions hitting him at once. It was Haley who had done it, and he was seized with the need to tell her. Bright light streamed through the windows and he wondered how late he'd slept—and more importantly, where was Haley?

"Haley!" He called for her, grabbing his wrap to head for the dressing room and see if she was there. "Haley?"

There was no sign of her in either the dressing room or the bath, and he hurried over to the bellpull to summon Bradley, yanking it with a humorous vigor that was sure to send the poor man running. Galen smiled at the image, elated beyond words at his newfound sleep, but determined to share his joy with Haley as soon as possible.

Enough of this! I love the woman and I'm going to find her and tell her—and when Michael tries to give me that knowing look, I'll ignore the hell out of him! I should have told her last night when—

Galen spotted the papers on the floor by his desk, and the

world ground to a horrific stop. On wooden legs, he made his way over to the familiar pages and then had to remind himself to breathe.

The damning caricature lay on the carpet, and Galen knew it was over.

She was gone.

Chapter
20

Before noon, the front bell at Galen's brownstone was ringing ferociously. Bradley sheepishly led Mrs. Shaw inside to the ground floor drawing room but hadn't needed to inform Galen because he'd run down the stairs taking them two at a time in the wild, irrational hope that Haley had returned.

"Mrs. Shaw." Disappointment tainted his words, but Galen knew that the time had passed for prevarication. Her appearance was a harbinger of the worst kind, and he tried to brace himself for the inevitable. "I can only imagine what you must think of me."

"Oh, you'll have no need for suppositions, young man," she replied tartly. "I have every intention of telling you exactly what I think of you!"

"If you'd just give me a chance to explain, I'm sure—"

She held up a gloved hand, cutting him off as crisply as a general dismissing a raw recruit. "Explanations are always plentiful after a man has been caught in some wretched business or another! It's a marvel to me that your sex doesn't think about explaining themselves *before* your schemes are uncovered and you look like the worst and vilest creatures on the earth. Why is it that eloquence only comes when it's too late?"

He shook his head. "I couldn't say." Galen winced at the inadvertent irony and almost groaned at the agony of knowing that he'd just made it so much worse than he'd ever thought possible by appearing glib.

Mrs. Shaw's eyes narrowed dangerously. "You think I'm some elderly dupe? Did you think I was just blindly giggling at my lovely luck to be a small cog in the romantic machinations of your masculine plans?"

Galen could only shake his head, not trusting himself to answer without adding more fuel to the fire in her eyes.

"I'm not new to the game, Mr. Hawke. But I liked you, and I allowed you to insert yourself into my niece's life because you seemed so . . ." She sighed in frustration before going on. "I had hoped that Haley would find the love she deserved and make a better life for herself. Frankly, I'd have done the same if you were a penniless tinker, but only because I thought I was dealing with an honorable man."

"I never—"

"I have no interest in hearing your denials!" Her chin lifted an inch, and she marched up until he was forced to look down directly into her eyes. "What I am interested in, Mr. Hawke, is obtaining possession of every libel-covered page from that desk of yours!"

He nodded dutifully, a sick twist in his gut at the thought of Haley seeing them again. "Of course. If it's any consolation, I wasn't going to . . . no one has ever seen them, Mrs. Shaw. It was a misguided plan that my heart overruled weeks ago, and I never—"

"The papers, Mr. Hawke." She poked him in the chest with one bony finger and then held out her hand. "I'll take them now."

He left her to retrieve them, overriding the instinct to hold the envelope like a snake in front of him. *I should have destroyed them when Michael came upon me that first night!*

And then later . . . but I was too stupid to even remember they were still in my desk!

He held it out to her. "Here, this is everything."

She took the envelope from him and then glanced at the contents to assure herself that this was no trick. "Burn it. I want to watch you burn it," she commanded.

Galen felt like a coward. It was easy enough to find matches and comply with her wishes. He threw the burning packet onto the fireplace grate and watched as the only evidence of his villainy disappeared into black leaves and embers.

Would that the deeds could be erased so easily . . .

"Are there any other copies? Is there anything else that she didn't accidentally uncover?" Mrs. Shaw asked behind him.

"No, that was everything."

"Good. Then I will bid you farewell, Mr. Hawke."

"Mrs. Shaw, wait, I beg you."

"Beg?" She halted her steps, giving him a look of astonishment. "Well, you don't know the game at all, do you?"

"It's no game, Mrs. Shaw."

"Of course it is! Allow me to refresh you on your next few moves! You pretend to be angry at this misfortune of being misunderstood! You insist on your innocence! You even go so far as to make foolish threats to prevent us from saying anything about this matter in public, although you know full well we can't without endangering poor Haley's status! You huff and puff, and then you pick up your manly pride and decide what lovely girl will next have the honor of falling for your obvious charms and finding herself completely destroyed as an unhappy result. That, Mr. Hawke, is the game. And if you're going to choose the black pieces on the board, then you'd better learn the rules!"

She sailed out of the room and then past a horrified Bradley, who barely managed to get the door open in time for her stormy departure.

* * *

She returned to find Haley, still prostrate with tears across her bed.

"How could anyone be so hateful? So horrible to . . ." She lifted her head to look at her aunt in miserable supplication. "He deliberately set out to ruin me! He never had any intentions of . . . and I was so blind and stupid, I never saw the danger!"

Haley put her head back down, closing her eyes. "No, that's not true," she corrected herself in a broken little whisper. "I saw the danger. I just convinced myself that somehow it didn't matter. That he . . . wouldn't let me be hurt."

"Did he promise to marry you, dearest?"

Haley sat up quickly, like a wounded tigress, lashing out at anyone foolish enough to draw near. "I want you to know that I blame you in some small part for this!"

"Me?" Alice sat down, astonished. "What did I have to do with it?"

"You! With your bells and your adventures, telling me to use both hands to reach for my happiness!" Haley lifted up from the bed, her face red from crying.

Alice shook her head slowly. "I thought . . . they say it is better to lose your heart than to not know your own heart, and I . . . I only wanted your happiness."

"Well, I should have remembered that if you use both hands to reach for what you want, then everything else is dropped, isn't it?"

"I only wanted the best for you! You're too young to—"

"And when am I too old, Aunt? When do I put the bells away in time to realize that there are no more adventures and that I have no husband and no future? When did you realize it? When did you realize that you'd held onto the wrong things with both hands and ended up with nothing and no one?"

Alice gasped, the words finding their mark. "I . . ."

Haley's malice crumbled into regret in a single breath and she threw herself against her dearest aunt, embracing her tightly. "Forgive me! Forgive me for being so monstrous!" Hot tears stained her aunt's shoulder as she sobbed. "I'm so . . . wrong at every turn that I don't know what to do or say! Please . . ."

Soft hands reached up to smooth her hair, and Haley was sure she would die with relief. "There now, my dearest girl. There's nothing to forgive! I'm a fool, and the world's worst chaperone, but—" She stepped back to lift Haley's chin and meet her eyes. "I *am* still your greatest ally, and no one can ever convince me that I do not love you the best."

"I'm ruined." Haley tasted her own heartache as she spoke the wretched words aloud.

"You are *not* ruined!" Aunt Alice gripped her shoulders, a new strength coming into her face that Haley had never seen before. "I've always hated that word! It's a man's word to set you back on your heels when you've defied them and chosen your own path."

"Aunt Alice?"

"To hell with *ruined*!" The older woman stamped her foot, her eyes blazing. "And damn any man who tries to say such a thing in my presence!"

Haley's mouth fell open in shock to hear her precious Aunt Alice curse for the first time in her presence.

"And no one will, Haley. No one will say it, and we will go on as if nothing has happened. You've ended an engagement to Mr. Trumble. Nothing more. Not as far as anyone beyond this room need speak of—and as for *him*, he'll say nothing if he values his life."

Haley shook her head, managing a weak smile through her tears. "You'd make a terrible assassin, Aunt Alice."

"Well, I meant it figuratively speaking, but . . . the rest of the sentiment holds true. He made false promises and we shall certainly threaten him with a libel suit if he so much as—"

"He—he never lied to me," Haley whispered.

"What? Well of course he did! He must have—"

Haley shook her head sadly. "Not a single untrue word. I've relived every conversation this morning, and . . . I . . . heard what I wished to hear."

"Well, that's no matter! You'll not miss a single party and there won't be a ripple of scandal connected to your good name, Haley."

"I don't know if I can just pretend that nothing has happened." Haley sank back down on the bed. "How can I just go on? I . . . love him. I love him with every fiber of my being, and I was so blind and stupid. How is it that I could have been so blind? I've spent years fussing at my father about his foolish romantic attachment to mother's memory and now . . . I swear if someone offered me laudanum, I'd take it!"

"Now you're truly talking nonsense!" Aunt Alice sat down, more like her usual self as she took command. "And I am an authority on nonsense, as you may have noticed." She smoothed out her skirts. "But we'll let you have this afternoon to finish up with these tears, and so I'd recommend that you cry until you cannot cry another drop! It's a luxury you won't always have, dearest."

"A luxury . . ." Haley echoed softly.

"I'll tell the maids you have a headache and that your rooms are off-limits. I'm sure I can manage a tray with something to tempt you to keep up your strength for it." Aunt Alice nodded her head. "A good old-fashioned bout of hysteria should do the trick!"

"What trick?"

Aunt Alice ignored the question. "And then we'll see about picking out just the right dress for Somerset's dinner party tomorrow night."

"I can't—"

"You can and you will!" Aunt Alice stood. "You've never been one to break when things become difficult, and I don't see how that could have changed. Men take only what you allow them to take, Haley. If he has your heart, even now, then it is because you allow him that gift. You can reclaim it whenever you wish. Your pride, your self-confidence, your honor . . . it's the same. Do you see?"

My heart. My pride. My honor. Mine to give and mine to retake. Yes, somehow I see it. A little late, but it's a good lesson all the same. But oh, would that I were getting them back in the same condition and not so battered and bruised!

Chapter
21

Galen left the house within minutes of Mrs. Shaw's dramatic departure, desperate for advice from a friend after the verbal lashing he'd taken. He'd bungled everything so completely that he wasn't sure how he could recover even a fraction of Haley's affections—but he was determined to try. Of all the Jaded, it was Rowan who always seemed to keep a level head and an unshielded heart, and it was because he was the least cynical among them that Galen sought his opinion now.

But when he arrived at the haven of West's small home, it became clear that Rowan might have other distractions on his mind. The servants showed him in quickly with baleful faces, and Galen froze in the doorway of his friend's beloved library.

It was in shambles.

Precious books were scattered over the floor, furniture overturned, and cushions torn open, transforming the haven into a room that spoke of violation and violence. Galen was sure that if he'd been punched in the stomach, it would have felt the same. A slight movement caught his eye, and he moved to find Rowan behind the overturned desk carefully gathering up the broken shards of what he'd once joked was the world's ugliest vase. But now, he was handling it as if it had been a porcelain Ming.

"I think I may be able to have it repaired." Rowan looked up at Galen, his eyes reflecting relief at the sight of his friend. "I'd offer you a chair, but . . ."

"What the hell happened?" Galen asked.

"Well, it wasn't burglars. Mr. Cotton may be losing a little of his hearing, but I would never insult him or the staff to even jest about them sleeping through *this*." Rowan stood slowly, holding a tray level with all the broken bits of pottery on it to set it on the side of his overturned desk. "No, you're actually looking at the remnants of a legal search."

"What?"

"The local police received a tip that I was the leader of a vast fencing ring . . . or was it smuggling? I wasn't here, and frankly, poor Mr. Cotton may have misheard them." Rowan shrugged. "The result is the same. Though you should see the bedroom! They cut open my feather mattress and I think the entire third floor is covered in down. It looks like it snowed up there."

"A tip? From whom?"

"I would say an enemy of the Jaded who wanted to see if a thorough toss could uncover anything of interest." Rowan crossed his arms. "They failed to leave a warrant in the confusion, but I don't think I'll be marching down to the authorities to make any claims."

"I had an encounter with an Indian mugger last night, but now, I think I'll consider myself lucky. I sent word to Michael but it never occurred to me that there might be more going on. . . ."

"Let's just hope the storm is over."

"You're taking this remarkably well." Galen bent down to retrieve one of the books and uncovered a small painted gourd that had survived the upheaval.

"They didn't tear the books apart, so it's just a matter of

sorting. As for my family's things . . ." His voice trailed off, battling the heartache of seeing the trinkets and treasures of lifetimes reduced to trash beneath his feet. "I'll recover everything I can."

"Did they find any of your jewels?"

Rowan shook his head. "I hadn't hidden them in the house. There's a bit of irony, eh?"

"Damn!" Galen overturned one of the leather chairs, his rage finally finding a single focus at the sight of the cut and ruined thing. "My favorite chair!"

"Let's talk about something else, Galen. Ashe tells me that you've lost your heart to a debutante after all. And not just any debutante!"

"I don't think I want to talk about it right now."

"I need the distraction, Galen, and from the look on your face, d say this is definitely a case of misery loving company." He began to rummage through the bar, discovered a single unbroken glass, and then poured himself a brandy from a bottle still hidden safely inside one of the covered nooks in the wall. He lifted his glass, toasting his friend. "To you and your . . . misery?"

Galen shook his head. "I'm past misery, Rowan."

Rowan set the glass down and came around the desk. "That was a stupid jest. You came to tell me something, or you wouldn't be here. Ashe made it sound as if you had gotten into a feminine tangle of some kind, but I didn't pay too much attention."

"A feminine tangle"—Galen sighed—"now there's a phrase you don't hear every day."

"Is it true?"

"Rowan." Galen took a deep breath, wondering how to ask for advice without being forced to reveal too much of his villainy to such a respected friend. "I've won and lost her, through my own stupidity."

"You're not a stupid man, my friend."

Galen managed a weak smile. "You'd be surprised." Galen knelt back down to gather up a few more books, handing them up to Rowan to place on the shelves, the physical act letting him frame his words as he continued. "I pursued her under false pretenses, and for all the wrong reasons. I hated her, Rowan, and I wanted to bring her down."

"Hated her? Why?"

"Because John Everly had loved her, and she'd repaid him by forgetting that he ever existed."

"Oh." Rowan was struck speechless, but he continued to take the books that Galen held out, and for a few moments they worked in silence until Galen continued his tale.

"After I had her, after I knew she was mine, heart and soul—I forgot to hate her, Rowan."

"It's no black mark against you, Galen, to forgive someone. To forget to hate them and discover that you love them, instead. John would have understood," he offered calmly.

"God, I miss him, but I'm not sure what John would say."

"Is that what's distressing you? Do you feel guilty at finding happiness with this woman, because of her connection to John?"

Galen closed his eyes, the sharp pang of a hundred emotions stilling him. "I'm distressed because she ended it with me. I'm *distressed* because she found out that I had intended to harm her, and I'm not sure how a man denies a truth, admits he's a liar, and has any chance of still earning her trust."

"You intended to harm her?" Rowan's voice had an alarmed edge.

"Her reputation, good doctor. I was going to expose her publicly in the press as a faithless, moneygrubbing whore. How does that sound for noble schemes and lofty plans?"

Rowan dropped the book in his hand on the desk and took a seat on an overturned chair's back. "It sounds. . . like another man I've never met. Suddenly, our conversation the other day begins to make sense. But Galen, you—you couldn't have done it."

"No, I couldn't. No matter how blackly appealing the cursed idea was before I met her, once I knew Haley . . . and then it was too late to tell her the truth. And then I convinced myself that she didn't have to ever know. I'd pursued her and won her. Why would that seem different from any other illicit courtship that ends in respectable matrimony? Except—"

"Except she found out your secret, and now it seems too different to ever be believed that you're not Lucifer himself," Rowan finished, retrieving his drink to take a steadying sip or two. "Well! This is starting to put my day into perspective."

"I should take comfort that she has a respectable and honorable man waiting to marry her. But I don't think I can live knowing that fat mud troll, Trumble, is going to be her husband."

"Ah! There's one problem solved."

"What do you mean?"

"I heard from Lady Pringley that the engagement is off. Apparently the fashionable Miss Moreland, for reasons unknown, broke off their agreement, but the gossips are convinced it's because Mr. Trumble may have met someone else."

"Off?" Galen felt numb. "When?"

"For some time, now." Rowan knelt next to his friend. "I'm surprised you hadn't heard."

"No. I've been so caught up in my own head, and . . . so distracted by . . ." Galen wasn't sure what was worse: the sick relief that Trumble would never touch her or the additional guilt of knowing that he'd callously and completely disrupted her life. The illusion that everything that had happened had been just between the two of them was shattered. "Any advice, Dr. West?"

Rowan leaned back on his heels, straightening up to use the furniture to stand, and then held out a hand to help Galen back up. "Are you sure you want to hear it?"

"Yes." Galen looked him squarely in the eyes. "Granted, I'm a little crazed, so don't ask me to swear that I'll follow it, West, but yes, I want to hear it."

"When did she discover all of this?"

"Last night."

Rowan drew his fingers over his chin, clearly thinking things through before speaking. "It's too soon."

"Pardon?"

"It's too soon to approach her. She'll be too emotional to hear anything you say, and I'm afraid you'll be no better off for the attempt, Galen." Rowan nodded, as if to underline his own wisdom by agreement. "I think you should wait a few days and let her catch her breath."

Galen held out his hand, shaking Rowan's hand. "I'll leave you to your sorting and repairing, West. Have you sent word to Michael?"

"You're not going to wait, are you?"

Galen's expression didn't change. "Send for Michael. Good day, Rowan, and be sure to let me know if there's anything I can do." He made a quick bow and left the library without another word.

Galen wasn't sure what he could do to win her back. He wasn't sure what words even existed to bridge the chasm his actions had carved between them or if there was a gesture grand enough to make her reconsider him.

But one thing he knew with absolute certainty.

He wasn't going to wait before he tried.

Chapter
22

🌰

"What a lovely gown!" A very young and beautiful Lady Forrester had befriended her for the evening, and Haley was grateful for the distraction. "I don't think I've ever seen such a clever sleeve! Everything else I see is endless draping and rouching, but this! It's like a delicate basket weave, but of silk."

"It's my own creation," she admitted, feeling braver about the subject because of Jacqueline's sincere compliments and sweet nature. "I enjoy making my own things."

"Well, I've heard from more than one woman this Season that there is a fierce quest to discover the cunning genius behind your dresses," she said, squeezing Haley's hand reassuringly. "But I'll keep your secret if you wish!"

"Thank you, Lady Forrester. I'm wishing I'd met you weeks ago . . ."

"Oh, I don't think I could have kept a delightful secret like this for *that* long!" Jacqueline teased. "It's perfect timing that we're friends now, for you'll think me an even-tempered and honorable creature, and be spared my worst traits."

"And what traits are those?" Haley asked with curiosity.

"I would never say!" she laughed. "But my husband even admits he has never met a woman more impossible, nor loved any other as much, so I cannot be too terrible!"

At the mention of a husband's love, Haley felt the pleasure she'd had in the conversation instantly bleed away. It felt petty to envy her new friend her happiness, but her own heartache was too recent. "No, not too terrible."

"You should be dancing! I would refer you to my cousin, Wilbur, but he was the worst dancer in London last Season and has now vowed to never make another attempt." She shook her head. "I'd be grateful, normally, to see all the toes of my friends safe at last, but what a social albatross to cart him around from party to party so that he can mope in corners."

"I wasn't going to dance this evening."

"Really?" Lady Forrester eyed her with new speculation. "I hope you don't mind my saying, but how is that possible?"

"I prefer not to." Haley hoped she didn't sound too cheeky. "How is that impossible?"

Jacqueline smiled. "It is impossible if it's true that you just recently ended your engagement to a certain successful industrialist! For that kind of brave or remarkably insane action simply *must* be followed up by a cavalier demonstration that you are, in fact, better off without him and ready for a happier and far wealthier blue-blooded prospect!"

"By dancing?"

"At the very least!" Lady Forrester looked back over the guests, as if openly seeking Haley's next prospect. "You are too lovely to be a good wallflower. Trust me, I know all about wallflowers! My older sisters were notorious at blending into the draperies, and I thought my mother would die from all the fuss she would make afterward. I still think they did it deliberately to enjoy my mother's theatrics. Mind you, they both made incredible matches once they'd determined to mend their ways!"

"As easy as that?" Haley asked, marveling at the elusive

idea that a woman could change the course of her life by determination alone.

"Well"—Jacqueline bit her lower lip, a mischievous gleam in her eyes giving a few of her secrets away—"they *may* have had a bit of a stealthy push from their younger sister, who wasn't going to be allowed to come out until they were married. But what is life without an adventure or two? And it all worked out in the end!"

Haley could only nod, beginning to realize that the sprightly Lady Forrester might indeed be the most charming troublemaker she had ever encountered. *Lord Forrester is bound to lead an adventurous and happy life, I suspect.*

"Shall I help you find a partner for the next dance?" Jacqueline offered brightly.

"If you wish, but . . ."

"Come, let's step forward and see who we can find in the crush to—"

"Miss Moreland!" Rand Bascombe addressed her as he approached the pair. "What a delight to see you out this evening! Ah, Lady Forrester, wasn't it?"

"It was and is." Jacqueline nodded. "I was just encouraging my new friend to dance, Mr. Bascombe."

"As well you should. Would you care to dance with me, Miss Moreland?"

Haley would rather have spent an evening with her back against a wall, but she couldn't afford to be rude in front of Lady Forrester. "Yes, thank you."

Bascombe bowed to Lady Forrester and swept Haley onto the floor before she could demur or say anything else to her new friend. "Aren't you enjoying yourself this evening, Miss Moreland?"

"Yes, of course." It was the proper answer, but hardly enthusiastic.

"Come now, I understand you've had a disappointment with your engagement ending so suddenly, and I am so sorry to hear of it. I thought you and Mr. Trumble were such a . . . lovely couple." He turned her perfunctorily around the dance floor. "But you are too beautiful a young woman to want for company, Miss Moreland, and I'm sure a dozen hearts in the Ton cheered to think you were not taken."

"It is not a cheerful subject, Mr. Bascombe. Please . . ."

"We'll leave it, then. But while I have you," he continued, "I must let you know that as a friend, I have a favor to ask— and of course, a favor to offer you in return."

"What kind of favor?" she asked warily.

"I want you to send word if Mr. Hawke contacts you again, or if you have a meeting. For you see, I still think you're the most likely person for him to share his secrets with—or perhaps he already has! And since I suspect he is no longer on good terms, you might feel differently about helping me in this regard."

Haley's mouth fell open involuntarily before she realized it, then she pursed her lips quickly in shock. "Mr. Bascombe, I—"

"It's no betrayal to speak of these things, Miss Moreland, when a man has treated you so cruelly. And how hard would it be to answer one of his letters and feign forgiveness if it suited you?" His grip on her fingers tightened to keep her from pulling away. "For if you will help me, I think I may be in a position to help your father with his financial straits."

She was speechless. That he knew of her relationship with Galen was too unfathomable—and too horrifying to absorb in a single waltz. "You cannot . . . believe . . ."

His expression became intensely serious, and his hold on her was suddenly a subtle prison as they made another turn around the floor. "I am relying on you, Miss Moreland. Any conversations regarding India that Mr. Hawke shared with you are quite literally worth their weight in gold to me and to others."

The music ended, and he took a step back, releasing her at last.

"Mr. Bascombe." Haley took a deep breath. "What in the world can have happened to Mr. Hawke in India that would fascinate you so much?"

"If you knew, you would know not to ask. But there's no

need to explain why I need this information, Miss Moreland. I'll depend on your discretion not to repeat this offer to any-one else—and you can depend on mine in return."

"You . . . are entirely serious."

"Never doubt it, Miss Moreland. We have a mutual enemy now, and that makes us even better friends, you and I." He bowed again. "I'll wait for your note."

Haley watched him walk away, trying to hide her astonish-ment and confusion.

"Miss Moreland?"

Haley turned, praying her distracted state wasn't too evi-dent on her face. "Yes." She realized instantly that Lady For-rester had made good on her promise to assist her friend in making a better show of the evening.

Jacqueline's smile was far too innocent. "May I present my cousin, Mr. Wilbur Parrish? It seems he's recovered his good humor enough to beg a dance!"

The surly expression on Mr. Parrish's face belied her words, but he bowed all the same. "May I have the next dance, Miss Moreland?"

Haley spared one look to Lady Forrester and accepted that there was nothing to be done. She was just going to have to make the best of it and keep hoping that she could stay one step ahead of the worst that the Fates had set out for her.

Only one thing was certain. Bascombe had spoken of en-emies and favors, and all she knew was that there wasn't a soul on the earth she'd betray at Rand Bascombe's bidding. Not even if it meant her life.

* * *

"Well? Will she cooperate or not?" Melrose barked from his corner in Bascombe's study.

"She is a waste of time! She's either too enamored to tell us what we want to know, or Galen has already paid her off to keep her mouth shut!" another man said from his seat by the fire.

"If he'd paid her off, then why are her father's creditors

starting to circle like vultures?" a third gentleman noted cynically, the whiskey in his glass sloshing onto the floor unnoticed.

"She'll send word to me when she's ready." Rand interrupted them all. "Hell hath no fury like a woman scorned, and once she accepts that her only choices are assisting me or marrying some rheumy baron who's out for a third young wife . . . Revenge will seem a sweet selection."

"It's not a subtle piece of business, old man." A voice full of ice made every man in the room involuntarily shudder, as the fifth man in their company spoke from the shadows along the far wall. "You've been promising a great deal to the Company for weeks. Be careful that you aren't the one in line for a bit of fury when they grow impatient with your games. For make no mistake"—his voice dropped in volume but carried to Bascombe as if he were whispering directly into his ears— "you'll bleed if you don't deliver the Jaded's secrets soon."

Chapter
23

Galen searched the room, nervously looking for any sign of Haley. Lord Kendall's card party was a dull affair, but Galen wouldn't have missed it for the world. So far, the social invitations and events on the family's calendar had yet to change, and he'd been able to plan his own evenings accordingly.

A ball would have been far preferable to this dreary gathering, but let's hope the quiet makes it easier to find her.

He deferred another invitation to sit at one of the tables and continued his surveillance, circling the rooms with all the various games and equally varied players. The wealth changing hands was something that wouldn't have arrested his attention years ago, but Galen had a new awareness of each coin's meaning. *It all goes so quickly. I could gamble until I'd won a thousand fortunes, and I would still feel like a pauper. Perhaps I should tell her that. That she's robbed me of my heart, and that I'll happily spend every penny I have on her happiness to ransom it back—*

"Mr. Hawke!"

Galen turned in surprise at Lord Moreland's friendly hail,

disappointed that he seemed to be alone. But the man looked much more robust than he had at their last meeting, his face a healthier color, and his cheeks had filled out slightly. "Lord Moreland, what a pleasure to see you again."

"A pleasure to be seen, I can say with all honesty. Though I'm not one for the tables." He eyed a game of casino longingly, but then turned back to Galen with a sober expression. "Are you a gambling man?"

"Only when society requires it, Lord Moreland." Galen took a deep breath and decided to take a direct strategy. "May I speak to you for a few minutes?"

"Yes, yes of course." The men stepped away from the tables and retreated to a conversational area near the windows. "Here, let's take our rest here and you may tell me what is on your mind."

"Thank you, your lordship."

"Though I warn you, from the way your notes seem to be flying back unopened out of the doors of my house, I am at a loss." Lord Moreland chose one end of the settee and gave Galen a searching look. "You seem like a perfectly reasonable choice to me, so if you've come to ask why my daughter seems to have taken leave of her senses, I pray you'll attempt another topic."

"I had a slightly different topic in mind." Galen was determined to see the ghost of his past addressed and set aside, once and for all.

"Thank God!" Lord Moreland leaned back in relief. "Then, let's have it."

"I was hoping you would tell me more about John Everly."

Lord Moreland's face betrayed his surprise, but he obliged Galen all the same. "The Everlys were our close neighbors years ago, when they resided for a short while at Frostbrook Manor. The family was extremely respectable, and Carlton Everly used to hunt with permission on our lands. I liked him a great deal, but his wife was a quiet, sickly woman. I don't really remember much of her, at all. Though my dear wife did deliver more than one basket of whatnots to cheer her when she could. My darling, Margaret, was forever thinking of others!"

"And John?"

"He and his brother used to come over and tease Haley to tears." He smiled at the memory. "But they became fast friends eventually, running wild through the countryside and getting into every manner of mischief. John even protected her from a local bully, according to Haley, and I marvel that he'd turned out so well—in light of their beginnings."

"But they came to love each other?"

Lord Moreland raised his eyebrows in surprise. "Love? Did I give you that impression?"

Galen's world ground to a halt. "You did."

"It was a jest, I'm sure. After all, they were far too young to do more than bounce about the village like puppies. We laughed when she came home with a ribbon tied around her wrist and said that they'd become engaged! It was a simple childish game, but sweet enough."

Galen's stomach clenched around a growing shard of ice. "How old was she?"

"Twelve? No, thirteen! For that was the year I bought Margaret thirteen bonnets to celebrate each year of our precious daughter's health and happiness." Lord Moreland's eyes had yet to shed their faraway sheen as memories of times gone by held him captive. "Then they moved off as Mr. Everly's business required him more in Town, I believe, and I don't think I could say much more of them—except I bought Carlton's stable out on a whim! Everly had a good eye for horseflesh, but no need for so many in Town. Too much expense, he said." He seemed to remember Galen's presence. "Was that helpful?"

Thirteen years of age. It was a boyish crush that John had spoken of, not any formal declarations from a man with any seriousness. He'd loved her, but not . . . Oh, God, I judged and condemned her on the word of a child. Because truly, John, you were a child to speak of her so! You never loved the woman! There was no betrothal! It was all wishful thinking and innocent nostalgia and I . . . I almost destroyed her for it—which officially makes me the worst villain to ever walk.

"Yes, thank you." His tongue felt as if it were coated with sand.

"We recently heard of John's death abroad." He shook his head sadly. "Are the Everlys acquaintances of yours, Mr. Hawke?"

And it gets worse. Because I don't think I can lie anymore.

"John Everly was a dear friend, Lord Moreland. He spoke of Miss Moreland with great affection."

"Oh! I'm grieved but comforted to hear it. I'd lost touch with them entirely over the years and always wondered if they remembered their neighbors. I'll have to see if I can find Carlton and send him a belated note of condolence."

"His parents reside in Chesterfield. I'll send you the address."

"Thank you." He shifted in his chair. "May I ask you, Mr. Hawke, what trespass have you committed that has my daughter so set against you?"

Self-loathing almost made him confess all, for the sheer pleasure of letting Lord Moreland kill him, but he thought better of it. "I've committed too many trespasses to name, your lordship, but I can only hope the lady's memory will prove forgiving."

Lord Moreland gave him a rueful laugh and stood to end their conference. "Haley forgets nothing, but I've never known a girl with a greater heart, so I'll just wish you luck, young man."

"Thank you, Lord Moreland. I'll need all the luck I can muster."

Galen started to make his way back to the main room and walked directly into the path of a jovial, red-faced Herbert Trumble. "Mr. Hawke! Now I know I am in the best of company!" Herbert had his hand in a vigorous shake before Galen could think of an escape. "Though I'm not one to gamble, sir! Make no mistake, if I lose any money it will be because I've not repaired a hole in my pockets and not for a silly game."

Galen did his best to keep his countenance unruffled, as other guests at the nearby tables began to look up in amusement at the odd tableau they presented, with Herbert still pumping his arm wildly and blathering on about the evils of gambling as if ignorant of his own presence in the middle of a card party. "You're a wiser man than most, Mr. Trumble, but I must beg the return of my hand."

"Oh, dear!" Herbert let go immediately. "What a dreadful habit! And even worse, I'm forgetting my manners when it comes to introductions." He glanced back and summoned the woman who had been waiting a few paces behind him with a gesture. "You must meet the incomparable angel who has graced me with her company! Darling, this is Mr. Galen Hawke, a good friend of mine who has been very generous to me during my stay in London."

Galen hoped the shock didn't show on his face as it was clear that Herbert Trumble had bounced back from his disappointment with amazing speed and versatility. "Miss Langston, a pleasure. I recognize you from the theatre, of course."

"Herbert has been so sweet to introduce me to all his friends, and I am happy to make your acquaintance, sir." She held out her hand, and he took it briefly, bowing over it without kissing it.

Herbert beamed, drawing his "angel" next to his side, but then looked embarrassed as he recalled Galen. "Oh, dear . . . this may look inappropriate . . . if you hadn't heard . . ."

Galen swallowed and was sure he could taste crow. "I'd heard."

"Ah! But not the latest happy news!" Herbert said. "I want you to be one of the first to know that for some miraculous reason, Miss Beatrice Langston has agreed to become my wife and we're to be wed at the end of this month!"

Miraculous reason?

"Herbert, please! You are too sweet!"

Galen eyed the beautiful actress towering three inches over her beloved's balding head, and would have consigned her to a dismissive and damning judgment of character, but in his next breath, he noticed something miraculous after all.

She was blushing, and not an overly pretty practiced blush, but the truly natural blush of a woman as the color crept up from her breasts and even altered the tint of her ears. She was holding his arm with *both* hands. And the most telling thing of all, she hadn't really taken her eyes off of Trumble the entire time.

"Congratulations, Mr. Trumble," Galen said, and meant it. *I suppose it's fitting that at least one man in the room finds a little happiness where he can.*

"Thank you, Hawke! Is she not a treasure?"

"She is. She is that, and more." His throat threatened to close, and he grimly held onto his composure. "If you'll excuse me."

He stepped away with a polite nod to the lady and made his way more purposefully toward the other room with every intention of leaving immediately. He'd had enough for one night. He'd received enough revelations and painful blows to fell a giant, in his opinion. He needed to retreat and regroup, sorting through the fact and fiction of the life he'd made for himself in the last few weeks, so that he could come to Haley with more than just apologies.

And then, as if the very thought of her magically summoned her, Galen saw her at one of the small tables at the far end of the room.

As beautiful as a cameo, Haley's profile was comprised of graceful and wistful lines, and Galen's chest ached to see her. She looked paler, and thinner, but there was nothing that could have dulled the luster of her skin and hair in the lamplight; nothing to dampen the quick fire that the sight of her invoked inside of him. Her shoulders were bared by the evening style of dress she wore, and his breath caught as he realized that the ribbon in her hair trailed the column of her neck and down her elegant back where his hands had once freely explored.

I could walk up and force her to speak to me. She wouldn't dare to snub me in public—I could . . .

The idea died quickly. Galen wasn't going to force Miss Haley Moreland to do anything for the rest of his days. And confronting her in public would only add to his woes. It wouldn't be a conversation. It would be a farce that would hurt her no matter how it turned out, and she would hardly thank him later. *Even if I honestly believed I was in any position to prostrate myself at a card party and bare my soul with Herbert Trumble ten yards off—I'd be ready for Bedlam.*

Galen gathered up what he could of his dignity and allowed reason to overrule passion just this once. He knew he would speak to her and make his case. But it would have to be another time and another place.

And then if she didn't kill him, he would just take it as a hopeful sign.

* * *

"A lovely party, wasn't it, dearest?" Mrs. Shaw asked as they settled inside the carriage.

"Lovely." Haley wasn't sure that an evening listening to Mrs. Greeley outlining the errors Lord Kendall had made in arranging the card tables as he had qualified as "lovely," but she couldn't muster the strength to complain. She was numb and exhausted after another night of pretending that she hadn't a care in the world.

"Lovely!" Lord Moreland agreed sarcastically. "In light of a sad lack of entertainment for a man who has neither the coins to gamble nor the comfort of a good glass of brandy, I'd say it wasn't too painful."

"Alfred, please!" Alice reached for her fan. "If you're going to mope at every turn, you could at least make yourself useful and see about a rich widow or two! I'm not clear as to why all the pressure is on poor Haley to marry us out of this stew! You're the one who got us into it. It only seems fair that you be the one to find a rich wife and take a quick march down the aisle!"

"Like hell!" he sputtered, then turned to Haley. "Any interesting prospects, dearest?"

"No, Father."

"Well, I don't think you were looking too hard. For you'll never guess who I saw this evening!" he said, ignoring Alice, who was rolling her eyes in the corner.

"Who?" she asked, trying to play along, a ghost of a smile on her face as she became aware of Aunt Alice's antics.

"Mr. Hawke!" he announced. "You remember him, don't you? I was sure I saw his name on several notes in the hallway and—"

"Out of the question!" It was Aunt Alice's turn to sputter. "Alfred, you're to have nothing to do with the man!"

Haley felt a wash of ice-cold air lash through her body at the sound of his name. "Mr. Hawke was . . . at Kendall's?"

"He was, indeed, and made a point of speaking to me," Lord Moreland said. "Frankly, I like the man. And although I'm no judge in these matters, he seems easy enough on the eyes, and I can make an inquiry or two into his finances to see if—"

"No! Alfred, please!" Alice was beside herself at the prospect.

"Father, please." Haley's softer plea commanded his complete attention. "I would rather that you didn't."

"Then can you tell me why?" he asked just as softly, and Haley thought her heart would break all over again at the gentle look of sympathy in his eyes. "Why are you sending back this man's notes and flowers? I know I'm generally thought of as too incoherent to pay attention to these things, but sober, I'm noticing quite a bit these days, Haley."

Haley shook her head. "I can't say why."

"Very well." He straightened in his seat, narrowing his eyes suspiciously and studying the pair of them. "You realize I could very well just assume the worst and call the man out!"

"First of all, dueling is illegal, and I can't remember the last time you shot a gun, drunk or sober." Alice challenged him with an arch look and put her fan down. "And secondly, how is your subsequent suicide going to help the situation?

And thirdly, if your assumption is off, which in this case, *it is*, Margaret will at last meet you in heaven with the ultimate confirmation that you are a fool! And if she doesn't throw you off for some other dead soul who displays more sense, I'd be shocked and disappointed in the justice of the afterlife!"

"Aunt Alice!" Haley gasped in shock, and her father just sat in stunned silence as the sound of the horse's hooves on the pavement was the only noise to be heard for the space of at least ten seconds.

Finally, Lord Moreland once again turned to his only child. "*Is* there something the patriarch of this family should know?"

"No!" both women replied simultaneously, but Haley recovered first, leaning over to take her father's hand. "Please, Father. If you ever loved me, please don't ask again. You must simply trust me to know what's best in this instance!"

He cradled her hand in his, and finally nodded. "I do trust you, Haley. So, we'll leave off the subject for now, and I'll do my very best not to send off for pistols at dawn or scare off any of your suitors."

"Thank you." Haley relaxed against the seat, wishing they were already home so that she could give in to her tears. One mention of *his* name and the spiral of memories was paralyzing. She pulled the fur around her cloak's collar a little closer and buried her nose in the softness. She hated the weak part of her that wanted to ask her father what they'd spoken of, or if Galen had asked after her.

What difference did it make what Galen said? Why do I care about a man who hates me enough to draw me as a whore for all the world to see? Her breath hiccupped as a new realization crept over her. *I am my mother's daughter. Once I was in love, I never saw anything else around me, and I lost all sense of logic and reason, just as she did. And no matter what Aunt Alice says about getting your heart back again and again whenever you wish, for me that will never be true. Because I'm my father's daughter, too. And we only love once in a lifetime.*

And at that, the tears wouldn't wait.

Chapter
24

Dearest Son,

It is with a heavy heart that I summon you home to Stamford Cross. Your elder brother has taken ill, and the doctor informs me that there is not much time left before he has passed from our hands back into those of our Maker. Fly home, Galen, and bring with you what comfort you can to your family.

> *Yours in Sorrow,*
>
> *L.*

Galen reread the note again, reeling at the quick turns of fate and folly that could bring any man down without warning. He'd been in the middle of trying to come up with an excuse not to storm Moreland's brownstone and refuse to leave until Haley forgave him when the messenger had come with the terrible news.

It didn't seem possible that Trevor was dying. The last

time he'd seen him they'd gone riding, and spent an entire day talking of nothing, as only brothers can. He'd left for London knowing that no matter what else happened in the world, Trevor would never change. And he had never wished him to.

But now the carriage was waiting and he could hear Bradley banging around the house coordinating his sudden and immediate departure for the country to sit vigil and wait for the unthinkable.

He'd sent word for Michael, asking him to come urgently, but the clock began to chime and Galen accepted that he'd run out of time to—

"Your note said it was life and death."

Michael stood in the doorway, and Galen was too grateful to ask how he'd managed it. "I'm leaving London."

"Is it anything to do with Miss Moreland?"

Galen shook his head then felt the refusal fade. *Doesn't everything now have to do with Miss Moreland? Isn't that why I summoned him?* "My brother is ill and may be dying. I'm praying that my father is overstating how serious it is, that he wrote his note in a state of unwarranted worry, but . . . I have no choice but to go home."

"I'm sorry, Galen."

"Thank you." He took a slow deep breath. "Trevor has always been one of the heartiest men I've ever known. I have to believe that this is a false alarm, but I cannot risk staying away. Not even when things in London are so . . ."

"Unfinished?"

"*Unsettled* was the word I would have used." Galen crossed his arms. "I was the worst cad to her—and for not a single reason that mattered! John did love her, but . . . they were literally children together and he never said a damn word after the age of thirteen to that girl! I tried to destroy her because John had a boyhood crush!" He began to pace, self-loathing coating every word. "I misunderstood it all, and then wouldn't listen to anything you said to try to ward off this unbelievable disaster! And now, before I can convince her to see me or even speak to me—damn it! The timing couldn't have been worse, Michael."

"Things can always be worse, Galen."

Galen smiled. "Ever the optimist!"

"Look on the bright side," Michael played along. "With you out of Town, our friends from the Company will just have to bother someone else for a while."

"So long as it's not Miss Moreland!" Galen retrieved a small leather packet from his desk. "Here, Michael. These are invitations to a few parties where I'm certain she'll be."

Michael's hand had automatically extended to take it, but with the words *invitations* and *parties*, his fingers froze mid-air. "You cannot be serious! I'm a soldier, not a gentleman to sashay about dusty drawing rooms and play parlor games."

"I need you to keep an eye on her, and even speak to her if you can. I don't want her to think I've simply abandoned her without cause, Michael."

"So send her a note! Tell her your brother is ill! Tell her you're sorry! But for the love of God, don't make me attend a string of fussy tea parties!"

Galen pressed the envelope into his hands, folding his own fingers over Michael's to guarantee that there would be no misunderstanding. "I've sent a dozen notes and emptied three flower shops to no avail, and now I'm out of time! I'm not asking you, Michael. I'm begging you to do what you can on my behalf until I can return." The muscles in his jaw flexed, the humiliation of the request outweighed by the pressing urgency of his heart. "Please do this for me."

Michael took the packet and slid it into the inside pocket of his coat. "I will. But I'd have been happier if you'd proposed kidnapping her."

"We'll make that our next plan of action if this one doesn't work." Galen smiled in spite of himself. "Thank you, Michael."

Michael left without preamble, aware of the pressure on Galen to depart immediately. And within moments, the time had come to go.

"All's ready, sir. It's a private coach all the way, so you can make great speed on the roads as best you can," Bradley advised as he helped Galen with his coat. "Cook packed a basket, so you won't suffer on that account, she says."

"Give her my thanks for her thoughtfulness, and . . ." Galen took a deep breath. "I can't think of anything else."

"Your hat, then." Bradley held it out. "Good journey, Mr. Hawke."

"Thank you, Bradley." Galen turned to go and then stopped for a moment, his own reflection in a small mirror on the wall catching his eye. He stared at the stranger staring back at him. *Love should leave a mark. That's what I told her, and by Jove, I believed it. But that man . . . that man doesn't look as if he's let anything touch him in a long time.* Galen walked over to his reflection.

"Sir?" Bradley followed him, confused at the sudden halt in his employer's momentum. "Are you all right?"

I was so sure that a person shouldn't be able to truly love another and then walk away, pure and untouched, as if the encounter with flame didn't burn you. . . . Can you be human and walk away from love without so much as a single tear?

But his reflection mocked him, and Galen finally turned away from the mirror. "I'm fine, Bradley. I just don't think I'm ever again going to judge another human being by their face or their appearance for as long as I live."

"Very good, sir," Bradley replied, a little mystified as he watched Galen head down the steps and into the coach to disappear into the fog like a ghost.

Chapter
25

◆

"Are you wearing that?"

Haley had to bite the inside of her lip to keep herself from saying anything inappropriate in response to such an impossible question. They were already late, and she'd taken particular care in choosing a dark blue satin gown that showed off her figure. Her father's temperament was deteriorating quickly, but Haley knew it was directly related to the mounting pressure he was suffering from their debts and creditors. He was trying to keep her from the worst of it, she suspected, to assist her in keeping a calm and more attractive demeanor on her hunt for a suitable husband. "I am, Father."

"I liked the red," he said in a surly tone. "You look like your mother in the red."

"I cannot wear red to every occasion." She leaned over to kiss his cheek as she reached the bottom of the staircase. "But for the dance at Milton's, I will, I promise."

"Promise me you'll have a good offer before the dance at Milton's and you can wear any color you choose!"

"Leave her be, Alfred!" Aunt Alice came down the stairs

at a more peaceful pace. "How in the world is a girl supposed to attract a husband when you keep haranguing her until she has the vapors?"

"I wasn't—" Lord Moreland cut himself off and took his daughter's hand with an apologetic sigh. "Ignore your father and enjoy yourself this evening, dearest."

"Thank you." She smiled and kissed him again, wishing once more that she could have managed both their happinesses instead of sacrificing her own to recover and make a match that would save them all from financial ruin.

For Haley, these last few days were a blur, and every smile tasted of ashes in her mouth when she thought of the caricature she was in danger of becoming—a woman who would sell herself to the highest bidder. Galen's memory haunted her at every turn, and she still caught herself looking for him before remembering their last night and the horrible revelation that had followed it. Bascombe's strange offer came back to mind, but again, she dismissed it, although more and more she wondered if she should send Galen a note to warn him that Mr. Bascombe's interest had taken a strange turn.

But writing Galen felt like an impossible choice, so she abandoned the idea.

She said nothing during the carriage ride to the next party, quietly sitting in the corner and reliving in turn her first kiss and her last, marveling that one could experience so much and still be so naïve. Before long, they'd arrived at Lady Pringley's great home, and she was forced to banish Mr. Hawke from her thoughts.

Even so, as the evening wore on, it was more and more difficult to cling to any hope at all, as inevitably her recent engagement came up with varied looks of pity and curiosity from the other guests. When she spotted Lady Pringley heading her way, she despaired at the lack of time to make any subtle escape.

"Miss Moreland! What news! I only just learned of your misfortune and would have called on you, but it has been such a whirlwind this year—and my cousin's daughter is planning a wedding, so you can imagine the upheaval!" She seized both of Haley's gloved hands into hers and then openly evaluated her evening gown. "I thought it plain from a distance, but my goodness, the drape of that cloth is so elegant that I am forgetting to breathe!"

It was a ridiculous compliment, and Haley forced herself to smile. "As usual, your ladyship is too kind."

"Nonsense!" She squeezed Haley's fingers, her look changing to vitriolic sympathy. "What mortification! To be sloughed off by a man like that!"

Haley's chest flooded with panic, unsure for a fleeting second to which man Lady Pringley referred.

"An industrialist! I'd sooner see you married off to a shopkeeper, and I imagine your father is feeling nothing but relief at this narrow escape." Lady Pringley released her fingers to allow her to snap open her fan for effect. "I said nothing earlier, to shield you of course!"

"Mr. Trumble is a fine man, and I wish him every happiness, Lady Pringley. I'm sure that is what you meant to say, was it not? That you wish him every happiness?" She held her ground, unwilling to play some spiteful game of gossip and libel to appease her host. *I've done enough to harm poor Mr. Trumble without listening to this horrible woman!*

Lady Pringley's eyebrows arched, reassessing her young guest. "Yes, something quite like that." She leaned closer, her voice dropping so that no one else would hear her. "Whatever the cause, he has left you in a terrible position. One only speculates why your father would have allowed such an uneven match in the first place, and if, as most people begin to suspect, your family's finances are not solid, then you may be hard-pressed to find a gentleman willing to risk so much as a single waltz, my dear Miss Moreland."

Haley gasped, unsure of how to answer, but then Lady Pringley went on with a cruel smile. "But I like you, so here is a small bit of priceless advice. Start crying 'foul!' whenever Trumble is mentioned and you may divert enough attention away from your father's wallet to yet ensnare a willing fool."

Haley was speechless as the woman straightened up, artfully fanning herself as she sailed off to another cluster of guests near an open doorway.

"Miss Moreland?"

Haley turned, only to find herself staring at the center of a man's chest where she'd expected a face. She looked up to take in what was undoubtedly the tallest and broadest gentleman she had ever met. "Yes."

"Miss Haley Moreland?" he asked again.

"Yes." She curtsied, some of her humor returning. "I believe so."

"I'm afraid we've not had the pleasure and . . ." He sighed. "I am not a man for these formal affairs."

"No? You seem to be holding your own better than some." She tried to offer him some encouragement. For all his intimidating size, she was amazed at how cautious his stance, as if he were expecting a firing squad instead of a room full of dowagers and debutantes.

"I meant to introduce myself. I'm Michael Rutherford."

"How do you do, Mr. Rutherford?" His hand swallowed hers, but his grip was as cautious as if her bones were made of glass.

"Well enough."

He had the look of a man who would rather be up to his neck in the Thames, but she did her best not to laugh for fear of being misunderstood and hurting his feelings. "Have you—"

"Ah! Haley! There you are!" Aunt Alice interrupted, her face flushed as she came hurrying toward them. "Your father promised your first dance this evening to Lord Willecourt—oh, my!" She stopped short as she suddenly noticed the masculine mountain her niece was addressing. "Pardon the interruption, Mr. . . . ?"

"Mr. Rutherford, wasn't it?" Haley tried to give the man an opening to reintroduce himself more properly, and potentially divert her aunt from her mission. Haley had briefly met Lord Willecourt earlier and her best guess put him a summer or two away from sixty.

"It was." Mr. Rutherford's succinct answer gave her nothing to cling to, and Mrs. Shaw merely shrugged.

"How nice to meet you"—Aunt Alice grasped her arm—"and if you'll excuse us, my niece has a previous engagement."

Haley could only nod a quick apology to Mr. Rutherford before Aunt Alice was pulling her relentlessly toward the ballroom. "Aunt Alice!" She lowered her voice, smiling just in case anyone was watching. "Father can't be serious!"

"There's no telling, dearest, but just placate the man if you can and let's try to keep an open mind, shall we?"

"I'm beginning to miss the days when you encouraged me to misbehave."

"As am I." Aunt Alice's look was one of sincere regret. "But even I can't ignore the realities pressing on our doorstep. Just do your best to impress his lordship, and remember that your father loves you above all else."

Haley had to swallow the lump in her throat but managed to paste a smile on her face as they reached her father and the waiting Lord Willecourt.

* * *

The instant they were home, her father summoned her to the library for a talk. "You have to move faster! Once the servants catch a whiff of all of this financial rot, the news will spread like wildfire and that will be that!"

"I'm doing the best I can, Father!"

"And how is that? I didn't see anything that amounted to a single fluttering eyelash during that dance with Willecourt! Hell! Alice showed the man more warm looks and welcoming touches!"

"Aunt Alice is closer to the man's age! And I apologize for not flushing with womanly flirtation while a man discusses sheep breeding and hoof diseases!" Haley stamped her foot in frustration. "What would you have me do?"

"I don't know! Just do it faster!"

She lifted her chin defiantly, unwilling to cower. "I am still a gentleman's daughter and not a complete eyesore, Father!"

"And you don't think there are a hundred girls who can top your lineage and bat their eyes convincingly? And *they* have dowries to offer that no fool would overlook! A man has to marry for gain whenever he can, Haley!"

"You didn't!"

"Yes, I did!" he shouted, then immediately turned the color of a beet at his inadvertent confession.

"Y-you married for gain?" Haley whispered, sitting down as her knees suddenly felt unsteady. "But you always said . . ."

"Your mother"—he sat down on the sofa next to her, nervously tugging at the tassels on one of the decorative pillows as he finished his story—"came with a tidy sum, and frankly, I don't remember being all too keen on marrying. But my father insisted and the matter had long been settled between our families before I'd had my first shave. She was the catch of the county, but I wasn't fishing. And by the time my father advised me I was betrothed, I almost made a run for it."

"I can't believe it."

"It's true! I don't think I spoke to her three times in my life before the wedding, I was so stubbornly determined to keep my distance for as long as I could. But then, it was done. We were married and I was sulking in a corner at the reception afterward, and she . . ." Her father's eyes had taken on that far-off look, as he gazed into the memory of happier days. "She started singing at the piano for the guests, and then I couldn't seem to stop looking at her—an angel in white silk and butter yellow taffeta. And then she laughed and smiled right at me, and I couldn't believe it! I'd been *sulking*! Like an idiot! And she was too sweet a miracle to hold it against me, can you imagine?"

"Oh, Father!" She put her head on his shoulder. "Why did you never tell me this story before?"

"I was too embarrassed! Besides, I loved her too greatly to let myself remember too often what a complete blind ass I'd been!" He put a hand on her head, smoothing out the silk of her curls. "I wanted the same happiness for you, Haley. And probably because of my own past, I was sure that it was possible, even if you were secretly digging in your heels about marrying Mr. Trumble. I thought, why not another miracle? She could just look up and think . . . him . . ." Her father's words trailed off as he faltered, and then finally he chuckled. "The handsomest little bald fat man in all of England!"

Haley laughed, then buried her nose in his coat, wishing that it could last; that this fleeting merriment wouldn't evaporate so quickly and return them to the harsh realities ahead.

"Marry, Haley. You must marry quickly."

"Who?" she asked, her eyes filling with tears. "Did you have anyone in mind?"

He shook his head, his face betraying his fears. "Not a single soul."

Haley buried her face against his shoulder again, but this time it was to cry her heart out.

Chapter
26

Michael rang the bell and forced himself not to nervously shift on his feet while he waited for an answer. He knew he should have left a card first, but he hadn't the time or patience for the foolish niceties that London society seemed to think vital. *I've never understood why a man has to stop by with a card to say that he's going to stop by. Whoever made up the rules had far too much time on their hands to sweat and worry about ten minutes of conversation where everyone generally seems to talk about the weather and nothing else.*

He rang it again, then pulled his hand back with guilty speed as the door instantly opened.

The butler's appraisal wasn't as icy as it might have been, but Michael knew his imposing size took the starch out of most men. "May I help you, sir?"

"I wish to see Miss Moreland. I mean, if she's home, I thought I would pay a call."

"Is she expecting you, sir?" The butler didn't move from the doorway, and Michael wished he'd bothered with the card nonsense after all.

"If you'll inform her that Michael Rutherford is here, I'll wait." He crossed his arms defensively and like any good soldier, held his position.

A male voice bellowed from inside the house, and Michael tried not to smile as the butler winced. "Who the hell is it, Weathers?"

Mr. Weathers altered his strategy quickly. "Won't you wait inside, sir? I'll advise the family of your presence."

Michael stepped in the door, straightening his coat, and offered Mr. Weathers his hat. "That would be fine."

The butler retreated to carry out his duties, leaving Michael as an unexpected and, for the moment, vastly uncategorized guest to wait in the foyer. To pass the time, Michael instinctively surveyed the house from a defensive point of view and inventoried the objects within view. It was an old habit, and generally useless in the urban homes of merry London, but it kept his mind occupied.

Although, if I ever decided to try my hand at burglary, I don't think the peerage would know what had befallen them. Not that I need to add any more black marks on my soul by taking some buffoon's portrait of his crusty great-uncle's—

"Mr. Rutherford?" She'd approached him without alerting his senses, and that startled him far more than her quiet voice.

He nodded, looking at her with a new measure of respect. That she was beautiful enough to have enslaved even a man like Galen Hawke was indisputable. But there was more to her than beauty, and Michael was glad for his friend. "Yes. We met at Lady Pringley's party."

"Yes, of course. I remember you." She stepped back, gesturing for him to enter one of the formal sitting rooms off the foyer. "But then, you are a difficult man to forget, Mr. Rutherford. Would you care to come in and take tea?"

He nodded, stepping into the room she'd pointed to. "Yes, that's very kind of you." He eyed the delicate legs of the sofa and decided that he'd be better off in one of the sturdy chairs when the moment came. "I should apologize for coming without . . . I am a disaster when it comes to social rituals, Miss Moreland."

She smiled, ringing the bell for their tea. "I like your plain way of speaking. It's refreshing to think that you might actually mean what you say, unlike . . . so many others. Would you care to sit?"

"Yes, thank you." He took the heaviest of the chairs, but even so, settled slowly and carefully to try to avoid an embarrassing bit of destruction. He was simply not built for delicate drawing rooms.

"I hope you'll forgive me for trying to speak just as plainly, Mr. Rutherford." She sat across from him, a pale queen in a gown with green flowers over ivory muslin.

"I would be grateful if you would forget all the rules of polite conversation, just for this once. A soldier's head has a bit of a struggle with all the airy small talk of the day. I had quite a headache after Lady Pringley's."

She gave him a sympathetic look, almost admitting that she felt the same way after three minutes in the woman's presence. But she honored his request and wasted no more time in getting to the question on her mind. "Very well. Why are you here, Mr. Rutherford?"

I like you more and more, Miss Moreland. "Galen asked me to come."

"Then"—she stood—"you'll understand if I ask you to leave. Good day, Mr. Rutherford."

Michael stood, hoping she didn't hear the creak of his kneecaps. "He's left London. Family tragedy is about all I can imagine that would have torn him away, and he was fairly wrecked not to be able to see you again. So, I guess . . . if I'm being shown the door, I've passed most of the message along that he charged me with and I'll leave with a clear conscience." He made an awkward bow and started to leave. "Good day, Miss Moreland."

"Wait." The command was so quiet, he almost missed it, but he turned immediately.

"Yes."

"What was the rest of the message for—"

"You'll pardon the interruption." Lord Moreland came through the doorway, his face red with anxiety. "But unless you've come to propose marriage, young man . . ." He trailed off, giving Michael a hopeful look.

"No!" Michael answered in shock. "No, your lordship!"

"Father!" Haley's shock was equally apparent.

"Well, if he's not come to court, then I'm afraid you'll have to ask your guest to leave, Haley." He gave her a look that forbade her to ask a single question or make any additional protests. "Now!"

"Mr. Rutherford, I'm so sorry, but if you would be so kind. Perhaps another day—"

"Yes, yes, another day!" her father echoed, leading them out toward the front door, rushing the giant man's exit as best as he could.

Michael barely managed to utter a word of farewell before the front door closed firmly in his face and he found himself exactly where he'd started, standing on Moreland's steps unsure of what to do next.

Ah! That didn't go as badly as I'd imagined it would. And to think I was worried that I might be rude . . . But whatever has Lord Moreland demanding marriage proposals and throwing guests from his threshold can't bode well.

He retreated, but with every intention of keeping track of the family and seeing if he could discover what was going on. He would do it for Galen. He only hoped he wasn't going to be the one to send him another bit of tragic news.

* * *

"What's happened? How could you be so horrible to a complete stranger?" Haley was mystified. Of all her father's faults, she'd never known him to be so abrupt and—odd. "H-have you been drinking?"

"No," he answered, "although if I had been, I'm sure even you wouldn't blame me." He moved to the windows and quickly began to pull all the draperies closed. "We're leaving London immediately. It's over."

"It's . . . over?" Haley asked, just as the sound of slamming cupboards and doors became evident in the rooms above, as if every servant were running around to pack them out of a burning house. "I don't understand."

"Just know, first of all, that I don't blame you. But we are out of time, my dear. I have received the worst of news from my solicitors. My debts are going to be called in, with warrants issued, and we must return to our estates immediately unless you'd like to visit me in a pauper's prison." He sank down in the chair just recently vacated by Mr. Rutherford, his face in his hands. "I'm ruined."

Haley moved to kneel before him, doing her best to soothe him, but also to understand how things had suddenly become so dire. "Father, there now. I know we have debts, but surely we can negotiate and retrench. Things are difficult but it's not as if we're—"

"Beggars?" He dropped his hands to look at her, the color in his face deepening. "We will be soon if I've the hand on the rudder! I'm a fool, Haley. Your father is a fool, drunk or sober, and I'm sorry for it."

"How can you say that? You're not a fool!"

"I am! I borrowed that money from Trumble and I thought if I got into a wonderful scheme, I could make it all back and more. I wanted to take the burden off of you to marry without affection! I wanted to provide for my family and be the valiant hero that saves the day and restores our honor."

"That's very sweet of you," she said softly, the dawning horror of where his tale was going robbing her of breath.

"Well, it's gone! Every last penny! One bungled investment after another, and everything I'd hoped to avoid has come to my doorstep sooner rather than later, my dear girl. And these aren't friends to wait for their payment! I lost the last of our reserves, and now if I'm caught in the city . . ." He started to cry into his hands. "I'm a failure! Thank heavens your mother is not here to see me like this!"

It's over. My one Season in London, my one chance at marriage, and truly, my life as I've known it. It's officially over.

Haley stood slowly, old habits dying hard. She would see to the family and do whatever needed to be done for their survival. She squared her shoulders and let the last of her dreams die. "Enough of that, Father! Let's get you upstairs and get your trunks packed. I'll ask Weathers to see to it and send immediately for a carriage to be pulled around to the servants' entrance."

She walked to the bellpull to give it two firm tugs. "We can leave more discreetly from there."

She left him and went out into the hall to intercept Mrs. Biron, who was flush with the sudden activity of the house and obviously already aware of their need for a quick departure. "Mrs. Biron, please tell the maids to pack only what we came with. Any gifts or acquisitions during the Season can be left behind and sorted out later. But all my dresses and every bolt of cloth and sundries, I want them sent separately and safely out of this house before we go. I'll write down the address where they're to be sent. And of course, please inform the staff that we are not at home for anyone who comes to call. Lock the doors and see to it, won't you?"

"Yes, Miss." Mrs. Biron nodded. "Your aunt is upstairs doing her best to direct the maids."

"I'll also help." She started up the stairs, but hesitated on the first riser. "Mrs. Biron, call for a carriage for my father at the servants' entrance and send him ahead. A small overnight case of a few traveling essentials should do for him, and I'll see to the rest of the household. But I want him out of London within the next half hour."

"Yes, Miss Moreland. I will see to it."

Haley turned back and continued calmly up the stairs, as if organizing hurried flights from their debtors were an everyday occurrence. *So much for worrying about what the servants will say! Let us just hope they're loyal enough to help us successfully escape with clothes on our backs. Thank Providence the house and lands are entailed away, but there will be no income to speak of and I'll have to begin to think of creative ways to keep us afloat or we'll starve in the comfort of our own home.*

Her heart ached at a sudden memory of Galen, standing at her back. And a longing for his strong arms around her, to make her feel shielded and safe, nearly choked her. Even after everything he'd done, she couldn't wish him ill. Losing Galen had been the cruelest blow of all, and made all the rest petty and fleeting.

I wished for the moon, and I touched it, after all. But now, I don't ever think I can bear to look up at it again.

Chapter
27

The rain fell in relentless sheets, and had turned most of the roads into treacherous and muddy courses more suited to stopping travel than anything else. Galen pulled the oilcloth of his riding coat a little tighter and ducked his head against the wind. He'd abandoned his own carriage several miles back, but had come too far to lose any more time in his quest to reach Haley.

It had been weeks since he'd been forced to leave London to head home, and Galen could only pray that he wasn't too late. Michael had sent word that Lord Moreland and his family had left London within a day of his own departure, retreating in haste due to some financial difficulties. It had caused a few tongues to wag about this unfortunate turn of events, especially since Miss Moreland had appeared to be so promising at the start of her Season. Now she was portrayed by the press with some speculation, having thrown off a perfectly good match, plunging her family into destitution. The anonymous reporter had asked if she had taken leave of her senses or was, in fact, a heartless and selfish girl to defy her father's direction.

All rubbish, but it made for good reading for the gossips, and Galen had been forced to accept that he'd managed to publicly ruin her, after all.

His horse's gait faltered, and Galen immediately dismounted to assess him. He ran gentle hands down the animal's front leg, wincing as he realized his horse was going lame. Galen shook his head and lowered the animal's hoof gently. "We're not having a good journey, Chaucer, old boy, but I'd say it's no less than I deserve." He patted his mount's neck. "You, on the other hand, are wondering why you couldn't have stayed with the carriage, aren't you my friend?"

The stallion whinnied softly, apparently agreeing.

"Well, she may not let me in the door, but we'll see about getting you some shelter." Galen rearranged the reins to let him lead his mount. "Come on, the weather won't improve with talking."

The last three miles to Moreland's estate were humbling. His boots became so caked with mud that he was forced to stop every few hundred yards to scrape them off, as the weight was extremely cumbersome. Galen did his best to keep his horse on the best footing possible, but it sacrificed his own more often than not, and he began to wonder if they'd both be lame by the time they arrived.

At last, he noticed the treelined drive off the lane that an innkeeper had described as Moreland's home, Mayfield. The grass along the drive was uncut and rough, but the fading grandeur of the lane was still apparent.

When the house came into view, Galen's pace slowed as he took it in. It was a gray hulking beast in want of more than one coat of paint, and the walled water feature in front of it had given way on one side, creating a strange underwater garden as the deluge had been allowed to simply flow off into what might at one time have been a rose garden of sorts. One end of the house had sagged, the roof and walls leaning just enough to give a man pause to consider his safety before entering the rest of the structure.

It's worse than I imagined it would be. Michael said there

*were financial troubles but . . . this—this is more than a few
passing debts.*

There were no lights that he could see through the windows and no sign of smoke from any of the chimneys to betray a hint of warmth or even occupancy. Even so, Galen tied his horse under the spare shelter of a tree and made his way to the front door.

The rusted bell rang clearly enough, and he was grateful not to resort to banging on the door like some invading ogre. While he waited for a servant, he scraped the last of the mud off of his boots and composed what he would say to convince them that their mistress was somehow expecting a social call in the middle of a rainstorm and gain him entrance to the house—and to her. His nerves were on edge, and he swallowed a knot of trepidation at just how badly this could all go.

Finally, he could hear the door being unbolted and took one last deep breath to ready himself for—

But it was Haley in the doorway, and not some servant. It was Haley in the palest blue day dress embroidered with a tiny pattern of yellow birds, like spring untouched by the gray gloom around her. Her hair was pulled back without adornment, and she had a black smudge on her cheek; and Galen was sure he had never seen anything or anyone so beautiful in his entire life.

"Oh!" she exclaimed in surprise, shock holding her very still as she realized that he was no phantom and was on her doorstep.

"May I come in?" he asked, discipline alone keeping him from stepping forward and pulling her into his arms. The joy at seeing her again was like a flame whose warmth left no room for doubt.

"I'm not . . ." He could almost hear her thoughts. The rain was so heavy that it was hard to see across the yard, and he must have made a pitiful sight with his ruined boots and dripping clothes on her steps. It was hard to send any man back into that kind of weather, even one she probably still hated.

"Please, Haley," he entreated softly.

She stepped back. "For a few minutes, then. Until the rain slows."

He didn't hesitate. Galen swept past her, grateful for any concession that meant he could finally speak to her again, face-to-face.

The inside of the house wasn't faring much better than its exterior, and Galen instantly noticed the paler square and rectangle spots on the walls where artwork must have hung until just recently. In fact, there was nothing on any wall that he could see, and not a single piece of furniture. It was only an hour or two past noon, but the darkened skies outside made the inside of the house shadowed and unwelcoming. In sconces that would have supported a dozen candles, there were only single tapers alit.

Whatever wealth Mayfield had once held, it had been stripped of it without ceremony, and he was saddened to think of a family's history and treasures collected by ham-fisted debtors with no mercy shown.

The air was cool, but at least he was out of the weather.

"Haley, I would have sent word I was coming, but I wasn't sure you'd have opened any letter of mine. So I confess, I resorted to a strategy of surprise."

"It worked. I think you're the last person I ever expected to see." She closed the door behind him, bolting it against the draft. She faced him, her expression serene and a little proud, as if there was nothing amiss. "May I take your coat and things?"

He had to nod, only because he was literally creating a puddle on the marble floor where he stood, but he hated to see her acting as a footman. "Here, let me put them somewhere for you. I'd hate to see you soaked from touching them."

"It's no trouble." She took his coat and hat, and even the sodden scarf, setting them aside to drip in the corner on a makeshift coat stand. "Why don't you come into the back drawing room? It's a little more comfortable there."

"Yes, thank you." He followed her down the hallway,

trying not to look too closely at the bared floors and damaged walls. He clenched his fingers into fists behind his back at the realization that she truly lived in this squalor and that he was partly to blame for it.

The back drawing room was a smaller room on the other side of the house and facing east; he suspected it would have been a brighter and warmer room on any other day. There was no fire in the corner grate, though it appeared she'd been in the midst of cleaning it when he'd rung the bell—and the black smudge on her face now made perfect sense. The furniture was mismatched and was obviously repaired bits and pieces salvaged from a storeroom that even the debt collectors wouldn't have bothered with. Even so, there were decorated pillows on the chairs and embroidered cloths over the back of the sofa, and he could see a woman's hand in making the best of it. As he approached the sofa he realized that one leg was missing altogether and had been replaced by a stack of books.

"Did you wish to sit down?"

Galen felt so awkward that he heard himself mumbling, "I'm afraid I'll leave a watermark."

A ghost of a smile slipped past her control. "I don't think the upholstery will be much worse for it, Mr. Hawke."

He waited until she chose a small wicker chair before taking a seat on the sofa. For a moment, it was all he could do to look at her. It was so strange, to see her like this, and so far, there'd been not a hint of emotion from her, beyond her initial surprise at seeing him. Of his own feelings, he had no questions, but suddenly, it struck him that too much time may have passed and that her heart may have already shed him completely.

No, it's not possible! Damn it, I'm not going to sit here and start nervously chatting about the rain and come to my senses only after I'm on the wrong side of that front door again!

"Haley, there's so much to tell you that I'm not sure where to begin. But I'd rather that you . . ." He took a deep breath, studying the first hints of a storm in her blue green eyes with a surge of relief. "I'd forgotten how beautiful you are, Haley."

"Had you? Is that a compliment?" Her eyes darkened with emotion. "That I'm so easily forgotten?" Her grip on the arms of her chair tightened reflexively. "I have forgotten nothing, Mr. Hawke. Was there anything else, or should I just see about fetching you a change of clothes so that you can be on your way?"

"I misspoke." He leaned back, a hunter settling back to see which way his quarry would break. *God, I love her temper!* "You have every right to hate me. And I'm not forgetting anything. Not one minute that I spent in your arms, not one kiss, not one—"

"How dare you! You speak of . . . what happened between us? As if it wasn't just part of your vile scheme? As if it meant anything to you beyond the twisted pleasure you took from . . . hurting me?" She stood, anger bringing her to her feet. "Did you come to see for yourself how far I'd fallen? Is that why you're here? To see where your attention and promises have led me and then make some moral point about a woman's sins? Does this give you pleasure? Well, I apologize for being abrupt, Mr. Hawke, but on your way to Hades, you can teach another girl the consequences of submitting to your kisses. I don't need any more lessons."

"No, I never—" He stood as well, determined to hold whatever ground he could.

"I want to know only one thing from you, Mr. Hawke." She took a step closer, some of the anger dying in her eyes, but Galen couldn't rejoice, as it was replaced by a raw pain that tore at his soul. "Why? Why did you hate me so? I had never met you before that night when I found you in the balcony. What did I ever do to deserve such . . . malice and treachery?"

All those days and weeks, he'd thought himself prepared. He'd considered every tactic, every sweet, soothing word, every gesture to try to bridge the chasm that he alone had forged between them, and now . . .

There was nothing left to do but lose her by telling the truth.

Chapter
28

"You did nothing." Galen could feel his heart pounding in his chest as the weight of his impending failure mounted. But he couldn't stop now. "I made a horrible mistake and at one point, actually believed I was doing the right thing. But that sense of righteous indignation was short-lived and I . . . I cannot describe the heaven and hell it was, to be so impossibly happy when I was with you, but to know that I had achieved your trust with the worst deception."

She stepped back, her balance unsteady, and he instantly guided her back to her chair, kneeling at her feet to complete his confession. "You're not making any sense."

"I'd almost convinced myself that it didn't matter anymore. That I would just ask you to marry me, and you need never know how falsely I'd behaved because I was going to spend the rest of my life making it up to you, Haley. But then you found the caricature . . ."

"It called me a whore, Galen. A fortune-hunting whore and I . . ." A single tear rolled down her cheek and Galen's stomach clenched in agony at the sight of it. "Why? Why would you ever think such a thing?"

"I was a fool. Hell, I probably still am! It was the worst kind of misunderstanding, and I am the worst villain to draw breath to be so determined to act so cruelly. But if you only knew—Haley, I don't think I can survive another day without asking for your forgiveness."

"Forgiveness?" she whispered, then her chin lifted defiantly, her eyes flashing. "I think you'd be amazed at what a person can survive, Mr. Hawke."

He smiled, a humorless grimace, as he realized that this was a debate he could sadly win. "No, I wouldn't. I wouldn't be amazed at all."

He stood and walked to the windows for a moment, taking in the dreary view of her rain-soaked kitchen garden and the overgrown remnants of a hedge knot pattern that had turned into an unsolvable puzzle. He finally spoke with his back to her. "I survived a fever as a child that took my younger brother. I survived India. I survived vermin and torture and hunger. I survived the Black in a dungeon that I thought would have broken my mind and rendered my soul from my body."

"Oh, Galen!"

He slowly turned back to look at her again, surrendering his pride. "I survived when others in our small group did not. And I think it was there, in India, where I started to love you a little—but only because it sounded so wonderful to think of an angel faithfully waiting for at least one of us to return safely. And when John Everly died, I didn't—and that was somehow harder than all of it combined. He was . . . so carefree. My opposite in every way. And a part of me was convinced that between us, he was the one who most deserved to make it out of there."

"John Everly?" She became very still in her seat, her face paler but very calm. "I knew him. We were friends—playmates, really." Her brow furrowed. "We'd heard word he'd died in India but . . . You were with him?"

"Your father said nothing?"

"My father?" Haley's look was pure confusion.

"I mentioned to him that I knew John when I spoke to him that night at Kendall's."

She shook her head. "He's never said a word, but . . ." Her cheeks colored. "When I recall the conversation after the party, I can understand how he might have forgotten it in the . . . heat of the moment."

"He died in my arms in India." Galen crossed back to sit down again, needing to be closer to her. "His last words were of you."

She gasped. "How is that possible? I mean . . . he was so dear, but I was hardly the love of his life."

Galen flinched as if she'd slapped him. "It seems you were." He ran a hand through his wet curls, praying that one word in ten sounded less jarring in her ears than it did in his. "John spoke of you often, and in his mind, you were perfect. Whenever he described you, it lifted our spirits, but I never realized that he'd enhanced his memories of a mere girl of thirteen. When he said he intended to marry you as soon as he returned to England, I assumed that you were, in fact, already betrothed—that you were waiting for him."

"To marry me?" She put a hand up to her lips. "I had no idea."

"I met him there, you know. We were all strangers to each other before the Troubles. Before we were each captured and brought to some sahib's hidden fortress to be held until he could decide how best to demonstrate his power, or use us to trade to the British to appease them, or . . . Hell! None of us ever really knew what the insane fiend intended. We just knew we were there to rot and suffer at his every whim and will. And after I lost track of the weeks and months, it was John who kept talking about you and England and how there was still hope."

She sighed but said nothing, simply listening now as if she knew he couldn't stop.

"He died in my arms just after we escaped, and I thought you were engaged to be married. And when I made a few inquiries, others confirmed that you were 'sweethearts' since childhood and I never thought to question it. So when I saw in the *Times* that you were already betrothed again so quickly to Trumble, I was . . . You hadn't mourned him and I hated you for appearing to have simply gone on without a single black crepe ribbon to show for it. I hated you as I have never hated another human being."

She shook her head at the horror of it, seeing now where the tale was heading.

"We'd suffered so much. And I'll never know why, but it twisted me into something else inside—something unfeeling and numb—until I saw your name in that article. I felt alive again, but only because I suddenly had a purpose: revenge." He took a slow shuddering breath. "I'd never met you when I decided I was going to teach you a lesson about love and loss. But once I had met you, it was I who seemed to keep learning things. It was I who learned about love. And now, it's I who have finally tasted my worst loss of all."

"Oh, Galen!"

"All at my own doing, Haley. Every blind step of it. And here's the final little cutting bite of irony. For all my righteous indignation about honoring the dead, here I am, barely a month after my brother Trevor's death, making the unlikeliest of proposals and giving very little thought to anything to do with convention. My father was furious, but as I'm the last surviving child he has, his heir apparent, and now Lord Winters . . . I don't think he'll hold a grudge for too long."

"I'm so sorry to hear about your brother. Michael said it must have been a family tragedy to take you away from London."

"Even a family tragedy almost didn't do it." He attempted a smile, but he couldn't manage it. "But it was Trevor, and I had to go."

"And so, all of this"—she opened her hands—"you did it for John?"

It sounded so stupid. I did all of this vengeful, petty, blind, wasteful nonsense for John Everly. And I did it for myself, so that I could sleep at night and forgive myself for not even throwing dirt on his face before walking away.

But all he managed to say was, "Yes."

"I see." Her voice sounded hollow, and Galen began to wish she were yelling at him again, for this was far worse.

"But there's still a chance, Haley!" He reached for her hands, but she pulled away and he forced himself not to press her. Instead, he pulled from his pocket a slim case, opening it so that she could see the fire and flash of the ruby and diamond necklace he'd commissioned just for her. He'd meant it as a token of his sincerity, but also as the symbol that could turn vengeance into healing. "There's still a chance for us. You know everything now, and as misguided as I've been, I can still set things right. I have a title of my own and an income, and in time, I'll be the Earl of Stamford and that should please your father. I can take care of you and your family and you'll never want for anything for the rest of your days! Every luxury, every desire, fulfilled beyond your dreams, if only you can see your way to forgiving me and allowing me to care for you as you deserve to be—"

She stood without touching the jewel-filled case, retreating to put the chair between them. "I'm not a fortune-hunting whore, Galen."

"God, no! You never were!"

She shook her head sadly. "Perhaps. I did agree to marry Herbert Trumble, and it was for his money alone. But as you can see"—she gestured to the room— "I've mended my ways."

"Haley, I—"

"And I have a plan of my own," she went on, her voice growing stronger. "Since I am no longer eligible for matrimony in light of my family's situation and my own flawed character, I'm going to save what funds I can and start a dressmaking venture. My mother left me a substantial amount of materials that I've been able to hoard, enough to fill two shops, I should think. Lady Pringley and a few other ladies in London made quite a point of admiring my designs, and I think I can manage a going concern. Of course, at first, I'll simply make what I can for the ladies of the country."

"A seamstress?" He was stunned. "But it's such a . . . grueling profession. And not necessary that you kill yourself bent over a sewing table for—"

"I'll determine what is necessary for me, Mr. Hawke. I have the right to make my own choices! You, sir"—her hands gripped the chair so tightly that her knuckles lost their color, and tears once again threatened to choke her—"you don't get to make any more choices on my behalf! You've done enough for me already!"

He couldn't look away, sure that if he bowed his head she would see it as defeat, as if he'd accepted her refusal. "Haley."

"But I have to accept responsibility, Galen, for my own part in all of this. You want to absorb all the guilt and then ask for absolution, but I'm not sure that's possible. Because I was the one who broke my engagement with Herbert, because I couldn't live a lie as easily as you could. Because once I'd kissed you in Hyde Park . . . once I knew what was possible . . . I forgot to think of anything else. I didn't see Aunt Alice's frayed sleeves, or my father's account books. I didn't pay attention to anything but you. And that was all *my* own doing. Every blind step."

"No."

"It's too easy to cast blame on the seducer, but I was . . . eager, wasn't I?" She began to shake. "I was so desperate to know passion and to feel wanted—I never stopped to question your motives or even examine my own. You were right, Galen, when you caught me at the exhibit staring at that couple. I was starving for love."

"And I fed you poison." Galen tasted the bitter truth and almost groaned.

"I . . ." She fought against her tears and stiffened her spine. "I need you to leave now. I need to think. And I can't seem to think with you standing there looking at me like that! Galen, please . . . just go."

For a moment, he considered refusing, but it was too much, the sight of her in such terrible pain and knowing that he alone was the cause. He closed the case and put it back inside his coat pocket. "For now, Haley. I'll go for now."

He bowed and left to show himself out, aware that it would take nothing short of a miracle to win her.

And he was patently out of prayers.

Chapter
29

In less than twenty minutes, the bell rang again, and Haley almost fainted. She wasn't sure she could withstand another encounter with Galen so quickly. Already her entire world felt as if it had tilted off its axis, and she was too close to the edge. From the instant she'd seen him, clothes wet and plastered to his body, his curls wet and every glorious line of his face and body beckoning for her touch, she'd been awash in lust, and too horrified at her body's betrayal to even think. And then when he'd begun to beg her forgiveness, to tell her the horrifying truth, to share the nightmares of his past—it was too much too quickly.

Weeks. Weeks of convincing myself that I am strong enough to put this behind me. If I love him, I'm lost, isn't that what I said? And now, he is here, and he has said that he'll marry me . . . but is it only to soothe his conscience? Am I to be some lifelong penance? And what happens when he tires of his guilt and just wants to forget all the tragedies of his past—and me along with them?

She reached the door, unsure of whether to scream at him

for not going as he'd promised or throw herself at him and give in to the madness that demanded he make love to her in the rain. She turned the handle and—

"Mr. B-Bascombe?" She looked past him for a moment, but there was no sign of Galen. Only the sight of Bascombe's carriage and rain-soaked driver and footman, awaiting their orders. "What a . . . surprise!"

"You never sent word," he announced, then pushed past her easily as she instinctively gave way. He started to take off his coat and hat and then held them out to her. "I would have sworn we had an understanding, Miss Moreland."

Haley took his things, her fingers numb. "Mr. Bascombe, I have no memory of any agreement between us, and frankly, none of an invitation for you to come to Mayfield."

"My goodness!" He ignored her, staring up at the high blank walls. "It's disastrous! I'd envisioned a few faded spots on your wallpaper, but this—this is unbelievable! Is that . . . is that a bucket on the floor?"

"The roof leaks." She held his things back out to him. "Thank you for stopping by, Mr. Bascombe, but my father is upstairs resting and we're not seeing—"

"Don't be stupid, Miss Moreland. I saw your father in the village making a call on friends, and he won't be returning home before there's a break in the weather." He gave her a knowing smile that sent a chill across her skin. "Not that your dear father needs any excuses to linger over his cups. And Mrs. Shaw has gone off to stay with an old friend in the Cotswolds. Word has it you've had to dismiss your servants, so that means you are alone, and I am sure that I am one caller you'll make an exception for."

"You seem sure of so many things, Mr. Bascombe, that I begin to wonder if you're correct about anything." Haley continued to hold his wet things out. "I am not a housemaid. I am the lady of this house and you should recall that on your ride home, sir. Good day."

"I'm not going anywhere. We have business, you and I. And I think you'll be grateful for this remarkable second chance that Providence has given you"—his eyes cast about the hall—"in light of your current circumstances."

She dropped his things without ceremony on the floor by the doorway, then crossed her arms defiantly. Haley had no idea what he was talking about, but she had no choice but to let him have his say since she lacked the physical strength to throw the man out into the rain. Hopefully, once he'd finished he would leave. "Very well. Let me show you to my sitting room."

Unlike Galen, Mr. Bascombe was hardly polite with his silence upon first seeing the room. Haley had done her best to make it a comfortable nest, and it wasn't as if they were receiving formal calls anymore. "Disastrous!" He eyed the chairs with suspicion and refused to take the risk of placing his weight on any of them. "You'll freeze to death come winter."

She bit the inside of her lip and simply stood still to wait for the man to say something more to his point.

"May I remind you that we are allies, you and I? I thought that you would have at least made an effort toward that small task I mentioned in regard to Mr. Hawke." He began to pace the room, openly inspecting the meager objects in his path as he went. "Especially since I, who could have filled in so many of the blanks for the social reporters who were trying to work out the story surrounding your broken engagement and sudden departure from London, held my tongue . . ."

"How very kind of you!" she said, her sarcasm impossible to mistake.

"I have been kind!" He turned quickly, his face reddening. "You were a guest in my home when you first arrived in London! I have been nothing but gracious to you and your family! And when I realized that Hawke had taken notice, I did nothing to spoil your little love affair! I would certainly call that kind, wouldn't you?"

"Kind?" Haley felt a new flash of annoyance at the man's audacity. "I don't understand why, but it's clear you were hoping that I was going to become some sort of . . . accomplice in a game involving Mr. Hawke. But as I told you in London, I am no spy, and whatever your interest in Mr. Hawke, I would suggest you make your inquiries directly to him."

Rand shook his head. "You have no idea what is at stake, Miss Moreland!"

"And I have no idea what you expect me to do for you. I no longer enjoy Mr. Hawke's confidences, sir." *And even if I did, I certainly won't change my mind about sharing them with the likes of you, Rand Bascombe!*

"And that is where Providence has intervened!" He took a quick step forward, and Haley flinched at the strange light in his eyes. "I have it on good authority that Mr. Hawke is on his way here to see you! What do you say to that?"

It was easy to feign surprise. The entire conversation had been so strange, she wasn't sure what to say. But every instinct insisted that she keep Galen's visit to herself, for his safety and perhaps for hers, too. "W-why would he come here?"

His eyes raked over her figure, openly enjoying her feminine charm. "He's missing your company, I'd say. And ready to make another proposition, this time, no doubt, to set you up as his mistress. I'm betting good odds he'll offer you a house and carriage."

"Why are *you* here, Mr. Bascombe?"

"To give you a more honorable option, my dear! Once again, I am offering to clear your father's debts if you'll but find out where Mr. Hawke was held in India—the name of the sahib, the names of his friends, and any details that will aid my associates in their search would be greatly appreciated as well." He started to move toward her again, and she took a careful step backward as he went on. "It's so simple, Miss Moreland. You tell me what I want to know, and all your worries are past."

"What associates are these? And why would you pay just to know those things?" she asked.

"You're so innocent, Miss Moreland. And the less you know of this business the better. But suffice it to say, Hawke and the others of the Jaded stole a few things from their captors on their way out, and my friends are very interested in gaining a share of that wealth."

"The Jaded?" Haley was completely mystified. "Is this . . . is this about . . . money?"

"It's about treasure!" He clapped his hands, like a greedy child at Christmas. "Now, will you aid us? After all, Hawke is no friend of yours, and I'm offering you every advantage for an easy enough task. And how is this? If you do as I bid, I'll even see about quelling a few gossiping tongues and even make a few introductions when I have the opportunity. You can come back to London for another Season next year, and I will sponsor you!"

She was almost speechless at his outrageous offer. "I . . ."

His eyes narrowed. "And don't worry, Miss Moreland. Your reputation can still be restored so long as no one else knows how you played the slut with Mr. Hawke." He took a seat on the sofa where Galen had been, and she panicked as she realized what the wet cushions might signify.

"Get out! You insinuate too much, Mr. Bascombe, and you know nothing of me!"

"I know enough." His expression grew vaguely irritated as his hand touched the damp fabric. "But I am fast out of time to receive your answer! Since you and Galen both left Town, it looks highly suspicious, and I am being called to account for you both! You'll help me bring Hawke to heel, Miss Moreland. You'll do this because it will benefit you and your family, or I'll forego every promise and you can work off your father's debt in a char house."

"How dare you threaten me in my own home to try to pressure me into somehow acting against Lord Winters! Well, I won't have it! If you want to go on a treasure hunt, then by all means, go!" Haley stood back and gestured at the door. "I don't care what you say about me to the London vultures—"

Bascombe stood and closed the distance so much faster than she would have thought possible, his grip on her arm bruising and merciless. "Get a lot of news from London and the outside world, do you?"

"W-what? Let go of me!" She tried to pull away, but his fingers only tightened and she whimpered involuntarily at the searing pain that held her captive.

"Lord Winters?" His eyes grew cold, and she realized her mistake. "He's been here already. You're dry as a bone and I'm over there sitting in a puddle like a fool! You've been sputtering little white lies to me the entire time."

"You're hurting me, Mr. Bascombe." Haley did her best to stay calm, aware as never before how isolated she was in a house without servants, with her father away, and no one to intervene.

"Damn it!" Bascombe's fury was palpable. "All I wanted was for you to ask the man a few questions and get me those answers! Is that really such an unreasonable thing in exchange for all the favor I've shown you? I have people who are growing very impatient, Miss Moreland, and I can't ask them to wait any longer, do you hear me?"

"Please, let go of my arm and we'll discuss—"

"The time for discussion has passed." His other hand whipped forward and caught her throat in the grip of a warm vise. "I think Hawke still has feelings for you. So I would think in exchange for your life, he may just give me what I want."

She began to fight in earnest, but her hands couldn't find any leverage on his arms and the panic and agony of his fingers against her windpipe made it even more difficult to think clearly. "No! Please!"

"You'll come with me to London, as calm and pretty as you please, and we'll just leave Mr. Hawke a little note, shall we? And you can tell your lover that if he doesn't cooperate, why then I'll see you killed at my leisure."

She kicked out but only tangled into a chair to send it crashing into the corner with the stove. Bascombe's fingers tightened in anger, and Haley was sure she didn't have much longer before he'd just be able to carry her from the house in a faint. The last vestige of civility evaporated and her fingers curved into claws as she struck out wildly at Rand's eyes and face.

Haley had a fleeting sensation of triumph as her fingernails made contact and she heard his hiss of pain, but then she was on the floor and he was on top of her, and the world was fading into a gray mist.

"I'll have my place in the inner circle of the East India Company, Miss Moreland, and I'll be one of the richest men in England! But you . . ." He lessened his hold just enough to let her come back to her senses. "You have no idea how much farther you're going to fall to pay for this little display of temper."

"He . . . won't . . . tell you . . . anything." Every word burned her throat, but fear for Galen overrode everything. "Please . . ."

"You'll wish you'd died, Miss Moreland." He hauled himself up, releasing her throat, only to clench his fingers into her hair to begin dragging her from the room. "I don't think your father will bother looking for you when you send a note advising him that you've run off to London to suck cocks for a living."

"You write one word of lies to my father, and I'll—"

Rand's hand twisted against her scalp and Haley's threat was cut off with a yelp. She screamed as she was forced to reach up to hold his wrists to prevent him from scalping her, but she did her best to kick out to slow his progress, her mind scrambling for a way to avoid being thrown into his carriage and lost forever. Even so, she was relentlessly being taken from the only home she'd ever known, and step by cruel step, Haley began to cry out in despair and horror at what might lie ahead.

Chapter
30

○

"Rand! You bastard!" Galen roared as he came through the front door. "Let go of her, you son of a bitch!"

Bascombe complied, letting go of her hair more out of shock than a probable spirit of compliance. She fell backward against the bucket on the floor, sprawling on the marble but safe for the moment. Galen wasted no time, his momentum and fury too great to allow Rand to rethink her release or use her as a shield. Like a tiger, he launched himself at the older man, who was spared slightly as the slick marble floor robbed Galen of the traction he needed to use every ounce of force at his command.

The men flew to the hard stone floor in a tangle of limbs, and Bascombe grunted at the impact, instinctively lifting his forearm to strike Galen across the jaw, and the true struggle began. Bascombe was older, and much stronger than he appeared, but Galen had the advantage of height and power.

Bascombe pulled his arm back again, to try to hold Galen at a distance or push him away, but Galen shifted back only far enough to give himself room to strike back as hard as he

could with his free hand. Bascombe kicked his legs and offset
the blow, groaning at the pain all the same as Galen's fist connected with his cheek. Galen's hold on Bascombe was like
iron, and he pulled back to hit him again only to lose his balance as Bascombe pushed directly against the floor instead of
his opponent for leverage.

Galen rolled easily, spinning back with a snarl to prepare
to launch himself at Rand again. But this time, he hesitated
and his fists were stilled in front of him.

For Rand now held a small pistol in his hand, and his eyes
were full of murderous loathing as he stared at Galen. The
only sounds in the bare hall were the ragged breaths of both
men.

"You're no hero, Hawke! You're an opportunistic thief, I
think, and a selfish bastard!"

"Really?" Galen asked calmly, determined to keep Rand's
attention focused entirely on him. "How is that?"

"You and your friends . . . what harm in sharing your good
fortune, eh? What harm in letting a few others in on your secrets? Many would have said it was a patriotic duty to crown
and country to spread that wealth. But nothing I've tried has
yielded any success—not even trying to bribe your dear Miss
Moreland. Stupid slut!" Rand lifted the gun, leveling it directly at Galen's chest. "And so here we are. But let's be civilized, shall we?"

"By all means."

"Tell me where the treasure is located and we'll call it
even, Lord Winters."

"Even? I give you the map to unimaginable wealth, and . . .
what do I get again?" he asked, deliberately not looking toward Haley, silently praying she'd quietly make an escape
while she could.

"I'll spare your life!"

"I'm naturally grateful for that, but then again, what assurances do I have that you'll keep your word after I've told you
everything you want to know?"

"None." Bascombe's look was pure venom as he smiled in triumph. "But you'll do it all the same if you want to live."

Galen made a show of considering his situation. "Hmmm. Sleepless nights, assassins at my doorstep, short-sighted treasure hunters waving pistols in my face, and . . . oh, yes, the nebulous threat of death to everyone I hold dear by relying on the honor of an openly unstable and stupid man." He made a subtle shift of his weight onto the balls of his feet. "It doesn't sound like much of a choice, Bascombe."

Bascombe hissed in displeasure and decided on another strategy. "Well, then, to hell with your life! What about hers?" He moved the gun away from Galen to aim it toward Haley—but Galen had been waiting for just such a moment and charged him once again, this time to reach with both hands to strike down Bascombe's arm and break it if he could.

"Get off!" Bascombe growled as they locked grips in a macabre dance trying to gain control of the gun and each other.

Galen rewarded him with a wicked grin. "Ah! There's that stupidity I'm coming to enjoy!"

Bascombe's rage was explosive and gave him a burst of strength, but Galen cared for nothing but the gun and keeping his opponent's emotions churned and distracted away from Haley. Blood from scratches on Rand's face gave him a demonic look, and Galen almost laughed at the strange twist of fate that would pit him against such a creature after so many nightmares—for this battle felt all too familiar—win or lose.

Bascombe must have seen the possessed look in Galen's face, for his grip on the gun tightened in desperation. Galen tried to keep his feet underneath him, but the slick floor and his soggy state were still working against him, and the barrel of the pistol was coming dangerously close to centering on the center of his chest. The peril was very real, and Bascombe's grimace turned into a smile as he realized how close he was to victory.

Galen growled and considered in a flash if he should just

let gravity do its worst and pray that the jolt of his body on Bascombe's when they hit the floor would yield him the gun without it firing by accident.

Damn it! I'm failing her! And this time it's final and fatal . . .

The sound of the bucket striking the back of Bascombe's skull was like a hollow barrel being dropped onto a stone. Rand Bascombe instantly crumbled at Galen's feet, and Galen looked up in stunned silence at the sight of Haley struggling to keep her balance as the bucket's momentum continued, nearly pulling her around.

"I've . . . killed him." She looked at Bascombe's prostrate form, her eyes wide with horror.

Galen climbed over the man to gain his feet, gently reaching for her and slowly unclasping her ice-cold fingers from the bucket's rope handle. "No, no, you didn't kill anyone, even if he deserved it for laying a single finger on you. But he'll have a headache on the morrow, and he may yet swing from the gallows, but that's for another day."

"Y-you're sure?"

He knelt down and checked the man's throat for a pulse, swallowing hard at the disappointment when he detected one. *Damn. But at least she's spared it.*

He stood, wishing he'd more of Rowan's compassion. "I've seen enough dead men to know the difference. But you most definitely saved my life." He set the bucket aside and anxiously ran his hands across her shoulders and cupped her face to assure himself that she was in fact, unharmed. He repeated the words and watched the shock fade from her expression. "You saved my life, Haley."

"You came back." She was looking at him as if he were an apparition.

"I . . . had to." Galen swallowed hard and spoke only the simplest truth. "My horse became too lame to make it to the village, so I had to double back. Then when Rand's carriage passed me on the lane, I had a strange feeling that something wasn't right."

"You saw him?"

"I recognized his carriage, and from the pace his coachman was setting, they certainly didn't slow to take notice of me. Then I overheard your screams . . ."

"Oh, my!" Her knees started to buckle, and he caught her easily to carry her back to the only room he was aware of that could offer her a soft place to recover. Settling her onto the sofa, he tried not to convey any sense of hurry, although he was eager to get back to Rand to finish the matter at hand.

"It's a good thing you never faint."

"You're an ogre to tease at such a moment, Galen."

He nodded. "It's the least of my sins, Haley. Stay here."

He left and quickly made his way back to a still unconscious Rand Bascombe. The temptation to kick him didn't pass, but Galen managed to ignore it all the same and refrain from murdering the man—barely. If he let himself remember Haley's cries or the way Rand had dared to touch and threaten her—a dark part of him beckoned with rational arguments about their future safety and the expedience of vermin removal in the grand scheme of things. But instead he went to the front door and called out to the waiting footmen. "Come for your man!"

"Yes, your lordship?" They came forward, clearly unaware of the situation.

"Your master is there!" Galen stepped back to give them a good view before he hauled Bascombe up with an ignoble grip on the back of his coat and pants and heaved the man out the front door to land facedown in the mud. "Take him back to London with the regards of the Jaded."

They complied with sheepish astonishment, managing to lift their filthy employer from the muck with efficiency, if not dignity, as his coat and feet dragged through the mud before they could leverage him into the carriage. Galen stood on the steps and watched the carriage pull away for Bascombe's uncomfortable journey home.

Serves the bastard right. I'd have killed him if I could,

but that may have to wait for another day. . . . I'll have to get word to the others that . . .

And the worst of it struck him.

Everything that Michael had said about being cautious and taking these threats seriously—he'd ignored almost all of it and mindlessly brought the worst kind of danger to her doorstep. He'd thought only of how much he loved her, how much he desperately wanted to make amends. He'd offered to marry her as if matrimony would insulate her in some way from the worst of the world.

Even that night when that man attacked us with a knife outside the brownstone—I never stopped to think past my own feelings. Like an idiot, I was blinded by the revelation that I truly loved her; so blind I never asked if it was right or wrong to pull her irrevocably into this.

Into the Black . . .

"Galen?" She stood in the arch of the doorway, her expression anxious. "You're never going to dry if you don't come out of the rain."

"Haley . . ." Despair washed through him at the sight of her, and he suspected that there wasn't an ounce of misery he could ever complain of that he hadn't earned. "I don't think anyone has ever . . ." He took a deep breath, then looked back up at her, forcing himself to drink in every detail. Her hair had come down, and she was so beautiful that it was painful to look into her eyes. "I'm so sorry."

"Galen, you—"

"I never should have come here." His spine stiffened, and he could have sworn that he could feel his heart turning to stone with each agony-evoking word. But this time, he was determined to put her happiness and well-being above his own. *I'm a selfish villain! I could have paid her father's debts from an anonymous distance and guaranteed her whatever life she desired without plopping myself on her doorstep and leading Bascombe to her.* "None of . . . Bascombe threatened you because of me, and I'll see to it. You'll have nothing to fear from him or any of his kind, ever again."

Her hand reached up against the doorframe, as if to steady herself. "You couldn't have known what Bascombe intended!" She held out her hand. "Come out of the rain, Galen."

He shook his head. "I'll send your father back from the village and make sure that you're not alone. You won't be troubled with any more of my petitions, Haley."

"W-what are you saying?" She took a step forward, her eyes darkening.

"It is hard to imagine loving a woman more, or thinking that anyone has ever felt this way . . . but I'll not see you cursed with me. I'm a fool not to have realized it before. But I'd rather die than see you harmed. Good-bye, Haley."

He turned and began to walk down the muddy driveway, determined not to look back at her, not to torture himself any longer. He would go back and wear black and have every excuse for sulking and grieving for as long as it took to—

"Galen!" She ran down the steps into the rain and pulled him around to face her.

"Go back, damn it! You'll catch your death!"

She was already drenched, but she put her hands on her hips defiantly, refusing to give ground. "I'm not made of glass, Mr. Hawke, and I don't see you rushing out of the weather to prevent your own death, so I'm not going anywhere until you stop this!" She stamped her foot in frustration, and Galen winced as the mud sloshed up onto her dress, effectively ruining it, but augmenting how human she looked, how vulnerable, and even now . . . alluring.

"I am stopping, Haley. I'm stopping all of it! I'm leaving you in peace!"

"In peace?" She grabbed the lapels of his overcoat, a flash of temper in her eyes making his breath catch in his throat in surprise. "If you loved me as you said, then how can I know any peace without you, Galen? If you truly meant it, then how can you even think of leaving me?"

"You heard Bascombe! You won't be safe with me, Haley. It doesn't even matter if there is a treasure or not! So long as the rumors exist about the Jaded, they'll keep trying to take it or uncover what secrets they can, and I don't know if I can keep you from harm."

Thunder rolled ominously, and Haley's grip tightened on his coat. "You wouldn't know that if you were a sheepherder, Galen. No one can know that they are safe—no man can promise it. So, you're saying all of this because you don't love me and you don't want to marry me, is that right?"

"No! I want you more than air! I'm . . . I'm a flawed man, Haley. I came here to secure my own happiness and never considered that it might cost you your life! How does that redeem me? How in the name of heaven can I ever excuse that?"

"You're human! Forgive yourself for being human, Galen!"

"After all that I've done to you, for all the wrong reasons, how could *you* ever forgive me?"

"Is that truly what you need, Galen? *My* forgiveness?"

He started to answer her but then held very still. Every noble impulse to set her aside for her own good dissipated and he was left with an icy sense of panic, like a man standing on the edge of a cliff. *God, yes, woman . . . pull me back! Help me find my way onto solid ground and see my way out of this tangle!*

"Haley . . ."

Her eyes filled with tears. "I forgive you, Galen. I forgive you for . . . John. I forgive you for leaving him there—and for leaving too much of yourself there, too. I forgive you for everything you've done to punish us both for living in a world that didn't really stop to notice any of it. I forgive you for breaking my heart into a thousand pieces . . . because I . . ." She released his coat, a rain-soaked Aphrodite freeing him to fly. "If hate blinds, then what of love? For I swear, I cannot see anything but you, Galen."

"Then keep me, Haley."

"Not unless you make me one promise." Tears flowed freely, undisguised by the rain, but her voice was steady.

"Name it."

"No more hiding."

And he knew exactly what she was asking, and every corner of his heart filled with light and heat. His beautiful Haley wasn't afraid of the Black. She would be with him from this moment on, and there wasn't a demon on any plane of existence that they couldn't vanquish together.

"Never, my love. Never again." He kissed her, as if with every touch and taste he reclaimed his soul, as if he would never let her go. She melted against him, and he couldn't surmise where he ended and she began, and Galen savored the sweet serenity of the world at last falling away. He pulled his lips from hers, only to whisper in her ear, "I'm going to tell you that I love you each day and every day that I have left until you command me to stop."

She smiled through her tears, joy fueling a playful light in her eyes. "You have never listened to a single command I've given you before, Mr. Hawke."

"I've obeyed every word!" He drew her back into his arms, a wicked grin on his face. "Of course, you'll have the rest of your life to test my husbandly compliance, Miss Moreland."

She gave him a look of equal mischief, and he could feel the seductive burn of it uncoil within him. "I'm going to look forward to that."

"You've saved my life, Haley." He kissed her again, restraint falling away as she mirrored his desire, and the weeks of separation and denial fueled a searing heat between them that gave no quarter. Every longing he'd been forced to ignore sprang into life and demanded her surrender. Galen's kiss claimed every soft, sweet corner of her mouth, experiencing every exquisite texture, and drawing from her all that he needed as the fire in his blood began to dismiss logic.

Her knees buckled and he held her weight, cupping her delectable bottom through the wet layers of her clothes, pressing her up against him, even as his own knees bent so that they were both kneeling in the mud and the rain, intertwined in an embrace that allowed for nothing between them. Haley's hand slid up inside his coat and across the wet silk of his shirt, and Galen growled in frustration. He dropped his arm to ready himself to tip her back and carry her inside the house where he could finally have his wicked way with her, when the sound of a carriage abruptly changed his plans.

Lord Moreland's mouth was open in shock as his light rig began to slow. "What the hell are you doing to my daughter?"

Galen helped Haley to her feet, suddenly aware of their muddy state and exactly what he'd been about to "do" to Lord Moreland's daughter. Galen braced for the man's justifiable reaction.

"Mr. Hawke!" Lord Moreland pulled hard on the reins, leaping from the carriage before it had genuinely come to a halt. "Unhand my daughter, you cad!"

"Father, please!" Haley tried to step between them. "He wasn't—"

"He was!" Her father stopped, his face red, although his expression was wavering from angry to simply perplexed. "Is this not the man you insisted I not so much as mention? I swear, Alice threatened to nail my doors shut if I interfered and he is . . . *kissing you! On the ground!* Without even the gentlemanly accord of a damn umbrella!"

Galen did his best not to smile and stepped out to prevent Haley from acting as a shield. He wasn't about to let his future father-in-law mistake him for a coward. "She is extremely stubborn, your lordship, as you may have warned me. I did attempt to send her back inside, but . . . well, as you can see, we may have forgotten the weather momentarily."

"Galen!" Haley elbowed him in the ribs.

"You've forgotten more than the weather, young man!" Lord Moreland crossed his arms. "This is absolutely unacceptable and—"

"I've asked your daughter to marry me, and as you noticed, she has agreed."

"M-marry?" He looked at them both for signs of madness—beyond their refusal to acknowledge that it was raining. "She accepted?"

Galen nodded. "In *spite* of my wealth and title, she has."

"Father"—she put her hand on his arm—"I am in love with Galen Hawke. I will have him, and no other."

Galen was sure that if a man could die of happiness, it would have occurred at that instant, hearing her proclaim her feelings to her father, so unashamedly and so sweetly.

"Th-then you should marry him." Her father kissed her forehead. "And let the rest of the world find its own way, dearest child."

Lord Moreland released her back to Galen's hands, shaking his head. "Speediest courtship I've ever seen!"

Galen swept her up, circling with her in his arms, until she threw her head back and began to laugh, and with each melodic peal of merriment, the last shadows vanished and Galen knew he'd finally made his way back home.

Epilogue

$\bullet$

Glasses raised high in Rowan's restored library, in unison the men hailed their friend's great fortune and unpredictable success in falling into nuptial bliss and his safe return from his honeymoon. "To Galen! To the new Lady Winters!"

Galen kept his arms crossed, enjoying their warm wishes and doing his best not to capitulate to the worst of their well-meant jibes.

"Thank heavens Josiah refused to take that bet on who would be the first among us to suffer a wife!" Ashe intoned, taking another drink. "I'd be bankrupt!"

Josiah rolled his eyes, but Rowan couldn't help himself. "And who did you say would be the first to fall?"

"Who else?" Ashe gave him a wry grin. "You! All those soulful good looks and romantic notions of yours—I don't believe you'll survive the summer!"

Darius nodded consolingly. "You seemed the likeliest candidate."

"Then he is sure to be the last!" Galen predicted confidently. "Which puts *you*, Ashe, directly into the fire!"

Ashe's look of horror was priceless, and the men savored the levity of the moment, imagining in varying degrees of failure their poor friend Ashe in the throes of love.

"I'll never marry!" Ashe vowed, lifting his glass to solemnify his claim.

Darius clapped him on the back. "And the Fates prepare to claim another victim! When you defy the gods, Blackwell, you invite them to prove you wrong—and they invariably do."

"I'm not defying the gods," Ashe clarified, returning to his chair, "I'm reminding them about a leopard's spots!" He downed the last of his drink and recovered his humor. "And if that doesn't work, I'll just redirect their attentions to poor Josiah slinking about over there."

"To me? I'm not fool enough to distract the Fates when they're busy teaching a man a well-earned lesson." Josiah leaned against a bookcase and studied a small statuette of Aphrodite. "Nor fool enough to try to guess what the future holds for any of us."

"Wise man," Michael noted quietly, stretching out his long legs by the fire. "Not to leave a happy subject, but we'd all be wiser to pay more attention to the world around us. The Jaded are spoken of more than I like."

"Some new novelty will come along soon and we'll be forgotten," Rowan said.

Michael shook his head firmly. "Not as long as men seek out secrets and lust for lost treasure. I hate to say it, for each of us has benefitted in our own ways, but I sometimes wish we'd never picked up a single stone out of that godforsaken hole."

"I'm not regretting a single stone!" Ashe stood quickly and crossed to refill his glass. "I regret that we didn't bother to steal a cart while we were at it . . . then we could have bought an empire of our own and not had to worry about poor Rowan's collection of African gewgaws getting rifled through!"

Rowan bowed his head, trying not to laugh. "That's very sweet of you, Ashe."

"No more talk of what we should have done. The issue at hand, gentlemen, is what do we do now?" Michael asked.

"We could simply be a bit more open about what happened. We've committed no criminal acts, and the talk may not last at all once the details were public."

It was Darius who shook his head. "Myth has a power all its own. No matter what we said, it would never slake the curiosity of those determined to believe differently. They would see it as a smoke screen to hide the truth, and the danger wouldn't lessen. But you'd have the public on your doorstep, and that . . ."

"Is unacceptable," Michael finished.

"Our first instinct was to keep ourselves to ourselves." Josiah took a sip of his brandy before he went on thoughtfully. "And I'm not proposing a drastic change to that strategy. But a variation may make all the difference in the world."

"And what variation is that?" Rowan asked.

"What if we fed just the rumors that worked best to our advantage? The Jaded aren't a secret anymore, thanks to that article and talk amidst the peerage, but what if we supplied a different answer to the nature of the Jaded? What if we quietly and carefully confessed that it were true that the Jaded are a secret club for gentlemen? A whisper about our notoriety and penchant for privacy and we'd blend in with every other informal society in this city—and then if it comes up, we can just laugh at any suggestion that there's more to our association and friendship than any other club."

Ashe smiled. "The Jaded does sound wicked. Perhaps a hint or two about all the women we secretly seduce for sport at our meetings?"

"No!" Galen straightened in his chair, his voice the loudest but not the only one as Rowan, Darius, and Michael also echoed his disapproval. "My bride has enough to concern herself with! And I'll forego the company if you insist on painting us as another hedonistic version of the Hellfire Club."

The men laughed, but it was Darius who finally spoke. "Let it be the truth, then, to ensure that we have Galen's continued friendship—if not his membership. If asked, the Jaded have no interest in the treacherous company of women beyond their temporary uses—a brutal assessment, but it will ward off more questions and keep more than one scheming mother off of Ashe's doorstep."

The lighthearted atmosphere evaporated as each man considered the grain of truth in Darius's proposal. All the names they'd whispered in the dark for comfort had proven to be ghosts unable to withstand the harsh light of day, and not a single faithful, feminine welcome had awaited them. Not one of them had returned to England without a harsh lesson in betrayal or loss—and none of them had been eager to risk another taste of heartbreak afterward.

"It sounds like an unsocial social club," Michael noted, but he nodded approval. "And that may be just what we need."

Josiah stood and raised his glass, his saturnine expression unreadable. "To the Weary and the Wicked, the Wanton and the Wandering—to the Unwanted! Gentlemen, a toast to the Jaded!"

"To the Weary and the Wicked, the Wanton and the Wandering—to the Unwanted!"

Their glasses touched again, and this time, it had the ring of a sacred oath, and the men knew that for all their bravado, the necessity of a haven for their small number was fundamental to their survival, and now that haven was something tangible—something named and defined—and each man knew without speaking the words aloud that they would willingly die to protect it. "To the Jaded!"

Turn the page for a sneak peek at
Renee Bernard's next historical romance

Seduction Wears Sapphires

Coming August 2010 from Berkley Sensation!

The quiet of the country ate at his nerves, and Ashe Blackwell had to force himself not to pace. Bellewood, his family's home, was less than a day's ride from Town, but it felt to Ashe like it sat on the farthest edges of civilization. His grandfather's library had always been his least favorite room as a child, with its gloomy colors and dusty shelves. It was here he'd been brought if there was a punishment to be determined or a stern reprimand was to be given. Gordon Walker Blackwell was not a man Ashe had ever wanted to face after he'd been caught at one childhood misadventure or another.

Damn! How is it a man can live for more than three decades and then suddenly feel like an eight-year-old in short pants? Hell, it's not like I've recently been around to break vases or get caught snogging the—

"Is that the style in London these days or did you not change your clothes after arriving?" His grandfather's voice was edged in familiar icy authority, but the years had robbed the older gentleman of the power of volume, and Ashe winced to hear it. It saddened him to see the dear monster losing his teeth. "Your coat is rumpled, Ashe, like a man who takes no care of himself."

Ashe managed a half bow and tamped down on his habitual sarcasm out of an old love for the codger. "I only just arrived, and meant to change after a muddy ride, but your butler brought me here and indicated that your business could not wait."

"Nor can it! I've no time to waste as you seem to have."

"I make the most of every day, Grandfather," Ashe countered gently.

"How dare you, sir! You make the most of your nights and I suspect you haven't seen much of a morning ever since you returned to England! You are a disgrace, Ashe. I hear report after report of your carousing in London and I marvel that you can stand before me without hanging your head in shame."

Ashe's spine stiffened; he was not enjoying the lecture. "I'm flattered that you would follow my pursuits so closely. But the gossips may exaggerate my—"

"Do they?" His grandfather stepped closer, cutting him off. "Is it all wrong? Am I misinformed? Are you a moral example of what a gentleman should be, my boy?"

Ashe hesitated at the strange new tone in the older man's voice. *Was that desperation?* But a lie wasn't possible. "No, Grandfather, you are not misinformed."

Silence strung out between them, and Ashe's chest ached at the stirring look of raw disappointment in the old man's eyes.

"Which brings me to the reason that I summoned you out of Town."

Here it comes. Lecture finished and now we'll get to whatever is troubling him.

"I'm dying."

Shock froze Ashe in place at the unvarnished announcement. His grandfather was older, yes, and looking a little slight, but on the verge of passing? Finally, he managed to reply, "Is this Dr. McAllister's opinion as well? Are you . . . ill?"

An impatient gesture cut off the awkward sympathetic line of Ashe's questions. "I hate doctors and of course I'm not ill! Don't be daft! Do I look desperately ill to you?"

"You just said you were dying. I'd say that was a logical inquiry."

"We are all mortal, and don't give me that knowing look. I'm sharper than men a fraction of my age and I've not gone soft in the skull."

"A relief to hear." Ashe struggled not to smile.

"Mind that wit of yours!" He straightened his shoulders, and Ashe caught a glimpse of the formidable younger man again. "I'm closer to the end of life than I care to contemplate! And who do I have before me to carry out even the saddest parody of a legacy?"

Damn. The lecture hadn't even gotten started.

Ashe's smile faded. "No one could match your legacy, sir."

"You could at least try!" The old man turned away, moving to the great marble fireplace over which his own great-grandfather's portrait looked down on them both. "When I lost your father—when your parents were killed, I took you on and never thought that all the promise and potential you held would be squandered before my eyes."

"I'm not an opium addict, Grandfather, and I'm certainly not squandering—"

"You had your moments of mischief before, but I was never alarmed. But ever since your return from India . . . I'm not even begging you to marry. Although, God knows, it's not a ridiculous thing to ask you to make a good match and provide us all with a healthy heir or two." A sigh rattled through his slender frame, and he leaned against the carved Italian marble mantel. "Give me some hint that you're not completely lost, my boy."

"I am not lost."

His grandfather turned back, the same odd, intense light in his eyes that had made Ashe wary at the start of their conversation. "You are so far into the dark woods, I don't think you remember who you are. It's whatever that India business was, but it's no matter. I have the solution, Ashe."

"Do you?"

"I could threaten to cut you off, naturally. I could tell my solicitors that your name is to be struck from the will. I could do it, Ashe."

"It's your right to do so. And since I've disappointed you, not even I would dare argue against that decision, Grandfather." Ashe spoke as honestly as he could. "I would rather forfeit ten fortunes than earn your disdain. And I'm sorry for it."

"Ah, hell!" His grandfather drew closer. "Enough! I know that even if I removed every farthing from the will, it wouldn't leave you destitute, since you clearly made some sort of fortune on your misadventures—but there is more to an inheritance than money, my boy."

"True."

"So"—he circled Ashe, as if assessing a new racehorse—"I understand you are a gambling man."

Ashe nodded slowly. "I've been known to take a risk or two."

"Then hear my proposal." His grandfather gestured toward two waiting chairs by a small side table, and the men settled in. "I want some reassurance that if you truly wanted to, you could rein yourself in. My fear is that you're beyond the call of discipline, my boy, and while I love you beyond measure, I will not leave our family's fortunes, land, and holdings in the hands of a jackass who can't keep his pants buttoned."

Ashe leaned back in his chair. "Some reassurance? Are you asking me to reform in a religious flash of fervor? Join a monastery? Or did you just want some kind of vow that I could, as you put it, rein myself in, if and when I wished to?"

A blank look answered his questions. "I'll take a simple demonstration."

"What kind of demonstration?"

"A single social Season in which you don't cause a solitary scandalous ripple in the wide and murky pond that is London." The older man leaned forward. "It's not much, Ashe, in the greater scheme of things, but I'd be hard-pressed to think you'd admit that you don't have the spine to behave for the briefest span of a few months. Or have you grown so weak that you're sitting over there wondering how you might possibly survive such an ordeal?"

"Not at all. I was wondering why you'd set the bar so low."

"Oh, it may not be as easy as it looks. After all, with a reputation like yours, a single unremarkable Season may not truly be possible. And I'm not going to allow you to hide in the country and wait it out, either. You'll be in Town with all your demons. But"—he sat back, shifting as if to feign indifference—"if you managed it, then all threats of cutting you out would forever be gone. I'll face my final years knowing that when the crisis comes, you still have the potential to live up to your lineage."

"And if I fail?" Ashe asked, aware that no dare was without consequences.

"Not only will I cut you out, but I will hand all things over to your second cousin, Mr. Yardley, who, by the way, has been less than subtle in expressing his desires to improve the house and make a better show of it."

Yardley? Winston Yardley is a sniveling excuse for a human! He'd met the man a scant three times and, even so, the memory of the ferret-faced man made his skin crawl. Of all the people to stand in the wings, Yardley was the last person on earth that Ashe wanted to see benefiting from a great man's passing. "Like hell he would!"

His grandfather's smile held no hint of mirth. "But that's not the last of it. For you see, Ashe, I would then see your name published with infamy and make it publicly known on both sides of the Atlantic that you are a scoundrel and irredeemable in your family's eyes."

My God, he's serious.

He went on before Ashe could respond. "I'll take an article out in every paper of note on this globe warning every woman of quality to shun you and every man of name to reconsider his friendships." The threat was quiet, but Ashe didn't think a gunshot would have resounded any harder.

"So, let me understand your meaning. I take this challenge, or . . ."

"Or the worst unfolds, just as I've described it."

Ashe hated feeling cornered, but it was difficult to think of a soothing argument that would divert his grandfather now. Once the old man was set on an idea, he was notoriously stubborn.

But this? What trap is this?

"One Season of impeccable behavior and all is forgiven?" Ashe asked. *I'm missing a step here, but if it means keeping Yardley's clammy hands off my grandfather's silverware . . .* "And it didn't occur to you to just ask without all this posturing?"

"I'm fairly certain I've already attempted simple requests—to no avail, Ashe." He shook his head. "I can't face seeing you drag our name through the mud, and while you may think your activities have gone unnoticed, I can assure you, they have not."

Ashe clenched his jaw, feeling defensive and impatient. "Have no fear, Grandfather. I'll be the consummate gentleman."

"You've agreed then?"

"Yes, but not because of the inheritance."

"No, of course not, but I am pleased to know that some small part of you cares enough about your reputation and the future of our family to give me the demonstration I need." His grandfather stood, and Ashe reflexively did the same. "Take my hand, Ashe, and swear to me that this Season, you won't so much as twitch off the respectable path of invitations and activities I've laid out for you. No gambling and no whores, my boy, or I'll prove that one of us, at least, is a man of his word, and I'll make good on my threats."

Invitations and activities he's laid out for me? I think a part of me is twitching already, but there's no out now.

"I swear it." Even as he spoke and shook his grandfather's cool, dry hand, Ashe felt the weight of his words for the first time. He was vowing to genuinely behave for a Season, which would have been challenging enough, but this Season had promised to be particularly wild and exciting—and the temptations that abounded in London would be hard to resist. *Well, at least Josiah and the others will get a chuckle out of this ironic twist of Fate.*

"Good." The elder Blackwell moved over to a sideboard to pour himself a small measure of port. "Oh, I forgot one small caveat."

Ah! Here's that missing piece. "And what was that?"

"You'll understand if I cannot simply take your word for this good behavior. Not that I don't trust you"—he lifted his glass in a token salute—"but I don't trust you, Ashe."

"Will you be accompanying me for the Season, then?" Ashe asked, praying the answer would be "no."

"Hardly! I'm too old for Town and, frankly, too old to try to keep some sort of watch on your person at every hour!" he scoffed, then downed his port to set the small glass aside.

Thank God. Not that I'm off to cheat this wager, but—

"No," he continued smoothly. "I've arranged for a chaperone."

Ashe blinked twice. "A what? You arranged for a . . ." He couldn't say it. It was too unbelievable.

"A chaperone." His grandfather's smile was far more genuine now, as he openly enjoyed his grandson's discomfort. "I have arranged for someone who will be at your elbow and accompany you at every event to guarantee that you don't forget what's at stake."

"You're serious! I'll be damned if I'm walking about like some virginal debutante with a dragon in tow!"

"Nonsense! Look on it as my way of showing support for your new moral effort. By providing a chaperone, you'll be less likely to stumble. And no one need know of the position you're in! Your chaperone won't declare their role openly or the nature of our arrangement."

"Well, there's one thing we agree on. I'm not about to announce to my peers the reason I'm playing choir boy and tooling about with a chaperone!"

"Mind your manners!" his grandfather said, his stern looks returning. "All this protesting makes me think you had every intention of botching this wager from the start! Well, if you want out, and your word means nothing, then say so now. Because if you meant your oath honestly, then it shouldn't matter if I hire a legion of chaperones and spies, should it?"

Well, there's a point of logic I should have anticipated. . . . Oh, well. I'm already in up to my eyebrows, so why complain about the temperature of the water?

Ashe let out a long, slow breath. "You're right, and I have no intention of backing out. I just—I have never heard of a man with a chaperone, so you'll have to give me a moment to accept the notion."

His grandfather nodded and moved over to the bellpull by the fireplace to give it a firm tug. Within seconds, the butler materialized in the doorway.

"Yes, sir," Mr. Frasier said with a curt nod.

"Bring in Townsend, Frasier." He walked back to Ashe, his hands behind his back. "Try to be polite when you meet your chaperone, my boy."

Ashe felt a twinge of confusion. *Why wouldn't I be polite to the chap? Hell, if he thinks we're the best of friends, I may actually get to take a deep breath this Season without a dispatch flying back here and setting off cries of alarm.* "I am always polite to your friends."

His grandfather said nothing but gave him an arched look full of skepticism. Within seconds, the library doors opened again, and Ashe turned to see what flavor of windbag his chaperone would be.

A petite woman in a pale gray gabardine dress that was several seasons out of fashion came toward them, and Ashe's first impression was that his grandfather's new housekeeper was a good bit younger than he'd have expected. But as she drew closer, a new and more startling idea occurred to him.

He wouldn't! She cannot possibly be—

"Allow me to introduce you to your chaperone and companion for the Season. This is Miss Caroline Townsend. A relation to my very best friend and American business partner, Mr. Matthew Townsend, now sadly passed away. I have invited her here to attend this very serious and delicate matter, and after a week in her company, I am convinced that she is entirely suited to the task at hand."

"This is preposterous!" Ashe turned to his grandfather, rudely ignoring her and cutting her out of the exchange. "I might have managed to accept this if you'd sailed in some granite-faced old dowager, but you cannot possibly think that a—how in God's name were you thinking that this might work?"

"It will work because a young woman gives you the perfect excuse! It will work because you will present her as a family friend and you will take the role of guardian! It will work because with her at your side, you may actually get admittance into respectable houses and decent company! It will work, because no one would suspect the truth!" The years dropped off his face as he spoke, and Ashe had to remind himself not to take a step backward as the old intimidation began to work its magic. "It will work because I'm telling you to make it work!"

For long seconds, they faced each other, until at last, Ashe was forced to blink. He reluctantly stepped back and barely spared a quick glance back at the woman before closing his eyes in frustration. *A plain, drab little pony of a thing, but the old man's probably guessed correctly. If I'm to have a dreary Season, she'll provide the perfect dreary excuse. Damn!*

"My grandson will apologize for his rudeness," the elder Blackwell said, his voice full of warning. "And I, too, Miss Townsend, for not preparing him and raising him properly to mind his manners in the presence of a lady."

"Not at all," she spoke, and the strong silk of her voice and strange, flat American accent caught Ashe's attention immediately. "Your grandson is a grown man and old enough to do and say what he pleases. And if it pleases him to be rude and boorish, then that's no reflection on you, Mr. Blackwell. You've been nothing but kind, sir."

Rude and boorish? Ashe clenched his jaw in frustration but managed to growl out his words. "I apologize, Miss Townsend. But as you've pointed out, I'm a grown man, and hardly in need of a chaperone, despite what my grandfather believes."

She tilted her head to one side, a small bird openly unafraid. "What you're in need of, sir, is not for me to say for fear of seeming equally rude, but I've promised your grandfather I'd do what I could to assist you, so we'll just have to make the best of it, won't we?"

Ashe forced himself not to sputter in astonishment at the woman's cheekiness. She'd openly insulted him, and then stood there as calmly as if they were discussing the weather. He looked at her more closely, his first impression of a gray dove giving way only slightly. Her brown eyes were large and framed with impossibly long lashes that gave her an inquisitive countenance, but not an owlish one. Her gaze was far too direct for an English woman of breeding, but the intelligence there made it difficult to look away. Her features were balanced and pleasing, but her color was far too high for the current fashion. Ladies were encouraged to look as porcelainlike as possible, hinting at a lofty station that allowed them to shun the sun and all excesses that might put a permanent stain on their faces. Instead of dainty curls and a lace headdress, her dark blonde hair was pulled back with a simple fall of waves down her back without a single ornament.

She was plain but for those mesmerizing eyes . . . But the Ton will tear her to pieces—an American! With the manners of a rough and tumble Colonial, no doubt, to match that saucy tongue of hers!

His grandfather laughed, and the surprising sound of it arrested the dark vein of his thoughts. "I'll leave you to get acquainted for a few moments."

"I hardly think that's necess—" Ashe started to protest.

"Nonsense! You'll talk and make amends to the lady." He turned to take Miss Townsend's hand. "I will see you both for a cordial dinner, and then you may both take your leave in the morning in my carriage. Ashe will take you into Town and see you settled at his home."

"Thank you, Mr. Blackwell."

He left without another glance at his grandson, and Ashe let out a long sigh before attempting another start with his "chaperone." "I am genuinely sorry, Miss Townsend, for my behavior. But I am also sorry that you seem to have been thrown to the wolves without your knowledge. I'm having trouble understanding why my grandfather thought to put you in such an untenable position, but as you seem to grasp, I have little say in the matter."

"Are you the wolf in question?"

He shook his head. "Not this time."

"Then I fail to see the difficulty, Mr. Blackwell."

His brow furrowed, unsure of how realistic a portrait to paint for her. After all, if she refused to proceed with the plan, he could hardly be blamed. But if she went into it without any idea of the obstacles ahead, he wasn't sure he'd be able to live with himself. "Are you well versed in the etiquette of a London Season, Miss Townsend?"

Ashe watched a flash of fiery temper alight in her eyes and knew the answer before she supplied it.

"Good manners are common sense, Mr. Blackwell, and I'm sure I'll pick up on things quickly enough. We are not entirely without the social niceties in Boston."

"No, I didn't imagine you all in mud-covered huts, Miss Townsend."

"Yet you seem to look at me as if I'm wearing animal hides, Mr. Blackwell."

"Now there's a wicked picture," he said, unable to keep from smiling at the thought of the little terrier of a woman in front of him wearing nothing but a few furs. He went over to the side table. "Port, Miss Townsend?"

"No, thank you."

Why am I not surprised? He smiled and turned back to lift his glass in a mock toast. "What kind of woman agrees to chaperone a rogue such as myself? What in the world would appeal to you to come so far for such a ridiculous task?"

Caroline Townsend fought the urge to throw something at his smug face and did her best to compose a reasonable answer. He was a rogue, without question, and while he was far more handsome and imposing than she'd expected, he was also the more annoying and ill-mannered. *So much for the superiority of an English gentleman!*

She stepped forward, tipping her head back to look up into his face with what she hoped was her sternest and most unforgiving expression. It had previously brought more than one pupil to tears, and while she didn't expect the pompous wall of a man to crumble, Caroline was determined not to give any ground. "I see nothing ridiculous in helping my grandfather's dearest friend."

"Your grandfather's dearest friend may not have considered all the risks when he asked you for this favor."

"You repeatedly speak of risk and I can't help but think you're trying to frighten me away, Mr. Blackwell." Her chin lifted a defiant inch, and Ashe had a small glimpse of just how immovable Miss Caroline Townsend could be when pressed. "And since you are a self-confessed rogue, I don't believe I need to defend or explain anything to you. Your grandfather said you couldn't be trusted not to disgrace him, and while I can only imagine what you've done to earn his censure, I don't care. My life and reasons for being here are my own."

It galled him a little that his grandfather would have said such a thing to an outsider, but then his chaperone would undoubtedly have to know the worst to understand her strange employment.

"As are mine! I have agreed to my grandfather's request, but know this, Miss Townsend——I won't waste any more time warning you away from your noble quest to play my moral guardian. And you can trust me when I tell you this, since you're so determined to have your way, I'll not interfere. I don't need you to keep me from disgrace. Rogue or no, I'm capable of holding my own without some drab little tight-lipped American nipping at my heels. Frankly, I would rather haul a tiger around on a bridle than cart you through a Season."

Hands fisted at her hips, she faced him squarely. "I'm glad we have an understanding, then, Mr. Blackwell. Especially since I am the one with the unhappy task of holding *your* bridle, which from here makes you look less and less like a tiger and more and more like an ass!"

She turned on her heels, her spine ramrod straight, and crisply left the room, the sound of the library door shutting in a most unladylike manner behind her that made his jaw drop open in astonishment.

Women blushed and fluttered at the sight of him, and generally yielded to his every whim, he reminded himself. *Hell, and that's the ones I don't pay! Damned if my grandfather hasn't found the one woman on this planet I believe I can genuinely confess to loathing at first sight—and who apparently shares the sentiment when it comes to me!*

Ashe's eyes narrowed as he considered his petite opponent in the upcoming game. The stakes were too high to underestimate her. Whatever his grandfather had promised her, the sooner he could find it out and match the offer, the better. Not to break his word, but to eliminate at least one miserable element from the Season ahead.

Though he had a sinking feeling the petite terrier was not going to be amenable to a bribe. His grandfather's business ventures had been very successful, and he'd heard him mention Townsend's phenomenal success across the Atlantic. The little chit had no doubt inherited enough to make her impervious to any offer he might make.

If she's incorruptible, then I'm trapped unless I can find another way. But no matter what, I'm not going to be outdone by an upstart American and forfeit my pride and abandon my family's honor into Yardley's sweaty hands. If I have to cart the chit around, I will—but I'll be damned if she doesn't

*regret every minute that she thought to hold the whip hand
with me.*

He lifted his glass in a quiet salute to the closed library
door. "You'll wish you'd stayed home, Miss Townsend, for
this is one favor you're going to beg me to release you from
before the month is out."